WHITE HEAT

**Center Point
Large Print**

**This Large Print Book carries the
Seal of Approval of N.A.V.H.**

WHITE HEAT

CHERRY ADAIR

CENTER POINT PUBLISHING
THORNDIKE, MAINE

This Center Point Large Print edition
is published in the year 2007 by arrangement with
The Random House Publishing Group,
a division of Random House, Inc.

Copyright © 2007 by Cherry Adair.

The text of this Large Print edition is unabridged. In other
aspects, this book may vary from the original edition.
Printed in the United States of America.
Set in 16-point Times New Roman type.

ISBN-10: 1-60285-072-0
ISBN-13: 978-1-60285-072-9

66E

Library of Congress Cataloging-in-Publication Data

Adair, Cherry, 1951-
    White heat / Cherry Adair.--Center Point large print ed.
        p. cm.
    ISBN-13: 978-1-60285-072-9 (lib. bdg. : alk. paper)
    1. Terrorism--Fiction. 2. Large type books. I. Title.

PS3601.D348W47 2007b
813'.6--dc22

2007018950

For my friend Rosella Re in Rome, Italy. Ti ringrazio molto *for jumping in to help me with research and all things Italian. Thank you for finding a beautiful palazzo for Emily, and also for showing me that magnificent villa for Daniel. Your assistance with translations, descriptions, and pictures was invaluable, and very much appreciated. All mistakes are one hundred percent mine.*
Baci e abbracci.

Acknowledgments

I'd like to thank the following people for enriching my writing experience and also my life:

Justin Smith at Squatch Media for building cherryadair.com and making it what I think is *the* most fabulous website in the galaxy.

Virginia Finucane at River Rock Studio Design Group, graphic artist extraordinaire and friend, for "getting me" and translating the pictures in my head into the most amazing graphics.

Theresa Meyers at Blue Moon Communications. Thank you for going above and beyond the call of duty as both a friend and a publicist.

One

COUNTERTERRORIST OPERATIVE MAX ARIES FLUNG A leg over the crumbling second-floor balustrade, then dropped lightly onto the narrow stone terrace. He'd spent some pretty damned phenomenal days and nights in this sixteenth-century palazzo. But he wasn't here to seduce Emily Greene. Not this time.

He presumed she was here. Her little yellow Maserati was parked out on the street, but she hadn't answered the doorbell when he'd rung a few minutes ago. Of course there were any number of places an attractive, single woman could be at two in the morning. If not for the urgency of her calls Max might have waited until a decent, civilized time to see her. He'd been awake for a straight ninety-seven hours, and he was punchy as hell. Sleep would've been good. A shower would probably be appreciated. But there hadn't been time for either.

He'd been on the T-FLAC jet, halfway home from an op in Grozny, when he'd called his answering service to check for messages during a break in debriefing. He rarely had personal messages; operatives didn't have time for real lives, so he was surprised to have received half a dozen.

9

All from Emily Greene. Apparently she'd been leaving messages for weeks. The messages had started out cool, but reasonable and sympathetic, then grown increasingly more annoyed as she'd practically summoned his ass to Florence for his father's funeral.

Message received loud and clear.

Fine. He was here, wasn't he? A few weeks late, and several dollars' worth of sincerity short, but he was here. He hadn't been that interested in the death of his sperm donor. But he was curious as hell to see Emily again. This was as good an excuse as any. And, he thought, amused, he'd practically been in the neighborhood.

The balcony doors were wide open to the chill damp air, and several of the spicy-scented potted geraniums crowding the patio were knocked over. There were dozens of possible reasons the pots had been toppled, but between one inhale and the next Max's hand went instinctively to the custom Glock in the small of his back. He left the SIG Sauer and Ka-Bar knife in their ankle holsters where they were. For now.

He wasn't the only one who'd entered her apartment this way.

Exhaustion dissipated as adrenaline reactivated his tired brain. Unless she had Romeo and Juliet fantasies, Emily had an intruder. First the old man's murder, now this? Max didn't believe in coincidences. He stepped over scattered dirt to slip through the open French doors where sheer white draperies fluttered in the rain-drenched air.

The delicate fragrance of woman was underscored by the familiar, but out of place, smell of male sweat and gun oil. The intruder had passed this way recently. Very recently.

Shit.

Moving quickly and soundlessly through the stygian darkness of the living room, he circumvented the enormous, down-filled floral sofa where he and Emily had made love their last time together. Max's night vision was excellent, and his eyes automatically adjusted to the almost-pitch-black interior even as he catalogued the blend of distinctive odors around him. The acrid smell of turpentine, the unmistakable smell of still-wet oil paint from Emily's first floor studio, dust, flowers, garlic—

The intruder.

He felt that familiar spike of adrenaline and smiled. *Now* he was wide awake. Alert to the smallest sound or hint of movement, he followed the man's trail like a bloodhound. Weaving his way at top speed through the overcrowded rooms, and heading toward the long hallway leading to the rest of the apartment.

Silently crossing the terrazzo floor of the entryway, he noted the flowers in a vase on the hall table, black in the darkness. A woman's purse lay beside the crystal vase. An umbrella and long raincoat hung from a hook nearby. No sign of moisture, indicating she'd been home awhile. Two suitcases stood sentinel nearby. Where was she going?

He noticed a dark shape lying twenty feet ahead on

11

the floor in the hallway, just this side of the open bedroom door. Max's heart double-clutched.

Emily—

He raced toward the still figure.

God damn it.

Between here and there was the slightly less dark opening to the kitchen where he sensed someone standing in wait. He spun on his heel just as a hard object struck his upper arm with a bone-jarring *thud.* He deflected the second blow, grabbed the assailant's wrist and twisted. A heavy object dropped to the tiled floor with a metallic clang. The second his fingers closed on the slender, bare arm, he knew his attacker was a woman.

He yanked her arm up behind her back, not letting up because his assailant was a *she.* He knew plenty of female tangos who could fuck a guy's brains out one minute and put a bullet between his eyes the next. He used a little more force on her arm. The woman let out a bloodcurdling shriek as she struggled for freedom.

He didn't ease up any. He wasn't using enough pressure, *yet,* to snap her fragile bones. She wiggled and squirmed in his hold. He backed her into the kitchen. Separating her from the dark lump a few yards away on the hallway floor. Divide and conquer. "Settle down, I—"

She wasn't listening. *"Mi lasci andare, figlio di puttana!"*

Emily?

The second he released her, she pivoted and

12

punched him in the stomach. "I killed your accomplice"—she yelled in rapid, almost unintelligible, Italian. Whack!—"and I won't"—Whack!—"hesitate to"—Whack!—"kill you, too. The police are on their way." Whack! "I'll get a *medal* for killing you bo—"

Definitely Emily.

"Emily," Max grabbed her arms—*much* more gently than he would have a tango—to stop the pummeling. "It's me, Ma—"

She kneed him in the balls.

"Jesus, Mary, and Joseph, woman!" Pain shot up into his brain with the intensity of a laser scalpel. He doubled over, fighting to remain conscious through the nausea. Direct hit. Christ, a rookie mistake not expecting *that.*

She used this opportunity to strike him on the back of the head with her clasped hands, then tried to knee him in the face. He shoved her leg aside just in time to avoid a broken nose.

Testicles lodged in his Adam's apple, he straightened with difficulty and pulled her tightly into his arms, lifting her off her feet and off balance. Screaming invectives, she struggled like a fish on a line, body arching, legs kicking.

Even in the dark he recognized the pale oval of her face. Her eyes glittered, reflecting the dim light on the cook top. She wasn't seeing anything but escape as she swung wildly again.

He gave her a shake, trying to make eye contact. Strands of her silky dark hair caught in the stubble on his jaw. She still smelled like paint thinner and roses. How had he missed that when he'd first grabbed her?

"For Christ's sake, Emily! It's me, *Max*. Settle down."

As his voice registered, she stopped fighting, freezing in his hold. "Max?" The fire went out of her like air out of a balloon and she sagged against him, dropping her forehead to his chest.

"Thank God."

She felt good in his arms, damn good, but he settled her carefully on her feet the second she acknowledged she knew who he was.

Jesus-fuck, his balls hurt like hell. "Okay now?" he asked gruffly, straightening as best he could.

"Not by a long shot." The light in the kitchen clicked on. Her chocolaty hair was wild around her shoulders and her dark eyes appeared almost black in her pale face as she blinked him into focus. The top of her head reached his chin, but she looked a lot taller as she glared up at him. "What the hell are you doing here?"

Jesus. He'd forgotten how incredibly beautiful she was. Not moderately pretty, not just attractive, but drop-dead, breath-stealing *stunning*. Her dark hair and eyes made her creamy skin seem to glow from the inside like a light inside alabaster. Her nose was small and perfectly shaped, her long-lashed eyes were large and expressive, and her mouth—Man. Her mouth was made for sin. Her body, now dressed in skimpy pajamas, was lithe, toned, and sensational. Her breasts

14

high and firm. Mouthwateringly perfect. Her legs were long, and Jesus, they'd been strong wrapped around his hips, his shoulders, his—*Focus*—

"You pretty much insisted," he said dryly, resisting running his hand around her smooth midriff to feel her bare skin again. He stuck his free hand in his pocket, and leaned against the door jamb. A quick sideways glance and he could see that the lump outside the door hadn't moved.

"Almost *three weeks* ago!" she snapped, running both hands through her thick glossy hair. The movement lifted the front of her small T-shirt just enough for him to get a view of the soft lower swell of her breasts and a tantalizing glimpse of her midriff.

His mouth went dry. Man oh man. She didn't fight fair.

"And while I'm pleased you finally decided to show up," she said with just a tinge of sarcasm, and oblivious to the fact that his tongue was stuck to the roof of his mouth, "waiting a few more hours and ringing the frigging *doorbell* would have been the polite thing to do."

She dropped her hands to her sides and glared at him. "But then *polite* isn't really your thing, is it, Max? What's the time anyway?"

She glanced at a clock over the stove. "Two bloody A.M.?" She spun back to him. "Are you and your friend *nuts*?"

The guy on the floor? "What friend?"

"*What* frie—" Her eyes, big, brown, and expressive,

15

went wide. "Oh, my God. You mean the guy out there wasn't with you? Then who *is* he?"

"Good question." Not sure if he could walk yet, he was excruciatingly aware of every single whimpering nerve ending in his balls as he straightened up a little more. White suns spiraled and shimmied in front of his eyes as he pushed off the door jamb.

Great. Just fucking great. "Wait here. I'll check."

She bent down, exposing her pretty heart-shaped ass draped in baby pink cotton pajama bottoms. Picking up the sixteen-inch cast iron frying pan in both hands, she handed it to him handle first. "Here. Be care— Oh." She noticed the Glock he'd managed to hang onto when she'd kneed him. Retaining his grip on the gun was a function of reflex and training. But even he was surprised to find it was still in his hand. She'd be excellent as a diversionary tactic in a T-FLAC training exercise.

She gave him a wary look. "Guess you won't be needing this." Despite her bravado he noticed the fine tremor in her hands as she slid the pan onto a nearby countertop.

They'd been together a handful of days and nights the last time they'd been together, and getting to know one another hadn't been part of his seduction plan. Emily had been a means to an end a year ago. The fact that they'd been combustible in bed had turned out to be a bonus. But they hadn't done a lot of talking. For all he knew she was pissed enough to brain him when his back was turned.

16

He shook his head, scared as hell that she could've been hurt when he grabbed her. Proud that she could hold her own. The frying pan was an effective weapon in a pinch, but nothing beat a speeding bullet. "Stay put."

Max went into the dimly lit hallway. The lump was still there on the floor, halfway between the kitchen and Emily's bedroom. He placed his foot firmly on the guy's back.

"Is he dead?" she demanded, automatically slipping back to Italian. She'd lived in Florence long enough for it to be her first language, although she was as American as he was.

Flipping the guy over with his foot, Max kept the Glock aimed directly at the guy's forehead. "Nope, you did a good job," he told her, impressed with her handiwork. Looked like she'd whaled the guy a couple of times after he was down. No defensive wounds. "He's just unconscious."

She'd gotten in a couple of excellent blows to the man's face with the pan. Good girl. There was a lot of blood and swelling, but the guy was still breathing. Which was a good thing. Dead men didn't offer a lot of answers. And Max had a shitload of questions.

"Thank God," she said on a shaky breath. She hadn't moved from the doorway, and he motioned her over.

"Come out here and tell me if you recognize him."

Emily had her weapon of choice, a sixteen-inch cast iron frying pan, gripped in both hands again as she stepped out of the kitchen doorway. "Light on or off?"

"On."

The hall light overhead clicked on, illuminating the unconscious man. It also illuminated Emily. This time the thin PJ pants she wore drooped to expose the three tiny dolphins leaping over her belly button. The tattoo was sexy as hell, but the soft, velvety skin of her belly was more so. He'd loved to nuzzle his face against the silky, fragrant warmth. Loved the rose soap and woman smell of her. He'd used the tip of his tongue to taste her skin there, and she'd sighed, he'd brushed his lips lower, and she'd moaned.

"Are you sure he isn't dead?" she asked quietly, coming up behind him, tension in every lovely line of her body. Her tall, lush, sexy body. Her full breasts were outlined by the skimpy cotton top. One side of the little pink satin bow holding up her pants was undone. The single loop sat just beneath the leaping dolphins. Sweet. Girly. *Hot.*

Not only was the guy *not* dead, Max was pleased to note that Emily's knee to his groin hadn't killed any lustful thoughts he had. Christ—that tat on her smooth, creamy skin had given him some extremely uncomfortable nights over the last few months. Good to know his dick was still fully functional.

He doubted if Emily Greene had been holding open the window of opportunity for him for a year. Fine and dandy with him. Max didn't do involvement. Ever. But she'd let him into her bed before. Perhaps—

"Yeah, I'm positive he isn't dead. Know him?"

He hauled the guy upright by his lapels. Cheap, dark

18

suit. Brown shirt. Dark sneakers. Stunk of Gauloise cigarettes and gun oil. Max patted him down, relieving him of the Heckler & Koch tucked in an underarm holster. A USP Tactical, Max noted. Cost twice as much as the guy's entire outfit, *plus* a thousand bucks.

A hired gun.

Put a whole different spin on the break-in.

Taking out the clip one-handed, Max slid the magazine and weapon along the floor behind him, out of reach. Then started searching his pockets. A knife in a leg holster. And a compact Smith & Wesson .357 in an ankle holster. The guy meant business.

What kind of business?

Max removed both weapons and stuck them on top of a nearby bookcase out of sight. Who the fuck *was* this guy? Not a tango. Not here. Not in Emily's apartment at two in the morning in a quiet residential neighborhood of Florence. Didn't make sense. But even though it wasn't likely, he considered it for a moment. Considered and dismissed it. Nah. But since terrorists were his business, he tended to see tangos behind every shrub and dung heap.

"Of course I don't know him." Her eyes gleamed in the semidarkness. She was so beautiful she stole his breath. "He broke in just like you did. *Friends,*" she said pointedly, bending to pinch the gun in two fingers, "don't climb up two stories to pay a social visit."

She took several steps closer, eyes running over the guy, whose head was flopped to his chest. Max used the barrel of his Glock to jerk up his chin so she could have a better look. She'd done a nice job breaking the intruder's nose, and she'd managed to get in several more strategic hits, as evidenced by the ugly bruise on one cheek and a knot above his left eye. Blood still ran sluggishly down the dude's temple.

"Did he touch you?" Max asked coldly. She had no idea the man could go from slightly battered to dead in two seconds or less depending on her answer.

When she didn't respond, he glanced over his shoulder in time to see her shaking her head. "Is that a no?"

She held the gun slightly away from her body like one would hold a dead rat. "He scared the bejesus out of me, but I saw him before he saw me."

Good enough. She was scared, but rational. Max needed answers. "Are the police really on their way?"

Could complicate matters. Max had his own people to deal with garbage detail. Not that he'd expected to need them since he was technically on vacation. Technically.

She hesitated. "I didn't have time to call them. I'd just come into the kitchen for a glass of milk when I heard him sneaking out of my bedroom—My God. I didn't even hear him go right past the kitchen and *into* my bedroom. I just grabbed the heaviest pan I could, and hit him as he passed the door. The sound was—" She grimaced.

Horrific. Max knew. He'd slammed heavy objects into any number of craniums. Had a few slammed into his own.

She glanced back at her victim. "What did he think I had that was worth stealing?"

It was rhetorical, but he answered anyway. "We'll find out." He continued searching the guy's pockets as he talked. If the intruder was a burglar he'd been flattened before he could lift anything. Odd, since he'd gone from one end of Emily's apartment to the other. "Anything missing?"

He was no expert, but Emily had some good stuff around. As he recalled she had antiques, objets d'art, and other presumably valuable bits and pieces cluttering every surface. The woman was not only untidy, he remembered, she was adorably absentminded.

"I don't know. There's nothing of any great value up here. The studio downstairs has better security. The insurance companies for the museums demand it."

The H&K and frying pan clanged together as she switched the gun to free her other hand. She reached down and picked up the clip, turning it end over end as she talked. She had pretty hands, with long slender fingers and short nails. He remembered her hands weren't quite as soft as they looked because of the paint and cleaners she used. But he'd loved the feel of them gliding over his skin, touching him, stroking him. God. He'd loved the feel of her hands.

And she always had paint on her, somewhere, that she'd missed when she cleaned up. This morning it was a smear of green on her elbow, and a smear in her hair. Five gradiated diamond studs sparkled and flashed in each ear as she moved. Those were new.

"I recently finished a copy of a very famous work, but no one except the client knew the original was h—What?"

"English, okay?" He switched from Italian, jerking his chin indicating the guy on the floor. Chances were he spoke English, but maybe he didn't.

Emily switched easily to her native English as she continued. "But I shipped both pieces back to Denver three days ago. So there's nothing of value downstairs right now, even if someone figured out *how* to break in. Do you want me to go down and check?" she offered. But she didn't move.

It hadn't occurred to him that she'd suggest going alone after what had just happened. Single woman. Could take care of herself. Except when an armed man broke in. Well hell. She'd even taken care of the intruder before he'd gotten there. "No. Go somewhere and lock the door till I'm done here."

She looked over her shoulder, and Max followed her gaze. Other than the dim light streaming through the kitchen doorway, and the overhead hall light, the entire apartment behind her was dark. A visible shiver ran across her shoulders.

"What if he wasn't alone?" Her voice was barely above a whisper.

He figured that a second intruder would be long gone, but he wasn't about to take any chances. "Maybe." He reached back for the flex-cuffs he just happened to be carrying. "I'll secure this one, and go take a l—"

The guy exploded up off the floor. Emily screamed. More in warning than fright.

Max shot out his elbow, striking his opponent's throat. The guy gagged, but came back with a punch to Max's solar plexus.

The party was on.

"Oh my God, oh my God, oh my God," Emily said hoarsely, backing up.

"Go back in the kitchen, shut the door. Lock it if you can," Max told her evenly as the man landed another solid blow, this time to his sternum. Pissed Max off, because he'd been thinking about Emily, not guarding himself sufficiently to deflect the blows. He threw a rear hand punch that knocked the bastard back a couple of steps, then pulled him in for a head butt. Both men cursed. It hurt like hell.

There wasn't enough room for three of them in the narrow hallway, and Max was afraid Emily would try to "help" him with her frying pan. And get hurt for her trouble.

"Emily—" The other man telegraphed by his body movement that he was going to deliver a punch to the side of Max's head. Max grabbed his arm high and low, and pulled him in for a knee to the belly. The man grunted, but came up swinging.

"I have his gun and this . . . thing."

Great. A weapon *and* the clip. "Put them—*separately*—somewhere out of the way." He relaxed his muscles, and transferred his weight, rotating his hips and shoulders into the attack, then moved straight forward, forcing the guy to back up with a series of fast punches to the face and chest. His rapid retraction prevented the man from grabbing Max's hand or arm, and kept him off balance.

Uppercut. Hook. Rear hand punch. Max kept them coming faster than the other man could deflect them.

"Kitchen," Max shouted to Emily, as the intruder tried a horizontal elbow strike. "Close, but no cigar," he told the other man in Italian, raising his right knee and driving hard, just above his opponent's knee. The guy's body sagged, and he grabbed onto Max's shirt front.

Max stepped forward and left at a forty-five degree angle, moving into the outside of the other man's body, then chopped up with both forearms, breaking the hold.

Damn it. He didn't want Emily holding the gun, and he sure as shit didn't want his opponent to wrestle it from her. The guy charged in, attempting a hip throw. Max was ready. Shaking off the man's hand on his right wrist, Max pulled him in close and off balance, then used a leg sweep to bring him to his knees.

He sensed that Emily was still with them in the hallway. With his forearm across his opponent's throat, he yelled, *"Now."*

Emily darted back into the kitchen as the two men wrestled in the hallway. This was surreal. The big gun felt ridiculously heavy in her hand as she tried to decide what to do with it. She'd never held a gun before. She didn't want to hold one now. Nothing good could come from her gripping the bloody thing, and she presumed Max was afraid if the guy got free he might take it from her by force and kill them both. Not a pleasant thought.

She wasn't about to grapple with a guy twice her weight for a weapon she had no idea how to use.

She tossed the bullet holder thingie behind the refrigerator, then opened the odds-and-ends drawer, carefully laid the big black gun inside, and closed the drawer as if it might detonate with the slightest movement.

For a moment she stood there in the semidarkness of her herb-scented kitchen, bare toes curled on the cold tile floor. Favorite frying pan still clutched in a death grip in her left hand, she stared at the closed door.

The sounds coming from just outside were enough to make her consider shimmying through the narrow kitchen window and making a break for it down the folding fire escape ladder to the street below. She should get *la polizia.*

The sickening crunch of a bone snapping made her hesitate. Hopefully it was the intruder's bone. As annoyed as she was with Max, she still didn't want to hear his bones splintering like kindling. Emily wiped her damp palm on her pajama bottom, switched the pan from one hand to the other, and wiped that hand as well.

Her gaze darted between the small window and the closed, not locked, door. She knew she could fit through the window. Not easily, but she'd done it on three occasions when she'd lost her keys. Of course she hadn't done it in the dark, or in the rain, any of those occasions. She hadn't done it when she was scared for her life either.

God—She couldn't leave Max alone with a motivated burglar. He could be killed.

Even reminding herself that Max had a gun didn't make leaving *him* to deal with *her* problem acceptable. Damn her own moral code of responsibility. It was frequently inconvenient. Using a double-handed grip on the handle of the pan, she raised it above her head, and stepped back out into the hallway again. Ready to help Max if necessary.

Heart pounding and breathing as if she'd been running, even though she'd barely walked ten feet, Emily gripped the handle so hard her hands went numb. Crossing the threshold from kitchen to hallway, she was just in time to see that the man's eyes were open. Not that he was looking at her. He was more focused on Max.

With good reason.

Max looked scary as hell. His strong jaw was unshaven, and the lights in the hallway threw his lean, hard features into shadow so that he looked not only enormous, but fierce and deadly. He had a gun in his left hand, pressed hard to the burglar's bleeding temple. His right had the guy's injured elbow high over the man's head, completely earning the menacing grimace the guy was sending him. Max didn't seem to notice, or care, as he warned the intruder not to move a muscle. In, Emily suddenly noticed, perfect Italian.

The Italian he'd claimed not to speak or understand just eleven months ago.

He was dressed all in black. But then so was the intruder. Which was the bad guy? They both looked dangerous and disreputable. Max's dark hair was far too long and shaggy. He needed a haircut. And a shave.

All she'd gotten was a glimpse of his eyes in the kitchen, and the coldness in those hazel eyes had chilled her to the marrow. It was as though he were looking at a stranger. Which was damn unflattering, all things considered.

He hadn't looked at her that way the last time they'd been eye-to-eye. Then the color of his eyes had been black-forest green. And hot. Smoldering hot. A sense of foreboding shuddered through her body and her fingers cramped on the frying pan.

Who was *this* Max Aries?

Two

MAX YANKED THE MAN TO HIS FEET. THE GUY bucked and heaved, for all his bulk as supple as an eel. He almost managed to wriggle free. Max held on and braced a forearm against the man's neck. "Oh, no you don't. What do you want? What did you steal, asshole?"

"Mi lasci andare. Non ho preso niente!" the man assured him hoarsely, gripping Max's forearm with

both hands, Emily presumed, to release some of the pressure threatening to collapse his airway. His face was turning red from lack of oxygen. Or anger. Probably both.

She spread her feet for better balance, tightening her grip on her weapon even though Max clearly had things under control. She didn't recognize him. The man who'd charmed his way into her bed within hours of their first meeting had looked nothing like this steely-eyed giant with a gun.

He'd been amusing, sexy, interesting, and . . . *benign*. Just as she preferred. Just like Franco, who would be here later today to accompany her to the airport.

There was nothing benign about the man standing in her hallway now. He seemed bigger, broader, *dangerous* tonight. Surely he hadn't been like this when she'd first met him? That Max had looked devastating and unbearably debonair in a stark black tux.

She couldn't imagine the man standing in her hallway tonight wearing anything as civilized as a tuxedo.

His voice was even, his breathing normal, his hand, and the gun, perfectly steady yet he radiated menace from every pore. "You've got ten seconds to tell me what you wanted, *and* who you work for. In ten point one seconds, I won't give a shit. I'll kill you."

Emily believed him. So did the guy.

He struggled for freedom like a fish on a line. Not a chance. It was obvious Max wasn't letting go until he had answers. Her stomach rolled uncomfortably as Max's forearm tightened around the man's throat. *"Uno. Due . . ."*

The guy clearly hadn't managed to steal anything, although art theft wasn't uncommon. Which was why the various galleries and museums that Emily did restoration work for insisted on the stringent security systems she had in her first floor studio. But anyone who knew anything in the closely knit art world would know that the Raphael she'd been working on had been picked up by courier three days ago. There was absolutely nothing of value downstairs.

She was going to be on holiday for a month, and she'd managed to finish the *Madonna* commission in plenty of time, ensuring a calm and relaxed vacation with Franco. They weren't going to spend *all* their time in Seattle. One day with her mother was about all either she or her mother could stand.

This guy *had* no rolled canvases on him. He'd headed straight for her bedroom. If he'd tried the downstairs studio first, the alarm would have sounded, and the police would already be here. A chill ran down her spine.

Had he come, not to steal something, but to *take* something?

Her?

Kidnapping was big business in Italy.

She'd done very well for herself over the years. Both copying and restoration were lucrative fields, and she was extremely good at what she did.

29

God. Her sister would've freaked if she'd been kid-napped. Which she *hadn't* been, Emily reminded herself. Thanks in part to Max. She glanced away from where he held the man pinned to the wall, and was hit with a pang of homesickness. She couldn't wait to be in Seattle. Which didn't even make any sense. Seattle hadn't been home in years. *Florence* was home. But every once in a while she forgot reality and bought into the dream.

The only home she'd ever had was the one she had made for herself here. And she was damned proud of what she'd achieved. Home was just a word. Every now and then she forgot.

"Sette . . . otto . . ."

She hadn't made it to Washington for Christmas because Richard Tillman had put a tight deadline on the *Madonna dell Granduca* commission. In this business, reputation was everything, and she'd worked damn hard to ensure that hers was above reproach. She'd also made a great deal of money doing something she loved doing.

And her mother had been in rehab—again—anyway. Susanna, her older sister, who lived in Boston, hadn't spoken to their mother in ten years. Emily was the only link between the three women.

"Scusi, sono venuto nella casa sbagliata." The burglar gasped as Max kept up the pressure on his throat.

Max wedged his knee into the man's kidneys. *"Merda.* I think you had the right house. What were you looking for?"

When the man refused to answer, Max tightened his hold. "Slow learner. Start talking. If not, I'll keep squeezing until your last breath is fucking begging for air."

"He's going blue," Emily observed, horrified that Max might actually kill the man right here in her hallway. "I'll call the police." Which she should have done long before now, she thought sickly. She turned to go and make the call.

"No. I'll take care of it."

"Don't—"

Max did something and the man made a horrible gagging/gasping noise just before she heard what sounded like a bone snapping. He was cut off in mid gag. Bile crowded the back of Emily's throat as she spun around, hand to her mouth. Aghast, she saw the man hanging lifelessly from Max's forearm.

Had Max broken his neck? "You killed him."

"He's not that lucky. He'll just be out for a while. I'm not done questioning him." Releasing the man to crumble onto the tile floor, Max secured his hands behind his back with quick efficient movements, never putting down his own weapon. He glanced up briefly as he pulled the ties secure on the other man's ankles. Why would a man have plastic ties in his pocket?

The million-dollar question was: Why would a man have plastic ties in his pocket *and* scale a wall to get into her home? She put a protective hand over the rapid, telltale pulse at her throat.

"Check in the bedroom. See if anything's missing."

She'd wanted him here for his father's funeral, which had taken place, damn him, three weeks ago.

His attitude was starting to get on Emily's last nerve. While she was grateful—*incredibly* grateful—that he'd been here to *help* with the burglar, Max Aries wasn't the boss of her. They'd spent less than a damned week together. And that was almost a year ago. He'd been her first, and last, one-night stand— well, a four-night stand. Which gave him no rights what-so-bloody-ever. Unfortunately, as annoyed as she was with him, she knew she wasn't being reason- able at the moment.

She sucked up her irritation at his past transgres- sions, and said as rationally as she could manage, "He didn't have anything on him when you search—"

"Take a quick look anyway."

"Okay." Not because Max asked, but because she wanted to go into the bedroom and get dressed. Her cotton jammies were thin, and she was bare under- neath. She needed a few more layers between her body and Max's penetrating gaze.

Skirting the two men, Emily darted into her bed- room, flicking on the lights as she went. Her rumpled bed was a dim reminder that she'd been snuggled under the covers mere moments ago. If she hadn't been unable to sleep . . . thoughts of the wrongness and rightness of going away for a month with Franco . . . If she hadn't gotten up to get that glass of milk . . . If Max hadn't arrived . . .

Quickly dressing warmly in jeans and a cream cashmere sweater, she went in search of the shoes she'd worn the day before. She found one under the clothes piled high on, and hanging off, the antique Portuguese rococo Fauteuil à la Reine chair in the corner. It was carved walnut, gilded and as uncomfortable as sitting on a rock, but it was beautiful. When she could clear it of cast-off clothing. A quick search now didn't uncover her shoe.

She'd kicked them off while finishing packing last night. As she neared the bed, she stepped on something with her bare foot. *"Ahi!"* Bending she picked up a small glass vial, then straightened and held it up to the light. Nothing in it, and no stopper. She'd never seen it before. Odd.

"Find something?" Max asked, strolling into the bedroom, looking rough, tough, disreputable, and far too appealing for his own good. How could a voice be seductive and deadly at the same time? Damn it, she'd barely caught her breath from the last time he'd knocked her off her feet, and now here he was, to steal it again. The man was a menace.

Franco. Franco. Franco.

The last time they'd been in this room together they'd torn off each other's clothes. Now *there* was a pair of shoes she'd never found. They'd left the party early and come straight to the bedroom, shedding their clothes as they went, stopping when they couldn't see to walk because their mouths were fused, and their hands hadn't wanted to stop exploring.

33

"It's nothing." She held the small vial out to him.

Max didn't take it. Instead he gripped her wrist hard enough to leave a bruise. "Drop it. *Now*."

Automatically responding to his implacable tone, she tossed it on the floor, even as she protested his rough treatment. "Wha—Hey!"

Face grim, he pulled her out of the room despite her protest. "Where'd you find it?" He was still gripping her wrist.

She twisted free, she suspected only because he'd let her, then rubbed the red marks with her other hand. "On the floor by the bed. Stop manhandling me. I understand simple sentences, Max. What the hell's going on?"

"See anything like that vial before?"

He'd answered a question with a question. Infuriating man. "No."

"Shit. Go downstairs and wait for me, we're going to have to get out of here fast. I have a call to make, then you're coming with me until I figure out what the hell *is* going on."

She shot him an annoyed glance. "You waltz in here and demand I come away with you? Get over yourself. You weren't that good. I'm not going anywhere with you, Max. My bags are already packed. I'm leaving for Seattle toni—"

"We'll talk about it later. Your guy wasn't stealing, he was *delivering*. That vial could have contained gas or some other biohazard—" He pulled out a small cell phone, raising a brow as if to say—*get going.*

34

Emily stood her ground. No contest who she was more afraid of right now. The burglar was tied up. Max gave her a look that should have sent her running from the room as if her hair was on fire. Instead of bolting, Emily lifted her chin and folded her arms beneath her breasts.

He didn't scare her. Much.

Even though she had mixed feelings about going to see her mother and spending a month with Franco, she wasn't going to postpone her trip now because Max Aries suddenly decided that he was in charge.

He'd barged back into her life at the most inconvenient time. Did he have radar to pick up when she was feeling her most vulnerable? If he'd come when she'd called three weeks ago, she'd have been prepared to fend off any residual attraction. Showing up on the very freaking day she was about to make a monumental *life* change, and weeks late—three weeks late—left her swinging in the wind and far too susceptible to his particular brand of sex appeal.

"Send a hazmat team to 16974 Piazza Santa Croce," he instructed into the phone. "One. No. Alive, but incapacitated. Have them suit up. The intruder deposited a vial of God only knows what, near Emily Greene's bed." He paused to listen.

She did not like the sound of *hazmat* team.

He gave her an are-you-still-here look, and broke off the conversation to bark an order. To her. "Downstairs. Now."

Sit? Stay? "Who the hell do y—This *my* home, and

that's *my* intruder. I'm staying right here until—"

"No. We'll be gone. Shit. Good point. Yeah, right. We'll wait," he said coldly into the phone before shoving it back in his pocket. He met her eyes and Emily rubbed her arms through the soft yarn of her sweater as a chill seemed to permeate her very bones.

"This guy probably put something into your bed, thinking you were in it," Max told her grimly. "Not some cuddly something, but a potentially *lethal* something. That vial could've contained *anything*. Want to hang around with bare feet to find out if it's animal, vegetable, or mineral?"

That gave her pause. For half a nanosecond. Frowning, she shook her head. Talk about overreacting. "Stop trying to scare me. The guy's a burglar, not some kind of . . . *terrorist*. I'll call *la polizia*. They can deal with him."

She took an involuntary step back as the guy on the floor opened one eye and reared up.

"No *poliz*—" He choked as Max pressed his foot to his throat without looking down.

"You don't get a vote, asshole." Max's attention hadn't shifted from her, and she found his one hundred percent focus unnerving under the circumstances.

"Any number of toxins can leech and kill on contact. What would be your guess as to what was in that thing, Emily? Five ccs of perfume? *Not*. The possibilities are goddamned chilling. Bio-chemicals, flesh-eating bacteria, a transdermal poison of some kind—

36

Christ. Any one of a thousand toxic substances can be carried in that small a vial. Whatever was in it is now somewhere in your bedroom. Likely in your *bed*.

"Do you really want to stand there and put it to the test just because you're pissed at me?"

"Who *are* you?"

He gave her an exasperated look. "Right now I'm a man with his foot on what could possibly be Typhoid Tommy's throat. Get cracking, Emily. I'm not kidding. We could be breathing in spores as we speak. Move it."

Emily might be stubborn, Max thought. But she wasn't stupid. Once she grasped the magnitude of the situation she went downstairs, leaving him to wait for backup.

The intruder still wasn't talking. He would eventually. They always did. Within fifteen minutes a full garbage team arrived and the guy was unceremoniously hauled out, strapped to a stretcher. While the hazmat team went in to sweep Emily's bedroom, Max and the medic went downstairs.

He'd never seen her studio before. He was impressed. The enormous room was brilliant with artificial, full-spectrum light that reflected off the whitewashed walls and ceiling. It was a working studio, crusted with paint and well-worn furniture. How the hell she found anything in here, he had no idea. There wasn't a clear inch of flat surface to be seen.

Simple wood shelving bulged and bowed with the

weight of countless art and art history books. She seemed to own tomes on every artist, living or dead, that he'd ever heard of and many he hadn't. She also collected auction and museum catalogues.

Pinned to every vertical surface were sketches, gesture drawings, and notes. Stretched canvases leaned haphazardly against the far wall in groups of tens and twenties, and in various sizes. Many others, removed from their stretchers, were simply stacked on the floor. An empty easel stood in the center of the room, and a long table nearby held paints and brushes and various boxes of charcoals, pastels, pencils.

Interesting place. But Max only had eyes for Emily, who was seated on a bar stool, sipping a cup of something that steamed around her face. She looked up as the two men came down the stairs. Her eyes appeared enormous, her skin stretched over the elegant bones of her face. She glanced from Max to the man clothed from head to toe in white hazmat gear.

Lowering the cup to her lap, she asked, "Did they find out what it was?"

"Not yet. Emily, this is Dr. Tesorieri. Doctor, Emily Greene. We need to be tested," he told her briskly, shoving up the long sleeve of his T-shirt and baring his forearm.

Within minutes they were swabbed and had blood drawn. Max's estimation of her went up several notches when he realized she didn't like needles, but bared her arm for the swabbing. The skin around the corners of her eyes twitched as the doctor approached her with the syringe. She didn't shut her eyes, but stared off into the middle distance, her even white teeth clamped down on her lower lip.

The doctor packed away his syringes, the nearly full, tightly sealed vials of blood—three from each of them—and disposed of the alcohol swabs inside a small, bright red medical waste container.

"I'll let you know our findings." The doctor's voice was muffled behind the face mask.

"Yeah, you do that," Max said, pulling his sleeve down. He glanced at Emily, who had her arm bent to hold on the cotton inside her elbow. She still looked pale and shell-shocked. He wanted to kiss away the indentation of her teeth marks on her lower lip.

It was fucking good to want things, he reminded himself.

Get over it.

She held up a pale bare foot with bright pink polish on her toes. "I need shoes."

Even her feet turned him on. Craziness. "Where can I find them?"

"I have some packed, or I can just get my rain boots when we go up."

"It's raining. The boots will work. Here." He handed her a large, black leather tote that had been sitting on top of one of her packed suitcases in the foyer. Damn thing weighed at least ten pounds. "I'll get your cases from upstairs," he told her, intentionally not sounding sympathetic, as he looked into those large, confused eyes. As scared as she was, he couldn't allow himself to give her any comfort. He didn't have time for her to fall apart. Time for explanations later. Right now he wanted her out of her house and somewhere far away.

He hoped she had some answers, even if she didn't know what the hell the questions were.

They faced each other in the cool, damp night air, out on the street. Emily wasn't surprised to find herself trembling. Delayed shock? It wasn't every day a girl had a guy break into her house, let alone two. Still, she could wrap her brain around *that*. What was incomprehensible was the necessity for a hazmat team. For blood tests. For her to leave her home in the hands of strangers.

For going off with Max.

She flinched when he reached out with both hands and pulled the hood of her bright yellow slicker up over her head. She hadn't even noticed it was raining. His knuckle accidentally brushed her cheek when he withdrew.

He put his hand out. "Keys."

She curled her fist around them. "It's a new car."

"Yeah. Nice. You're not driving it right now, you can hardly stand. Get in."

Emily wanted to protest, she really did. She just didn't have the energy. Silently she handed them over and climbed into the passenger seat of her own car. That about summed up her morning, she thought. She'd somehow lost control of her own free will. Just for now, she told herself. Just for now. It didn't pay to depend on anyone but herself. But she could relax her rules and let the man drive her new car because she was shaking too badly to take the wheel.

When Max closed her door, she leaned her head back on the butter-soft black leather seat and closed her eyes.

He seemed to take up more than his fair share of the interior of her car as he adjusted the seat and familiarized himself with the controls. His dark hair was shaggy, falling into his eyes, which didn't seem to bother him. Emily's fingers itched to push it back out of his face. Instead, she clasped her hands in her lap, and reminded herself that this Max wasn't in any way the same Max she'd made love to on every available surface of her palazzo last year.

Her skin prickled as she glanced at him out of the corner of her eye. She didn't trust him, although she couldn't put her finger on why. He'd changed in some indefinable way that was unmistakable. She hadn't seen this ominous rough side of him before. A side that, while it intrigued her, also scared the crap out of her.

Perhaps because he hadn't had to use it? No. This was ingrained. Part of his DNA.

She'd foolishly expected *that* Max to call her to apologize. But she'd never be stupid enough to expect anything from *this* Max. She'd learned more about him in the last hour than she had in the four days they'd spent together last year. His personality then and now was like night and day. Light and dark.

She suspected this dark side was the real Max. The lines on either side of his mouth seemed deeper than before, but that might just be a trick of the streetlights playing on the rough stubble on his face. She couldn't imagine suave, debonair Franco leaving home looking this disreputable; what a pity.

Adrenaline seeped out of her, leaving her limp and dazed in the aftermath of so much violence. "I've never struck anyone in my life."

"Could've fooled me. That trick with your knee must've taken a lot of practice. Buckle up," Max adjusted his own seat belt to cross his large body. His deep voice stroked across her nerve endings like a mink glove, and she absently rubbed her arms through her soft sweater.

"How can you joke about it? I thought I was fighting for my life."

"Believe me. I'm not. Good thing I don't want kids, I think you gave me a knee vasectomy."

"Glad to be of service," she told him shortly, glancing at the familiar cars parked up and down her street. Her house was teeming with anonymous men in hazmat suits. Yet there were no strange vehicles anywhere on her street. "Where did those men inside park their cars? More important, where did they take the intruder?"

"Somewhere they don't have visiting hours." His tone was ironic.

His irony pissed her off. Her attraction to this man was as irrational as it was irritating. Emily dragged in

42

a shaky breath. After four months, her Maserati still had that new car smell. Unfortunately, it was obliterated with the achingly familiar scent of *him* instead.

She loved how he smelled. Fresh air with a hint of laundry soap underscored with a tang of clean, male sweat. Why the combination made her pulse race and her mouth go dry was illogical. Franco always smelled of expensive Bulgari Blu, but *his* cologne never made her pulse race or her heart do flip-flops.

Because she was the round hole she was trying to fit Franco's square peg into. The analogy almost made her smile. Almost. Seeing Max again made her realize what a horrible mistake it would be to take Franco with her to Seattle, no matter how much she wished a relationship with Franco could work. Seeing Max again squashed those thoughts flat. On the other hand, spending time with Franco away from his rather demanding family might be just what their relationship needed. Just because Max was here again didn't mean her entire life had to change.

She resented him just for *being,* and dismissed her thoughts as mere chemistry. She'd get over it. Her irritation with him would soon dispel those pesky chemicals once and for all.

She had even less in common with Max Aries than she did with Franco. She should just stick to painting and start collecting cats.

She assured herself that her stomach was doing somersaults because of recent events, but her rational mind knew that wasn't the only reason she felt off center. Where had he gone when he'd left? Where had he gone? And what had he done? She wondered about the scar she'd kissed on his left hip. She no longer believed his story of a childhood bicycle accident. Not after she'd seen him in action an hour ago.

The man was a fighter. He had other scars, too. All of which he'd explained away easily and with humor that reminded her about all the things his father had—reluctantly—told her after Max had left without a word. Now they made her wonder, too, if he was more of a liar than she'd first thought.

Daniel had been right.

She remembered the feel of his hot skin against her lips, and the way he seemed to know her body better than she did. She didn't want to remember. But she did. He'd left her without a word. No call. No e-mail. Not even a bloody fax to explain his sudden disappearance.

She'd felt foolish for feeling as though her heart had been ripped out after only a few days of knowing him. It defied logic. For months after he'd gone, she'd ached for him.

"You met him through your mother, right?"

Either Max had a short memory, or he hadn't really been as attentive as she'd thought at the time the two of *them* had met. The only thing they'd had to talk about in the first hour of meeting was his father. After the first hour they hadn't done a lot of talking. She rolled her head and opened her eyes. "Him who?"

"Daniel."

"You should have asked him that yourself." She resented the hell out of Max for ignoring his father over the years. Another straw on the pyre of her emotions about him.

"You're here."

Only because she didn't have the energy to be anywhere else right now. "He attended a fashion show in Milan," she repeated what she'd told him when they'd first met last year. "My mother was one of the models. I was eleven." Even at that age she'd known, and had been in awe of, the great Daniel Aries. He was a legend in the art world. "One thing led to another, and by the end of the week he agreed to mentor me." Years later she suspected that Daniel and her mother had had a hot and steamy affair that lasted a year or more, but all she cared about was that she was permitted to attend a string of high-profile art schools in Italy.

"How come you didn't live with him?"

"Because I went to a boarding school in Rome. And loved it." No one depended on her. She'd been allowed to make her own decisions and choices based on what *she* wanted and needed. It had been the most liberating, peaceful time of her life. "You lived with your mother after the divorce, right?"

"They never divorced," Max informed her.

"Really?" Max hadn't mentioned that before, but then neither had Daniel. The Aries men certainly kept things close to their chests. "I could have sworn Daniel told me they divorced when you were in your early teens."

45

"He walked out when I was eleven. Literally went out for cigarettes and never came back. My mother cried a hell of a lot less with him out of the picture."

"You must've been devastated, too," she said gently. Awful for any child, but she suspected particularly hard on a boy that age.

"I barely noticed he was gone."

"Your mom died a couple of years ago, right?"

He glanced at her with a small frown. "Yeah. How do you know?"

"Daniel got very drunk the day he heard." Max had sent a fax with the news. That was it. A fax to tell his father that the mother of Daniel's child was dead. "Breast cancer, right?"

"Yeah."

Was the breakup of his parents' marriage what had turned Max from a conscientious student into a wild kid? Last year, after Max had left, Daniel had admitted that he was aware of his son's wild lifestyle. Emily had immediately gone to see her doctor after her mentor had given her the gory details of his son's sex-capades.

She'd been furious—not at Daniel, who wouldn't have imagined she'd fall into bed with his promiscuous son. But with herself for blindly doing the unthinkable with a man she knew nothing about. Because of her mother's lifestyle, which included drugs, two unwanted pregnancies, and who knew *what* else unpleasant, Emily was always so damned cautious before starting any relationship.

46

Not with Max. They'd used condoms. *Most* of the time, but for months afterward she'd waited for the STD shoe to drop.

That, coupled with the way she'd allowed herself to be seduced by him within hours of their first meeting, had left her with a tangle of unsorted emotions she still hadn't resolved. She'd always had the option of saying no. She just hadn't wanted to. Hardly his fault she'd succumbed to his considerable allure.

Lots of men had tried, with considerably more charm and finesse, to get her into their beds. She'd hadn't collapsed like a soufflé into *their* arms.

Meeting Franco a few months later had gone a long way in helping her forget Max. Of course, even after four months of dating him, she hadn't slept with Franco. She wanted to be sure. Or as sure as a woman *could* be before falling into bed with a man.

Too bad she hadn't been as smart and cautious before falling like a rock for Max. She'd toppled into bed with a man she knew she shouldn't want, but just had to have. More fool her.

She'd learned her lesson.

For the millionth time, she wondered why Max had left her waiting for him at La Baraonda last March without a word. Alone in the restaurant, she'd waited for him for three ridiculous hours sipping Chianti, looking at her watch, worrying that something terrible must've happened to keep him from her. She hadn't been back to her favorite restaurant since, although Franco was dying to try it.

What had kept Max from her that night? Why had he never called to offer an apology or, at a minimum, a lame excuse? The questions had stopped twirling around in her head after several months. She'd met Franco at the Uffizi. And she'd almost forgotten Max Aries, damn it. Now he and all the unanswered questions were back.

"Why didn't you return my calls in time to come to your father's funeral, Max?" She'd girded herself to hear his voice again, but, in the end, hadn't had to face her demons because she'd left half a dozen messages on an impersonal machine. Which only added more fuel to her annoyance.

"I was out of town." He glanced in the rearview mirror before turning down a side street. "Your messages didn't reach me until yesterday."

"Are you telling me that you were on *assignment* for more than three weeks?"

He gave her a somewhat surprised look, then his face evened out and he muttered, "Yeah."

"For the magazine?"

"My boss sent me out of town."

The words were right but she knew he was lying. Why and about what was a completely different matter. But, as Daniel had often cautioned, "If Max is talking, he's lying." She knew that despite his efforts, Daniel had been rebuffed by Max over the years. But Daniel had clearly been kept apprised of his son's goings on. By Max's mother? she wondered. Daniel had never said.

"You aren't a reporter at all, are you?" Not unless he worked for *Soldier of Fortune* magazine.

"No."

He must've used all his words the first time they'd met. Now he'd run out.

"You knew exactly what you were doing in there. And you have a gun on you. Not too many reporters I know carry a loaded weapon."

The confrontation between Max and the intruder hadn't taken long, and even Emily, who hated violence of any kind, including in movies, knew that those movements were practiced. Very practiced.

"Are you some kind of policeman in the States?" It was a logical conclusion after what he'd done earlier, except that he was too . . . *steely* to be a police officer.

"Sort of. Yeah."

Anger made her grit her teeth. "What does 'sort of ' mean exactly?" At three in the morning, the wet streets were all but deserted. The tires hissed on the wet pavement, and the wipers *thump-thump-thumped* slowly across the windshield. And the smell of him, the *heat* of him, made her feel as steamy as the windows. She pressed the defrost button.

"I work for a counterterrorist organization."

Could be another bullshit story. She wasn't quite sure she believed him. But such a thing existed, so she didn't call him a liar. Yet. "I presume for the United States government?"

"Privately funded."

"You're making it up."

He shrugged.

"You're serious?"

"As death."

"Don't say that." She shivered. "Does it have a name?"

"Terrorist Force Logistic Assault Command. T-FLAC for short."

"Why did you tell me you were a photojournalist when we first met? I'm not a terrorist."

If Max really was a counterterrorist operative as he claimed to be, had *Daniel* known? Was that one more thing about his son that Daniel had conveniently omitted telling her the night he casually mentioned that his son wanted to go to the Castelreighs' party with her?

"No. But a man at that party was."

And? her brain encouraged. She turned her head to stare at him. "Was *sleeping* with me part of your way in, too? Or was that just a side benefit?" She wanted not to be hurt about it. She wanted not to be angry. She wanted, damn it, not to care one way or the other.

It was unfortunate that the memory of their short fling had made such a lasting impact. With any luck propinquity would take care of *that* problem. Her stupid heart fluttered as she caught him watching her. She turned her head to look out of the window, but it was too late to stop the heated throb of her blood. He'd had that ability. One look and she'd been toast. No, she thought, feeling a little panicky. She was the melted butter to his hot toast.

50

It was a good thing she had changed her mind about Franco, and would be seeing him soon. Their flight left in less than eight hours. Max could have Florence while she was in the States. With Franco. By the time she returned, Aries would be long gone and there'd be no need for them ever to see each other again.

She was just fine with that.

Three

BIOTOXINS. *SPORES. ASSASSINS.* EMILY SHIVERED. A second later warm air rushed out of the vent in front of her as Max turned on the heat.

The wipers sounded like a heartbeat, faster now as the rain fell harder. They sped through the shiny, dark streets of Florence toward God—and Max—only knew where.

She glanced at his profile in the bluish illumination from the dash. Her heart wouldn't behave, no matter how much she reminded herself that he was a lying, father-disrespecting, thoughtless bastard she shouldn't care a thing about.

Franco.

Her mantra wasn't working. Her breasts ached as she stared at Max's strong, tanned hands on the steering wheel and remembered what those hands had felt like on her bare skin. Or the way he'd brushed her hair back from her face to see her smile, or—Damn. Damn. Damn.

The rain was coming down in sheets, and the wipers

automatically adjusted to the conditions. "I hope we're not going too far." She had to raise her voice a little, as she changed the subject to something less inflammatory. For now. "I have to be at Galileo Galilei airport in Pisa by six tonight. And I still have a hundred things to do before I—" Even as she said it, Emily knew it didn't matter how adamant she was, or how great her desire, she wouldn't be going any-where. Not yet anyway.

Max slid her an unreadable glance. Fear churned in her stomach as she accepted that arguing with him wasn't going to change the fact that she was stuck. Everything inside her rebelled, but she said reasonably, "I won't be going anywhere for a while, will I? Did they give you any idea how long we'll be in quarantine?"

"Until they know what was in that vial, and we've both been cleared. So settle back and enjoy the scenery. We'll be staying at his place for the duration."

"By 'his' I presume you mean your father's?" Daniel's home was located on the outskirts of Flo-rence in the Certosa hills of Impruenta, only twenty minutes away. The villa was large enough to avoid seeing Max for a year. Not that it would take that long for them to get a clean bill of health, and not that Max would stick around for a hundredth of that. According to his father, a lot of women knew what the back of Max Aries looked like. She'd just been unlucky enough to be one of many.

"I imagine," Max said matter-of-factly, "he left the villa and everything else to you."

"To me? Don't be ridiculous." Emily rolled her head on the headrest to look at him. "Why on earth would he do that? You're his heir."

"Biologically."

More alike than either would admit. It tore at her knowing that it was their stubborn gene, obviously hereditary, that had thwarted any chance of a father/son relationship. Now of course it was too bloody late. "My God. The apple didn't fall far from the tree, did it? You and your father both got the same dogged stubborn streak. Biological or any other way you look at it, you were his only child. There's no reason to suppose he didn't leave everything to you. Who else would he name in his will?"

"You were more a daughter to him than I was ever his son. He loved you," Max told her flatly. "Enough reason to leave all his worldly possessions to *you*. He always did have his priorities straight."

"He loved you, too." *In his own way.*

Max's hands tightened on the steering wheel. Instead of defending Daniel she kept her mouth shut. She was sure his father had loved him. But she had no illusions about the man who had helped her rise to the top in a field where not just talent, but who you knew, could make or break you.

Daniel had loved Daniel best of all.

She'd adored him. Daniel Aries had been an amazing, if oblivious, mentor. Emily also acknowledged he'd been a shitty and oblivious parent, too. But it was partly Max's fault that he and his father had had a lousy relationship. As long as she'd known him, Daniel had tried his best to make a connection with Max. Max hadn't been interested.

"I suspect that his death and your intruder are somehow linked," Max said evenly, shoving his seat back a little more to accommodate his long legs. "Tell me what you know about his day-to-day life in the months before he died."

Emily frowned, tucking one leg under her, and turning in her seat to face him. "What an odd thing to say. Why would you think Daniel's suicide had anything to do with this morning? You might not have gotten my messages in a timely fashion, but it's been almost a month since your father died."

"It wasn't suicide. And your friend back there didn't drop in for a social call. He was there to kill you."

"Ki—My God, Max! Scare the crap out of me, why don't you? That's a hell of a stretch. I'm an artist. There might be someone who doesn't like my technique, but I doubt they'd want to kill me for it."

"Someone killed the old man. You two were close. And less than a month later, someone breaks into your house and deposits a vial of an unknown substance in *your* bedroom. I don't believe in coincidence."

"There are all sorts of different reasons," Emily pointed out. "How about *this* scenario? That guy showed up at my place to wait for *you*. No, really. Think about it. I've lived in my palazzo for more than ten years without anyone ever breaking in. Then suddenly, on the same night—ten minutes before *you* show up—*he* arrives.

"You have a gun. He has a gun. You know how to restrain a guy and knock him out, he knows how to throw some pretty impressive punches, too."

Max made a growling noise, which Emily wisely ignored. She adjusted the controls so the warm air blew on her feet. "Or not. I really don't know what that guy was up to in my house, but as hard as it is for us both to believe, as awful as it is to imagine, your father threw himself from the balcony outside his tower studio." Dramatic and theatrical and *typical* of Daniel. "He left a note."

"If he were going to kill himself he would have used pills. Not a gunshot, which tends to be messy as hell, and *not* by jumping off a third-floor balcony to splat on the driveway below and be seen by a bunch of servants and house guests, which is messier still. Trust me," he said wryly. "He didn't jump."

Emily reached over and almost touched his arm. He'd pushed up the long sleeves of his black T-shirt, baring strong forearms dusted with crisp dark hair. Her mouth went dry. She could almost feel the heat of his skin, almost feel the dark hair tickling her palm. Her body listed toward him as though he were a magnet, and she a sliver of metal.

Danger, oh Lord. Danger.

She redirected her hand, adjusting one of the air vents instead. Then straightened out in her seat, still looking at him, but not quite as engaged. The car felt extremely small and confined, and she was enveloped by the delicious and familiar smell of him that seemed to permeate her very pores and fill her brain with wicked and unwanted memories. Pheromones, nothing but pheromones. Whatever the hell it was made her want to rub her body against his like a purring cat.

"But that's what he did," she said gently, understanding his disbelief because she'd felt it, too, when she'd heard the news.

Max shook his head. "A, he was too vain a man to end up splattered on the driveway. B, the trajectory was wrong. If he'd jumped, he'd've landed closer to the building. He was thrown."

For someone who'd barely known his father, Max seemed to know Daniel pretty well. He was right. Daniel had been extremely vain. He'd been a striking-looking man even at seventy plus. And had kept his hair the same rich, dark brown color as Max's. Daniel had also had a face-lift when he'd turned sixty, and several other minor procedures—"tune-ups" he'd called them—over the past few years. "Are you sure?"

"I have someone doing a tox screen and checking his body for suspicious marks. I'll know more in a couple of days."

The seat belt tightened as she turned her entire body to stare at him. "Your father's been *buried* for three weeks. What are you saying? That you had his body *exhumed* on *conjecture*?"

"Yeah."

Emily tried to digest what he was telling her as she observed the rain sheeting the windows, blurring the dark houses as they passed through the empty streets. She also *tried* not to let her own feelings for him, and her own guilt, cloud her judgment. She glanced away, refusing to be drawn in by his tight jaw or the way his knuckles showed white as they gripped the leather-covered wheel.

Max wasn't here to see *her.* He was here to say good-bye to a man he'd barely known. She needed to keep reminding herself that his presence in Italy wasn't personal. Her feelings for Max were jumbled and disjointed. She missed Daniel. She was still mourning his loss. She'd forgotten Max—*almost.* She'd thought she wanted a life with Franco. Now she wasn't sure. Damn it.

How had life gotten so screwed up in such a short time?

Her stomach wasn't clenching just because of Daniel's recent death. Or even wholly attributable to the intruder. Or the fight. Or the vial. Or the hazmat guys.

Not hearing from Max right away had given her perspective and a plan of action. Even when she was leaving him curt messages and silently cursing his answering machine, she was rehearsing different scenarios. He'd walk back into her life and she'd be calm, collected, and immune.

Why wouldn't she be? She had an incredible new man in her life. A man who cared deeply for her. A man she'd considered marrying. A man she'd been taking home to meet her family. The final test. That seemed a lot of past tenses all of a sudden. She'd been prepared for seeing Max again. What she hadn't been prepared for was the resurgence of heat. Not the kind of thing a girl could prep for. At least not this girl.

She'd had all year to try to sort the wheat from the chaff. And she'd just about come to terms with what had happened between them the first time around. Now Max was back to muddy her emotional waters all over again. *The big jerk.*

Just for a few hours, she reminded herself. She could deal with him for those hours. And then go back to forgetting him.

Sure. Just like I forgot him for the last eleven months, one week, and three days? Right.

Think Franco.

This time tomorrow, she told herself firmly, they'd be in Seattle, and Max would be nothing more than a distant and annoying memory.

This was about Daniel. Only Daniel. "The suicide note was handwritten," she told Max, recognizing where they were, and feeling a strange combination of fear and anticipation. "The police asked me to identify his handwriting. It was very distinctive. There was no doubt at all that it was Daniel's."

"Then either we're dealing with an excellent forger, or they used something he'd written for something else. What did it say?"

Daniel's strong, unmistakable handwriting on that white sheet of paper would forever be indelibly etched in her mind. "He wrote, 'I'm sorry, I can't do it. It's just not worth it anymore.'"

"Could have meant anything."

She'd thought it was odd, too. But in context it made some sort of sense. "But it didn't." She'd never get over the fact that she hadn't been there for Daniel when he'd really needed her. He'd seemed a bit more subdued than usual when they'd last spoken, but that was understandable considering his hands had been bothering him more than usual.

Max turned the car into the long, tree-lined road leading up to the villa just as the sky was lightening from black to charcoal. "I'm sure you'll find things at the villa that will help you connect with your father. He would've liked that."

"How he felt is irrelevant to me."

"Any relationship requires that two people make some kind of effort to communicate. Neither of you ever did. You hurt each other."

Max barked a sound that was supposed to pass for a laugh. "Hurt me? He was barely aware of my existence. And I didn't give a damn enough to be hurt by him."

She'd touched a raw nerve. Emily decided to drop the subject. For now. "Have you ever been here?"

"No."

The tall wrought iron gates illuminated by their headlights opened slowly on well-oiled hinges, as if welcoming them with open arms.

"*You* must've spent a lot of time here if he had a

microchip put in the car to activate the gates for you."

He. No name. "I did. But it was also more convenient. I tended to lose the gate control. He has five cars, all of them have the opener installed. I think the lawyer had them taken into Florence to have them appraised—"

"He did."

"Then I'm sure you'll want to take at least one of them with you when you leave."

"Maybe," Max said blandly.

Maybe? He couldn't have sounded less interested. Fine. Emily had no desire to spend any more time with Max than she absolutely had to. If this was the real him, she'd come to realize in the last hour that he'd probably done her a favor by leaving. Too bad he intrigued her now more than ever, she thought with a glimmer of annoyance. She wasn't fond of puzzles, and she was too linear and straightforward to read between his lines and try and figure out who or what he was. Still, there was a strength about him, a strength that had nothing to do with what he'd done to her intruder, that captivated her. Ticked her off, too.

The gates slowly closed behind the car, and they continued up the ancient cypress tree-lined driveway that cut a pale swath between acres of lawn and trees. In the predawn light the usually vibrant and lush gardens were stark and somber, as if painted in grisaille, draped in the incredible tonality of a black-and-white Sickle's chiaroscuro. Emily loved the grounds austere like this almost as much as she did in midsummer when everything was in a Technicolor of full bloom.

"Last summer your father had a hundred new trees planted in the olive groves," she told Max, whether he wanted to know or not. The eerie stillness of the estate, and the villa ahead, dark and grim, unnerved her. She wasn't given to idle chitchat. She spent too much time alone for that, but needing to break the thick, uncomfortable silence was changing her usual desire for peaceful quiet.

If Max knew what was going on he wasn't being chatty with the information. And she didn't want to talk about the things that had gone bump in the night until she was in brilliant light. Be it sunlight, or a good one-twenty bulb.

"Your father's gardens were quite famous, you know," she said, almost desperately. Anything not to think about what had happened in her palazzo earlier. Who *was* that man? What had he brought with him? God. This was like a surreal movie. The kind she didn't enjoy watching.

She tried to think how she'd explain this to Franco, and almost smiled trying to imagine him, in his Armani suit, his razor-cut hair, and his seven-hundred-dollar shoes, battling the thug in her hallway. The image wouldn't form.

"Earth to Emily? Gardens?"

"Not that Daniel worked in them." She tried to block out the memory of Max's grim expression as he'd knocked the vial from her hand in her bedroom earlier. Her brain couldn't even *comprehend* things like biotoxins and hazmat teams.

"He loved to look down from the tower when he was painting." She knew she was talking too fast. Worse, she knew Max had absolutely no interest in what she was saying. And she didn't want to think about the tower that had taken her mentor's life.

"It's exquisitely beautiful, particularly in the spring and summer. Of course to maintain it, he has upward of a hundred people working in the garden and the house."

"A hundred and twelve," Max inserted, his eyes glittering in the backlight of the headlights. He turned off the wipers as the rain stopped. "As of three days ago, they're on vacation indefinitely."

"I thought you'd never been here."

"I haven't. Talked to his lawyer on the way."

With Max's stewardship the place would go to ruin. But it was his right to do whatever he wanted with the property.

The villa was empty. She and Max, and all the scary events of their morning, would be alone in the enormous house for the duration of their quarantine. Emily found her heart beating much too fast as they drew closer to the main building. She prayed "the duration" was very, very short. The tires crunched on the wet gravel, and the headlights cut through the gloom, reflecting in the dark windows ahead.

The muted burnt umber of the ancient walls was set off with *pietra serena,* a local gray sandstone, to beautifully enhance the corbels and graceful columns holding up the arches.

"That's the Cedar Garden over there." She pointed to the side of the house where a sweeping lawn could be glimpsed between high hedges and ancient trees. She'd picked roses from the antique rosebushes growing there, and fresh tart fruit from the potted lemon trees planted in the enormous *pietra serena* pedestals that made graceful architectural statements between the trees.

She loved everything about the villa and surrounding gardens, and had painted some of her best work here over the years. The fifteenth century villa, originally a Medici family palace, was reputed to be one of the finest examples of Renaissance architecture in the world. By the time Max was done with neglecting it, it would go wild and overgrown.

They pulled to a stop in front of the villa. Emily didn't want to get out of the car. And God—she did not want to go inside.

The thought that it would no longer look as it did now, and no longer be available to her, gave her a hollow ache in her stomach. But right now she had bigger concerns. She may have breathed, touched, or absorbed some god-awful bloody toxin and be dead by lunchtime.

"The garden was named for the three-hundred-year-old cedar of Lebanon planted in the mid—" He looked at her, one eyebrow raised. "You don't give a damn, do you?"

No, Max thought, he sure as hell *didn't* give a rat's ass about anything that had to do with his sperm

63

donor. But Emily was obviously scared and confused, and by the look of her pale face, and the dark circles under her pretty eyes, she was ready to collapse. She had a sexy, husky voice that was a pleasure to listen to, though. If talking kept her upright, then she could chat away until he could get her secured within the compound Daniel had called a home.

He stopped the car as close to the house as possible. Emily rubbed a hand across the bridge of her nose. The gesture showed her vulnerability and was strangely appealing. Max wondered what the hell she and his donor had gotten themselves involved in. A murder and an attempted murder.

Somebody had pissed somebody off.

Or?

Hell if he knew. But he'd sure as shit find out.

"Damn it," Emily said with a small catch in her voice as she looked up at the villa. "I miss Daniel. I can't believe he's gone."

Didn't bother Max any, but he kept his expression inscrutable and waited her out.

"This whole . . . thing. Daniel dying. That creepy guy at my place . . . None of it feels real." She didn't move, but her chest swelled as she dragged in a deep breath.

"Wait here. I want to search the house before we go in."

The blood drained from her already pale face. "You think there's someone inside waiting for us?"

"Want to take the chance?"

"No. But I'm not going to be a sitting duck in the car if someone wants to use me for target practice." She got out and closed her door with an expensive click. "I'll take my chances inside." Shaking off the apathy that had kept her pinned, she took off with purposeful strides toward the door. Her unbound hair billowing behind her reminded Max of a matador approaching a bull, cape flying.

"Besides," she said briskly. "I have the code to get in."

She headed for the entry keypad beside the double front doors.

Emily, as Daniel's friend and protégé, had full access to the villa. Max had to have intel get him the address. He hadn't known nor cared for the specifics before today. He'd been given the access code, as well as the security code for the alarm located just inside the front door.

I'm here, you old bastard. "Hang back a second," he told her, Glock in hand.

"I have to turn off the alarm inside first."

She didn't move out of the way, so he had to brush her body to get close enough to the pad on the wall. The scent of her reminded him of sun-warmed sheets, rain, and roses. Fragrances that always conjured memories of the Sunday they'd spent making love in her big, soft bed. And on the sofa. And on the floor. And in the bathtub . . .

"I've got it." He tried not to breathe too deeply as he stabbed in the code on the keypad. 11–21–19–72. Ironically, his birthday.

Emily frowned. "How do you know the codes?"

"I know people." With other pertinent intel, Daniel's security codes, as well as Emily's, had been sent to him before the T-FLAC jet touched down at the Amerigo Vespucci airport at one this morning. And if his people assured him the death had been murder, not suicide, then there was no doubt in Max's mind.

The front door unlatched with a muted click. Weapon ready, he brought a finger to his lips, then held up his palm for her to stay put. Eyes wide, she nodded. Stepping around her, he opened the heavy door. He was relatively sure the house was empty. It had been swept by a local T-FLAC team in the last fifteen minutes. His cell phone had vibrated in his back pocket with the all clear code as they'd approached the front gate.

Still, Max had a bad feeling he couldn't shake.

When his team's lives, and his own, depended on him making the right split-second judgment calls, he trusted his intuition. That and experience, which had been honed and proven on countless missions. Shit happened.

He didn't want shit happening when Emily was involved.

So, even though the villa and extensive grounds had been given the all clear, he'd do his own sweep before he'd relax for what was left of the night. Which wasn't much. The sun was making a valiant attempt to rise. He needed at least a couple of hours of sleep to function on all cylinders. And Emily was clearly at the end of her emotional rope as she leaned against the door jamb, waiting for him to tell her the alarm system had been disarmed.

He found the sophisticated security system keypad just inside the door, and started disarming it.

"You only have twenty seconds."

It took him five. "Come in and close the door so I can activate it again." His voice was just loud enough to carry the few feet to where she stood. As soon as she was in, front door locked behind her, he instructed, "Wait here. I'm going to look around."

Four

IS IT OKAY IF I TURN ON SOME LIGHTS?" SHE WHISpered. He saw the nervous shift of her eyes. She was justifiably scared, but she wasn't making a production out of it. He had to admire her grit.

Lights on or off weren't going to matter if there was a determined killer in the house whose eyes had already adjusted to the dark. "Sure."

Emily turned on the lights, illuminating a big, ostentatious foyer. The domed ceiling was frescoed, and enormous gilt-framed paintings lined the walls above while spindly antique tables and chairs hugged the walls below.

Place was ornate as hell. Max hated it.

It was also cold, and smelled of stale air. Max couldn't picture his warmhearted mother ever living here. It had all the cozy warmth of a sterile museum.

Utilizing his "cell phone" as a thermal monitor, he quickly—the term relative considering the size of the place—searched the villa bottom to top. It was a ridiculously large home for one man and his ego. Three floors of overdone, expensive furniture. As he searched for an intruder, or whatever the hell was poking his intuition, he imagined Emily at ease among all of the antiques and gilt. Personally, he liked plain comfortable furniture that he could put his feet on and relax without worrying about dropping the resale value.

He wasn't impressed with the villa.

But he *was* impressed as hell with the state-of-the-art security system. Must've cost the bastard a pretty penny to keep his precious art inviolate. Hadn't kept his killer out. Which meant the old man had known, had invited, his murderer inside.

Satisfied that the building was secure, he jogged downstairs to find Emily exactly where he'd left her. She hadn't even taken off her yellow coat, merely pushed the hood back off her face.

She looked as exhausted as he felt, yet, as if she'd hostessed here a thousand times, she asked, "Would you like a cup of tea? Or something to eat?"

No. What he'd like to do was take her up to one of the bedrooms upstairs and strip her naked, then bury himself in her soft warm body and fall asleep that way. "Sure."

"I'll turn on the heat on the way. It's freezing in here." She started removing her coat, but a strand of dark hair got tangled on a button.

"Here, let me," Max said before she ripped her hair out at the root. Touching her could be a big mistake. Gritting his teeth, he reached out, freeing her hair of the button. The scent of roses and linseed oil, the most unlikely combination of seductive fragrances, made his body stiffen.

He stepped away from her. "One cup and we're going to bed." He only noticed her shoulders tense because he was so acutely aware of her. "Five bedrooms upstairs, right?"

They entered the vast kitchen, where he'd left all the lights on after his search.

"There's a bedroom down here, too."

Max knew. He'd been through the kitchen and bedroom and large walk-in pantry on his sweep. Emily tossed her yellow rain slicker over a chair at the big farmhouse table in the middle of the room and went to fill the kettle.

Clearly she was familiar with the kitchen, as she took out cups and a bowl of sugar. Watching her graceful movements, he pulled out a chair, sitting down cautiously. His balls still ached from her knee action.

"I'll take that one."

She glanced over her shoulder, eyes shadowed. "What one?"

"Bedroom downstairs."

"Damn," she muttered, obviously suddenly remembering something. "I have to make a phone call."

"At three-thirty in the morning?"

"Oh." She looked at her watch. Biting the corner of

her lower lip, she shook her head. "I'll call him later."

Her lips were beautifully shaped. He'd like to be the one doing the biting. "Him?"

"My friend, Franco, is coming with me to Seattle."

"Taking him home to meet the folks?"

She gave him a cool look from large, hot-chocolate-colored eyes. "None of your business."

Didn't mean he couldn't make it his fucking business, Max thought with unexpected savagery. What had he expected? That she'd wait for him to come back? Indefinitely? Hell, ever? And after he hadn't bothered to call her?

Since he'd had absolutely zero intention of returning—ever—he wondered almost abstractly why the thought that she hadn't waited pissed him off. He was a logical, rational man. His reaction to this woman was anything but.

Still, it pissed him off royally knowing that she'd found some other man to warm her bed. "Does Frank have a last name?" he asked as pleasantly as he could through gritted teeth.

"*Franco* Bozzato." She took a pack of cookies out of an enameled tin on the counter, then moved the kettle off the burner before it whistled. "You wouldn't know him."

Max would know more about Signore Franco Bozzato by morning than Emily ever would. "Probably not," he said agreeably as she filled their cups, added sugar to both, and brought them to the table. She went back for the cookies.

"We don't need a plate," he muttered as she reached into the upper cupboard for one. "What does your boyfriend do?" Max felt an insane spurt of jealousy, which he quickly interpreted as heartburn. The woman had a life that had nothing to do with him. He felt mildly guilty about using her last year to get a low key intro to Arkady Strugatsky, a high-level Russian terrorist who considered himself a patron of the arts.

T-FLAC had tried various ways to separate the Russian from his bodyguards. The man had been as inviolable as Fort Knox. The party, a high-society, high-profile black-tie event with a silent auction, had been held at a private castle on the outskirts of Rome. Because many of the items up for bid had been valued in the millions, security had been straitjacket tight. Even Strugatsky's phalanx of guards had been instructed to wait for him outside. No arms were permitted through the metal detectors.

Getting in undetected would have been impossible. Getting out wasn't that big a problem. Not for someone whose name was on the printed guest list. Photographed, fingerprinted, and vouched for by the highly respectable Miss Emily Greene. Talk about provenance.

He and his team had gotten what they wanted, Strugatsky without his bodyguards. It had been a relatively simple matter to escort him out of the party and into the limo waiting at the back door. Max hadn't needed to return to the party, or to Emily. Nor had he needed to spend the next couple of days with her.

He considered the extra time he'd spent with her a bonus. He'd liked her, she'd liked him—two consenting adults.

Thanks to her, Strugatsky was some Bubba's bitch in Leavenworth.

The end had justified the means. No harm, no foul.

Nobody needed to know how hard it had been to walk away from her when the job had been done. And if he hadn't been called suddenly to another op, he might have stayed a few more days if she'd been willing. And she would have been.

Still. It had all worked out in the end.

"Franco is an investment banker." Emily remained standing, cradling her cup between her hands as she inhaled the fragrant steam. Light refracted off the studs in her ears, and Max noticed one was missing, and another had green paint on it. "It's weird being here when there isn't anyone around. Your father always had a house full of people."

"I'm sure he did."

She narrowed her eyes. "You don't have to say it as though this was the . . . *Kasbah,* and he had a smorgasbord of drugs, and hot and cold naked women running around. He didn't have wild sex parties. He was a sophisticated, well-educated man. His social circle was filled with people who were smart and interesting. People admired him. Loved him. He had a lot—" her breath caught. "A *lot* of friends."

He was an asshole, a womanizer, and a sorry excuse for a human being. And if you believe he didn't have a parade of women in and out of this mausoleum, you were sadly duped. He was just smart enough to keep his two lives separate, one behind closed doors. Just because he and Daniel didn't have any contact, didn't mean Max hadn't kept a weather eye on him. Not out of any personal interest. But Max hadn't wanted the son of a bitch to suddenly show up on his mother's doorstep one day.

She'd died two years ago, and then he just didn't give a damn what the man did or to whom. But the reports still came in. He hadn't bothered reading any of them in years. Their tenuous tie was gone.

He'd known just enough to "convince" the bastard to invite him to the party last year. He hadn't told him why he wanted to go, and Daniel had never asked. He'd thrown Emily to his son without knowing who or what Max was, or why he wanted to be accompanied to the event by someone everyone there knew and liked.

"I didn't say anything," Max said mildly, drinking the tepid tea he didn't want. Emily's loyalty to Daniel was sorely misplaced. But he wasn't going to be the one to burst her bubble.

"You didn't have to. Your eyes sneered."

"Eyes can sneer?"

She covered a yawn with her hand. "Yours do."

He'd heard worse. Did Frank Bozzo's eyes sneer? Max bet not.

Emily sipped from her cup, watching him over the rim. She had gorgeous eyes, but right now they were heavy-lidded with exhaustion. He could go another couple of hours. But he was going to need to sleep soon. He had an unexpected but familiar itch that told him something murky, and relevant, was rearing its ugly head out of his sperm donor's past. Max didn't know what, or where, but he sure as shit suspected that there was something going on. Something bad. Something urgent.

He'd arranged to get copies of those reports he hadn't bothered reading. Perhaps there'd be some clues to be found there. It was a start.

"You speak Italian very well." Emily rubbed her eye and yawned. "You had an excellent teacher. You know all the nuances of the language. Did you learn at— where was that? Stanford?"

Max hadn't shared that information with her. A year ago, he'd made sure she'd done most of the talking. That nugget could only have come from her mentor. The old man had known that much about him. Interesting. He wondered if her source had also known he'd attended MIT.

"Yeah. Turns out that I have a natural aptitude for languages." *Especially after T-FLAC recruited me in my first year of college.*

"Do you still live in San Francisco?" she asked, her speech a little slurred with exhaustion. Max knew he was postponing going their separate ways to get some sleep. But looking at this woman was enough to turn a saint into a sinner. And he'd never been a saint.

"Yeah. Off and on. More off. I travel a lot."

He knew she'd been born in Seattle, Washington. But with her dark hair and eyes she could easily pass as Italian. He knew more about her than he'd let on in the car. He knew her mother had been a model. He knew where and when she'd gone to her fancy, over-priced boarding school, and that she'd stayed to attend Istituto statale d'arte di Venezi, the art school in Venice, followed by several years at Accademia di belle arti di Roma.

She'd graduated top of her class and been sought after, and fought over, by top museums all over the world. She was *that* good as a fine art restorer. Her CV was long and impressive. In art circles she was considered number one, having surpassed her mentor several years ago.

And through it all, Daniel Aries had been beside her. Teaching and guiding her. Her mentor and surrogate father.

Max wondered if her mother and his sperm donor had had an affair fifteen years ago. Probably, if the mother looked anything like the daughter.

Emily yawned again, then lifted her arms over her head, hands clasped, and arched her back, stretching like a lazy cat. Dropping her arms she leaned a jean-clad hip on the table. She waved a vague hand around the room. "Would you consider living here?"

"Hell no."

She gave him a disapproving look. "Then you should sell. Everything in the villa should be donated

75

to museums. Your father's talent made him an extremely wealthy man. He spent his money on what he loved most—"

Wine, women . . . "Himself?"

"Art," she said crossly. "He has—had—an enviable collection that people would kill for—" Her eyes widened. "Lord, Max. Do you think that—no. Now I'm believing your nonsense. Nobody killed your father. Not for his art collection," she trailed off, shaking her head. "Of *course* nobody killed him for his collection. Nothing was stolen."

She had a clever imagination, and the ability to rein in the quantum leap of logic her tired brain had just made. At least she was now tacitly acknowledging that the man had been murdered.

She rubbed a hand over her face, fatigue evident in every line of her slender body. The early morning events had taken a toll on her. In the last couple of hours, she'd knocked a would-be assassin out cold and brought a highly trained T-FLAC operative to his knees. It wouldn't take long for her to believe as he did, that her intruder had come to kill her.

And while Max felt zero emotion over the death, accidental or otherwise, of Daniel, a man he'd never known, Emily had loved the son of a bitch. She was hurting, exhausted, and scared.

And Max suspected it wasn't going to get better real soon. He glanced away from the distracting glossy shine of her hair in the soft lighting above the table, the sparkle of the diamond studs in her ears, and the way her wide eyes looked weighted with sleep as she valiantly tried to stay awake.

His pulse kicked. Beneath those jeans and sweater were three little dolphins waiting to be rediscovered.

Christ.

She rotated her head. Max wanted to run his tongue over the tendons and nerves there. He reminded himself that he wasn't here for *her*. He was here because she'd called him. That was the *only* reason. Oh, yeah. Minor detail. And because someone had tried to kill her tonight.

"God. I don't know anymore." she pushed her cup aside, her dark gaze drifting over him, and shifted away a little too quickly. "I need some sleep. Maybe we can think more cohesively in the morning."

She met his gaze. "I loved your father, and I love this villa. Not for the value, but for the history and beauty of the things it took him forty years to collect."

"Fine with me. If he didn't leave it to you outright, you could pay me a buck, and all this Liberace-esque splendor will be yours."

Emily straightened. "You're a Philistine, do you know that?"

Max's lips quirked. He'd been called much, much worse.

Emily woke to find the sun shining through the window to warm her bare skin. She'd been so tired by the time she'd gone upstairs to bed that she'd stripped and fallen face-first between the lavender-scented sheets.

She blinked open her eyes. The room was golden and toasty warm, tempting her to go back to sleep. She pulled the covers up to her shoulders, knowing she had to get up.

For one thing she still had a plane to catch. *If* she was cleared of any dire disease. She also wanted to call Franco and let him know she might have to meet him in Pisa instead of having him pick her up at her palazzo.

She didn't want to consider the ramifications if she had to cancel her flight. She felt fine though. Better than fine. Surely if she'd contracted something god-awful it would have manifested itself by now?

She smelled coffee and sat up.

Uh-oh. The clothes she'd left on the floor were now neatly folded on a chair. Her suitcase, last seen in the trunk of her car, was now on the bench at the foot of the bed.

Max had apparently paid her an early morning visit while she slept. She hoped she'd kicked off the covers *after* his visit. Her face went hot. Silly to blush like a teenager because Max might possibly have seen her naked.

"It's not like he hasn't seen my naked parts before," she reminded herself out loud, jumping down off the high mattress and heading for the en suite bathroom with its walls of mirrors. As she inspected her body—front and back—for anything out of the ordinary, she remembered the roughness of his jaw as he'd kissed his way up her body a year ago. The sensual memory solicited almost the same response from her body as the real thing. Her nipples remembered the wet heat of his mouth, and the exquisite sensation of his teeth scouring the tight buds.

Get a grip.

After a nice hot shower, she dressed in jeans and a long-sleeved, shocking-pink sweater with matching pink socks. Not bothering with makeup, she combed back her wet hair and went downstairs in her stockinged feet in search of coffee.

The sun-bright kitchen was empty. But the coffeepot was full. After pouring a large mug and adding sugar, she went in search of Max, sipping as she walked through the large rooms of the villa. The black coffee was strong and bitter, and with just a little milk added would have been perfect. Still, the caffeine did its job and finished the waking-up process. Daniel's son was probably counting the silver and calling an appraiser in to tell him how much money he could get when he sold everything.

It had taken Daniel most of his life to amass an enviable art collection. From what she knew of Max, he'd probably sell the lot to the highest bidder. Emily tried not to resent him for his greed. Hell, she didn't know him, just *of* him from the stories Daniel had shared. Time would tell.

She wasn't ready to see Daniel's studio without Daniel in it. She also wasn't ready to see *Max*. She was still annoyed at him for not arriving in time to attend his own father's funeral. And for leaving her without a backward glance. And for being a player with the moral fiber of a fruit fly.

Worst of all, she admitted to herself as she headed to the tower and Daniel's studio, *worst of all* was the way her traitorous body responded to him whenever he was within sight. Her brain and her hormones were in violent conflict.

"My new mantra," she muttered, climbing the stairs to the tower's second-floor studio. *"Mind over matter." My mind, and Max Aries doesn't matter. I can do this. It's only for a few more hours at most.* She smiled as she reached the landing.

She was woman. Hear her ignore.

Earpiece in place, Max leaned his shoulder against the casement of the open French door. He stared unseeing at the vast stretch of lawn and the leafless trees as he filled in his Control, Darius, about the events of the early hours of that morning. The rain had finally stopped about half an hour ago, and the landscape had been washed clean. Water sparkled like diamonds as it dripped off bare branches.

The subject switched to operative Catherine Seymour's, code name "Savage," recent activities. "We fucking know Savage is a rogue operative," he snapped. "Why the hell would you—Yeah, I hear you." Keep your enemy close. He got it. But it pissed him off that the powers-that-be at T-FLAC headquarters were still sending Savage out on ops. Minor ones, true. But they had confirmation that she'd almost killed Taylor Kincaid in the op in South Africa three months ago. Hunt St. John was gunning for Savage's blood, and Max didn't blame him.

The more they'd dug, the more crap they'd unearthed about one of their best sharpshooters. Savage had been with T-FLAC for almost ten years. While they'd been fucking chasing their tails trying to track down the head of the Black Rose terrorist organization, one of that slithery tango group had been working right alongside them.

They knew Savage was a Black Rose asset. Catching her was easy. But keeping her close and still active would lead them to the head of the tango group. And that's what they wanted. Savage couldn't sneeze without them knowing the velocity.

"Where's she now?" Max listened, then gave a short bark of laughter. "Not a shitload of tangos in Portland. Anything else of interest?" He'd called in to see if their medical team had discovered anything interesting about the old man's body after exhumation. So far they hadn't. Still, Max knew how thorough they were. If there was anything hinky, other than being tossed off a three-story balcony, they'd find it.

He listened absently as his Control, Darius gave him a thumbnail sketch of what had happened—tango related—in the world at large in the last twenty-four hours. The U.S. embassy in Mauritius had had several bomb threats. A church had been blown up in Brazil, thirty dead. A bunch of lilies had been left near the site. A synagogue in Rio had a minor explosion, more lilies. *That* was a pattern they were following, and keeping a tight watch on. A train had been derailed in Hong Kong—three hundred dead or injured. T-FLAC had dispatched teams to the various locations.

Business as usual.

He stepped out onto the narrow balcony. Gripping the smooth stone balustrade, he looked down. There was still a stain on the driveway below. He felt nothing for the man who'd died there. Nothing but curiosity as to *why* he'd been killed. And even that would've been mild if Emily hadn't somehow been dragged into whatever it was.

Max had been offered the help of T-FLAC resources, and he'd taken them up on their offer. T-FLAC had the best—of everything. While this was a personal matter, he needed T-FLAC's vast resources to bring the investigation to a close quickly. He had better things to do than look into the dark corners of the life of a man he didn't know or like.

Daniel must've had hundreds of enemies. Max decided he'd make a list, cross-check that with anyone connected to Emily, then check out the most likely suspects. Then leave the rest to the local police.

This time when he left, he'd tell Emily good-bye.

He'd be back at work by Monday.

Emily walked into Daniel's studio and inhaled the familiar, pungent smells. Even though he'd been gone for weeks the stinky French cigarettes he'd chain-smoked, against doctor's orders, warred with the overlying odor of paint thinner and brush cleaners.

The scent, and the organized chaos, made Emily's chest ache with suppressed emotion. It looked as if Daniel had paused for a cigarette break and would be right back. Her throat constricted. It was hard to comprehend that a man as vital as Daniel Aries was dead.

The double French doors leading out to the balcony were wide open. She imagined it was Max's attempt at getting rid of the strong smells in the room. It wasn't working, but no way was she going to shut the doors, despite the chill. In fact, she had no intention of getting anywhere near that balcony. Whether her friend had been pushed or jumped, she didn't want to see where he'd spent the last few moments of his life.

Max sat at his father's battered antique oak desk in the far corner of the studio, his back to her. She'd heard his deep voice as she'd come up the stairs and she presumed he'd been on the phone. He wasn't now, but he didn't turn around. She'd bet her last American dollar that he knew exactly where she was as she crossed behind him, her socks silent on the paint-splattered wood floor.

She'd love to paint him. Just as he was, limned by a stray shimmer of sunlight. His shaggy hair was damp, and, despite the lingering reek of stale tobacco, she could smell the soap on his skin. A shiver that had nothing to do with the damp air traveled across her skin.

God, it should be a crime for a man to be that sexy and appealing. And really, she thought, getting just a glimpse of his profile as he bent over whatever he was reading, he shouldn't be appealing at all. Especially not to her. Once bitten, twice stupid.

The problem was her brain and body weren't in sync.

Her brain, considerably more intelligent than her body, told her to hop that flight with Franco. To check into the hotel in Seattle and immediately jump his bones. They'd been dating for four months. He'd unknowingly paid for the mistake she'd made with Max, whom she'd fallen into bed with in *four* seconds flat.

So far, Franco had been very patient.

It had been so good with Max that she hadn't been interested in okay. She'd *wanted* the bells and whistles. Unfortunately, her body—even though the guy had ditched her and she had no idea that she would ever see him again—had waited eleven months and so many weeks to see *Max's* again. While her brain told her Franco was a good guy who genuinely cared about her, her body just wasn't that interested.

Her traitorous body felt urgent, aroused, and downright anticipatory just looking at Max. Who wasn't a good guy at all. He was a womanizer, a liar, and a socially irresponsible player.

Said womanizer, liar, and socially irresponsible player was currently putting out enough pheromones to render her incapable of rational speech. *She didn't need speech. She needed one word—no.*

N.O.

Her body *needed* a long walk in the rain to cool off as she repeated the word over and over. And over. Until it sank in.

N.O.

Not to Max. But to herself.

It wasn't a smart move to look at him, she decided, and she looked down at her hands gripping the table. Her hands were, to her, her most attractive feature. Her nails were short, usually grubby, and the closest they got to polish was oil paint. Her fingers seemed to have a creativity all their own, and even she was frequently astounded at what and how she painted. But that was her secret. Her vanity.

She wanted to put her hands creatively all over Max.

Crazy. Dangerous. Tempting.

But really, really, *really* stupid.

Draining the last of her now tepid coffee, she placed the mug on the table holding Daniel's state-of-the-art DïLonghi coffeemaker, a microwave, and a small refrigerator. When Daniel had been working he'd frequently camped out up here. Her heart felt heavy. That hadn't been for a long time. Yet she knew he'd come up here every day anyway. Not to work, although knowing Daniel, he was sure to have tried.

How sad to be unable to do the thing one loved the most.

Which was worse? Daniel killing himself because he couldn't bear to no longer paint? Or some stranger taking his life? Both were unthinkable.

Emily leaned her hip on the table. Since Max was

low on social graces she figured she might as well cut right to the chase. There was still plenty of time to go home, get her stuff, then hit the airport to make her six p.m. flight. "Did you talk to whoever you're supposed to talk to about us getting out of here this morning?"

Her pulse jumped as he turned, one elbow over the back of the chair. Unshaven but bright-eyed, he leveled her with a dark look that melted her insides into a pool of liquid without an ounce of effort.

No.

"They haven't figured out what was in the vial. Yet. We stay put for another twelve hours."

Emily pressed her palm hard against the table on either side of her hips to dispel the ridiculous, uncalled for, unwanted attraction. He was *just* a man.

Been there, done that, she thought crossly. On the other hand, as scared as she was by her visceral response to Max, she'd rather deal with that than the pee-in-your-pants thought of being eaten alive by some god-awful bacteria that could make her eyeballs bleed and turn her inside out. She'd seen one too many horror movies.

"If they don't know what was in it, how can they know we need to stay quarantined for another twelve hours? Why not *five* hours? Why not a *week*?"

A slight crinkle appeared beside his left eye. The start of a smile? An impending scowl? Who knew?

"They know things."

She waited for the punch line. Of course there wasn't one. Sighing, she said, "That is totally ridiculous, Max." She wasn't happy that they had to remain in quarantine for another twelve minutes, let alone twelve more freaking hours. The intensity of his eyes, very green this morning, made her edgy. She reminded herself to breathe. That was good. Do it again.

"If we're not dead by now, if we haven't already broken out in oozing green pustules, chances are we're fine and dandy. I want to make my flight tonight."

"Let's say the incubation period is under twelve hours, and not, say, twenty-four. Let's say neither of us shows any sign of infection. The odds of two unrelated people having immunity and carrying a disease/virus while staying asymptomatic doesn't follow the biological reality of disease transmission."

Emily rubbed the bone deep chill from her arms. "Let's say not." Her mouth was dry. She picked up her mug and brought it to her lips. It was empty. She clutched the mug in a white-knuckled grip.

"They're more concerned that we could be dealing with an agent that takes twenty-four hours to show symptoms," Max said matter-of-factly.

Nobody could be this calm about something this potentially horrific, she thought, scared stupid by the possibilities. Still, she wouldn't want to be with anyone else if her life was hanging in the balance. Max *exuded* calm and rational.

"We have to wait it out. Do you really want to board a transatlantic flight and take that kind of risk? You could pass along a virus as if it were the common cold." His eyes held hers. They were very green, and as still and . . . safe as the massive pine trees in her home state of Washington.

"Of course not." The thought that she had some nasty little . . . *something* . . . inside her, something that she could breathe on some innocent person, possibly even kill them, gave her the willies. This was like waiting for the other shoe to drop. And waiting. And waiting. With Max.

"Okay. So we wait," Which didn't mean she had to be happy about it. "Let's at least make this time productive. What are *we* looking *for*?" she asked, frowning as he started to read a letter addressed to his father.

"Proof that he was murdered."

"I'm sure the police did a thorough search when they were here."

"And I'll search again. I have nothing but time."

"Well I don't," she told him, annoyed. "What do you think you're going to find?"

"I'll know it when I see it."

Irritation, fear, and frustration rose to beat wings of panic against her breastbone. Emily glanced around. "How will *I* know it when I see it?" Canvases, painting supplies, half-filled coffee cups, and overflowing ashtrays littered every surface. Daniel, bless his heart, was a complete slob. They had untidiness in common. He had an enormous staff, yet refused to allow anyone inside his studio to clean.

It had started raining again. She poured herself a

fresh cup of coffee, trying to figure out where to start looking for something she didn't know she was looking for.

At the moment pretty much all she could think about was some flesh-eating bacteria dining on her liver. "I was always on your father's case about giving up smoking," she told Max as she carried her coffee across the room to where Daniel had all his canvases stacked, ten to fifteen deep, against the wall.

It would hurt, wouldn't it? Having something eating—

Stop it! Really. Stop.

Thinking about what scary thing could be happening inside her own body wasn't productive, and could make her insane. Better to look for the—whatever they were looking for. If nothing else she could bring a little order to the studio while she searched.

She lowered herself to sit cross-legged on the floor. "If not because of his health, then because of the gross smell, *and* getting nicotine all over his work." *And I'm talking to myself just to break the silence. Max doesn't give a flying crap about anything I have to say about his father.*

"Of course, Daniel being Daniel," *and you being so like him it's scary,* "he stubbornly refused even to consider quitting." She suddenly remembered a long-ago conversation she and Daniel had had one bright spring day. "He told me once he was sure he'd die young." Emily shot a glance at the back of Max's head. "Are you even listening to me?"

"I presumed your monologue was rhetorical."

She angled a small canvas to the light, looking at it instead of finding a heavy object to beat Max about the head with. Taking a deep breath, she focused on the painting instead of violent thoughts. *Really. The man was an ass.*

An ass with big strong hands. And lean powerful hips . . .

For God's sake, Emily Rose Greene, get a bloody grip, why don't you? Wherever her mind wandered was dangerous territory.

The break-in.

Max.

A mysterious bacteria . . .

She stared unseeingly at the painting in her hands. Max couldn't be any more *dis*interested if he tried. If she couldn't listen to her own admonishments to keep the hell away from him, then *his* clear indifference should make her job easy.

Concentrate on Daniel's work. The painting was of a simple, clear glass bowl filled with ripe peaches against a velvet drape of gentian blue. Her mouth watered just looking at the dewy, downy fruit. Emily could almost taste the sweetness, feel the cool hardness of the glass, and touch the voluptuous warmth of the fabric.

The painting was dated seven years before. She knew he'd come up here every day with his cigarettes and his unending cups of coffee, no longer able to paint. Her heart had broken imagining Daniel *trying* to hold a brush. *Trying* to paint. Knowing he never would again. His frustration level must have been as vast as his ego. She couldn't imagine not being able to do what she loved to do. For Daniel it must've been a hundred times worse. That's why when she heard he'd committed suicide she hadn't doubted it.

"God. What a loss his death was to the art world." *And to me.* "Daniel was absolutely brilliant."

Max's silence said, *"Whatever."*

She was tempted to give him the finger, but took the high road instead. She went back to the stacks of canvases. In addition to his work as a restorer, Daniel had been a brilliant artist in his own right. A lifetime of work he'd deemed "not good enough" was stacked up along the walls. Not only had he been a perfectionist, he'd refused to reuse canvases. His "mistakes," as he'd called them, would be any art collector's treasures.

A lump formed in her throat, and she got up to take some of the trash downstairs so she could pull herself together. More than half her life had been spent here. Daniel still had a bunch of Emily's canvases mixed in with his.

She made a dozen trips up and down the stairs carrying Daniel's forgotten, dirty dishes to the kitchen, then running the dishwasher. Bags of trash sat just outside the door to be taken out later. Max read or looked at every piece of paper before disposing of it.

She'd squeezed in a call to Franco on one of her many trips downstairs. She'd called him knowing that she should probably tell him that she couldn't . . . she shouldn't take him with her to the States. Or continue their relationship. And shouldn't, she admitted feeling small, use him to get over Max. But she'd pretended that other than a flesh-eating bacteria, everything was fine.

It was bad enough lying to a good man. It was almost worse lying to herself. But the reality was she needed Franco as a buffer against her feelings for Max. It was shitty to use him that way, but she'd make it up to him.

She hadn't told him *everything*. She hadn't mentioned Max, nor did she tell Franco that she could possibly be contaminated by . . . something. She'd merely told him she'd had a break in, and that the police had requested she not leave the country until they'd had time to question the man they'd apprehended. She was staying at Daniel's villa tonight because he had excellent security.

Franco had wanted to rush to her side, which was very sweet. But she didn't want to risk giving him whatever it was she might be carrying. At least that's what she'd told herself. So he'd changed their flight to the next evening.

With the trip reset, with a man she didn't love, Emily returned upstairs feeling guilty and defensive.

"We changed our flight until tomorrow," she told Max, as she went back to a box of papers she'd half sorted through. "We should be out of here by then, right?"

"I'm presuming the *we* you're referring to is you and Frank?"

She didn't bother correcting him.

Hours later, Max was still searching for God only knew what. Daniel, being Daniel, had shoved bills, receipts, and half-finished sketches into every drawer and pigeonhole of his desk. Max pulled everything out, attempting to create order out of chaos. She inspected a pinprick-sized red bump on her arm. Had it been there yesterday? Almost hyperventilating, she tried to remember. Yes. Oh, thank God, yes. She'd noticed it in the shower yesterday morning. *Before* the break-in. A spider bite?

As it got later and later, the weather reflected her mood. Still, the studio was brilliant with what appeared to be natural light. Like herself, Daniel liked to work at night, and no expense had been spared on special custom lighting for their studios.

She and Max had only started searching at mid-morning. This was where Daniel had spent the majority of his time, the most logical place, Max insisted, to find clues. Clues of what? Emily wasn't sure. It would take her a month to go through the canvases alone. "Your father was a pack rat. *Look* at all this stuff. He never threw a thing out. This is going to take forever, and frankly Max, I don't want to *be* here forever!"

"Fine," he said, not looking up. "Go bake a cake or something."

"That's incredibly insulting. Even for you."

"I can't help you, Emily. I didn't make the rules. If you don't want to help me solve his murder, then find something else to do."

She wished she had her frying pan. "That is *so* freaking unfair! I've been working as diligently as you have, so don't give me that 'go amuse yourself, honey,' crap."

A faintly amused smile flickered across his face. "I never called you honey."

No. He'd called her darling. And sweetheart. And love. The rat fink bastard. "Shut up."

She and Max worked silently for several hours. Dusk and rain pushed at the windows, and a tree branch kept giving eerie taps on the glass, ratcheting up her tension. Every now and then Max would ask her a question about something he came across. Emily answered. There wasn't any companionable chitchat.

They weren't companions. And giving the back of his head a hot look, she doubted if the man unbent enough to speak, let alone chit or chat. He was about as much company as a vacuum cleaner.

"What was he working on before he died?" Max asked without turning around.

He speaks. She wondered how many more conversations Max could manage without ever referring to his father as either Dad, father, or Daniel. Daniel was just *he* or *him.* "As far as I know, your *father,*" she stressed the word just to see if it would get a reaction out of him—it didn't—"finished painting a reproduction of Titian's *Penitent Mary Magdalene* for Mr.

Tillman about a week before he died. If he started something else after that, there's no evidence of it here."

She'd done the commission in Daniel's name, but that wasn't any of Max's business, nor was it relevant.

"He forged it."

The derision in Max's tone made her hackles rise. No. Not just rise. Rise *more*. His damned attitude—about his father, the work he and *she* did, and his clear desire to be anywhere but *here*—was really getting on her last nerve. He was as annoying as fingernails screeching on a blackboard.

"No," she told him firmly, "he *copied* it. Unless the copy is done with the intent to defraud, it's just that. A copy. Richard Tillman is an American multi-gazillionaire in his eighties, and has an *amazing* art collection. Both Daniel and I have done work for him over the years. Mr. Tillman wants the copies to enjoy in his home gallery, while he donates his entire collection of originals."

Max shook his head. "Basically he's screwing his heirs out of zillions of dollars of priceless works of art."

"This isn't out of the norm. It's fairly common for collectors to request good copies to keep in their homes. It's his money. He can do whatever he likes with it. I think it's an amazingly generous undertaking."

"I know who Tillman is." Max tossed a handful of papers into the trash bag beside him. "Hard to believe he'd give away a half-eaten tuna sandwich, let alone billions of dollars' worth of artwork. He's never been known as a philanthropist."

"Well apparently he's changed. Now he *is* one. According to what I've heard he's become a bit of a religious fanatic. Donating his art to the world is part of his newly acquired morality. I suppose doing good works—like sharing his art with the masses—is in keeping with his new philosophy on life. Lately he's been in a hurry. At his age, I guess he doesn't think he has much time to make amends for a lifetime of selfish hoarding."

Max turned around, one dark brow arched, his elbow on the back of the chair. "This from the horse's mouth? You've met Tillman?"

"No. I've never seen him. But I've been dealing with his assistant Norcroft for years. He lets things slip once in a while. According to him, Mr. Tillman is desperate to do his penance before his time on earth is, well . . . up."

"Giving away billions in artwork is a last-ditch effort at erasing his dictatorial, self-serving business dealings?" Max's tone conveyed exactly how he viewed *that*. "His fortune was built on the shoulders of sweatshop laborers and golden parachute recipients." He shook his head. "Interesting that he thinks giving away some paintings is all it takes for redemption."

"Redemption or not, I'm just happy he's taking things out of his private museum and giving the rest of the world a chance to see these priceless master-pieces."

"Yeah. Truly commendable." He held up a sheet of paper. "This is good."

Emily blinked at the non sequitur. "What's good?"

"This sketch of you."

"He did a sketch of me?" As far as Emily knew, Daniel had never drawn her. Intrigued she got to her feet and walked over to look. She held out her hand. "Let me see."

Max handed it over almost reluctantly. "He got your expression mid-laugh. A pretty remarkable snapshot really."

He *had* gotten her mid-laugh, her head thrown back, her eyes filled with humor. Her hair hung around her shoulders, making her look wild and wanton. She didn't remember Daniel doing this, but it was about six years old. She remembered that blouse. It had been one of her favorites.

She swallowed a lump in her throat, then frowned as she inspected the sketch. Not looking at her own face, but at the medium and pen strokes. "This is so odd. He didn't use one of the dozens of sketch pads lying all over the place. Look at this. It's plain bond paper. Probably from that printer over there."

"So? He grabbed the closest thing."

"Not Daniel. Besides, the closest thing *would* have been a sketch pad. He was never without one. And another thing—this is done in *ink*. He always sketched in pencil. Always."

"I'm more interested in the writing down there at the bottom. See that? 'A nine departmental gym.' Any idea what that means?"

"Haven't a clue. Maybe he was trying to write a poem. There's a bunch of gibberish on the back as we—"

Max's cell phone rang. "Aries." Emily was still standing beside his chair, and Max took her wrist to hold her beside him before she started to wander off. Her pulse throbbed beneath his fingertips.

"Nothing?" he demanded incredulously into the phone. There'd been no toxins of any kind in the vial. "Illogical. Either the container contained something you people haven't tested for—" he paused to listen. "Exactly. Or the intruder was there to *take* something, not bring it." But *what*?

Max listened to the lab guy speculate. Fuck speculation. He wanted answers. Now. "No," he interrupted. "He went directly to her bedroom, not her studio."

Beside him Emily's pulse leapt from a hard beat to manic. He soothed his thumb across the thin skin of her pale inner wrist. "Yeah. My thought exactly." The son of a bitch had wanted a sample from *Emily.*

Max scrubbed a hand across his jaw. "Hair? Skin? Testing for DNA? Jesus. *What?*"

So far T-FLAC's European lab had no idea if there was an unknown substance in the vial, or if the guy had wanted a sample of Emily's DNA. But with the vial, and the man in custody, they'd eventually have an answer.

For now he and Emily had the all clear, physically, to go about their business. Except that Max wasn't letting her out of his sight until he had concrete answers. There was no such fucking thing as coincidence.

"Yeah. Make that sooner than later," Max flipped the sat phone closed. Emily tried to liberate her wrist. "We're free to go. But—"

"Oh, no you don't. There *is* no but." She glanced at her watch. "I have time to pick up my other bag, and make my original flight. And that's *exactly* what I'm going to do."

"Not negotiable. Flight was cancelled, remember?" He rose, still holding her gaze.

"I have things to do."

"You stay until we ascertain what the hell is going on."

Her eyes jerked up to meet his, annoyed. "Nothing is *going on* anymore. Who are you? James bloody Bond? You can't keep me here. I have a life. Plans. People who are expecting me."

"Who? Franco?"

"He's one of the people. Yes."

"I'll drive you home."

"No thanks," she said annoyed. "I'm perfectly capable of driving myself."

"I said," he said through his teeth. "*I'll* drive you."

"Fine. If you'd let go of my arm—thank you—I'll go and get my suitcase from my room. I'll meet you in the kitchen in ten minutes."

"I'll take you home, and I'll deliver you safely to the airport. Agreed?"

99

"If you insist."

"I insist."

"Then I agree."

As soon as she was gone, he made another call. She might *think* she was going to be allowed to fly off unattended, but he'd have his people watching over her every minute of every day until he knew what the hell was going o—

"*Fucking* hell!"

He watched red taillights disappear into the drumming rain as Emily's Maserati screamed down the driveway, spitting gravel.

Five

SLOWING DOWN TO ACCOMMODATE CITY TRAFFIC, Emily hit redial on the speakerphone attached to her console. She was away from Max, bacteria-free, and not quite ready to go home. Had the men in their white space suits left her palazzo a disaster?

Would she see the intruder in every corner? Or Max, coming to her aid like some heroic, twenty-first-century Galahad?

"Franco, pick up—come on. Help save me from myself." He lived with his mother, grandmother, and sister on Via dell Neri, several blocks from Emily's place.

God, Max was probably pissed off.

I can not *believe I left him there,* she thought, half triumphant, and half amused. Listening to Franco's cell phone ring and ring, she told herself that she didn't care about Max. He deserved to be left at Daniel's. Without transportation. "He's got a phone, he can call a cab."

She couldn't hang around him anymore; she couldn't take it and keep her sanity. Max made her breathless, jumpy—reckless. Not a term anyone would usually apply to her.

Max . . . agitated her. Unlike Franco, who made her feel mellow and rational. Attractive without making her feel as though she'd expire if he didn't put his hands on her—

"Earth to Emily? N and a big O, remember?" she reminded herself out loud as she tried Franco's house number again. Still busy. The rain-washed streets were empty save for a few hearty souls braving the crappy weather to go to the local market to pick up their dinner.

She was sorry she and Franco had had to postpone their flight, but at least they could spend the evening together.

She'd just show up. His grandmother would ply her with food, his mother would interrogate her about where they were going, and his sister would want to know where she'd bought her sweater, so she could have the exact same one. It was one of Janna's more annoying habits to copy everything Emily wore.

She and Franco wouldn't have a second alone. Emily rather suspected that was how Signora campaigned. She made no bones about wanting a nice Catholic, *Italian* girl for her son.

So much for *that* plan. Signora Bozzato probably wanted Franco to hold out for a virgin as well. Emily shook her head as she disconnected the phone. Franco was forty. He'd be lucky to find anyone over seventeen in his mother's social circle who was a virgin. But Signora Bozzato kept lobbying.

She'd take him to La Baraonda, Emily decided. Time to exorcise old demons. A lovely meal, a few kisses from a man who cared deeply for her, and her equilibrium would be restored. A great start to their vacation.

This was possibly the most important trip of her life. Taking Franco home to meet her mother. If he could pass *that* test he'd be worth keeping. Except hadn't she already decided *not* to take him with her? Damn. She'd better make up her mind *soon*.

She squeezed into a small parking space a block from the Bozzato home. Right behind an identical yellow Maserati.

"Damn it, Janna!" She glared at the mirror image of her own, brand new, specially ordered car. "Copycat!" Franco's sister had gone and bought the same damned car the second she'd seen hers. Emily shook her head in disgust. She didn't care about imitation being the sincerest form of flattery. It was getting bloody annoying having spoiled brat Miss Janna Bozzato copy every damn thing she wore, ate, said, or *drove*.

"And I'd better deal with it now, or make peace with it, because she's going to be my sister-in-law."

Maybe.

Oh, shit. She was going to have to figure this out fast. It wasn't fair in any way to string Franco along if she couldn't let go of the past.

She might not have a ring on her finger, but Franco had started talking seriously about the M word. She hadn't said no, but she hadn't said yes either. Although it was pretty much implied if she was taking him all the way to Seattle to meet her family.

Crap. Why did life have to be so complicated?

Perhaps she'd take him to her place later. More, she admitted, because she was a little twitchy about going home alone, than any mad desire to start a deeper relationship with him.

"Which makes me, what?" she asked as she swung her legs out of the car and immediately stepped into a puddle in her already wet socks. *"Stava piovendo a catinelle."* The equivalent of raining cats and dogs. Within minutes wet feet were the least of her problems. Drenched from top to toe, she hesitated. Continue to the Bozzatos'? Or turn around and go home to a hot shower and dry clothes?

Going home made a whole lot of sense. Franco wasn't expecting her after all. Unfortunately, a little niggle of residual fear kept Emily trudging through the rain. She really, really didn't want to go home alone. She really didn't.

So she'd arrive looking like a drowned rat. Franco could see her at her worst. Shivering, she pressed the downstairs doorbell, and when no one responded, she tried Franco's house number again. The line was busy, so she knew someone had to be home.

Sometimes the family gathered in the kitchen to watch TV. With the noise from that, and the pounding rain, they probably couldn't hear the bell. Emily knocked twice more, then pushed open the heavy door, and walked in. All the lights were on in the living room, but the only sound she heard was the drum of the rain on the windows.

No sound of the TV. More disturbing, no sign of Franco or his family. "Franco? Signora? Janna?" Nonna Maria was as deaf as a post. The place smelled sickly sweet, and she wondered if Franco's mother had allowed him to smoke one of his Cuban cigars inside, which would be a first.

His mother's church shawl hung in its customary place next to his favorite camel raincoat, on hooks by the front door beside a painting of the Blessed Virgin. And so did a bright red slicker. Identical to the one Emily had ordered from a catalog two weeks ago. She and Miss Janna were going to have words. "Signora?"

She didn't like this. She didn't like it a *lot*. The drip-drip-drip of the rain against the windows, and the throbbing, unnatural silence of the apartment made her heart race, and her nerves vibrate.

The faint beep-beep-beep of a phone off the hook made the little hairs on the back of her neck stand up. Seeing the phone receiver dangling off the edge of the vestibule table ratcheted up her alarm.

Emily's shoulders tensed as she took her cell phone

104

from her pocket. What were the chances that she would be witness to two separate break-ins? She should get out of here. Dial 113 for *la polizia,* and have them come and check to see that everything was all right.

God. She was *way* overreacting. Wasn't she?

A slither of unease made its way down her spine as she stopped just inside the doorway. Cold water runneled off her clothes to pool on the worn oriental rug underfoot. *Back up.*

She'd never given intuition much thought. But every nerve in her body was screaming for her to get out of there fast.

Because of her own scare this morning, she told herself. But her intruder was under lock and key somewhere. Franco's mother had heart problems, and Nonna Maria was old. What if they'd had a medical emergency?

Her socks made squishy noises on the carpet as she moved forward slowly. She felt ridiculous scaring herself to death like this. Every light in the place was on. Everything looked as immaculate as it always did.

The furnishings were straight out of the fifties, with the yellow-and-brown floral sofa, and two matching chairs with lace doilies over the backs and arms, and plastic on the lampshades.

Nonna Maria's worn bedroom slippers sat neatly in front of her chair.

Franco's reading glasses, marking his place in the latest spy thriller, lay on the end table, as if he'd just stepped away. A half glass of pinot grigio sat on a hand-crocheted coaster next to the book. He always had a glass of wine after coming home from work, and before his mother put dinner on the table.

They should just be sitting down to their evening meal now. Whatever Franco's mother had cooked smelled disgusting. Probably his all-time favorite *salsicce di cinghiale.* She didn't like wild boar, and hoped they didn't insist she stay for dinner.

It was too quiet.

No one was home.

Maybe they'd decided to go out to a movie. Or they were visiting a neighbor. Nonna could have knocked the phone over with her walker and not even noticed. Which made perfect sense. Emily's shoulders eased. Man, Signora was *not* going to be happy about her tracking in dirty water from the street when she came home and saw the trail Emily was leaving.

She rounded the corner into the kitchen and wished desperately that she hadn't. Dear God in Heaven!

Red. Blood. Death.

The room whirled. Her muscles turned to jelly, her knees gave out. She braced herself on the doorjamb so she wouldn't fall into the nightmare. Not capable of drawing in the next breath she hung on.

No, God, no. No-no-no-no-no . . .

The family was home. They were all in the kitchen. They'd been violently, *brutally* butchered.

Six

"WHERE IS SHE NOW?" MAX DEMANDED INTO THE SAT phone. He'd been picked up within minutes of Emily hauling ass, and was talking to the operatives tailing her. They'd been on her as she'd zoomed out the gate. He was pissed enough to chew nails and spit out bullets. It was damn fortunate that a T-FLAC security team was patrolling the grounds and outer perimeters of the estate at the time and had vehicles available within seconds.

The driver, an attractive, forty-something oriental woman named Niigata, was in full, black T-FLAC LockOut garb, as were the others on the security team. She handled the vehicle like a race-car driver, taking both the straightaway and corners with high speed and finesse. Two more operatives sat in back.

"Looks like she's at the Bozzato residence," Emily's tail, Mike Ragusa, reported in Max's ear. Max cradled the Glock on his lap, his jaw tight. The kid on the phone was barely out of T-FLAC training. The man he was with, Boyle, Doyle—something like that—hadn't been out that much longer. First real assignment, security. And Emily's best hope if she got herself into any immediate trouble. Which there was no reason for her to do.

Still, Max felt a sense of impending danger he couldn't shake.

She'd be safe at the boyfriend's until he got there, he

rationalized, irritated that she'd given him the slip. And for some odd reason, annoyed as hell that she'd run from *him* straight to Bozzato's arms. It wasn't just his usually dormant ego that had taken a licking; he had a bad, a fucking *really* bad feeling in his gut. A feeling logic wouldn't shake.

He'd stick her in a local safe house with round-the-clock security until he unraveled what had happened to the old man. And/or until the lab and the interrogators could tell him what that vial had been for, and why the guy in custody had broken into her apartment.

Emily wasn't going to be able to take a pee without someone accompanying her to the bathroom. If not himself, then people he trusted. There'd be no negotiation. "Stay with her. ETA six minutes."

A second after he disconnected, the phone rang. "Aries."

"Vacation over, Aries," Darius informed him. "As of now, your ass is officially T-FLAC's again. We've had a third bombing. This one right there in your backyard. I want you wheels up within the hour. You'll be in Córdoba in time for dinner. Which you won't have time for. I'm dispatching your team, they'll be there at 0 dark thirty."

"I wouldn't exactly call Spain my backyard," Max said dryly. "What went bang?"

"La Mezquita. Familiar with it?"

"Moorish palace converted into a Roman Catholic cathedral."

"Good enough. I'll fax you more. EMTs have gone

in and collected the bodies, as for now we have control of the scene. But the locals are champing at the bit to get in to comb the rubble. I want you there before they tamper with things they know nothing about."

"Got it." Max thought for a moment. "Send Cooper."

"You think you'll need a sharpshooter?"

To watch over Emily? "Yeah." And AJ Cooper was the best.

"Done."

He'd trust Cooper to keep Emily safe while he was gone—a few days at most. The phone rang again. *"What?"*

"She's gone inside," Ragusa hesitated.

"And?"

"I don't know if this means anything. But there's an identical yellow Maserati parked right in front of hers."

Max's heart leapt. "You'd fucking better be as close to her as white on rice, Ragusa! Go. Go. Go!"

He was three minutes away. Might as well be on the fucking moon. The driver didn't need to be told to put her foot flat on the gas. She did that on her own.

Emily's fingers gripped the door frame once she'd finished retching. Impossible to move. Impossible to breathe. There was so much blood, it looked like red paint. Blood pooling on the floor. Blood splattered on the walls. Even the ceiling had a confetti of red spray. She blinked, trying to assimilate what she was seeing.

They'd been interrupted at a meal. Dinner. They'd been eating an early dinner. She must've missed the killer by mere minutes.

Go, her brain screamed. *Go. Go. Go.*

She couldn't move.

It was impossible to tell how many . . . Oh, God— *bodies* there were. Her hearing was muted as if she were underwater, but she felt the frantic beating of her heart in her ears as her brain tried to comprehend what kind of madman would do something like this.

Bile rose in the back of her throat again, and her knees felt weak. She saw a movement out of the corner of her eye, and whipped her head around. A man was silently running across the living room, as if following the dark wet spots her footsteps had left on the Signora's carpet. Dressed completely in black, his face covered, he was a terrifying sight. The big black gun was overkill. He shouted something she couldn't comprehend, let alone separate the syllables into a language.

Caught between a Scylla and a Charybdis she had nowhere to run. Stuck with no choice, Emily pushed away from the doorjamb and propelled herself into the bloody kitchen. Her foot, covered in nothing more than a wet wool sock, slid in one of the large, sticky red puddles on the linoleum floor. Her arms cartwheeled for balance, and she screamed as she went down on one knee, her hand shooting out to brace herself.

She stared into Janna's vacant eyes. Hyperventilating, terrified, Emily snatched her blood-soaked hand off Franco's sister's hip and scrambled to her feet, sliding on the gore on the slick floor.

The man in black was at the doorway, his gun pointing right at her. He couldn't miss, she was only ten feet away. "Don't! Please d—"

An arm wrapped around her throat, cutting off her words. She gagged, trying to drag in a breath. She hadn't even seen the second man, he must've been hiding behind the door.

He jerked up his other hand, and she caught a brief glimpse of a knife, a gleam of silver, a blur of dark red. She recognized the knife instantly. It was Nonna Maria's favorite boning knife. Flexible, and wickedly sharp. She never allowed anyone to use it, Emily thought numbly.

The hand, covered in tacky blood, started bringing the knife to her throat as in slow motion. The surgical steel blade glinted in the light.

Brain blank with abject terror, she saw that yet another shadowy figure had materialized in the doorway. Emily squeezed her eyes shut just as a loud explosion sounded, so close it seemed to suck all the air out of the room. The man behind her fell away. Ears ringing, she dropped to her knees as her vision spun and darkened.

Bull's-eye, Max thought savagely and lowered his Glock as the now faceless assailant crumpled to the bloody floor behind Emily.

"You fucking shoot *before* the son of a bitch brings

a knife to the hostage's throat, Ragusa," he said bitingly, not looking at the younger man who hadn't discharged his weapon. Ragusa was still standing with the pistol raised, staring blankly at the spot the assailant had been seconds before.

Emily was crumpled on the floor. Jesus Mother of God. Had she been cut? There was so much blood on her Max couldn't tell.

"I-I was waiting for a clear s-shot."

Kicking the dead assailant out of the way, Max dropped to one knee, lifting Emily in his arms. She looked at him from wounded brown eyes, glassy with shock. He could tell she wasn't seeing anything. Jesus. "*Make* a clear shot."

Her arms went around his neck, and she gripped the back of his shirt in both hands as she pressed her face against his chest. She didn't make a sound as he stood and walked swiftly through the kitchen.

"You and you." he jerked his head at two more men standing nearby. "Search the place. Now."

Emily was practically insubstantial in his arms as he strode out into the living room.

"Get the garbage detail in here," he instructed as two of the security people followed after him at a trot. "I want this location swept and sanitized, and swept again. Impound both Maseratis. I want to know how they found this place and why."

He was almost sorry he'd blown off the asshole's face before asking him questions. Almost. He crossed to the car, which was double-parked and still running.

Niigata sat behind the wheel. One of the men opened the back door and Max climbed in, still cradling Emily in his arms.

She clung to him, her arms wound tightly around his neck, her face pressed against his throat. She took a deep shuddering breath and her fingers clenched and unclenched on the back of his T-shirt before she lifted her head.

"I—Give me a m-minute, okay?"

He wasn't a touchy-feely kinda guy. But he found himself strangely disappointed when she slid off his lap and moved across the seat. Pretty much as far away from him as possible.

She was holding it together, but her bloodstained face was pale and taut, her eyes glassy with shock. That'd wear off. But she wasn't going to forget what she'd seen or experienced any time soon.

He shoved a foot against the door when the man tried to close it. "I want to know everything about that guy. Including where he went to kindergarten and what he had for lunch in fifth grade, got it? Every fucking detail."

He slammed the door. "Airport. Fast."

"Wait. Stop. Let me out first," Emily said, cracking her door as Niigata brought the car to a sudden stop. "I have to call the police, then I'm going—" She blinked, looking around as if coming out of a fog. "Somewhere."

Max leaned across her body and yanked the door shut. Emily's breast brushed his cheek, and the subtle rose scent of her skin was intensified by the heat of her body. He was capable of blocking out the familiar stench of the blood saturating the shoulder of her sweater and splattered on her hair and face.

They were both covered in blood, he hoped to hell none of it hers. He reached over and turned her to face him. She tensed, resisting the hand cupping her jaw. "You're in shock, sweetheart. Let me see if you were cut," he told her calmly, holding her chin so he could inspect the smears and blotches of dried blood on her face and neck. This time she stayed passively in his hold.

"I wasn't," she responded tonelessly.

"Humor me." As Max ran his fingers over her skin in thorough exploration, her eyes stared unblinkingly somewhere in the middle distance. Through the familiar metallic odor of blood was the tinny smell of her fear and horror. She shouldn't have to live with the image of that bloodbath. No civilian should.

He could tell she wasn't cut, but he wanted to touch her warm skin, needed to feel the steady beat of her pulse. She might not need the physical contact, but he sure as shit did.

"It's going to be okay," he told her softly, running a finger across her silky cheek. Electricity seemed to spark at the contact point, making him keenly aware of the softness of her skin. Her eyes showed the measure of her guilt and remorse, but they also reflected her astounding inner strength. He sensed how hard she was working to keep herself together and his admiration for her jumped several notches.

She pushed his hand away. *"Merda,"* she said thickly, coming out of her fog. "How can what happened ever be *okay*?"

"It can't. But you will be." It had been close. Too fucking close. A killer, a rookie operative, two more seconds and . . . "I'll make damn sure of it."

He changed his depth perception to stare out at the sparkling rain beaded on the windows and reflecting the streetlights. The old man's murder, the break-in, the mysterious vial, now this? An entire family slaughtered. For no other reason than that someone had been driving the same car as Emily's?

She was the only common denominator.

What in God's name could she have done, real or imagined, that would piss someone off enough to kill five people?

"Tell me exactly what happened when you got there."

Not turning her head, she shuddered. "Not now. I just want to go—"

"You're not going anywhere," he told her flatly, not giving her time to finish. *Anywhere without* me, *God damn it.* "Not yet."

She sucked in a breath, then shoved his shoulder to get him away from her. "Who the hell do you think you are?"

Max straightened, wiping a bloody hand—transfer from Emily's jeans—onto his black pants. "Are we not moving for a good reason?" he demanded of

Niigata. "I'm the man who just saved your ass from a knife-wielding killer," he told Emily succinctly as the car moved forward again.

"And God knows I appreciate it." Stubborn little witch put one hand back on the door handle. "But that doesn't mean we have to be joined at the hip."

He wondered if she was even aware that she was arguing, or if it was second nature to want to take care of herself, and she thought, somewhere in her shocked brain, that this was a good time to exert her independence. It wasn't. Telling her she wasn't being rational right now was not a wise move. But he'd do whatever needed doing to keep her with him.

She was struggling to keep her breathing slow and rhythmic, trying to control the hysteria he sensed was building inside her. With her free hand she bunched her hair off her face, looking bewildered. Max was amazed she still had the goods to argue with him. She looked ready to collapse.

Strands of her hair were sticky with her assailant's blood. She was going to need a long shower to get rid of the remaining gore. He'd shot the fucker at close range. She had brain matter on her hair and clothing. If she saw herself right now she'd probably faint.

"I just want to go home." Her eyes welled, and she dashed the tears away with her fingertips. "Seattle. I just want to see my m-mother. However stupid it sounds, I just want my mom. The irony is, I don't th-think she'd even know or *care* that I was there. But I w-want my mom."

Tears made white streaks through the redness on her skin. "I'm tired, and scared, and cold and c-confused. Not to mention overwhelmed with—with *guilt*. Tonight I lost people that I cared deeply about, and it was my fault. Janna—Janna bought the *exact* same bloody car as mine. Whoever did this was after *me*."

He lifted the bottom of his T-shirt and wiped her face. It smeared the blood, making her look worse, but it made him feel better to touch her. He desperately wanted to haul her back into his lap and wrap his arms around her tightly. He removed his hand from her face, but slid it soothingly down her arm, then picked up her hand in his.

It felt small, soft, and ice cold. After a second or two, her fingers curled around his tightly as if he were her lifeline in a storm-tossed sea. Her brows were drawn together, and her teeth showed white as she bit her lower lip. Her eyes were filled with the horror she'd just seen.

"This was not your fault." He kept his voice quiet, and rubbed his thumb across the back of her hand. Her fingers gripped his hard enough for her fingertips to turn white. "Not your fault. It was the fault of some sick fuck who took pleasure in slicing up innocent people. All the more reason why I want you with me."

"It's good to w-want things," she said softly, fighting him for the door handle again. She tugged on her hand. "Damn it." She turned a tortured face to him. "Let go. You can't force me to go with you."

Yeah. He could. Especially the condition she was in

117

right now. But it would ease the way if she came willingly. "At least come with me to Córdoba until my people can figure out what's going on."

"No." She looked around almost wildly. "I—No. Really and truly, Max. No. I'm not haring off to Spain in the middle of the night with you." The throbbing pulse at the base of her throat showed him how agitated she was. She tugged to free her hand. He didn't want to hurt her and reluctantly let go.

"I'm not stupid. I won't go to my palazzo, I'll go to Seattle, which is where I was supposed to b-be tonight any-anyway." She shuddered, her face bloodstained and pale in the bright lights of an oncoming vehicle.

"I just want to go home," she said again, sounding forlorn. "Clearly there's some crazy person out there. And I just—" She waved a vague hand.

"Yeah," he said, trying to gentle his voice. "There is a crazy out there. And the last thing you're going to want is to lead him to your family in Seattle. Understand?"

Horror dawned on her. "Oh, God." Emily hated the tremor in her voice. She couldn't bear to think of her mother's kitchen looking anything like the poor Bozzatos'. The graphic scene was fresh in her mind, the images so bright and vivid that she felt nauseated all over again. She swallowed, fighting the thick lump in her throat that indicated that tears—a torrent of them—were imminent.

Her skin felt cold and clammy. She wished Max would take her hand again. She glanced up to find him watching her. His mouth was a grim line as he reached up and brushed her hair off her face. "Hey." Their gazes locked, making a connection that Emily couldn't seem to break. His hazel eyes were dark with concern for her, and he cupped her jaw in one large, warm hand. "I'm sorry about your friends." He skimmed his thumb across her lips. "But what happened wasn't your fault."

"I—" She turned her head to look outside. God damn it, she would not cry in front of him. She bit her lip and stared unseeingly out of the window. The spurt of anger had only lasted a minute. She needed to hold onto that or lose her mind. Fighting with Max made her feel as though she was *doing* something. As ridiculous as that sounded even to her own mind.

She couldn't be near him, she really couldn't. She was coming unraveled, and the last person she wanted to see her vulnerable was Max Aries. If he was sympathetic, if he held her, if he tried to comfort her, she wasn't going to be able to hold herself together.

And she couldn't fall apart now. She just couldn't. Not with everything that was going on. She needed to pull herself together and help him with this, not hinder him by being a weeping, fragile female incapable of thinking on her feet.

In other words, her mother.

She wouldn't lead the killer to her friends or family. But there was nothing that said she couldn't hide in a hotel until . . . Until *what*? Until *when*? her mind screamed.

She wanted to get away. Out of the too-close confines of the car. Away from Max. Because she wanted his arms around her right now more than anything she could think of, other than complete oblivion, or going back in time to warn Franco and his family. She rubbed a cold hand over her eyes. Confused. Frightened. And sad.

Her escape fantasy was foolish, and she'd be the first one to acknowledge that. She hated admitting that Max was the only person who could keep her safe. Wasn't he?

They hadn't made it two blocks when four unmarked Lamborghini Gallardos, the vehicles typically driven by the *Polizia di Stato* surrounded them in a screech of tires and flashing lights, sirens blaring. Suddenly there wasn't another vehicle on the road.

"Shit," Max muttered. Someone had called in the cops.

"Go through, or wait?" Niigata asked, as a quartet of men emerged from each car. They weren't in uniform, but they were well armed. The headlights from the Lamborghinis pinned them in a circle of bright light, leaving the street around them in rain-drenched darkness. Something about them made the back of Max's neck itch.

There was a chance they'd make it through the blockade. A chance. The airport, and the waiting jet, were less than twenty minutes away. He'd bet a T-FLAC vehicle against anything on the road. But was he willing to bet Emily's safety to prove they could outrun and outsmart the local cops? Sixteen men, dark silhouettes against the light, fanned out around their vehicle.

"Lock the doors and keep the engine running, I'll talk to them," Max sprung his door, then shot Emily a quick look. "Stay put, I'll be right back."

Niigata and Mauro Zampieri, a local, more seasoned operative, had subtly unholstered their weapons, placing them within easy reach, but out of sight. Max's custom Glock was in his shoulder holster in view. He'd get out, hands in plain sight to show he wasn't a threat, but no one was getting their hands on his Glock. It was practically a part of his body.

"They'll want to talk to me, too," Emily told him, still shaken. "In fact their timing is perfect. When we're done here, I'll have one of them take me back to my car and follow me to a hotel."

Max had one foot out in the rain. "Your car's been impounded for an investigation. Do *not* get out."

Several men closed in on the car, guns drawn. They motioned with their weapons for everyone to get out of the vehicle. Hands up. *Pronto.* Shit.

Max complied, but paused before getting out. He didn't want one of these low-level cops suddenly getting trigger-happy. If she exited behind him at least he could keep her between himself and the heavy vehicle until he sorted this out. "Come out on my side—"

His words were cut off as Emily's door was yanked

open, and one of the men grabbed her arm, practically dragging her out of the car.

"Get your hands off her. *Now.*" Max snarled, incensed that the man would grab her when it was obvious she was in no condition . . . Fuck. They didn't know her. All they were seeing was a woman in blood-stained clothing, with glassy eyes.

All the police saw were four people fleeing the scene of a grisly murder.

No wonder they all had their weapons drawn. Max needed to defuse this possibly volatile situation ASAP. He glanced over the roof of the car at Emily. It was obvious she was still very much in shock, so much so that he wasn't even sure if she was aware of the activity surrounding her.

"I'll have this sorted out in a minute and we can be on our way."

"It's okay. *I'm* okay. I'll just—" she waved her free hand vaguely toward the surrounding police vehicles, her bloodstained face drawn and stark in the flashing blue lights as she looked at him with dark haunted eyes. "I . . . I'm okay," she repeated, a small frown pleating her brow.

Two men flanked her, leading her across the street to an overhang to get out of the rain. Out of the rain and also out of the light. He could barely make out her pink sweater and bright socks beyond the bright aura of the headlights. He'd forgotten she hadn't been wearing shoes when she'd run out on him this after-noon.

Alarm bells rang in his head. Basic police training would dictate that the officers assess the situation, then focus on the biggest potential threat. Him. But almost all of the cops had their attention on Emily.

Max held his hands out away from his body as three guys approached him. The fourth was behind him at eleven o' clock, hidden in the shadows. Zampieri and Niigata were instructed at gunpoint to exit the vehicle. Separated, they were each taken aside for questioning.

One guy stepped up, and grabbed Max's arm. Wrong fucking move. With the least amount of drama, Max disengaged. He greeted them politely enough, then asked for and saw ID.

Emily appeared to be the only one not aware of just how precarious their position was.

They walked like ducks and talked like ducks, but the itch on Max's neck persisted. He shot a glance across the street to where Emily stood, animatedly talking with her hands.

Max summed up the situation. His other men were still inside the Bozzato home several blocks away waiting for the T-FLAC forensic people to show. Sixteen men against himself and the two operatives, one of whom was still a rookie. Sixteen to two? Three? Doable odds. Would Niigata be waiting for his signal? Max glanced her way. She gave him the subtle sign that she was ready. Zampieri, he knew, was poised and waiting for his order.

Max answered the rudimentary interrogation,

keeping Emily in his peripheral vision. He frowned as she tried to pull away from the man gripping her upper arm.

This wasn't an interrogation.

This, God damn it, was a *kidnapping*.

The second Emily got out of the car, one of the men grabbed her arm, the other shoved a gun in her ribs. She gave a start of surprise, but before she could do more than gasp they herded her across the street toward one of the police vehicles.

Annoyance at their rough, inappropriate handling morphed into super awareness. Although the back passenger door was open, and the engine running, she noticed the interior light wasn't on. She realized her grave error. She should have listened to Max and stayed put, damn it. She had been incredibly stupid to get out of the car.

"A few questions, Signorina Greene." The officer's fingers dug painfully into her arm as he drew her away from Max and the others.

"How do you know my name?" *Don't be paranoid,* she told herself. But was it paranoia to now be convinced that someone really *did* want to kill her? Nausea churned in her stomach. Her heart started beating in a slow hard thud against her ribs and her mouth went dry. Knowing she was still in shock, since it had been mere minutes since they'd left Franco's palazzo, she tamped down her suspicions.

The police must've seen the slaughter at the Bozzatos'. For all they knew, she, Max, and the others were the killers. She tried to relax. They were just doing their job. Weren't they? God. Now she was seeing conspiracy behind every action.

The man with the gun was of medium height and medium build, even his hair was medium brown. Other than a small scar across one corner of his upper lip, his face was unremarkable. He smelled quite strongly of some kind of herb, marjoram? And wore a badly crumpled dark gray suit, with a dingy white, open-necked dress shirt.

"I repeat. How do you know my name? I didn't give it to you."

"Someone at the scene gave it to us."

Nobody at Franco's had known her name except Max, Emily thought, feeling sick. "I'm not going anywhere," she said coolly to the second man as the barrel of the gun pressed against her ribs. "Please put the gun away." He was a little taller, but as unremarkable as his friend. He, too, wore a dress shirt with an inexpensive dark suit.

It was pouring now, hard, cold drops. Her hair and clothing were already soaked, and her feet, clad only in socks, were freezing. She tasted watery blood in her mouth, and thought almost absently that Max had shot the man in the kitchen right behind her. Maybe an inch from her head. Her ears still rang.

Her stomach heaved and she felt dizzy with nausea as she realized that she had that man's blood all over her. Black dots buzzed in her vision, but she forced herself to take deep steadying breaths. She needed to keep her wits about her if she was going to get away from these men. And go where? She glanced over her shoulder to search for Max, but the gunman pulled her forward hard enough to make her stumble.

"Signorina Greene?" His Italian was pretty good. Swiss? Possibly German Swiss? "What was your relationship with the Bozzato family, hmm?" She saw the bodies and the blood, and blinked her wet lashes to clear the image. Her stomach roiled. "They were my friends. Ouch! You're cutting off my circulation. Release my arm, I'm quite capable of crossing the street on my own. In fact I'd rather conduct this interview tomorrow at your—"

The other man shook her, his face contorted in anger. "Shut up." His annoyance was disproportionate and she gave him a hard look. His face was oily with sweat, his eyes manic. He was scared. The fact that *he* was scared, scared *her* even more.

Emily's brain finally managed to sound an alarm. Delayed, yes. But accurate. She should have listened to her own instincts the second these guys put their hands on her.

It didn't take a rocket scientist to put two and two together. If she hadn't been horrified, shocked, and sick about what had just happened, maybe she'd have trusted the faint alarm bells ringing in her head sooner.

Despite the cars they were driving and the guns they all carried, they weren't police officers.

It didn't occur to her to yell for Max. She wasn't

accustomed to relying on anyone else, and everything was happening so fast, she only had time to react. "What do you want? Who sent you?" she demanded. "What in God's name could you *possibly* want from me?"

"Keep walking calmly, Signorina, and get into the car. There will be no trouble."

"You see, that's where you are dead wrong. There *will* be trouble." She tried to yank her arm out of the man's tight grip. If he pulled the trigger at this range she'd be nothing but splatter on the street. If she went with them her odds of survival were about the same. Zero.

She stopped in her tracks, her socks providing no traction at all. "I'm not going anywhere with y—"

Not deterred, they merely yanked her into motion by pulling her along. The open door of their car was less than six or eight feet away. Once she was in, there'd be no turning back.

Shooting another frantic glance across the street, Emily watched Max talking to three men, half turned away from her. Although traffic had been stopped by the four vehicles slewed all over the street, to reach him, she'd have to re-cross four lanes of road. A wide open space, with nowhere to hide.

Then she heard a loud pop and flinched, half-expecting to feel the searing pain of a bullet tearing through her flesh. Nothing. Except the frenetic pounding of her heart slamming against her ribs.

Just beyond their car was a narrow alley leading to

several other narrow alleys and a popular, always crowded trattoria. There were lots of people, and dark corners, and deep doorways to conceal her until she could contact the real police. Or until she could exit on the other side, and make her way to a hotel, or . . . or Max realized that things weren't what they appeared to be.

If I'm fast and lucky, she thought desperately, *I can reach the alley.* She had to take the risk that they wouldn't walk into a crowded public place and open fire. No. She had to *pray* they wouldn't. Because minutes had become seconds.

She had to call it. Or die.

Seven

WITHOUT WARNING EMILY WENT COMPLETELY LIMP, dropping bonelessly to the sidewalk in midstride. She was no athlete and it was neither a graceful nor a painless drop. Her funny bone smacked on the curb, but she barely noticed the buzzing pain jarring all the way up her arm as she heard, over the pounding of her head, a staccato, *bang! bang! bang!* of gunfire. It sounded exactly like her automatic stapler.

Max and his team had realized what was happening. Thank God.

Her sudden deadweight dragged the two men down with her. One fell, the other staggered but caught his balance.

Rolling out of their reach she scrambled up on all

fours. Something nearby made a reverberating *piiii-iing* sound.

Cursing, the man closest to her grabbed her by the hair, painfully yanking her head back. "You won't get away, bitch." Winding the wet strands around his fist, he tried to pull her to her feet using her long hair for leverage. "I'll cap you here and be done with you!"

Tears of pain blurred her vision, and her scalp burned. But as hard as he pulled *she* resisted, using gravity to keep herself down on the ground, even though the force snapped her neck forward. If he was going to shoot her, wouldn't he have done it by now?

He grunted and cursed as he continued to try and force her to her feet. By sheer will, Emily refused to stand, even though her hair felt as though it were being pulled out by the roots. If the son of a bitch wanted her in his car, he'd have to drag her kicking and screaming.

Over the thundering of her heart, she heard shouting and a loud *pop-pop-pop-poppopopopop*. Arms flailing, she finally found her attacker's head and gouged her short nails into his cheeks and scalp hard enough to feel his skin split. He barked in pain, letting her go, but not before she got a booted foot in the ribs for her effort.

Flying backward, she managed to correct herself and staggered to her feet. Half crouched, she ran, the rain striking her face like icy pellets, the streetlights a blur of movement as she passed.

Bangbangbang.

She was still out in the open, fully exposed and half expecting a bullet to hit her at any second. Breath sawing in and out of her aching lungs, Emily jumped on the hood of a parked car, rolling across the slick surface before tumbling to the pavement on the opposite side. Bullets *pinged* and ricocheted off parked cars, and sparks flew like Fourth of July sparklers.

A car's alarm started shrieking, adding to the din and chaos. She was cut off from Max. Knowing she had to get into the dubious protection of the alley, Emily ran in a crouched, semi-protected stance. She'd passed three, maybe four, parked cars when she heard a staccato burst of gunfire behind her. It was louder and close enough that she could taste the acrid smell of gunpowder.

Run run run run run.

Straightening, she ran flat-out toward the brightly lit opening of the narrow street and the safety of a crowded restaurant.

Pleasepleaseplease.

A second later, it wasn't a bullet that slammed into her back. It was the full force and heavy weight of a man. God. Another few yards and she'd have made it. She saw the gun in his right hand as they went down hard. They fell to the wet ground in a tangle of arms and legs, his arms wrapped around her from behind.

At the last instant he twisted, taking the brunt of the fall with her gripped in his arms. On her back like an overturned turtle, the man beneath her, Emily fought him tooth and nail. But this guy was stronger, more

130

persistent than the others, and he subdued her easily by wrapping his arms and legs around her. She could barely move as he rolled them between two parked cars, his body as un-damned-resilient as the hard surface of the street.

This time it occurred to her that she needed help, and she opened her mouth and screamed, "Maaaax!" at the top of her lungs.

"Emily," Max yelled against the side of her face as she bucked and heaved in his arms, shouting his name. "It's me, Max." They were sprawled halfway in the alley. "Calm down, I'm going to let you go, but for Christ's sake, do *not* knee me."

Apparently he thought it prudent to issue the warning. Emily was pretty sure every nerve and muscle in her body had liquefied with fear; she had no more fight left in her.

Two men sprinted around the fender of the car. They were only feet away. One arm around her, Max extended his other arm over her head and fired. *Pop. Pop.*

He pulled her to her feet before the bodies hit the ground. Then there was silence. No more shots, nothing but the sound of her pulse echoing in her ears, and her breath sawing unsteadily.

Grabbing her already bruised upper arm, Max searched her face in the iffy light. "Are you hurt?"

Elbow. Knee. Butt. The list was growing. "No. These guys aren't *Polizia di Stato*."

"Yeah. Got that." He scowled, sharp eyes fixed on

her face, clearly not happy with what he saw. He grabbed her hand. His was big and solid, and unlike hers, dry. "We've got to get to the car. Run like hell. Don't stop, don't even fucking pause. Got it?"

"Hell yes, I get it." Max was big. Max had a gun. She was sticking to him like glue.

He took off, Emily in tow.

Their car seemed a million miles away, skewed across the middle of the street, headlights still on. Max dodged two bodies sprawled in their way. He was nimble and light on his feet, and she felt like a buffalo in comparison. The surreal morning had turned into an even more surreal afternoon and night.

A man stepped out of a doorway, right into their path. The gun he held looked enormous. He was too close to miss. Emily flinched, as if by not looking she could somehow deflect the bullet. When she opened her eyes again the man was sliding down the side of a storefront, a look of utter surprise on half his face. The other half of his head was . . . gone.

Bile rose in the back of her throat. *OhGodohGodohGod!*

"Don't look," Max told her.

Horrified and somehow unable to follow his instruction, she turned to glance over her shoulder. They hadn't even paused in their running. There were bodies all over the place. Insanely, attracted to the noise and drama, some people were hanging out of their windows up and down the street to see what was going on below. Some had even come out in their

132

bathrobes to see the action. Though the noise and commotion were deafening, most of the shutters and doors along the street remained tightly closed, the residents no doubt fearful for their lives. Inconvenient for Emily and Max, but smart of them. Any good Samaritan risked becoming Swiss cheese for his pains.

Where the *hell* were the real police?

Max got off another shot, effectively deterring a guy sneaking up alongside them. The bullet went through the man's throat, then ricocheted off a wall behind him in a shower of sparks and bits of stone. The plate glass window in the butcher shop shattered from yet another bullet. One meant for them.

Someone grabbed Emily from behind, yanking her away from Max, almost pulling her arm from its socket. Another man closed in from his right. Before she could drag in a breath to scream, Max had taken down the man who'd grabbed her by kicking him in the jaw. The guy went flying, then slid a dozen feet along the ground and lay still.

"Go. Go. Go." Spinning in a half circle he did some improbable movement that had his entire body suspended in the air while his ankles hooked around the second man's neck.

They came down together in a bone-jarring tangle against the curb. "Go, damn it!"

Go where? As if she'd leave him here. She looked around for something to use as a weapon. The only thing she could see was a still spinning hubcap. Swooping down, Emily grabbed it and started

133

swinging it at Max's opponent's head, connecting with a resounding *clang* that made *her* wince.

Max landed a punch to the man's face, and he crumpled against a parked car. Seizing her hand again, Max pulled her along, keeping his body slightly in front of hers.

By the time they reached the car, Emily was sweating and lightheaded. Max pulled open the back door and shoved her inside. "Bulletproof windows." He slammed a fist on the lock, then slammed the door closed.

"Stay the fuck inside."

Then the crazy man went back into the fray.

Wonder of wonders, this time Emily had obeyed his goddamned orders. By the time Max returned to the car, eleven of the sixteen men were dead, and the local T-FLAC operatives had arrived from the Bozzato house just in time to take the remaining men into custody. *La polizia, I carabinieri,* and *Polizia di Stato,* plus several ambulances arrived minutes later, sirens screeching, lights blazing. So good of them to finally get their asses on the scene.

People were out in droves, umbrellas bobbing as they tried to see what was going on. A big night in the streets of Florence. All they needed was a fucking marching band, and someone handing out hot cappuccinos.

Local law enforcement usually deferred to T-FLAC when it was a matter of their own national security.

Max knew this situation didn't qualify; he lied by omission as he gave a statement. This situation, while lethal, was not an act of terrorism. While his focus *was* combating acts of terror, it was usually on a global or national scale.

Whatever was going on with Emily had something to do with an artist and his protégé. Or with her boyfriend, Max thought, annoyed by the possibility that some suave yahoo had gotten Emily into this kind of danger.

What the connection was Max had no idea. But when the police knew T-FLAC was involved it was a natural assumption that terrorism was their reason for being there. He didn't divulge the truth because he didn't want the local cops to take the remaining five men into their custody. He trusted T-FLAC's manner of interrogation more than he trusted the rigid guidelines local authorities were required to follow.

They could have what was left of Emily's attempted kidnappers when T-FLAC was done with them.

"That was fun," Keiko Niigata said dryly, wiping blood off her face with a filthy hand as she unlocked the driver's side door. She was slightly out of breath, her short black hair matted down with rain and blood.

Max gave her the once-over. She looked like hell, but she also had a familiar expression on her face. A look that said "Damn, I love my job." He saw it in his own mirror every day. "First time in close combat?"

"Yeah." She indicated her LockOut suit. The black, body-hugging material was almost impervious to penetration, and clung faithfully to her stocky frame. Although from the white, already healing streaks across the dense black fabric on her chest and shoulder, someone had attempted to cut her. "Think I'll wear this twenty-four-seven," she said cheerfully.

"Get that taken care of when we board." He indicated the seeping wound on her cheek. It would need stitches, but the suit had saved her from more serious injury. "Seen Zampieri?"

She jerked her chin to indicate the direction of the other man, then slid into her seat and started the engine.

"Good?" Max asked the older man as he approached.

Zampieri shrugged. "No complaints."

Max hadn't expected a different answer. Evidence of a bullet's path on his upper left arm and the nasal tone caused by his badly swollen nose indicated Zampieri had taken some licks. Still, the three of them had kicked the ass of sixteen determined men, and saved the girl. A good night's work by any standards.

They were all banged up, had lacerations, and were soaking wet and cold. Situation normal.

After sending a hand signal indicating their departure to the men he'd left behind and were still talking to the cops, he reluctantly opened the door and climbed into the backseat. He didn't know what to make of his reluctance, but it didn't matter. They needed to get to the airport, ASAP.

Emily had her head back, eyes closed. She wasn't

asleep. God knew, considering her day, it would have made sense. He'd expected to find her curled in a ball on the floor crying hysterically. Which was what most women—other than the ones in his line of work—would be doing right about now.

The passing streetlights flashed an intermittent striped pattern on her still face. Taking the opportunity to observe her while she played possum, Max scrutinized this woman who was a study in contradiction.

The pulse at her pale throat beat a staccato tattoo, and her lids fluttered as she feigned sleep. She'd make a crappy poker player. But, man, she was such a pleasure to look at. Looking past the blood in her hair and the smears of red on her face, he noticed everything about her.

Even wet and bedraggled, she was heart-catchingly beautiful. The kind of unconscious sexiness that women strove for but rarely achieved. Emily Greene was as lovely as an airbrushed model in some high-end magazine. Except she was the real deal. Again he felt the rage that had swamped him when he'd seen those bastards with their hands on her.

Max had a strong and irrational need to reach out and touch her creamy skin, the curve of her cheek, the gentle sweep of her soft mouth to confirm that she was real.

He rarely lied to himself, although he was damn good at lying to others. Yeah, looking at her was a pleasure. But even when he'd closed his eyes that first night they'd had sex, he'd felt a hard knock to his equilibrium.

Pheromones. Nothing more. Powerful, but merely a chemical reaction. What concerned him was how many *different* pheromones her body was transmitting for him to pick up on. He understood the aggregation pheromones. Those were the ones that said, "Hi baby. I'm attracted to you." He sure as hell understood the sex pheromone that said, "I'm available. Let's have sex. Here. Now. Often."

She was gorgeous, he wanted her. Physically. He got that. In spades.

But mixed in with the sexual attraction were a boatload of powerful *territorial* pheromones. The overpowering need to protect Emily at all costs was a new one for him. Max didn't know whether to be amused or alarmed. Territorial pheromones were what dogs had in their urine, and how they marked their territory.

"Were you hurt anywhere?" He couldn't tell. He wanted to touch her, check her out, but he didn't dare. What he was feeling right now was too uncontrolled, too wild to express in the backseat of a car. With Emily looking as though she'd—narrowly escaped death. Again.

"I'm okay. Shaky, but okay. How about you? Were you hurt back there?"

Was *he* hurt? No one had asked him that in decades and really meant it.

"I'm good."

"Yeah, I can see that." She touched his cheek briefly, then dropped her hand. "But were you hurt?"

Humans had a different way of marking their territory. It was called marriage. And since *that* wasn't in his vocabulary, he discounted all of the chemical mumbo jumbo and stuck to facts. Of course he was powerfully sexually attracted to this woman. What heterosexual man wouldn't be?

"No. I wasn't hurt. And neither were you, thanks to your smart thinking. Jesus, Emily. Thought the bastards had shot you before I could get over there." He brushed his hand over the silky disorder of her hair so he could see her face, then tucked the damp strands behind her ears, out of the way. "You're coming with us to Córdoba," he told her quietly, casually resting his fingers on her neck to check her pulse. He noticed she'd lost another earring in the fray.

Opening her eyes, she pushed herself upright. The skin beneath the smears of blood on her face was milk white, her eyes were dark. Yet it was clear she was determined to participate in whatever he threw at her. Max admired her inner strength.

"Who's doing this, Max? And *why?*"

"I'll find out," he assured her grimly. And he would. As soon as he discovered who the hell had bombed two churches and a synagogue.

Here was the whole Life vs. T-FLAC thing he'd thought he'd never have to deal with.

Shivering, she rubbed her arms through her pink sweater, which was dark with moisture. "*Before* more innocent people get killed?"

He sure as shit hoped so. Unfortunately, in his line of work it didn't always end up that way. "I won't let

139

anything happen to you. I swear it." It would be redundant to mention that his heart had almost fucking stopped earlier when he'd seen her drop to the ground. He'd thought she'd been shot, and had been stunned at the visceral desperation that had knotted his stomach when he'd imagined her sprawled lifeless on the sidewalk, him not thirty feet away.

"A great sentiment. But you can't make that kind of promise. You won't always be around, will you?"

No, he wouldn't be. In fact, if it weren't for the current situation he would have blown her off long before she'd walked out of the old man's villa this afternoon. Women and work, especially his work, didn't mix. Ever. Oh, he knew a few T-FLAC operatives who claimed rather fervently that they'd found the Holy Grail of love and happily ever after, but Max was a pragmatist. While he'd never experienced love himself, he supposed it existed on some level. More likely it was a pretty bow of a euphemism wrapped around sex. Chemical attraction. Back to pheromones.

"I'll be around until I discover who's behind this," he assured her, dismissing his inane thoughts. A pointless, fruitless tangent he'd do well to ignore. He'd stick to thoughts of a different kind of hunger. He'd missed both lunch and dinner. A thick steak, a baked potato, and a beer sounded good right now. "Any threat will be history."

"Nicely fielded." She met his eyes. "If *that's* the case then I hope on every level that you get this figured out sooner than later, and go on your merry way again."

Talk about gratitude, he thought, suddenly indignant. Jesus. "That's pretty damn cold all things considered."

"I know."

He hadn't expected the admission. A bitchy woman was a bitchy woman was a bitchy woman. "You know?"

Color rose in her face. "I need to stay mad for a while. I'm hanging on by a thread here, Max. I feel like—like—like a soufflé and someone opened the oven."

"Okay." He had no idea what dessert had to do with what was going on, but if she wanted to stay mad, and make reference to cooking, he figured he'd better keep his mouth shut.

"You should have been here for your father's funeral. And frankly I'm still not convinced that all this doesn't have more to do with you than it does me."

Was he supposed to yell back? Kiss her? Shut the hell up? Damn it to hell, but she was complicated.

Someone had tried their damnedest to kidnap her. In full view of dozens of people. *He* didn't have a single connection to Franco or his family. Max and the old man had been estranged most of his life. He'd only made contact last year for the express purpose of getting into that damned party. Other than that one time, they'd rarely spoken.

"Nothing to do with me." He no longer believed this had anything to do with himself or his work for T-FLAC.

"You showed up seconds after my intruder," Emily said, like a dog with a bone. "Don't you find that a little too convenient for coincidence?"

She wrapped her arms tightly around her midriff, doing what Max wanted to do. Hold her tightly.

Dismissing that as *luck,* rather than coincidence, he slouched back in his seat. "I don't believe in coincidence." What the fuck was he missing? What was the common denominator in all these seemingly random events?

"Me neither, not anymore." She turned to look out of her window. And apparently that argument was over.

Interesting.

Confusing, but interesting.

This evening's developments had taken the old man's death, and Emily's break-in, to a whole new level. He was tempted to take a leave of absence and get to the bottom of it. But his job took precedence. In the meantime, nothing was going to happen to her. He'd make fucking sure of it.

Eight

NIIGATA AND ZAMPIERI BOARDED WITH MAX. OPERatives were skilled in triage, and they grabbed a first-aid kit, then settled into their seats near the front of the aircraft to tend their wounds. The aircraft was spacious and well appointed with whatever the operatives might need going to or from an op. The galley was always fully stocked with fresh food and quick frozen meals. A doctor could perform surgery, and frequently had, with the state-of-the-art medical equipment onboard. The copilot on all the T-FLAC jets was also always a medic.

Every piece of high-tech equipment on the market (and a lot that weren't) was available at the touch of a button.

Max didn't care one way or another about the navy-and-camel décor, other than that the swivel, reclining, navy leather seats were comfortable, and big enough to stretch out flat. Sometimes the flight was long, and catching a nap was all the sleep they would get until the op was completed.

Emily was halfway down the aisle, headed to the back of the plane as Max stopped to grab a few essentials from the galley, a second first aid kit, and a blanket from one of the overheads. She was a little unsteady on her feet, but she walked the length of the plane before picking one of the chairs near the back. The seats weren't in rows, but in groupings of four with a table that could be folded open between them.

By the time he got to her she was staring unblinkingly out of the dark window. Her reflection showed him that she was hanging on by a thread. He had no idea how she'd react when the shock wore off. Everyone reacted to trauma differently. Anger. Tears. Depression.

She didn't acknowledge him when he sat down beside her. "Want a blanket?"

She shook her head.

"Buckle up," he instructed. The pilot didn't give a shit who was onboard or what their condition. He wouldn't take off until everyone was seated and strapped in. Max wanted to help her with the buckle on her belt, but when he reached over, she put up a hand to prevent him touching it, or her, and—eventually—managed it herself, even though her blood-smudged hands were shaking badly.

Twisting off the cap, he handed her the bottle he'd grabbed from the galley. "Water?" Max tamped down the urge to yank her into his lap again. This time holding on. *Tightly.* Jesus.

Like a robot, she lifted the bottle to her mouth, took a sip, then lowered it to the holder in the console of the armrest. She leaned her head back, but didn't close her eyes as the jet taxied down the long runway. Strain tightened her features, making her more starkly beautiful than ever. Her large brown eyes were still glassy, her shoulders unnaturally stiff as she tried unsuccessfully to control the tremors racking her body.

Shit.

Life vs. T-FLAC.

Here he was: dragging his personal life into an op. Insane.

"Wanna argue?" he asked, half joking.

"Maybe later."

Yeah. Maybe later. She was safe on the T-FLAC jet. Nothing was going to hurt her for the duration. What he needed to concentrate on was the *op*.

The latest explosions in the mosque, following the church and the synagogue, were part of a pattern; a string of bombings. In a few hours a T-FLAC team would be assembled and in Spain. Ready to hunt down the tangos responsible for this latest explosion. As yet no demands had been made. Just the mysterious bouquet of lilies left near the bomb site. Max knew that a demand would come. It was just a matter of time. Tangos *always* had an agenda, no matter how convoluted it might be or how many of them there were.

He couldn't drag Emily from pillar to post with him wherever the fuck the trail led. No matter how badly he wanted to keep her close. She'd have to be stashed in a safe house until he ascertained what the hell was going on.

He was pleased he'd asked for Cooper. As part of his team she'd already been dispatched to Córdoba. The woman was an excellent operative; he'd trust her to keep Emily safe until he returned. Damn it, that could be six hours, or six months.

Maybe he could piece together more of the puzzle before he put Emily in the safe house. The one in Wiesbaden, he decided. Keep her close.

With any luck he'd have some answers from his people in Florence by the time he got back as well.

One team was doing their thing at the scene of tonight's crime right now. Another was tirelessly interrogating the man who'd broken into her palazzo. Yet another group was still at Emily's home, searching for any clue that might reveal what the man had left or taken. Perhaps something that hadn't made it as far as the vial? Or something that didn't leave any trace inside it?

They still didn't know.

The man's fingerprints had been on the glass vial. But a match hadn't been found in any of T-FLAC's extensive databases, which included AFIS and the records from hundreds of law enforcement and governmental agencies around the world. God damn it. He didn't want to go haring off to Spain without knowing what the fuck was going on. More immediately, he wanted to see her body for himself to confirm she hadn't been physically harmed. Something he could only ascertain once the transferred blood had been washed off.

"How long were you and Bozzato an item?"

She rolled her head to look at him. "About five months. Why?"

"How much did you know about him?"

"What are you doing? Taking a survey?"

"Trying to figure out who the target really is. You or your boyfriend. Answer the question."

"I know he was decent, hardworking, and kind."

"Sounds like a regular AKC champion," Max told her shortly. "What else? Did he have enemies?"

"He was a financial consultant. Maybe someone didn't like what he told them—God. I don't know. Whoever did, did . . . *that,* wasn't an enemy. He was a butcher. Besides, I know Franco, he wasn't capable of making an enemy that would want him, or me, dead."

"Did you notice anyone suspicious hanging around when the two of you went out?"

"No."

"How about when you were out alone? Ever get the sensation someone was watching you? Maybe at the market, or the florist, or the bank?" The problem was, she was so gorgeous that people would be looking at her all the time. She probably wouldn't notice one more pair of eyes.

"No."

"Any strange cars outside your palazzo? Or perhaps showing up more often than could be coincidence when you were driving around?"

"No."

"How about hang ups? Wrong numbers? Crank calls?"

"No. No. And no."

"Other than Franco, made any new friends lately? One who asked a lot of questions?"

She shook her head.

"Filled in a survey or opened a new account? How about filling in a credit ap for that new car of yours?"

"I paid cash."

He raised a brow. "That's a big chunk of change."

"I could afford it."

"Restoration work pays that well?"

"If you're as good as I am, yes. But I also received a large payment for the work I did for a private client. I bought the Maserati in celebration when I turned in the last painting."

The Maserati Quattroporte Sport GT ran well over a hundred grand, more for all the bells and whistles Emily had. That was serious bank.

"Are we talking about the work you did for Richard Tillman?"

"You think a sick, eighty-year-old multimillionaire in Denver is trying to kill me? For God's sake, Max! What kind of people do you associate with? None of this has *anything* to do with Tillman. *Or* Franco," she added.

Maybe not. But he made a mental note to go to Denver and pay a call on the reclusive, born-again philanthropist to ask him some questions. In the meantime, he'd have T-FLAC intel check into Tillman's activities for the past year.

"Your mentor worked for him as well, right?"

"Why don't you at least call your father by name?"

"Because sperm donors are anonymous by nature. I like to keep it that way."

"That's a terrible thing to say, and a worse thing to believe. He gave you life, he cared about yo—"

"No. He did not. I hate to burst your rosy bubble about Daniel Aries, but the man was a pathological liar, a serially unfaithful husband, and he had no interest—let me repeat—*no interest* in having a son. Ever. And lest you think that this has had any bearing on my life as an adult, let me assure you that it hasn't," Max said flatly.

"My mother, who loved the son of a bitch to the bitter end, always welcomed him back with open

148

arms. He'd cheat, she'd forgive him." Elbows on the armrests he tapped his fingertips lightly on the leather. When he realized what he was doing, he bunched his hands into light fists and made a point of holding them still. "I loved the hell out of her, but it drove me insane to see her crying every time he left. And leave he did. Often."

Emily's brow knit. "*He* cheated?"

"Oh, yeah."

She let out a breath she'd been holding. "Oh, Daniel." She reached out and touched Max's arm, regarding him from those hot chocolate eyes that melted his brain and made him want to do and say things that weren't—had never been—in his repertoire.

"I'm sorry, Max. I really am. For years your father told me all these wild, improbable stories about you and your life. I suspected that most of them weren't true. If they *had* been, you would have to have been in your sixties to fit all of that in."

"Only the name was changed to protect the guilty. Yeah. That was my old man describing himself. Why the hell he'd do that I have no idea."

"Because it made him look better in comparison?" she suggested, pressing a fist against her solar plexus. He noticed that her eyes had lost focus, and guessed she was back to thinking about the murders. Her struggle to distract herself and concentrate on what she was saying, impressed the hell out of him. He could tell she was holding herself together by a very thin thread of sheer guts and determination.

She blinked herself back into the conversation and continued almost without pause. If someone hadn't been observing her as closely as Max was, they would have missed it. "Or perhaps he was merely tarring you with his own brush?" She bit her lower lip. "I have to admit I never could understand how he frequently complained that he had no relationship with you, yet he insisted that he knew you so well. I suspect your mother wrote to him for years off and on. But even if that were true, I doubt she'd know, or even *think* that about you. And even if she did, she wouldn't have shared that with Daniel."

"Why not?" he asked curiously.

"Because she loved you," Emily said matter-of-factly. "She'd never tell tales about you, especially not to your father. Is that what Daniel was like in his youth? A philanderer?"

"Big time."

Instead of answering she stretched the hem of her sweater away from her body and grimaced, then noticed Max still watching her and glanced away, folding her arms tightly over her chest.

"After he left for the last time things were considerably better at home," he said to the curve of her cheek. She was maintaining her composure, but barely. "My mother attempted to divorce him a couple of times. I suspect she didn't try that hard. Still, he ignored the papers she had her lawyer send." He shrugged. "After a while he didn't seem to matter to her. He was gone, and she went back to building a life."

"That was their relationship," she told him quietly. "And sad as that was, you and Daniel could have, should have, made some sort of connection, don't you think?"

Although she was keeping up her end of the conversation, she still looked too fragile for his peace of mind. Max felt uncharacteristically helpless. "Obviously not." The last damn person he wanted to discuss was his father. On the other hand, talking about her mentor, hell, *defending* her mentor, put a lively fire in Emily's wounded brown eyes, and brought a flush to her pale cheeks.

He decided to piss her off a little more, in the hope that she'd forget, if only for a few more minutes, the horror she'd witnessed. "Drop it," he told her, his voice grim. He wanted to get her in the shower, where he would personally wash the blood from her skin. He couldn't stand seeing it on her. Couldn't stand that she'd bear the memory of what had happened to her friends whenever she closed her eyes.

He couldn't fix that. Couldn't erase those memories.

Crap. He didn't remember when he'd ever felt this helpless. The knowledge made him feel hollow inside.

He knew she wouldn't appreciate that the only way he could think to help her was to fuck her brains out until neither of them remembered their names, let alone the bloody massacre. And then he wanted to do it again until they were both too exhausted to move.

Damn it to hell, he wanted that look gone from her eyes. He wanted the hard, grim line of her mouth to go back to the soft sweet curve he was familiar with.

"Drop it?" She gave him just the exasperated look he'd expected. "*Drop it*? We don't always have to *like* the people we love. Sometimes we don't even know our parents, or who they are. Every parent/child relationship takes *work*." She took a swig out of her water bottle. "Connections can't flourish unless one of you is willing to do more than fifty percent to *make* that happen," she told him flatly.

"Who are we talking about here?" He kept his voice carefully neutral. "Me or you?"

"You." She sounded genuinely angry now.

"Hmm. We didn't *love* each other. We were strangers." Even he wasn't sure if they were still talking about his relationship with his father, or if somehow the conversation had veered off into something a damn sight more personal. And dangerous.

"You should have tried harder."

He shifted in his seat, stretching out his legs, getting more comfortable. No. Not getting more comfortable. Feeling less *un*comfortable, damn it. "This conversation is a dead end."

"Fine. But don't sit here interrogating me, when you refuse to answer a simple damn question."

The plane leveled off at altitude. "Nothing is that simple."

"Well, I'm simply tired of answering your questions. How about that?" She got out of her seat and stepped into the aisle.

Max released the polished chrome clip on his seatbelt. "Come on." He got up, too. Not liking the way he crowded her, Emily stepped back. "You'll feel better once you've showered and put on some clean clothes."

"I doubt if a *hundred* showers will make me feel better," she replied. "But, yes. I would like to shower and get on some fresh clothes."

They'd been sitting close to the mahogany door leading to the aft cabin, and Max slid the door open, preceding her inside. The room contained a compact, but extremely efficient, high-tech office and second bathroom. Wall units discreetly housed a small conference table, and a couple of fairly comfortable beds.

He opened the narrow door to the bathroom and flicked on the light. Despite its small size, the bathroom, like the rest of the jet, was the height of both luxury and efficiency. Bronze mirrors covered the walls, plush carpet lay underfoot, and a man-sized, glass-enclosed, navy-and-gold tiled shower stood in the corner. The liquid soap in the dispenser was specially formulated with active enzymes. No smell, and it would remove any stain, particularly blood. But that was TMI for Emily right now. "There's plenty of hot water," he told her. "Take as long as you like. I'll leave you something to change into when you're done."

"Okay."

"Towels." He removed several from the cabinet beneath the sink, placing them on the closed toilet seat. "Yell if you need anything." *Me for instance.*

"I won't."

He stepped through the doorway. "I'll be in the forward cabin."

Her response was to slam the door in his face.

The moment she was alone, Emily's knees gave way and she dropped to the carpeted floor. Arms wrapped around herself, she folded over at the waist, face pressed against her knees. The band of pressure across her chest was so tight she could barely breathe.

OhGodohGodohGod.

If Max had expected her to respond intelligently to one more question she would have started screaming and never stopped. Her stomach churned and her heart pounded so fast she thought she was going to pass out.

Eyes open or closed, her brain was filled to capacity with *red.* She'd had no idea blood was as bright, as shiny, as slick as what she'd seen in the Bozzatos' kitchen. She'd never get the grotesque images out of her head.

Never.

Now, co-existing with those horrific images were images of the violence and terror of the gunfight in the streets of her neighborhood. The world gone mad.

As sickening as it had been to see the blood and gore there, she didn't know those men. Nothing could compare to what had happened to Franco and his family.

Details she hadn't realized she'd absorbed at the time were coming back in a sickening flood of hideous, Technicolor images that turned her stomach and made the vise around her chest ratchet even tighter. Like a vile and vivid copy of a Jackson Pollock painting, the walls and ceiling had been splattered with blood. The savagery of the attack was almost incomprehensible.

It had taken a few seconds for Emily's brain to process the scene. Janna—her neck practically sliced through—lay half-on, half-off the kitchen chair.

Emily's stomach clenched. Janna's lifeless eyes had been open, communicating the terror she'd suffered long before the life had drained from her body. Nonna Maria— Oh God! Nonna Maria's blue dress had been black with wet blood. They'd cut her chest and face so that she'd been unrecognizable, then taken one leg of her walker and jabbed it into the gaping knife wound on her chest.

While Nonna Maria and Janna were victims of a blitz attack, Franco hadn't been as fortunate. His body was riddled with stab wounds. Three of his fingers had been sliced off. Defensive wounds, she thought, sickly. In what was surely a fight for his life, Franco had grabbed at the knife in a futile gesture that had only added to the brutality. The killer had gone out of his way to inflict a maximum amount of wounds. Neck, chest, forearms, upper thighs.

As part of her training, she'd gone beyond the normal life drawing classes and studied nudes, and taken pre-med classes in anatomy. The assassin had purposefully hit every major artery in Franco's body. With each frantic heartbeat, Franco's blood had pulsed from his body.

Why would *anyone* slaughter an entire family? It didn't make sense.

Bile rose in the back of her throat.

If someone had wanted them dead, why not a bullet to the head? Why the massacre?

Why? Why? Why?

She pressed her forehead hard against her knees. God. She wished she could at least cry to relieve some of the intense pressure squeezing her chest. But though her eyes burned with unshed tears the situation was way beyond crying.

Somehow *she'd* brought *that* on the Bozzato family. *How* or *why* she didn't know. But there was no doubt in her mind that, but for her, they'd all be alive right now. A raw, painful sob caught between her chest and throat, but there were no cathartic tears to ease their path.

Emily pressed her clenched fists hard into her diaphragm where an ever-tightening band squeezed so hard she could barely draw a breath. Folding over on herself she rocked, unable to contain the overwhelming pain that had accumulated over the last several weeks.

Her teeth chattered. Cold. Cold. Cold. She couldn't get warm. It was as if the whole emptiness of her was filled with brittle shards of ice. Slivers that sliced and cut her deep inside.

Intense, unrelenting emotion had been building, giving her no time to decompress or figure things out before the next God-awful thing body-slammed her emotions.

Daniel's death, followed by the break-in, followed by the emotional whirlwind of Max's return, followed by the Bozzatos' grisly murders, followed by the attempted kidnapping and gunfight in the streets had left her emotionally reeling.

She should get up, she thought vaguely as she pressed her face against her knees and rocked. In a minute or two when she was sure she could stand without screaming. A sob ripped up her throat, followed by another. She didn't even attempt to stop them no matter how badly they hurt.

"Christ—" Strong hands closed around her shoulders, jolting her back to her surroundings. Max pulled her to her feet in mid-sob. Eyes more green than hazel met her startled tear-drenched gaze with such compassion Emily's heart wrenched. Tears clogged her throat as he wrapped her in his arms, holding her tightly.

"I— P—please g—g—" She didn't trust herself to finish. She wanted to climb inside him where she'd feel warm and safe. Insane. Max wasn't safe. Far from it.

"Ah, sweetheart." He wiped her wet cheek with a gentle thumb, then cradled the back of her head in his palm and pulled her wet face against his chest, his fingers tangled in her hair. He rubbed a big, warm hand up and down her back in a sweetly tender attempt at consolation.

For a moment she felt too brittle to accept that comfort, but after a moment her body recognized the safe haven he offered and she responded by wrapping her arms tightly around his waist. Fisting the back of his shirt, Emily pressed her cheek against his chest and cried in jerky sobs that hurt her throat.

"Yes, that's right," he murmured, pressing his lips against her hair as he cradled her against the furnace heat of his body. "Get it out. Let it go."

She wanted him to leave her alone until she could get a grip on her emotions. She wanted him to hold and comfort her. Hell. She didn't know *what* she wanted at the moment.

Yes she did.

She wanted *Max*.

Emily tightened her grip on the back of his shirt and lifted her head. She looked up at him through a blur of tears. "I-I'll be o-okay in a m-minute." She would if she could get her feet under her emotionally and pull herself together. Right now that wasn't even close to a possibility.

"Yeah," Max told her gently. "But in the meantime let me take care of you, okay?" His tone belied the taut planes of his face, and the grim set of his lips. "Let's get your clothes off so you can take a shower, okay?"

"In a m-minute." For a moment she rested against him, drawing in his quiet strength. She'd hit an emotional wall and she didn't have the strength to fight it. She was drained, and tired of being frightened. She wanted to forget everything and shut off her brain.

But of course when her brain woke up again, every-thing would be right where it had been before. What she had to do was pull herself together, she knew that better than most. She made an effort to push him away. It was a pretty puny effort, she admitted, as her eyes welled again. Having him here, now, when she was at her most vulnerable, was dangerous.

But God, it was seductive, too.

"Make love to me." Standing on her toes, Emily wrapped her arms around his neck and pulled his mouth down to hers. She didn't want gentle. She didn't even want *emotion*. Just sex. Hard fast driving sex until she couldn't think or feel any more.

"No. Fuck me."

He froze, and for a moment she thought he was going to resist. He didn't, thank God. He looked down at her for the space of several erratic heartbeats, his eyes a hard, glittering green. The look was hot enough to make her blood race like quicksilver through her veins. He was going to take her now. Here. Standing pressed against the tiny sink, in the equally tiny bathroom.

A muscle ticked at the corner of his mouth as he lowered his head, his hands splayed possessively on her back, drawing her flush against him. She felt his hardness, and shifted against him as her lips parted beneath his.

But instead of ravishing her the way she wanted him to do, Max's mouth closed over hers in a slow, hot kiss that made her ache. She whimpered as his tongue sought and found the slick velvety recess of her mouth. His kiss curled around her jangled senses as sweetly as warm honey. Tightening her arms around his neck Emily relished the deepening of the kiss, but she wanted more.

She wanted him to fuck her. To batter her body and leave her limp and satiated and without a cognizant thought. She wanted him. Harder. Faster. Still, the maddeningly slow thorough exploration made her heart hammer, and her body burn.

Max didn't give her what she was asking for, he gave her what she needed.

Tenderness. Understanding.

He kissed her eyes, her cheeks, her jaw. His mouth trailed up to her ear, and the damp heat of his breath made her shudder. And all the while he cradled her protectively in his arms.

She was vaguely aware when he removed his hand from her back, and a moment later she heard the rush of water. He'd reached over and turned on the shower. Bringing his hand back, he wove his fingers in her hair, while the other slid down to cup her bottom. If he was trying to calm her, it wasn't working. His touch made something deep inside her spiral more tightly. She deepened the kiss. Made it harder. Hotter.

Kissing him shamelessly, her fingers gripped his hair to hold him where she wanted him. Not caring if he knew how desperately she needed this connection. This affirmation of life. His erection, trapped behind the zipper of his pants, nudged her mound, sending shards of sensation to her every nerve ending, making her hypersensitive and already so aroused she knew she wouldn't need much to push her over the edge. Moisture gathered between her legs, and her nipples, crushed against the hard plane of his chest, ached.

"Help me forget," she whispered against his lips. "Just for a few minutes, help me forget."

His hands bracketed her face, and drawing her mouth up to his, he kissed her with controlled gentleness as he crowded her backward until he had her pressed between the furnace of his body and the cool porcelain sink.

"Lift your arms," he murmured against her eagerly seeking mouth as he reached down and pulled her sweater up. The wet wool did nothing to cool her burning skin as he yanked the garment over her head one-handed, tossing it somewhere on the floor behind him.

"Come back." She grabbed the front of his damp T-shirt in both hands and tugged. "You're wearing too many clothes."

"You first." He tugged down her pants and thong while he bent his dark head and his mouth found her nipple. He sucked hard as he shoved her garments down her legs. Her back arched as she kicked her feet free.

"Hurry. Hurry. I want it hard and fast and *now*, Max. *Right* now."

"Hold that thought," he murmured, his lips twitching as he backed her into the shower, then followed her into the stall. His big body crowded her against the cool tiled wall beneath the heavy beat of the showerhead as the stall filled with steam.

Emily closed her eyes and let the hot water beat on her head and down her back as Max pumped shampoo into his hand from a dispenser on the tiled wall. He gently put her from him, and lathered her hair. Murmuring a protest, she nevertheless closed her eyes, staying where she was. Hot water sluiced down her back, tickling as it ran down her legs.

"Lift your face," he instructed, positioning her to rinse the lather out of her hair. "Keep your eyes closed," he instructed, as he gently washed the blood off her skin, then rinsed the soap off her cheeks with his wet hands.

He bathed her from top to bottom while the water beat on her back in a stupefying rhythm that lulled her into a kind of a trance. Her mind told her that Max's touch was efficient and impersonal, but her body begged to differ. Max was keeping her at a high level of arousal. Her entire body was vibrating like a tuning fork as he turned her into the spray, lathering and rinsing her back.

"You do k-know," she mumbled as he turned her around then knelt before her, lifting her foot on his thigh. "That you're in here with all your clothes on, right?" She grabbed his shoulder as she teetered on one foot.

"I noticed." His voice was as dry as he was wet. His clothes lovingly molded to his body, his dripping hair was flattened against his skull and neck, showing off the sharp planes of his features, making his eyes look as dark and fathomless as a mountain pool.

He stroked his hand slowly up her calf, then bent to press a kiss to the inside of her knee. When he licked and kissed a path up the sensitive skin on the inside of her thigh the sensation made her shudder and burn.

"I've thought of nothing but tasting you for months," he admitted hoarsely, his tongue cool as it slid across her shower-warmed skin.

"Please—" she whispered in a raw, almost unrecognizable voice as she found herself leaning against the tiles, Max's head between her legs, his large hands cupping her ass.

A hot electric pulse shot through her body as his mouth explored more intimately and he tasted and explored with his slick, hard tongue. Her short nails dug into his broad shoulders as she tried to maintain her balance in a watery world gone hazy.

Her breasts ached, and she cupped one, pinching the aching hardness of her nipple between her fingers as Max's mouth brought her to a hard, fast orgasm.

Shaken and limp she leaned against the wall, watching him as he rose to tower over her. She clung to him, her fingers digging into the corded, water-slick muscles of his shoulders as he kept eye contact and yanked down the zipper of his sodden jeans.

Grabbing fistfuls of his T-shirt she pulled it up his body and over his head, then grabbed his hair in her fists and pulled him back to kiss her. His laughter was muffled by her mouth, but she felt the vibration all the way through her body.

He pulled away to finish unzipping his jeans and

finally—*finally*—sprang free. Heavy, thick, rigid. And right now—all hers. She reached for him greedily, cupping his heavy sex as he kicked off the rest his wet clothes.

"Bed," he said, taking her mouth in a kiss that left no doubt in Emily's mind about what was going to happen next.

When he lifted his mouth from hers to drag in a heavy breath, she demanded, *"Now,"* and pulled his mouth back to hers. Wrapping one leg around his narrow flank, she tried to position him where she was once again throbbing and aching.

Max bit back a laughing groan as Emily tried to climb his body. *"Bed,"* he repeated, pulling both her legs up around his waist, and supporting her sweet, creamy ass in his palms.

She buried her face against his neck and gave a gurgle of laughter. "I hope we don't hit an air pocket."

"What a way to go." He exited the shower with her in his arms. "Off." He paused just outside the glass door to let her shut off the water. The tiny bathroom was jungle-steamy, and sliding open the narrow door into the aft cabin let in a draft of much cooler air. Emily bit the side of his neck, making him groan.

He placed her on the narrow bed he'd pulled down from the wall unit earlier, then followed her down. Her legs were still wrapped around his hips, her heel digging into the flexing muscles of his ass.

Sliding his hands up the sensitive inside of her arms,

he pushed them against the mattress, then twined his fingers with hers on either side of her head. Her big brown eyes had lost the dazed, terrified sheen he'd hated to see there earlier, now they looked up at him with a fierceness, and a determination that made his pulses race, and his cock throb.

She kissed a path down his chest as far as she could go. "I need it fast and hard."

His lips twitched. "Hmm," he murmured, bringing her head up so he could kiss her throat. "I believe I made a note of that earlier."

She scowled, wiggling her hips under his, which made his body tighten and his teeth clench. "Well?" she demanded, narrow-eyed. Crossing her ankles in the small of his back, she pulled him tightly against her body. She'd never been shy about what she wanted. Thank God that hadn't changed, he thought taking her mouth in a kiss that stole his own breath and made his heart trip-hammer in his chest.

He dragged his mouth off hers, and lifted his head. He was done teasing. "I want you," he said roughly as he guided himself to her entrance. She was wet, her muscles already clenching as he slid two fingers inside her.

"Have m. . ."

More chatting than he was used to. Max rammed inside her wet sheath. Arms around his neck, Emily buried her face against his chest, and shuddered. "Haaa— Don't—m—" She came so fast he knew she'd been hanging on a precipice.

165

His own orgasm was blinding and instantaneous, and robbed him completely of breath. It was a few minutes before he could speak.

"Fast enough for you?" His fingers combed through her wet tangled hair, holding her tightly as he slanted his mouth over hers.

Her lips clung as he lifted his head. She brushed a quick kiss to his mouth. "Hmm. I'm not sure I'm done with you yet."

"Insatiable."

"With you," she said running her hand across his torso and the line of hair that traveled down to where their bodies were still joined. "I think I am."

Wrapping his arms around her, Max cradled her against his chest, their damp skin slick and binding them together. He brushed a kiss to her hair. "Sleep."

She closed her eyes and dropped into dreamless oblivion.

He'd done what she'd asked. Made her forget. For an hour.

But forgetting didn't make the problems, or the questions, go away. Not by a long shot.

"Fucking hell," Max whispered harshly into the darkness. He lay there, Emily's damp body curled against his, their hearts picking up each other's rhythm so that the two heartbeats were like one. "Fucking, *fucking* hell."

He hadn't been able to stop thinking about her for months. A dangerous distraction in his line of work. Now here he was again. Screwing up by screwing her.

No, he thought, a chill traveling through his body. He hadn't just *screwed* Emily Greene.

They'd made love.

He needed to get this business with her resolved and walk away. Fast. Her hair, tickling his nose, smelled—impossibly—of roses. "Triple fuck."

Nine

EMILY'S BODY TWITCHED AND SHE CRIED OUT AS SHE revisited the Bozzatos' kitchen in her dreams. In the world of nightmares she stood immobilized in the doorway, watching as the killer hacked and gutted his victims. Blood sprayed from Nonna Maria's chest as her rheumy eyes begged Emily to save her. But Emily's feet were glued to the sticky floor. She looked down and saw that her pink socks were wicking up a pool of brilliant red blood.

The viscous liquid moved up her bare legs, cutting like sharp little razor blades as it clawed its way up, and up, and up— Her own scream woke her. Panting, clammy with perspiration, she sat up and forced herself to take calm, even breaths. A dream. Just a dream.

By the angle of the light coming through the small windows it was early morning and from the lack of motion, she assumed the plane was on the ground, although she didn't remember landing. She didn't think she'd slept long, but the few hours of oblivion had helped.

The great sex had helped even more. For that hour

she hadn't been capable of any kind of coherent thought.

Don't read anything into it, she told herself firmly. The whole "leopard *doesn't* change its spots" thing. As long as she could accept Max for what he was, she'd be okay.

Stretching out the slight soreness in muscles unused to mattress calisthenics, she tossed back the blanket and got up to peer outside. From the size of the building—small—she realized they must be at a private airport. There was no international airport in Córdoba.

Max had mentioned just before she fell asleep that he'd be gone when she woke up. But that he'd be back later that morning. She needed to take the time alone to get herself on track and centered. Falling apart again wasn't going to accomplish a damn thing. Other than mind-blowing sex.

"What do I know for sure?" she asked herself, trying to be logical and reasonable when her life was anything but.

Fact. She had good cause to be afraid for her life. Fact. She was safe here with Max. For now. "But what about when he rides off into the sunset again?" It wasn't a case of *if,* but a case of *when.*

Daniel had told her a lot about his son. Pretty much all of it unsavory, and unappealing. But if what Max said was true, then his father had lied. Then where had Daniel gotten his information? Nothing her mentor had told her meshed with the Max she was seeing.

Why would Daniel lie? Other than to make himself appear in a better light. Maybe. "Or am I just seeing what I want to see?"

God. How would she *know,* considering what was going on? Was she allowing the physical attraction, which was unmistakable, to blend in with Max's heroic behavior? What woman wouldn't fall for a man who was big and strong and could literally save her from the bad guys?

And Daniel hadn't been as pure as the driven snow either. He'd had his dark side, too.

She didn't *have* to make a life-altering decision about Max. Whatever happened between them wasn't long-term. And all the rest was incidental to the physical attraction.

"Fool me once . . ." *Yeah, yeah, yeah.* She ignored her own caution. The reality was she was so hot for the man she didn't give a damn how short this interlude might be. He turned her inside out sexually, and the chemistry between them was hot enough to go supernova every time they touched. Every time their eyes met.

They were two consenting adults. This time she *knew* he'd be walking away without a backward glance. But for now—"Why *not* enjoy what he's offering?" *Think like a man.*

Maybe for once she should be willing to accept low expectations. There'd be no regrets on either side. She ignored the little twinge of irritation at herself. Since when did she settle? For anything?

She hadn't *settled* for art school in Seattle when she knew the very best were in Italy. She hadn't *settled* when she'd bought a custom, special order Maserati instead of a Jag off the lot. She hadn't *settled* when she'd been courted by some of the top galleries and museums in the world.

Hell no. She'd always kept her eye on the prize, whatever it had been, and she'd gone for it.

"For all I know, he's already mounted his black horse and ridden off into the sunrise," she muttered under her breath, then shook her head at how ridiculous she was, bargaining with herself. "Great! What did I just decide?"

She really had to get her brain and body in sync to make these kinds of decisions.

Although the air-conditioning seemed to be working, she wasn't sure of the water situation when the plane was stationary. Not taking any chances, she hastily showered, then dried off and went back into the small cabin. Max had left black jeans and a black T-shirt tossed over a desk chair. Thoughtful. Thought-provoking.

Going commando was a new, and not altogether unpleasant experience, but the muted sound of voices from the forward cabin made her dress quickly.

She flinched at the unexpected knock on the door, then cursed the way her heart leapt into overdrive. Max was back.

"Are you decent?" a woman called, opening the door a crack.

As if Max would knock. "Sure."

Emily's first reaction as the woman strolled into the room was that Max had a girlfriend. And here she was, with her striking red hair and fascinating face. Earth Mother. Emily imagined her against a dark teal background, looking over one bare shoulder—Good God. She wasn't going to *paint* this woman.

Hell. The rat fink bastard had had sex with *her* three times in the past few hours, and he wanted to introduce her to his *girlfriend*? The redhead put out her hand, ice-green eyes warm. Her skin was lovely, lightly tanned and without a blemish. She was probably a few years older than Emily, but she was in superb physical condition in close-fitting black jeans, and a long-sleeved black T-shirt. In fact, Emily was wearing an identical outfit, and presumed it belonged to Max's "friend."

"AJ Cooper. Wright really, but that confuses things."

Emily shook her hand automatically. Slender fingers, but calloused. Short nails. No polish. No jewelry other than a large-faced wristwatch. "What things?"

"I started as an operative before I got married, and everyone knows me by my maiden name. It's just easier to keep it simple."

So Daniel hadn't been *all* wrong. Max was having an affair with a colleague. A *married* colleague. It didn't surprise her, but it pissed her off. Daniel had been right. Max was a very smooth player. The fact that she'd slept with him again made him an asshole, but worse, made her feel damned stupid. So much for giving herself the pep talk.

"You're married?"

The redhead smiled, her eyes filled with pleasure. "Kane Wright. He also works for T-FLAC. We met on an op."

"Really?" Emily said coolly, wondering how fast she could find something else to wear. "That's pretty dangerous, isn't it? Having your husband *and* lover both in the killing business?"

"Yikes. You sure leap to conclusions, don't you?" AJ grinned. "Max and Kane are friends. And Max is *not,* nor has he ever been, my lover."

"God. I'm so sorry." Emily rubbed her forehead, feeling like an idiot. She had jumped to conclusions based on nothing but her own insecurities.

"Hey, no sweat." AJ dismissed with a smile.

"Ready to grab something to eat? Max filled me in on the happenings. He went into town with the team, but he should be back in an hour or so."

Another bullet averted, Emily thought, not amused that the thought of Max and this woman together had annoyed her. Her stomach rumbled. "Breakfast sounds good." *And I'm too involved with Max to be rational.* And she needed to keep her chin above water if she was to survive this.

"Great, come on." AJ pushed through the door. "I introduced myself to Keiko Niigata an hour ago. We let you sleep as long as we could. What Max didn't fill me in on, Keiko did. She told me you whipped some guy's ass with a hubcap." She gave Emily a high five.

"I bet Max forgot to mention I hit him with a cast-iron frying pan, then kneed him in the family jewels, didn't he?" Emily mentioned dryly.

AJ laughed. "I love a girl who's resourceful. Smell that? Keiko has the whole bacon and eggs and waffles thing going. Yum. I'm starving, too."

And apparently AJ was used to doing a monologue. She glanced over her shoulder, her red-gold braid a long snake down her back. "Sorry to talk your ear off. Comes from being married to, and working with, Alpha males who are great in a battle but hard on a woman's ego when she wants a little conversation. Monosyllabic hardly covers it."

Emily smiled. "Part of their training?"

"As a male? Yeah. God that looks as great as it smells," she told the Asian woman without drawing a breath between subjects. "Let's eat before the testosterone brigade gets back."

Emily glanced at the open door. The guy who'd been in the car with them yesterday stood guard at the top of the steps, a large, menacing gun over his arm.

"Morning," Emily greeted Keiko. "Thanks, this looks great." She accepted the offered plate, nodding at the man situated outside. They never had been introduced. "What's with the wet suit? You were wearing the same thing yesterday."

The matte black material clung to every curve and valley of his body, and made hiding anything pretty much impossible.

The woman wore jeans and a dark brown sweater now, but yesterday she'd been painted into that strange-looking bodysuit. And unless one had a killer body, it was not the most flattering outfit Emily had ever seen.

"The LockOut suit protects from injury," Keiko explained. "Similar to a Kevlar vest, but thinner and more impervious. I wouldn't want to be without it in the field, but boy, gain a few pounds, and everyone knows it."

"Apparently counterterrorist operatives are all in excellent shape," Emily said, reaching for the pepper. In fact, she'd very much like to see Max in this getup. Then she'd like to peel it off him. Slowly.

"Geez," AJ said with a laugh as the three women sat in the large leather swivel chairs at a table with their meals. "You look ready to take a bite out of a large, juicy steak."

Keiko met Emily's eyes, but she made no comment. *Thank God I didn't blush,* Emily thought, digging into her breakfast. The plane wasn't that big, and the interior walls were thin. She'd forgotten that she and Max hadn't been alone onboard for the hour they'd spent behind closed doors.

Emily didn't hear a ring, but AJ quickly removed a small black phone from her breast pocket. "Cooper. Yeah." Her eyes met Emily's across the table. "Right here eating breakfast. Got it. Want Zampieri to— Yeah. I hear you. We'll be there in—?" She checked her watch. "Twenty minutes? Yeah." She rose, putting the phone back in her pocket.

"Sorry. Breakfast is going to have to wait. Max wants you to take a look at something."

With just a couple of phone calls, Max's two worlds collided.

Asher Daklin and Rafael Navarro, both chemical and explosives experts with T-FLAC, were traveling by car with him to this third bomb site.

The streets surrounding La Mezquita were clogged with press and curious bystanders. It took some clever maneuvering for Navarro to navigate the crowds. A bombing of this magnitude, in one of the largest, most unique mosque/churches in the world, was big news. Media from around the world had a presence on-site. Camera crews, vans, cars, and people crowded the narrow streets outside the massive, fortresslike walls.

The team had received an overview about the site early this morning via fax from Control. Originally a smallish Christian church, La Mezquita had been built by Visigoths in 500 CE, then taken over for the worship of Janus, the double-headed Roman god of doorways and gates.

In the fifth century, Córdoba had been the capital of Spanish Muslims, and they'd built, and rebuilt, the mosque over the next couple of hundred years to make it one of the largest structures of the Muslim world. Several centuries later the Arabian mosque was captured by the Christian Spanish king and it was converted back to a Christian sanctuary.

All Max needed to know was that the bomb site had connections to Christians and Muslims. A bonanza for any antireligious group with an agenda.

And the place was big and important. La Mezquita took up a city block, and was considered one of the finest examples of Arabian architecture in the world. Apparently it combined Roman, Gothic, Byzantine, Syrian, and Persian elements. Not that Max gave a rat's ass about the architecture, no matter how stunning and unique it was purported to be.

He wanted to know what sick fuck had bombed another place of worship. The third in as many weeks on T-FLAC's radar. Had it been one of numerous radical fundamental Islamic groups? One of the anti-Christian groups? Jesus, the possibilities were pretty much goddamned endless.

His phone vibrated. "Aries."

"This is Greg Sandoval. My apologies, mist— Aries," Sandoval said. "The prisoner is um—well, er. He's *dead,* sir."

Their car slowed so Navarro could show ID to the local cops guarding the entrance gates. The barricade was lifted, and they were waved through. Place was still crawling with local forensic teams, bomb squad, and law enforcement. A pall of black smoke lingered in the air.

It took a second for Max to connect Sandoval's name with the T-FLAC operatives who'd been entrusted with taking the prisoner from Emily's palazzo into custody. "And how," Max demanded, "did the prisoner, with the answer I needed, *die*?"

Even with the windows closed, the smell of the explosion was cloying.

"W-would you um like to speak with Kleiver?" San-doval offered hopefully.

"Does he have a note pinned to his diaper from his mother with an explanation?" Max didn't bother hiding his sarcasm. He wanted to put a fist through the console. It had been a simple job of interrogation. A job two operatives should have been able to handle with their eyes closed. It had always been consider-ably more fun in training to be the interrogator, rather than the interrogatee. Hadn't these assholes learned anything? And, God damn it, were all the T-FLAC operatives in Italy this week frigging *trainees*?

"We were questioning the prisoner, and he started gagging—coughing, you know? Um, er, well then . . . *Then* Kleiver had to go get him some water. While he was out of the room the guy must've taken the cap-sule. I didn't realize it until he started foami—"

Furious, Max cut him off. "Jesus fuck! You mean none of you did a cavity check? *And* you left his hands untied? Did you get anything from him at all?"

Shaking his head at the conversation, Navarro turned into the cathedral's north parking lot. From this side the building looked pristine, but the wisps of black smoke hovered over the rooftops to the south. He continued across the lot. Max covered the mouth-piece of his phone.

"Go around to the south side," he instructed Rafe. The Patio de los Naranjos gate appeared to be locked up tight, and there were no cars in this lot. "San-doval?"

"Yes, sir. I mean, no s-sir." Sandoval stammered in Max's ear. "We didn't manage to break him before he—died."

Damn, and double fucking damn. That trail was now cold. No fingerprints on file, no form of ID. Even the intruder's clothing had been poorly sewn crap from Thailand—impossible to trace back beyond one of the hundreds of sweatshops dotting the poorer sections of southeast Asia.

Just as Max was about to cut him off again, Sandoval cleared his throat. "But we do have good news. Sir."

"Yeah? What? He had his mother's phone number tattooed on his ass?"

"Close. He has a tattoo of a black rose on his back. Could be a coincidence, but could mean he might be inside the Black Rose organization."

Max straightened from his slouched position. "It means he was a Black Rose asset." Jesus. A link between Emily and *Black Rose*?

"You're shitting me!" Excitement rose in the young operative's voice. He was too far down the local food chain to be involved in dealing with the larger, more lethal tangos. Uncovering a member of the very secretive Black Rose tangos was definitely a career advancement—too bad he'd also shot himself in the foot by allowing the prisoner to commit suicide. Asshole.

Black Rose. The news chilled Max to the bone. What in God's name was a member of the Black Rose

178

tango group doing in the home of an art restorer?

Now there *was* a connection between the players.

Max worked with Catherine Seymour. Seymour, known for good reason as Savage, was a known member of Black Rose. They were watching her every fucking move.

But that particular tango group's connection to this Italian mess . . . He hadn't seen that one coming.

The Black Rose were into extortion, money laundering, weapons trafficking and their methods . . . Whoever was in charge had given a green light on violence. In fact, the bloodier the better. His brain flashed a clip of the murder scene in Franco Bozzato's kitchen. Definitely met the high gore factor that was quintessential Black Rose. Learning that Emily's would-be assassin was a *tango* changed everything.

Knowing what they were capable of, Max needed to take an up close, personal look into investigating what Black Rose wanted from Emily. And why they'd killed his father. If BR was responsible for the hits in Florence then the situation shifted from personal to business.

"I'll have the body picked up," he told the junior operative as he and the other men climbed out of the car. "You and Kleiver stay with it until someone gets there. Don't even step outside to take a leak, you got that, Sandoval?" He disconnected before the hapless man could respond.

"Shit," he muttered under his breath.

"We're dealing with Black Rose again?" Daklin

demanded. "Christ. I thought we'd finished them off three months ago."

"Savage," Max said as a reminder. T-FLAC was keeping a close eye on the rogue operative, waiting for her to lead them to bigger fish higher up the Black Rose food chain.

"If I had my druthers that bitch would be on death row waiting her turn at a lethal injection," Rafael Navarro said. The three of them had been on the S.A. op with St. John, and been there when he'd been at the hospital waiting for word on Taylor Kincaid's recovery. He'd been like a fucking madman as he paced those corridors chomping at the bit for news on his lady.

"I know we're waiting for Savage to trip up," Navarro continued. "But Jesus Christ, that woman is as lethal as a black widow goddamn spider, and fifty times more calculating."

"Seduced all four men on her 'team' in Rio last month," Max told them, half listening. What in fuck's name did a Black Rose tango want with Emily? Had they also had something to do with the old man's death? It seemed so far-fetched, it was hard to believe.

Christ, was it something he could have prevented?

"Seduced four," Max rubbed a hand across his jaw. "Put two in the hospital. Now we have her on an op in—" His smile wasn't meant to be pleasant. "*Portland.* Seven-person team. There'll be no seductions, and no bodily injuries. They've been well briefed.

"Just because the dead man had a Black Rose

insignia on him doesn't mean he was at Emily's place under their command," Max pointed out reasonably. "He could've been Black Rose and killing Emily was just a side job." One thing he knew about bad guys is they rarely turned down opportunities to make some extra cash.

Navarro's expression was half hidden by his shades, but his mouth tightened. "Treason?"

"You got it." A T-FLAC operative who turned rogue was even worse than the scum they hunted. There was no wiggle room for a traitor. Catherine Seymour was like a loaded weapon in the hands of a psychotic drunk. She was beautiful, lethal, and used her Mensa mentality to outsmart and outwit the men and women with whom she was supposed to work to keep the world safe.

"Their job is to sit on her without her knowing she's having her every move watched and recorded."

Daklin made a rude noise. "Unless St. John gets to her ass first."

Savage had tried to kill Hunt St. John's lady, Taylor Kincaid, in the clever trap set by *Mano del Dios* a few months ago in South Africa. It had been close. Damn close. Hunt was out for Savage's blood. And if they didn't close the net around her soon, Max was inclined to let his friend have her.

"Haven't heard any whispers about Black Rose in this neck of the European woods lately, have either of you?"

"We haven't heard anything about them since the

South African op. But that doesn't mean there wasn't a sub-cell waiting in the wings to go active."

"Think this bombing is Black Rose?" Daklin leaned forward.

"I don't know," Navarro said. "What about the lilies left at the two other sites? Do we know if we were left the same floral clue here, too?"

"I'll check when we get inside. Could be someone else. Could be Black Rose." Although Max thought that would be just too coincidental. Problem was, he didn't believe in coincidence. Still, the leap from art restoration to the bombing of a Catholic church was pretty big.

There were any number of religious zealots out there. They couldn't discount that the bombing had been a hate crime.

"Why hasn't anyone jumped on taking the credit by now?"

"No one has come forward on the others yet, either." Max pointed out. "On the subject of Black Rose and the dead guy . . ." He quickly filled the other two men in on the situation with Emily and his father.

"Neither situation sounds like Black Rose's MO, does it?" Navarro murmured, turning into the south parking lot of the cathedral. "*This,* however, *does.*" He indicated, unnecessarily, the giant gaping hole in the centuries-old wall.

"Or Oslukivati." Max offered up another tango group. "Or any one of a *hundred* tango cells that could blow up something of this magnitude in the name of their god."

He opened his door, and waited until the others climbed out. "Always makes the job more interesting to have multiple choices."

"Ever think of chucking all this and retiring to a deserted island somewhere with a blond, a brunette, and a redhead?" Daklin asked pensively as they strode toward the smoldering remnants of the building.

The thought of spending a few weeks with a certain brunette appealed to Max a great deal. It shouldn't. It never had in the past. Well, that wasn't *exactly* true. After those days and nights with Emily last year, Max had considered the possibility of continuing the relationship. Considered and dismissed. His job and its lifestyle didn't exactly lend itself to a relationship. A reality that suited him just fine. Until Emily.

He wasn't just having great sex with an incredible woman, this was screwing with his brain. New and dangerous territory.

"No, thanks. One lady at a time works for me, and the idea of being stuck on some barren island with the same woman *indefinitely* is markedly unappeali—" His phone vibrated in his pocket as they skipped going through the massive, highly decorated door, and opted instead to go in through the new and not improved entrance. It was one mother of a hole.

"Aries."

His second call was from Control.

Darius informed him that a woman named Jacoba Brill, a restoration artist in Holland, had died in the early hours of the morning.

"Was a small glass vial found anywhere near the body?" Max asked, the hair on the back of his neck rising. He'd bet his custom Glock that the woman's death and Emily's break-in were related. "No? Well, look again."

The body was being autopsied now. Max knew the woman's death was no coincidence, even if the exam indicated natural causes. They could call it a heart attack from now until the earth changed orbits, but he wasn't buying it. Not when there were about a hundred different poisons and toxins that could mock the symptoms of a heart attack without leaving a trace in the body. Further, more sophisticated testing might reveal the underlying cause of death. Darius was already on it.

Max shoved the phone back in his pocket. "When we're done here," he told the others, "I'm taking Emily, with Cooper, Zampieri, and Niigata, to a safe house."

Max didn't say *which* safe house. He trusted these two men with his life. But he didn't trust them with Emily's.

"Then I'm going to Holland to check this out. I'll connect with you when we decide the next step."

"With Emily's thing, or the bombings?"

"Both," Max told him shortly.

Ten

CONFIRMED HUNDRED AND TWENTY-THREE TOURISTS and two priests dead," Max said, joining Navarro and Daklin. They'd split up, each to do what they did best. Max to ask questions. Daklin and Navarro combing the Capilla Villaviciosa, the small chapel that had been the central point for the explosion. There was little left of centuries of priceless artwork, painting, statues, and tapestries. Not to mention the pile of rubble that now represented what had once been a highly regarded example of thirteenth-century architecture.

"What do we think?" he asked the others. "Same signature as the Madrid train bombing in '04?" He didn't think so, but he wasn't leaving any stone unturned.

"Spanish judiciary," Daklin murmured. "Loose group of Moroccan, Syrian, and Algerian Muslims inspired by al-Qaeda and two Guardia Civil and Spanish police informants. Still doing their time."

Navarro considered it. "Ahmed was extradited from Italy. There's your connection."

Max rubbed the back of his neck. "Doesn't feel right."

"To me either," Daklin admitted. Navarro nodded.

"Hell. Back to square one."

While the answers he'd gotten might let them form a more complete picture of the hours and days before, during, and directly after the explosion, it was the bits and pieces they'd collected that would give them the complete picture. Even in the midst of nearly complete obliteration, Max knew T-FLAC's bomb techs would find enough pieces to reconstruct the important components.

Find the bomb's signature, find the bomb's builder. The trick was getting to the source before another fatal explosion shook the world's religious communities.

Absently, Max ran a hand around the back of his neck as he stared at the remains of the small chapel inside the enormous building. He knew two things: One, whoever blew up the building knew what they were doing and two, he'd made sure there was a body count to go along with the structural damage. The building was only open to the public from nine to six. The son of a bitch who'd done this had intentionally detonated when the place was teeming with tourists.

The three men stood in the mihrab, the central prayer hall, and just outside what was basically a large hole in the mosaic floor. Bits of the small chapel's stalactite ceiling, and chunks of plaster lacework had been flung across the floor for yards.

Where the hell was Emily? Max glanced down the length of the enormous hall. Thick, oily black smoke hung in the still air inside the vast building, almost blocking the view of the geometric white-and-rust-red double horseshoe arches, and what was probably a magnificent ceiling. A forest of a thousand black marble pillars supported the arches, the stone polished at hand height to a shiny black gloss from countless hands running over them for centuries.

He had a theory, Christ it was a wild theory, but until they could send in samples from the bomb site and get some definitive answers, it was all they had.

"Five vehicles melted to the ground, and fifty plus people injured in the parking lot. The explosion was localized, and this area," Max paused, pointing toward the starburst-shaped point of origin, "was destroyed." Steam rose off some of the smoking rubble. "Sprinklers activated?"

Daklin nodded. "Just for a few minutes in response to the heat. As soon as they cleared the building of survivors, they started moving the art into other areas of the building to prevent further damage. According to the curator, several paintings were ripped, torn, blackened by smoke or soaked by water."

"We'll want to take a look at the paintings they moved to storage."

Daklin took out a black square of linen and wiped his equally blackened hands. "Besides Black Rose, we have a smorgasbord of bad guys to pin this on." His half smile was mocking. T-FLAC was unlikely to be out of work any millennium soon. His specialty was toxic chemicals, but he dressed like a fricking model for a perfume ad.

A smart man would be wise not to believe the suave façade. Max remembered how the man had once single-handedly taken on a dozen hyped-up druggies in a dockside bar.

Daklin had walked away without one sun-streaked hair out of place. The man was a machine.

"No, but this stinks of Black Rose," Max said, giving voice to what they were all thinking. This was a well thought out, meticulous strike. Contained. Controlled.

He caught the eye of a man approaching them at a fast clip. "Hang on, that's the chief of police. Let's see if he has anything." He walked off to intercept him halfway.

"There *were* lilies at this site," Max informed the others when he returned to them a few minutes later. "A dozen, left out in a protected courtyard. No one connected their significance, until I asked, and it was only after the chief questioned those in charge that he found out someone had seen them, and taken them home to his girlfriend. They're bringing the guy in for questioning."

Daklin smiled. "And wrestling the flowers away from the girlfriend, I presume?"

A message.

A message they had to interpret fast. *Before* the tangos struck again.

"Definitely one of the larger groups responsible for this." Daklin offered, digging his hands into his elegant black slacks. "I managed to get a good enough sample of the Semtex used to send it in for analysis. As soon as we piece together the trigger, we can pinpoint where it originated, then see where it leads. It's not going to surprise me if this shit stemmed from the

Bosnian jihadist support network. Same as the syna-gogue and other church."

"No doubt about the derivation of the explosion, however." Max held up the large chunk of ornate, gilded picture frame he was holding.

"None," Daklin assured him. "The explosive device was in the frame. Slick, sophisticated. Interesting housing." His eyes gleamed. "Haven't seen anything like this before. I'll know more when I check it out in the lab."

Max let his gaze drift down the length of the hall again. It was completely empty. "I'm hoping Emily can tell us something about the painting." *And hoping like hell she can't.* Because if she *could,* it meant that somehow she was linked, however tenuously, to these latest three bombings. And as far-fetched as that sounded to him, Max couldn't shake the certainty that Daniel, Emily, and the bombings were in some way connected.

Connected by the now dead Black Rose asset in Emily's palazzo. Connected to him? Jesus. He didn't know.

Navarro shrugged. "We got what we needed from Father Antonio. It was called *The Holy Family,* and was done by Raphael in the sixteenth century. We have photographs of the piece, and all the necessary documentation and provenance in here." He tapped the thick file in his other hand.

"And out of all the paintings and other artwork," Daklin indicated the space filled with a plethora of priceless antiquities and art objects, "*this* is what the tangos chose to blow up?"

"They got a twofer," Max pointed out. "An Islamic mosque and Roman Catholic cathedral in one big boom. My vote is for a religious hate crime. Let's start there."

Navarro leaned against a pillar, crossing one ankle over the other. "Lisa Maki was thought to be head of the Black Rose and worked out of Barcelona."

Savage had killed the woman in South Africa three months ago. "Even though some of her work had religious undertones, we know she's not setting bombs from the grave. And her preferred kill was large groups, and more up close and personal," Max reminded them. "Like that student uprising, or the embassy bombing on the night of a gala event. Even if she were alive, this doesn't feel like Maki."

Max had that familiar itch at the base of his neck as a chill pervaded his body. They'd believed that the angelic-looking blonde had been head of the Black Rose. But they were now learning they'd been wrong. Maki had been in charge of one cell of the tango group, but she had *not* been the principal. They were hoping that Savage would lead them to the guy at the top. The only reason she was still at liberty and not locked up for treason.

Before Maki could be interrogated, she'd been killed by Savage in *Mano del Dios*'s underground bunker. St. John's jewel thief lady friend had sworn to it, and Max and the others had believed her.

"Let's invite Savage to join the party," Daklin said with relish. "We can keep the bitch close until we know what the hell is going on."

Max shook his head. "Under different circumstances, I'd agree with you. But I don't want her around on this op." He didn't want Emily anywhere *near* anything to do with Black Rose again. And that meant Catherine Seymour. Not until he knew the what and the *why* of how a Black Rose asset had broken into her palazzo.

If Savage had anything to do with the attempts on Emily's life, he'd kill her himself. Slowly.

It had been several years since Emily had been to La Mezquita. Then it had been crowded with tourists and worshipers, and had smelled faintly of orange blossoms from the grove of trees lining the Patio de los Naranjos on the north side of the building.

Today she was escorted by two heavily armed women through the south entrance. Only a handful of vehicles were parked in the lot, and half of those were blackened hulls. The sight took her breath away, and the thought of all that history and art gone caused a physical ache in her chest. She couldn't even begin to imagine how many people had died or been injured in the kind of blast that could melt a car.

"Holy crap," AJ breathed, looking around at the aftermath. "The blast was hot enough to melt the metal. Look over there." She pointed to a stand of trees at the edge of the parking lot, some three hundred yards away. Chunks of cars and other debris hung from the charred tree limbs like macabre Christmas ornaments.

AJ and Keiko had filled Emily in on the bombing. But knowing was different from *seeing*. She was overwhelmed by the smell of smoke as soon as they stopped and opened the car doors. The thick, oily stench brought black paint strokes to mind, an artist's rendering with undertones of centuries-old pain, framed with hand-hewn stone and crushed dreams.

So much art and history, ruined. Her heels crunched gravel as she rounded a corner, then received the full, devastating impact of the gaping hole in the side of the building. "God. Who could do something like this?"

"Unfortunately a *lot* of people," AJ answered as they took the shallow stone steps up to a partially open, magnificent bronze door and went inside.

"I didn't know what to expect," Emily murmured. The stench of smoke was stronger inside, and drifts of diaphanous charcoal-colored vapor floated in the air currents overhead like black ghosts. Goose bumps rose on her skin, and she rubbed her arms through the long sleeves of her borrowed T-shirt.

"This is—God. I don't even want to imagine how many people died, or how much priceless artwork has been lost." She brushed her fingers across one of the black marble pillars as they walked, the stone cold and hand-smoothed. If walls could talk.

Max stood with two men several hundred yards away. It looked as though he were waiting for her. And he was.

Just not the way her heart was interpreting his expectant stance. She felt an irrational urge to run the length of the prayer hall and fling herself into his arms.

Instead she walked sedately between the two women on Max's team. It felt like the longest mile stretched between herself and where he waited. Other than a brief respite in his arms, tension had been twining itself around her nerve endings for what felt like forever.

He didn't see her, and glanced at his watch. A tiny show of his impatience that surprised her. She observed him curiously as she closed the gap between them. She'd had him pigeonholed long before she'd ever met him. More so afterward when his father had admitted the kind of man his son was. But Max surprised her at every turn. He was *nothing* like the man his father had claimed him to be.

He hadn't lied and professed undying love and a rosy future. She had to respect him for being honest. At least about that. It was easier to deal with the truth than it was making whole cloth out of lies.

He knocked her off balance. And that surprised her because she usually kept her emotions very much in check. She'd learned to do that to protect herself, she supposed. Whatever. Now it was ingrained. Yet Max, whether he wanted to or not, was chipping away at her tough outer shell.

It was emotionally terrifying.

It was keeping her on her toes, she thought with the start of a smile for him.

"Did you know Jacoba Brill?" Max asked when she was still twenty feet away. Her smile faded. There was no tenderness in his voice, no softening in his hazel eyes. He was all business.

She hadn't known why Max had sent for her, obviously not to declare his undying love. But she hadn't expected him to ask about another restorer. Or, God help her, maybe she had. First Daniel. Then her break-in, then Franco's family . . .

With his question she literally felt her scalp tingle as her hair tried to stand on end. "Only by reputation."

Her heart started pounding way too fast, and she rubbed her damp palms on the legs of her borrowed jeans as the rubber bands around her nerves stretched another notch. She had to lick her lips to push the word out. "Why?"

"She died this morning."

"Please tell me of natural causes," Emily was amazed at how calm and controlled her voice was, when inside she was screaming like a frightened child. "She couldn't have been over fifty-five."

"They claimed a heart attack."

She could tell his opinion by his closed expression. She had to lock her knees so she didn't fall to the beautiful inlaid floor. This was an insane, terrifying, out-of-body experience. She wanted, no, *needed,* to wake up from this nightmare, in her own bed, preferably in Max's arms. She dragged in a deep breath. Let it out slowly before she could speak again. "You don't believe the diagnosis?"

"We're having our own people do an autopsy now."

The only way she was going to make it through this was to focus on things she could control. There didn't appear to be much at the moment. Glancing at the two men standing beside Max she put out her hand and introduced herself. It seemed a rational, civilized thing to do in a world gone mad.

The one on the left with the tortoiseshell-colored hair looked like a fallen angel. Tall and well dressed, he slipped a large, tanned hand into hers with a charming smile. "Asher Daklin."

The second man had eyes almost as black as his dead-straight, shoulder-length hair. He had a lean, clever face, and a mouth that looked as though he never smiled. Despite looking like some exotic member of royalty, Emily wouldn't want to meet him in a dark alley. Not unless she had Max with her. He took his hands out of his pockets, but didn't shake her hand. "Rafael Navarro."

She stuffed her fingers into the front pocket of her jeans, and glanced back at Max. "I can't imagine *how*—but what can I do to help?"

Max handed her what looked like a corner of an elaborate gilt frame. "There's a little painted wood under the frame that wasn't blackened by the explosion. Enough for you to tell us anything about the painting?"

She traced a jagged triangle of charred wood across the corner, grateful for even this small thing she could do to help. "I can tell you something about even the blackened piece here. But not with the naked eye. I'd have to test it back at my studio and/or send it to the lab I use. But yes, I think there's enough to work with. What am I looking for?"

"Can you authenticate what's here as the original work?"

"Sure. As I said, with testing. I can do most of the chemical testing in my studio. But for the X-ray, infrared, ultraviolet tests, it has to be sent elsewhere. But I can certainly get started on this right away if you like."

"You're not going back to your studio. But if you give Zampieri a list, and where he'll find the stuff at your place, he'll buy what you'll need. Is there anything you can tell us now, just by looking at this?"

Oil on wood. "What was the painting?" But suddenly she knew. God. It was exactly the right size. She just *knew.* The bottom dropped out of her stomach as she braced herself for Max's answer as one would brace for a punch to the chest.

"The Holy Family."

At his words the other shoe dropped in her mind with a resounding crash. Black sparkles filled her vision. The blood drained from her head, and it took a concerted effort to say through stiff lips, *"Canigiani Holy Family.* Raphael. I'm familiar with it. I-I did the restoration of this work six years ago."

"Did you paint a copy?"

"I removed a distorting blue overpaint done sometime in the eighteenth century—"

The truth, but not all of it.

She felt the prickle of nervous perspiration along her hairline. She'd seen this exquisite work a lot more recently than six years ago when she'd done the restoration for Richard Tillman.

She'd seen it nine months ago. While she'd been copying it in Daniel's studio.

Three hours later they were in Utrecht, the Netherlands, on their way to the home of Miss Brill. A car was waiting for them at Soesterberg Air Base. Max took her arm and led her to the black limo with tinted windows.

"Bulletproof?" she asked as he slid across the backseat to join her.

"Yeah. I told you I wouldn't let anything hurt you. As soon as you've taken a look at Brill's studio we'll get you to the safe house. Zampieri will help you set up a studio there with anything you need to test what's left of the painting."

The truth, if he ever found out, could hurt her big time. Right now she didn't see a need to tell Max anything. Because it wasn't relevant. If that changed, she'd have to tell him about the arrangement she'd had with his father.

If things changed.

And if things changed it would mean that her suspicions about Daniel had been correct all along. Emily really, really didn't want to be right.

Because if she were right her life would be irrevocably changed forever. "My mother's expecting me in Seattle." *If she remembered I was coming at all.*

"She'll see you in—"

"A few days?" Emily interrupted as they left the air base behind. "A week? Two?"

Not only was she aware that she wasn't being logical to ask him to pinpoint how long he'd need to keep her safe, it was immaterial how long she would have to stay locked up in a "safe house." He was keeping his promise to protect her. As much as she was chafing at all this cloak-and-dagger stuff going on, if she couldn't have her first option—going back to her normal life—then she was grateful to be secreted away somewhere out of the range of a maniacal killer.

If she believed for a moment that what she'd done had any bearing in this, she'd bite the bullet and tell Max now. But what would it serve to tell him that she'd been the one doing Daniel's work for the last seven years? Not a damn thing. He already had zero sympathy or compassion for the man who was his father. But even Max couldn't deny that Daniel had been a brilliant painter in his own right, a phenomenally successful restorer, and a man his peers considered a genius. Daniel Aries had been one of a kind.

She'd at least like to leave his professional life pristine for Max and the art world. She'd made that promise to Daniel. And she always tried to keep her promises.

The irony didn't escape her. As long as she'd been in the business she'd been number two. And she was okay with that. Daniel deserved to win the prize. His work over a lifetime warranted it. Nobody, especially Max, needed to know his secret.

Her secret now.

Set in a clearing, and surrounded by pine trees, Jacoba Brill's small white house was picture-perfect. The lush spring-green lawn was bordered with flowerbeds bursting with early red-and-white striped parrot tulips, underplanted with sweet-smelling purple hyacinths. The glossy red window boxes beneath the four windows matched the paint on the front door, and were massed with brilliant yellow King Alfred daffodils waving heavy heads in the light breeze. The new leaves in the surrounding trees rustled like a taffeta skirt.

Emily filled her mind with the happy colors. "Beautiful."

"Isolated," Navarro observed, pulling up to the curving walkway.

"Yeah." Max motioned to AJ. "Find a vantage point."

With a nod, AJ got out of the car. She carried what Emily presumed was a sniper rifle. "Is that really necessary way out here?" she asked Max. The artist's house was way off the beaten path, with no nearby neighbors. The scene was so idyllic it was impossible to believe anything bad could possibly have happened here.

Looks, Emily knew, could be deceiving.

Max shot her a glance. "We always prepare for the worst. Back." He gestured toward Navarro, then to Daklin, "Perimeter. I'll take inside. You," he told Emily, "stay put until I come get you."

She almost saluted. "No problem." And it wasn't. As much as she disliked the way Max issued orders, she was now more than happy to stay in a bulletproof car while trained professionals scoured the area for bad guys. She'd learned something from the past few hours at least.

From behind smoked glass she observed Max's team go to work. Each held a weapon and appeared ready for anything. AJ, nimble and amazingly quick, climbed a tree near the bottom of the driveway, then lay across a thick branch like a lithe cat sunning herself.

Navarro moved like smoke around the side of the house and disappeared from view. Daklin vanished into the trees. One moment Max was standing at the poppy-red front door, the next the door opened, then closed behind him.

She didn't realize she'd been holding her breath until Max came back to the car to get her a few minutes later. She let out the suppressed air in a rush as he opened the door for her.

He held out his hand. "All clear inside, let's go."

His hand was large and warm, and she would have enjoyed holding it as they walked. Just like regular people. But he wasn't even close to a "regular person," he was a counterterrorist operative, and he was working.

Releasing his hand before he let go of her, she adjusted the strap of her tote on her shoulder. It was enough that his strong, solid presence was beside her. She felt safe with him there. Physically, at least. Her rapidly racing heart was another matter altogether.

But that was just for her to know.

She took a deep breath of the crisp country air. The sight of the flowers, combined with their intoxicating scent, temporarily obliterated the stench of burning rubble imprinted in her mind. She was enchanted with the crisp colors and the charm of the cottage, but miserably sad that the woman who had lived here and lovingly tended this garden was gone.

Max placed his hand at the small of her back, urging her to walk faster. "Move it. It's too exposed out here. I want you inside."

"Great," she muttered dryly, picking up speed. "That immediately conjures up the image of a bull's-eye painted on my back."

"*I*'ve got your back."

Yes. He did. He'd slipped his arm around her waist, his hard forearm and splayed hand across her middle. He wasn't just touching her, his body was angled to cover as much of her as possible. She'd never in her life needed, or thought she wanted, to be physically protected, but having Max do so was sexy as hell. She couldn't figure out why she felt the prick of tears.

"There isn't a neighbor for miles, and she lived alone, didn't she? How sad." Emily's voice was not quite steady. "However it happened, by natural causes, or someone else's hand. She was all alone when she died."

"She wasn't alone."

"Good. It would be awful to—Oh." The artist hadn't been alone when she'd died. Right. The killer had been with her. Or at the very least, his was the last face she'd seen before succumbing to . . . to . . . whatever.

The only reason they were here was because a hazmat team had already been inside to take samples and had given the house the all clear. Max had wanted to look at the place before some other team came in to search.

Spreading his warm fingers on her midriff as they walked, he scanned her face. "How're you holding up?"

It was chilly, but the sun was shining and visually it was a beautiful day, but nerves had a clamp on her neck and shoulder muscles, and she wasn't sure she'd ever feel serene again. "I'm scared," she admitted. "But I'm also furious that someone I don't even *know* is capable of making me feel this way."

"It's not easy being a victim."

"I'm only a victim if I allow myself to be," she told him with asperity. "Believe me, I'm not planning on doing anything stupid. And I'll try to be hyperaware of my surroundings at all times." She suddenly froze. "My God, Max. Is my family in danger?"

"Nope. Got it covered. Someone followed what they thought was your car to the Bozzatos', but it's unlikely that anyone knows who or where your family is. I had to have my people dig deep to track down both your mother and sister so I could send people to watch them."

A slither went up and down her spine. "You have people watching them? In Seattle? In Boston?"

"Yeah. Got a problem with that?"

"I'd not only be ungrateful if I was, I'd be pretty damn stupid with a killer on the loose. Thank you, Max. I appreciate you doing that." She was stunned. Not only that he'd thought of protecting her family, but that he'd gone to the trouble of taking care of it so quickly.

"Tell me what you know about Brill." Max followed her inside, then closed the door behind him.

"Nothing more than I've read." Curiously, Emily glanced around the small room. She felt like a voyeur. "She had a good reputation as a restorer. She was—I think—unmarried." She shrugged. "That's about all I remember.

"I can tell you she was a very private woman," she observed as they walked through the parlor. "See? Not just drapes, but sheers and blinds as well. She could have let the drapes drop, but she loved the look of the flowery tiebacks, and left them that way."

"Well, she sure as hell wasn't worried about security. She's got an excellent system, but it was turned off."

"She was done with whatever she was working on, maybe?"

"Maybe. What else do you see?"

"Quintessentially feminine, precise, and prided herself on her neatness," Emily added, perusing the room with sharp eyes.

"You get all that walking through a ten by ten living room?"

"You know about iconography? It's the study of subjects in art, and their deeper meaning. The same applies to our surroundings. Her pillows are trimmed with ruffles, her books are strictly alphabetized, and there isn't a speck of dust or a thing out of place. The house is as neat as a pin. It wasn't for show. Usually people's living rooms, the public spaces in a house, show others who we'd *like* to be, but not who we really are. The rooms that visitors don't see show us more of their real personality."

"You're very observant."

"I have to be to do my job."

Simple botanical paintings in identical white frames were lined up with military precision along the pale yellow walls above a red, white, and yellow striped sofa. The fireplace was flanked by similar antique wingback chairs covered in crisp yellow linen. A crystal vase shaped like a flower basket sat on the mantel and was filled with slightly drooping red-and-white parrot tulips from the garden.

A simple bunch of hyacinths filled a white bowl on the cherry-wood coffee table, perfuming the air with their sweet scent.

"No kids. No animals," she told Max as they walked down a picture-lined hallway to the back of the house.

The style of clothing in the photographs was dated, the color faded. Old photographs. "Too neat and clean."

So was the woman's glass-enclosed studio, which ran the full length of the back of the house. Almost a greenhouse, the room was flooded with light and had a breathtaking view of the landscaped backyard, surrounded by trees and overrun with flowers. Unlike the neatness and symmetry of the front garden, the one in back was a wild riot of color and texture with no apparent attempt at order.

Sunlight flooded the stone floor through the glass ceiling.

Like the rest of her home, Brill's studio was immaculate, with everything neatly in its place. Besides the expected canvases, magazines and newspapers were neatly stacked on built-in shelving. Art books, sketch pads, and supplies filled various containers, from what looked like a Georgian, hand-chased silver soup tureen filled with paint tubes, to a child's plastic rain boot filled with brushes. Emily touched the tureen. "She did pretty well for herself. This is worth about twenty thousand American dollars."

An easel stood in the center of the room. She walked over to look at the stretched canvas. The impasto, the paint layer, was thick and raised from the surface. "The paint's smudged. Is this the room where she died?"

"Yeah." Max was crouched down looking through a stack of files in the bottom drawer of a bright red lacquered metal file cabinet. "How do you know?"

"She must've been working when she fell. The

paint's wet. Someone righted the easel and painting. You can see the fingerprints on the edge here where they held it on either side to pick it up off the floor. Something brushed against the high points of the wet paint, leaving a faint imprint." She looked down at the stone floor. "The brush fell and then bounced here and here. See the orange splatter?"

"Nice catch. Let's just hope those prints belong to the killer and not the sister, who found the body, or the EMTs."

"Her sister picked this up."

Max lifted a brow. "And you know this how?"

"Small hands. But I think if her sister came here to visit her and found her dead, after she called for help, and after she tried everything to save her, she would have spent the time waiting for medical help tidying up."

Max raised a brow. "Her sister is lying dead on the floor, and she straightens up the room?"

Emily nodded. "Jacoba was concerned about appearances. She liked people knowing she was orderly. Her sister gave her order before the EMTs arrived."

"Damn. That's good. Logical."

"Talking about good—" The painting was neither a restoration piece, nor a copy. "This is . . . interesting."

Not to speak ill of the dead, but the painting was dreadful.

Head tilted, Max glanced at the painting. "Jesus. What's it supposed to be?"

"An orange dog?" A very strange looking, five-eyed orange dog with only two legs. And either a super long penis, or a strangely shaped tail growing out of its front. The background was a slightly deeper shade of blotchy orange with a murky brown line running down the middle.

He smiled. "I think it's a sofa with an antenna."

"No, look. These are ears. Hmm, maybe they're cushions—"

Max's slid his arms around her from behind and she jumped a little because she'd thought he was on the far side of the room. He moved as stealthily as a ghost. "What are you doing?"

He turned her in his arms. "If you have to ask," he murmured against her mouth. "Then I'm not doing it right."

Eleven

SHE TOOK ADVANTAGE OF HIS OPEN MOUTH AND pulled his head down, taking his mouth like he'd taken hers when they'd made love. Like she owned it. Like she owned *him*. For a moment she pretended that she did. She teased him with her tongue, and when he groaned deeply, she felt heady with her own power. He stood perfectly still for a moment, letting her take the lead, then tightened his arms around her waist and pulled her harder against him.

His lips were warm and firm, and responded instantly as she probed inside the heated cavern of his mouth, challenging his tongue with hers. Her body did a slow, delicious burn as she did some slow exploring of her own.

His response was electrifying as he kissed her back, participating fully, his mouth hungry and hard, delicious. Her soft breasts snuggled against the solid plane of his chest, and her nipples ached for harder contact. Making a soft sound of need, Emily stood on her toes, wrapping her arms around his neck, and pressed her body hard against his, wanting more. Threading her fingers through his hair, she grabbed fistfuls, kissing him with a loss of control that stunned her. The taste of him went straight to her head and made her dizzy with longing. And allowed her to forget, for just a few precious moments, what else had happened here.

He was crushing her against his body, his arms wrapped tightly around her, one hand on the back of her neck, the other pressing her hips against the ridge between them. Her heart slammed against her rib cage, and she kissed him back as if she'd die if she didn't.

"Uh-oh." Daklin came into the studio and skidded to a stop. "Sorry."

Max lifted his head, but didn't release her, although he shifted their bodies so her flaming face was shielded from his friend's view. "What do you have?" The sound rumbled from his chest.

"Brill did work for Tillman as well. I found these in her office."

Uncomfortable and suddenly aware of how exposed they'd been in a room made of glass, Emily dropped her arms and stepped back. Daklin handed Max a sheaf of papers that all carried a familiar letterhead. Max absently smoothed his hair down as he took them.

She'd done enough work for Tillman to know what his contracts read, pretty much verbatim. "Richard Tillman's contract. I have similar ones in my files. He had us sign one for each painting to be copied. A date and time when the original would be delivered to the studio, and the date and time when each would be picked up. It also specified that he'd have extra security installed before the start of the project, and said security would belong to the artist after the work was completed."

"That covers it," Daklin told Max.

"Only one thing wrong with that," Max pointed out. "There's no security. All the equipment in the world doesn't help if you don't turn it on."

"But don't you think she *had* it on?"

"The sister and the EMTs got in."

"Oh. Right."

"FYI," Daklin told them. "I called in and told the autopsy team to do a Western blotting test on Brill's body. Also to take a serum sample to check for antibodies against *Borrelia burgdorferi*."

Max looked up from the paper he was scanning. He frowned slightly. "*Lyme* disease? You've lost me."

"Forestry workers in the area are known to contract

Lyme borreliosis. Brill lived in a pine forest, and did a lot of cutting back there. Seemed she was doing some art project with the limbs and leaves. Nature crap."

Emily glanced from Max to the other man. "I know this sounds insane, but I *hope* that's what she died of."

"It's just a theory at this point," Daklin admitted. "Still, we'll cover every avenue until we find concrete evidence of COD."

"Cause of death," Max explained.

She'd figured that one out herself. "So it wasn't murder? Please tell me this poor woman died of something easily explainable." It wouldn't make her death less awful, but at least it wouldn't be part of the whole macabre pattern.

"I'm all for leaving no stone unturned. But there's no doubt in my mind she was murdered," Max said unequivocally. "The only questions remains how and why."

Emily rubbed her arms. There was no doubt in her mind either. And she also wanted to know the how and why. Suddenly being in the woman's home seemed disrespectful. And being in an all glass room made her feel ill at ease. Anyone could be hiding in the trees, looking in. Even with AJ in the tree and Max and the other man here with their guns, she felt far too exposed. "Can we leave now?"

"In a while," Max nodded to Daklin, who took the papers, and left. "Look around the studio. See if anything is out of place. Anything doesn't belong. Take your time."

She took her time, but there didn't seem to be a thing out of place. This much tidiness would make *her* crazy in about five minutes, but since everything *was* set precisely in its place, it was pretty easy to see nothing had been disturbed. Or nothing she could see.

She crouched down next to a bookcase to read the titles of some of Brill's books on the bottom shelf. They had very similar reference and research materials, Emily noticed. "If I had a clue as to what I'm supposed to be looking for, it would make this a lot easier."

"It's like pornography, you'll know it when you see it."

No I won't, Emily thought impatiently. "We've done this before. At your father's studio. We didn't find any—Max?"

"Yeah?"

It was impossible to breathe, let alone speak. "I found something." Something casually hidden in plain sight among a collection of seaglass in a little boat on the bottom shelf.

Max came up behind her. "What?"

"An empty vial." Her voice was thin, and she was frozen in a half crouch beside the extremely neat and tidy bookcase.

"Daklin?" He barely raised his voice, but the other man appeared in the doorway as if by magic. Max reached down and pulled Emily to her feet. "Get her to the car and stay with her."

Her face was as still and pale as a mask, her eyes

211

dark with fear. "Come wi—" She bit her lower lip, cutting herself off, clearly realizing that this was his job, then nodded. Her boot heels clicked on the stone floor as she walked away with Daklin. At the door she turned around. "Don't *touch* it!"

"Go."

She went. Crouching down, he used his pen to push the small glass vial away from the bits of smooth glass. There was no stopper, and of course, nothing inside. How the fucking hell had the team missed this in their earlier sweep? A tiny smudge of bright orange paint was smeared down the side. He took out the sat phone as he rose and walked over to look at Jacoba Brill's last painting.

"Aries," he identified himself to his Control as he left the studio to finish his call in the hallway. "Found another empty glass vial at this location. Studio in back, on the floor in the southeast corner of the room at the base of the bookcase. Send another hazmat team ASAP to Jacoba Brill's home at Kruislaan 409. Yeah, Utrecht. Take the orange painting in for analysis as well. There's a faint impression of the vial on the bottom left-hand corner. Let me know what the lab makes of it." He paused to listen.

"No shit. I don't have to be told twice." He strode down the hall. "Anything else— Want to hang on? I have another call coming in. Okay. Keep me informed."

Max switched to the other call as he walked through the house. "Aries."

"Sir, this is asset Raymond Ackart. Wiesbaden."

Max paused inside the front door. He could see the sun reflecting off the top of the waiting car at the bottom of the walkway, and knew Emily was safely inside, but the hair on the back of his neck rose. "And?"

"I was ordered to report to the safe house on Tempelhof Strasse. I just arrived, sir. Zampieri, Kurtz, Banther, and four unknowns are dead."

Max bit off a curse. "Describe the scene."

"Someone was pretty pissed off, sir. Our guys are all sliced and diced. They gave as good as they got before they went—but holy Mother of God, there's a shitload of blood. It's bad, really bad."

"I have an idea," Max said, picturing the scene in the Bozzato family kitchen. *Fuck. Fuck. Fuck.* "Have you called for the garbage detail?"

"Waited to talk to you first." The guy sounded ready to puke.

"Call, then wait for further orders." Max shoved the phone back in his pocket as he strode down the walkway, his attention not on the pale oval of Emily's face behind the darkened window of the car, but the surrounding woods and trees. "God damn it."

Wiesbaden was one safe house out of many, but who had known that Emily was supposed to be secreted there within hours? Only himself, Control, and Zampieri.

And someone else.

Emily stacked the used plates on the tray. The aft cabin of the jet looked like a high-end boardroom, and at the moment, smelled of strong coffee, tomato soup, and delicious, gooey grilled cheese sandwiches made with provolone. She was impressed. Not only had Max fixed the meal for everyone, he'd also brought it—on a tray no less—to them at the table. Emily, along with AJ, Keiko, and Max, had fallen on the food like starving animals.

When she complimented him, Max muttered that the soup was out of cans, and the cheese sandwiches were the only thing he knew how to cook. It was kind of endearing to realize that making a meal for three women didn't diminish his masculinity in any way. Before he'd brought the tray in, AJ had told her that everyone on the team had to pull their own weight. Still, Emily was charmed by this culinary side of the man whom she imagined slept with his gun in one hand. If he slept at all.

The cabin was all mahogany paneled walls and high-tech electronic equipment, the beds tucked away behind the paneling. With the push of a button, a section slid back, revealing an enormous sleek video screen embedded in the wall behind Emily. The tiny red eye of a camera blinked in the left-hand corner.

Daklin and Navarro were on one half of the split screen, a man with a puckered scar across his face took up the other half. His name was Darius. Whether that was his first or last name, Emily had no idea.

Maybe he was like Cher. One name. He had the build of a linebacker, and the well-modulated voice of a seasoned Rotarian. The scar, and a pair of dark glasses, effectively obscured his features, making them unreadable.

Max worked with some interesting people.

A picture flashed up on the monitor of an almost eerily striking woman, with long, improbable red hair, and crystalline green eyes. Barbie with red hair, Emily thought, not liking the woman's eyes. They looked both cold and creepy.

"Sorry, wrong screen," the man said apologetically, bringing up Navarro and Daklin again.

"That," said AJ flatly to Emily, "was Catherine Seymour. If you ever run into her—run like hell. She's vicious, untrustworthy, and lethal."

"Emily and Savage wouldn't ever come into contact," Max told everyone, his voice cool and flat. "She's under surveillance and won't be making a damn move we don't know about. Right, Darius?"

"Closing in as we speak."

"As we should be. Let's make that sooner than later. Okay, let's get started, people." Max took a swig of coffee. He seemed to survive and thrive on adrenaline and coffee. Other than a five o'clock shadow on his strong jaw, and his hair pushed back off his forehead by running his fingers through it a time or two, he looked and sounded relaxed, fresh and as though he'd had eight hours' sleep.

Emily bet she'd had three times as much rest as he

215

had, and she was exhausted. Her adrenaline had come and gone, and come and gone again, leaving her limp and lethargic. AJ and Keiko also looked the worse for wear, although Keiko had managed to squeeze in a quick shower while Max was out in the galley. AJ shot Emily a sympathetic glance.

"This is a long flight," Max said, speaking to the camera as he placed his empty mug back on the table. "I'm planning to use some of that time to catch some z's. I've asked Emily to sit in on the briefing because she is, I believe, central to this op. Let me recap, then if anyone has questions or observations you can have at it when I'm through."

He spent several minutes bringing everyone up to speed on the timeline of events, from his father's murder to the death of Jacoba Brill. Emily had been present for most of what Max was recapping for the others. Still, when clumped all together in the retelling, it sounded exactly as bad and scary as she'd remembered it. Maybe more so because Max was giving the recap in a calm, matter-of-fact voice with no drama or fanfare.

He paused briefly to bite into his sandwich, chew, and swallow. "Point. One: Daniel Aries copied several of Richard Tillman's masterpieces over a span of ten years. As did Emily, here. As did Brill. Two out of the three are dead—"

"Make that three out of *four*," the man with the dark glasses inserted, not glancing up as his attention was snagged by a computer monitor on the table in front of him. "Just got intel. Alaire Drousé died in his home half an hour ago. Apparent heart attack."

Keiko folded her arms on the table and leaned forward, her black eyes gleaming with suppressed excitement. "Another art restorer?"

Emily had noticed how quiet the older woman was; she seldom asked questions, but she was clearly always listening and learning. She was sure Keiko wasn't happy to hear someone else had died, but she was clearly excited to be included in this briefing.

Emily knew of Drousé. "He's an authenticator for the Louvre."

Max's glance touched hers briefly. "Know him?"

She rubbed her arms, feeling a chill that didn't seem to want to leave her. "Only by reputation."

"Get those toxicology reports back to us ASAP," Max instructed. "And three attempts," he continued as if he hadn't been interrupted by the report of a fourth death, "that we're aware of, have been made on Emily's life."

Three close attempts, she wanted to point out, but she bit her lip and kept quiet instead. Her emotions were in turmoil with all of this. For Max and the others, this was business as usual. How in God's name did they ever get used to so much violence? So much darkness?

"Two," Max continued. "The man sent to Emily's palazzo was a Black Rose asset. Whether he was working for BR, or freelancing, has yet to be ascertained.

"Three: An incendiary device was found in a painting's frame at La Mezquita. That makes three paintings used as vehicles for bombs." Max wiped his hands on a paper towel, crumpled it, and tossed it on his empty plate. "Four: That makes *three* bombings. *Three* paintings, and *three* places of worship."

Emily got up to pour him another cup of coffee, and he shot her a grateful glance as she dropped in several cubes of sugar. She refilled her own mug, and AJ's as well. Keiko hadn't even picked up her still-full mug, she was too engrossed, and hanging on Max's every word.

"Five," he said, drinking his hot coffee, "according to the provenance papers we received from Father Antonio in Córdoba, the painting there leads us right back to Tillman."

"I have one more piece to add." Emily almost raised her hand before voicing a question as she'd been taught to do in boarding school.

"Can it wait?" Max asked, a tinge of impatience in his voice.

She shook her head. "Daniel did a copy of *The Holy Family* for Mr. Tillman about a year ago." She'd realized on the way back to the air base that she could no longer keep that piece of information a secret.

While she knew she had to tell Max of his father's involvement in the painting, there was no point, she'd decided, in telling Max that *she'd* done it instead of Daniel. Tillman had hired Daniel, and paid Daniel's exorbitant prices. Not only would Tillman be furious

218

if he found out that Daniel hadn't done what he was contracted to do, he'd be pissed he'd paid him double what Emily would have charged him.

Not that that mattered since Daniel was dead and there was no reason to suppose that Max would divulge the information to him anyway. Still, what *did* matter was Daniel's sterling reputation, which would be history if knowledge of his debilitating illness ever became public. Which was how and why this masquerade had started in the first place. The knowledge that Emily had done some of his work would put *all* of his work under intense scrutiny and debate. And that would ensure that his well-deserved reputation would be lost forever.

"From Tillman to your father, to Emily, to Black Rose, to a bombing? I'd be more convinced if the other two bombings carry the same signature. You two bozos on that?" Darius was, presumably, talking to Navarro and Daklin, because Daklin nodded and said, "Yeah."

"Tillman in bed with Black Rose?" Navarro asked, his expression bland. There was a black marble pillar behind him, so Emily knew he and Daklin were back at La Mezquita.

"Yeah, that's where I've gone, too," Max told him, polishing off his second sandwich and picking up a third. "What better way to launder their money than through a suddenly philanthropic old man?"

AJ leaned her elbows on the table, hcr soup mug clasped between her hands. "I suppose it's possible, but isn't he like a hundred years old?"

Max half-smiled. "Mid-eighties. I've known octoge-narians who are as sharp as tacks, so I don't think his age would exclude him from consideration. I want a look at him soon." He looked into the nearby camera mounted above the screen. "Dare. How soon can you get me that intel?"

The linebacker's dark brows rose over the top of his shades. "Depends how deep you want me to dig."

"Right down to pay dirt," Max told him.

"Will you be able to sleep, or do you need some-thing?" Max asked Emily as she came out of the for-ward cabin's bathroom. The cabin was dim, with only the light over Max's chair to illuminate her way. He'd offered the aft cabin with the beds to AJ and Keiko. She knew there were six beds back there, but he hadn't offered to let her sleep with the other women.

He'd settled himself in one of the comfortable chairs in the middle of the cabin, and when she came out of the bathroom, he looked up from the papers he was reading. Even in the subdued lighting, and from this far away she saw the flare of heat in his eyes as she walked toward him, a towel around her shoulders.

She yawned as she padded toward him. AJ had given her a pair of shorts and a tank top—black, of course—to put on after her shower. Going commando was starting to grow on her, Emily thought as she moved barefoot down the thick carpet toward him.

"Believe me," she told him softly as she blotted her

wet hair on the towel and yawned again. "The second I close my eyes I'll be out like a light."

"Will you," he murmured, putting out his hand to guide her into the seat between himself and the bulkhead. A pillow and a luxuriously soft red wool throw had been tossed on the footrest. Looked like bliss to her.

"Forget it, Aries," she told him, seeing the glimmer of the devil in his dark green eyes as she sank into a seat as wide and soft as a cloud. Max leaned over the few inches separating them, and pressed a button on her armrest. The chair slowly reclined so she could stretch out full length. In thirty seconds she'd be fast asleep.

She got a good look at this man who made her pulse race, and her heart did somersaults. She wanted to take his image with her to dreamland. "The brain is willing," she told him firmly, pulling up the blanket over her shoulders. "But the body is too tired to make its own decisions. I'm so tired I might fall asleep *before* I close my eyes."

"I'll hold you while you sleep," he offered as angelically as a choirboy as she settled into the big leather chair beside him with a moan of pure pleasure. Bunching the pillow under her cheek, she curled on her side to look at him through sleepy eyes.

His rumpled dark hair indicated that he'd showered, too, and he was wearing black drawstring pants. He was bare chested and barefoot. Temptation personified. His skin was tanned and other than an assortment of scars, nicks, and dents, as hard and solid as polished bronze.

She found the crisp hair on his chest sexy as hell, and wanted to rub her face in it. Tamping down the pang of lust, she gave him a stern look. "There are two people back there, and two more people in the cockpit," she mumbled, snugging the soft blanket around her throat as her lids fluttered. *And if they* weren't *there, I'd be sitting astride your lap right this second, with you deep inside me.* The image of it was so clear in her mind's eye she had to suppress a little groan of need.

"I know that." His voice was a low rumble as he dimmed the lights from the control panel on the arm of his chair.

She smiled at his deep, low-pitched voice. She loved the sound of—Her eyes shot open as he hauled her, pillow, blanket and all, onto his chair beside him in a preemptive strike that left her breathless. "What are you doing?"

Pushing his chair back to lay flat, he wrapped her in his arms, tucking her against his naked chest, the soft blanket covering them both. His warm breath fanned her damp hair. "I told you I'd protect you, didn't I?"

And who's going to protect me from you? "Where's your gun?"

"Wanna touch it?"

She smacked him lightly on the chest. "What are you protecting me from? Bedbugs?" Kissing the steady beat of his heart, she tucked her arm around his waist under the blanket.

"I'd hate anything to hurt this beautiful bottom of yours." Slipping his hand under the elastic waistband of her borrowed shorts, Max palmed one butt cheek, stroking it with his big warm hand. There was a devilish glint in his eyes. "My God, your skin is soft. I think there's a broken spring in that chair. Very dangerous to sweet, tender asses. You'd better share mine."

"Your sweet tender ass?" she mocked, huffing out a weak laugh. "I think there's a spring loose in your *head*. You *know* we can't . . ."

"Shhh," he said softly, tilting her face up. "Close your eyes." Gently he trailed his lips across her cheekbone, then brushed each eyelid with a tender kiss. "You have the prettiest eyes," he murmured. "Big and brown, and far too damned trusting." His lips drifted down to hers. "Your mouth could drive a man mad just looking at it. This little dip right here"—his teeth closed lightly on her upper lip, and the sensation of his teeth on her skin made Emily's temperature rise, and her heart start beating a little faster—"is the sexiest thing I've ever seen."

Increasing the pressure of his mouth on hers, Max kissed her, long and slow and deep, until she melted in his arms and forgot that they were on a very small aircraft with four other people.

Warm and sleepy and turned on by his hand stroking her bottom and his mouth on hers, Emily let herself rise and fall with the tide of needs and eddies drifting through her body.

Eyes closed, she felt the delicate graze of the finger-tips of his other hand brush her cheek as he kissed her slowly and thoroughly. His fingers trailed down her throat, pausing to feel the rapid beat there. His hand traveled to her breast, teasing her nipple through the thin cotton of her T-shirt, and she arched into his hand.

The hand cupping her breast moved down her midriff, causing all sorts of sparks to wake up body parts that had thought they were ready to sleep. His hand felt cool on her hot skin as he slipped past the barrier of her shorts and traced lazy patterns on her belly.

"I'd dream about your little dolphins," Max murmured thickly against her temple as he slid his fingers around her midriff and stroked the dolphins leaping over her belly button. She automatically drew up her knee to grant him better access. The movement made her exquisitely aware of the dampness between her thighs, and the rapid beat of her heart which she felt all over her body.

His nostrils flared, and she knew he scented her need. "Sometimes when I can't sleep," he said thickly as he continued to trail his fingers over her increasingly more sensitive skin. "I'd count these little guys over and over, imagining how many times I'd have to kiss each one before I'd drop off." His fingers slid lower to tangle in the damp curls at the apex of her thighs. Her breath caught, and she shifted, spreading her knees a little. With a little moan of greed, she arched her hips as his fingers delved between the damp folds, stroking deeply. She shuddered with the sweet pleasure of his intimate touch and lifted her mouth to brush her lips over his slowly, tasting him with the tip of her tongue.

Gripping her hair in his clenched fists, he covered her mouth with his, tasting and touching her until she shuddered. She had to pull her lips away from his to bury her face against his neck as his thumb drove her to the very edge.

She contracted around his fingers pushing deep inside her. Her hips rocked as he withdrew, then thrust again, leaving her hanging on a sharp precipice of need. Every time she thought she'd tip right over for a free fall, Max paused, keeping her poised on a razor sharp edge of pleasure again and again, until she couldn't catch her breath, and all her senses seemed amplified and sharpened.

She arched her hips off his lap, pressing her mons into his palm. "Max. . ."

The climax rolled through her body in an avalanche of pure pleasure. The moment seemed to go on forever, as Max's clever fingers and kisses kept her riding the rush of sensations for what felt like an eternity.

A last wave crashed through her body making her shake and moan. He slid one hand up her back to cradle her head against his chest, while his fingers glided slowly out of her ultra sensitive folds, making her arch and shudder again.

"Christ, you're responsive."

"If I had my hand in a corresponding position on you, I guarantee, I'd have your undivided attention, too." The hard length of his penis pushed against her hip as she sprawled beside him.

"I look forward to it, but I'm afraid you'd fall asleep mid-stroke."

Sleep pulled at her, and her jaw popped as she yawned. "Rain check?"

In a few hours they'd say good-bye in front of his team members when they landed in Denver, and she might very well never see him again. Her chest felt tight. But she knew it was a good thing. She and Max had nothing in common but sexual attraction. A boatload of sexual attraction, but that wasn't enough to build a future on. And then, she thought, as her brain started shutting down, there was his job.

Compatible in bed. It had to be good enough.

She felt as limp as overcooked spaghetti. Limp and satiated and bonelessly relaxed. Max played with her hair which relaxed her even more.

"Everytime I look at you," he murmured. "I'm staggered by just how damn beautiful you are. I know you've got incredible talent, but did you ever think that you don't have to work as hard as you do?" He gently massaged her scalp with the pads of his fingers. Which would've felt wonderful, if she'd been stone deaf.

"What you do, while amazing, is too solitary. You're so beautiful, why do you choose to isolate yourself when you could surround yourself with people who adore you?"

A little sleep dissipated as he hit her Achilles' heel. "Adore *me*? Adore what I look like, you mean. And of course, how it makes *them* look when they're seen with me." She wasn't thinking about herself. She was thinking about her mother. "My appearance isn't who I am, Max. It's not a skill, or a talent."

"Beautiful women tend to choose more public professions, that's all," he murmured, stroking her nape and causing goose bumps on her skin. "Hell, you could easily have done what your mother did— become a model."

Become a crackhead junkie who'd spent most of the past twenty years in and out of rehab, and in between sleeping with anyone who told her she was beautiful?

She stiffened. "Exactly."

Max had just done what every other man she'd gone out with had done. Made a big freaking deal about her appearance. As if a pretty face was all there was of her. *Good,* Emily thought, annoyed to find tears stinging her eyes. *I'm glad that's all he sees. Because he's just put this whole sex thing back into perspective.*

"I thought you were on your way to see your mother in Seattle. Don't you two get along?" he asked lazily, stroking her back. "I imagine with two such beautiful women you must've had a complicated relationship."

She laughed; it sounded rusty and hurt her chest. "You could say that. First of all there were three of us. My sister Susanna is nine months older than I am."

She rested her head against the curve of his shoulder. A perfect fit. But she felt brittle, and somehow unprotected lying practically naked and vulnerable in his arms while she dragged out her family for show-and-tell.

"I love my mother. I do. But the line between parent and kid is pretty blurred with us. She was one of the first supermodels. The cameras loved her. And while they were on, she was happy. Unfortunately she's an arid sponge when it comes to getting attention. It's never enough. No matter that they called her 'The Beauty.' There was always someone younger, or prettier, or smarter. They always got more callbacks than she did. More jobs, better jobs. So she started to drink when she didn't get the job. And then she started taking drugs here and there. And then she'd look and feel worse, so she'd take more."

His fingers tangled in her hair as he listened, combing through the damp strands in a rhythmic caress that was as soothing as it was arousing. Emily was driven to reveal this part of herself to him, even if she wasn't sure what underlying emotions caused her to do so. Usually she did her best not to bring up her family.

"Where was your father in all this?" His breath was warm on her forehead. Sensation and need rippled through her. So easy for him. So complex and foolish for her. She inhaled the familiar scent of his skin. No soap smell, just Max. Just the smell of his skin made her melt. Crazy. Stupid. Dangerous.

She rarely mentioned her family because it made her feel a little too exposed, a little too vulnerable. A little too defensive. She had no idea why she was telling Max of all people.

"Suz and I had different fathers. And to be honest, I'm not sure Mom *knew* who our fathers were. According to her, we were both mistakes. She did her best, God only knows. But by the ages of ten and eleven Suz and I were already cooking all the meals and trying to take care of each other while Mom was sleeping, or working, or dating. We were pretty much left to our own devices most of the time."

She didn't mention that they had been terrified that the authorities would realize that there was frequently no adult home with them for weeks at a time. They were always at school on time, made their own lunches, and wrote their own excuse notes. If nothing else, they'd both grown up independent women.

"Daniel was a godsend for me. He convinced my mother that I was seriously talented. And because, I think, they were sleeping together, she did whatever he suggested. So I stayed in Italy and went to boarding school, and she went back to Seattle. Daniel paid for my education, an amazingly generous thing to do considering his short-lived affair with my mother."

Her mother's finances at that time went from insanely high to crying because she couldn't pay the rent, flat-out broke.

"Social services went and got Suz. She was almost thirteen by then. She went to live with a foster family who adored, and eventually adopted, her. She and my mother didn't get on very well, and they don't have much of a relationship. Suz is smart and ressourceful, and coincidentally, more beautiful than our mother, and boy, my mother does *not* like competition."

"How's your mother doing now?"

Emily shrugged. "She's in and out of rehab. In, at the moment. At least she's making an attempt to get clean and sober. Or that's what I try to convince myself. But truthfully, I think she considers it a spa. When life gets too difficult she checks herself in. They make a fuss over her and stabilize her with meds, and for a few weeks she's really happy."

She rubbed her cheek on the crisp hair of Max's chest, eyes closed. "I still feel guilty that I've made a life for myself far away from her. But it took several years of therapy to realize that I couldn't fix her. Nor was it my job. It was hard, but eventually I had to let go. She sighed and shifted.

"So she's in Seattle. My sister's in Boston. Married, with a houseful of amazing children, and a husband who loves her. Not for her looks, but because she's an incredible wife and mother. And I'm in Florence. End of story."

"That's a hell of a story. But my God, look at what you've accomplished by yourself."

"Thanks in large part to your father."

"He had nothing to do with your talent," he said, his voice filled with admiration. "Everything you accomplished, you pretty much did on your own. Look at you. You're beautiful, talented, wealthy, and at the top of your career. Yet with all that you could easily have made your fortune the easy way. In front of a camera, instead of behind an easel."

She pushed away from him and sat up. He'd missed the point. Although she was too damn tired to know what the point was herself. "I'd like to stretch out. I'll be more comfortable over here." She managed to switch seats with her dignity intact by hauling the blanket with her. She punched the pillow into shape and crammed it under her cheek.

He gave her a searching look. "Are you okay?"

Only a man over his head and unaware of his imminent demise could ask such a bloody stupid question. "Are you kidding? I'm relaxed and sexually satisfied and ready to sleep. Thanks, Max. That was better than any sleeping pill." She rolled over because she could not look at him for one more second through the film of angry, stupid, stupid, *stupid* tears.

"I don't want anything to hurt you, Emily. Anything or anyone."

The vise around her chest pressed down on her aching heart. "*You* won't hurt me," she said, reading him loud and clear. And he wouldn't. As long as he didn't realize that she was falling a little more in love with him every hour they were together. She wrapped the blanket around her like armor.

"I didn't mean—Yeah. I guess I did. I'm married to my work. T-FLAC is everything I want. Will always want. But God only knows you've thrown me a curveball. I *like* you. You're funny and tough and damned courageous. Not to mention talented and beautiful. You're the whole package. . . ."

He *liked* her? She didn't really register all of his words over the grinding of her teeth. Why did it always come down to the packaging? It took a while, but somehow she managed to fall asleep in the middle of Max trying to dig himself out of the hole he'd dug.

Denver International Airport was one of the three largest airports in the world, and not even for T-FLAC would air traffic control change the flight patterns circling above their designated landing strip. The Bombardier Challenger just had to wait its turn, which meant circling fourteen thousand feet away from Tillman and his answers.

The plan was to make a pit stop to drop Max off in Denver, then his two operatives would accompany Emily to HQ in Montana. Even so, Max didn't feel comfortable letting her out of his sight. But there was no logical reason to keep her with him when she'd be safer at T-FLAC's secure underground facility.

Unfortunately, logic didn't come into play when her safety was of utmost importance to him.

Utmost importance? No. But of *prime* importance, and a matter of international security, was getting to the bottom of Tillman's involvement in all this. Emily'd gone from soft and malleable in his arms to prickly and unresponsive in a heartbeat. He had no idea what he'd said or done to turn her off like that. But it was for the best.

He'd never regretted giving a woman the "T-FLAC is my world" speech more than he'd regretted giving it to Emily. But he respected her too much to lie to her and make false promises. On the other hand, she'd gone from hot to cold before he made his point.

There was no future for them. No permanency. He loved the work he did for T-FLAC. It wasn't a job. It was his life. It was who he was. T-FLAC took everything, leaving nothing behind for him to offer a woman.

No matter how strong the desire.

It just was.

Life vs. T-FLAC.

No contest.

Women. "Don't take your eyes off her," he told Keiko as he sat the two female operatives down for a final briefing in the aft cabin.

"I won't," Keiko assured him. She was so new, so intense, so eager it hurt his teeth.

He was depending on her. Cooper, he knew, had eyes in the back of her head. He was trusting these two women to keep Emily safe while he was thousands of miles away.

She was up front in the cockpit, fascinated by all the dials, and, Max bet, talking the pilot into letting her handle the controls for a while. Or grabbing a parachute and jumping to get away from him.

Hell if he knew.

She hadn't spoken directly to him since she'd woken up this morning. "I don't expect them to know about her Seattle connection, which is in our favor. And even if somehow it does occur to them, she has at least six hours' head start. Unless—" He paused. "Unless they planned ahead and are waiting for her there. She wants to go and see her mother in rehab. Says an hour will do it."

"We'll be ready," AJ assured him. "We always anticipate the worst."

"Yeah, and we're usually right," Max muttered, rubbing a rough hand around the tension gripping the back of his neck. He pulled his buzzing phone out of his pocket. "Aries."

It was Darius with more fucking bad news. "The Blessed Virgin of Vladimir in Brisbane was hit three hours ago," he said in his well-modulated, nothing-fazes-me tone. "Russian orthodox. Two hundred seventeen people dead. Hundred and eleven injured. A team from Sydney is already on the scene. I'm coordinating with Navarro and Daklin on this. Shit. Hold."

Max switched his communication from his phone to the monitor so the two operatives in the room with him could see and hear Dare's latest intel. "We seem to be in a permanent holding pattern," he told the two women. The T-FLAC emblem blinked on the large black screen, waiting for Dare to finish his other call. "Might as well make yourselves comfortable."

The coffee had been turned off in anticipation of landing, but he got up to pour himself a cup of luke-warm sludge anyway. He didn't care if his caffeine fix was warm, hot, or cold. Caffeine was caffeine. He drained the mug and poured another while he waited.

The T-FLAC logo blinked out, and Dare's face filled the screen. He had a face only a mother could love, and now he was sporting a long, angry scratch on the cheek opposite his scar. It was a tight shot of him, just head and shoulders, but from the little Max could see in the background Dare wasn't in T-FLAC's underground facility in Montana, he was somewhere else.

Christ. Was the poor bastard still on Paradise? It was a sore spot, so Max wasn't going to ask. "Problems?" he asked instead.

"Problem—singular, but new intel, too. First, we received the autopsy results on your father. The bruising on his upper arms and chest indicated that he was grabbed from behind while he was in a seated position. The trajectory of the body, as you mentioned before, proves he was thrown. The tox screen shows he was on some high-powered cocktail of pharmaceuticals. But those had nothing to do with his death. Conclusion, he was literally picked up and tossed over the balcony."

Nothing new there. "What else?"

"Another art restorer has turned up dead. An Elaine Ludwig of Bellevue, Washington. See what, if anything, Miss Greene can tell you about her."

Max nodded to Keiko to go get Emily. The woman quickly pushed away from the table and strode off to the cockpit. "Do we have the body?"

"Affirmative. We also got someone else. The man who killed her. Ludwig's husband's a Marine. Just got back from Iraq. Literally. Came in the house unexpectedly in the early hours to discover the man leaving the bedroom. Didn't ask any questions, just took him out with his Beretta 9mm."

"Semper Fi," Max said, pleased they had another lead to follow. Emily and Keiko came back into the room, and Emily shot Max an inquiring glance before looking at Darius on the monitor.

Dare's eyes connected with Emily's and her shoulders stiffened as if preparing for a blow.

"What do you know about Elaine—"

"Ludwig," Emily finished dully. "I knew her well enough to say hello to. Is she dead?" At Dare's nod she reached over and gripped Max's hand. Her fingers were like ice. "This is insane."

"Hmph," Dare agreed. "Yeah. But we'll get to the bottom of it. Stay with Max. Your plane will be next to land. I'll keep you posted."

"What's the new intel?" Max wasn't about to let Dare off the hook.

"The guy our Marine offed?" Darius said. "Black rose tattooed on his ass. And our Queensland bombing? Traced the Semtex to the Black Rose cell responsible for the bombing in New Zealand last September." There was a tense pause.

"You've got yourself an authenticated Black Rose clusterfuck, here, my man."

Twelve

THE FORTY-FIVE-MINUTE DRIVE TO TILLMAN'S ESTATE just outside Denver was a long time to be sitting in a confined space with a man Emily couldn't seem to take her eyes off of. She tried her best not to find anything interesting to look at out of Max's window, because she didn't want to inadvertently look at *him*. She needn't have worried. They were about as far apart as they could be without one of them straddling the outside of the car. While he seemed to fill the entire space with his presence, Max appeared completely oblivious to her, and the desultory conversation she was having with the two women in the front seat.

Because of the death of Elaine Ludwig, Max had decreed that she remain with them, and not go on ahead to Seattle. Emily was fine with that. People in her world seemed to be dropping like flies. She wasn't safe with Max emotionally, but she was a hundred percent sure of her physical safety when they were together.

For the past half hour, he'd been poking, amazingly rapidly, a chrome stylus at a small black handheld device. Even though he was in his customary uniform of unrelieved black, today he'd opted for black dress slacks and a beautifully cut jacket over his black silk T-shirt. Black suited him.

She, however, had protested wearing the all-black,

all-the-time outfit that AJ had offered her on the plane. Instead she'd opted to wear her own clothes. Jeans, tan high-heeled boots, a navy cashmere sweater, and a camel hair jacket. It wasn't until she was dressed that she realized she was color-coordinated with the T-FLAC jet.

The short jacket might be attractive, but she was going to freeze her ass off when she got out of the car. More so because she'd gotten bold, and adopted the "go commando" part of the T-FLAC dress code.

Max's appearance had very little to do with what she found so appealing about this annoying man. Looks weren't that important to her for obvious reasons. Yes, he was handsome in a rugged, get-the-hell-out-of-my-way way. But she was intrigued by his focus. His drive. His chivalry, even if it was somewhat over-whelming when directed at her, was ingrained. She liked the way he treated his two female operatives exactly the same way he treated the men he worked with. She loved his big, tanned hands, and the way his eyes turned to green when he looked at her, like a barometer of how much he wanted her.

This probably wasn't the best time to try to make sense of her feelings for Max. She was on too much sensory overload as it was. *I'm in such big trouble here,* she thought as her heart clenched. She turned her head to look blindly out of her side window at the passing scenery.

It was a glorious day, with not a cloud in the crystal blue sky. The stands of pine trees on either side of the narrow rural road were laden with snow. Rust-and-white Hereford cattle stood ankle deep in it, big brown eyes watchful as the car passed beyond their fence. It was a beautifully serene, bucolic scene. She took a mental snapshot so she could paint it later.

But she'd add action and drama to the serenity by painting Max, leaning over the neck of a running black stallion, its tail flying in the wind as it soared over the snowy hills. She'd paint speed in the chunks of white spewing behind the horse's hooves, and a plume of steam misting from the horse's mouth as it galloped.

"Do you ride?" she asked Max casually.

He glanced up from whatever he was doing to give her a slightly puzzled glance at the non sequitur.

"Anything from a horse to a Harley. Why?"

Of course he rode a motorcycle. She'd dress him in black leather. Hell, she'd like to paint him in nothing at all. "No reason. It's hard to believe we've been on his property for the past half hour," she said, changing the subject fast.

"Tillman has some serious bank," Max pointed out, his attention back on the device in his hand.

"No kidding." Emily tried to figure out what some of the buildings were that they passed. Barns. Out-buildings holding farm equipment. Several large homes at the end of long, snow-covered driveways. According to Darius, Richard Tillman's twenty-five-million-dollar, five-hundred-acre ranch, nestled in the hills between Denver and Colorado Springs, was a money machine. Besides owning one of the largest commercial real estate development companies in the Northern Hemisphere, he also raised cattle and bred quarter horses, both here and in Montana. He was *that* kind of wealthy.

None of that made Emily's heart beat faster. What gave her heart palpitations and made her mouth go dry was the man's art collection. "I'm going to ask—okay, *beg* Mr. Tillman to let me go into his private museum while you two talk," Emily confessed as they drove down the tree-lined drive. "He has the most extensive collection of Renaissance paintings in the world," she said aloud while mentally cataloguing the works she knew he had. Rembrandt, Raphael, and Da Vinci . . . and dozens of other masters.

She almost salivated knowing that in a few minutes she was going to have the sheer, unadulterated plea-sure of seeing them without hordes of tourists jostling for a better vantage point, or without having to work on them. She'd enjoy just looking at them for the pure pleasure of doing so. Without analyzing every brush-stroke and technique, or having a hundred other people breathing down her neck. "And," she added happily, "two full-time curators to oversee them. I have some serious art envy."

"You haven't met Tillman, have you?" Max asked, powering down the device, and shoving it into his pocket.

She shook her head. "I've always dealt with his assistant, Alistair Norcroft. Nice guy."

Max rested his ankle on his opposite knee. "You get any kind of vibe from him?"

Not at all. I go for tall, dark, broody, James Bond types with whom I have no future. "I only met him a few times. And each meeting was pretty brief. Usually he had a courier deliver and pick up the paintings, but sometimes he'd come himself. He appears to be incredibly efficient, and from the way he talked about his boss, devoted."

"A hefty paycheck would go a long way in paying for that devotion."

"That's a cynical way to look at it. I suppose you could be right, but Alistair didn't strike me as all that money-grubbing when we talked. You'll see what I mean when you meet him. He's a pretty low-key guy. He's got an incredibly responsible job, but he's extremely laid-back and calm. And boy, is he organized. I've never met anyone as compulsively organized as he is.

"Funny, I'm not even sure how old he is. He could be anywhere from thirty to sixty." Like Daniel, he'd admitted to having a couple of procedures done. Very metrosexual of him.

"Maybe he had an eye lift . . . or chin jobs are common among men, aren't they, Max?" AJ twisted around from her position in the passenger seat.

He lifted a brow. "Not among the men *I* know. But yeah—Norcroft had a face-lift in 1997, and some god-awful thing called a chemical face peel in '03," Max said, surprising Emily. Why on earth would T-FLAC know or care about that? "He's fifty-six.

241

"Went to Harvard," he continued. "First in his class. Never practiced law. After a ten-year stint with another wealthy guy straight out of law school, he went to work for Tillman. Been with him ever since."

They passed a heliport and more outbuildings. "If you know all that why did you ask me?"

"Because you might give me some insight that wasn't in the dossier I got this morning. How about Prescott? Ever meet him?"

"Nope, but I'm sure *you* know everything including what Prescott Tillman ate for breakfast this morning." Prescott was Richard Tillman's only son.

"Want to know?"

"If you tell me, will you have to kill me?" Emily teased as a way to keep the conversation in perspective.

Max's eyes narrowed to shards of green glass. "Not funny."

Under the circumstances, probably not. "Depends if I'm talking to the checker at Wal-Mart or an international counterterrorist operative, doesn't it?" She glanced through the front window as the car went under a high metal arch forged with an inlay of the initials RT. "What on earth . . ."

AJ gave a gurgle of laughter as Keiko turned the car into the drive of the biggest home on the property. Richard Tillman's home. "Oh, Lord," the redhead laughed. "Check this out." She rolled down her tinted window to get a better view.

A blast of frigid air swirled around Emily's Choos.

The spectacle was hard to miss. She stared at the rows of larger than life-sized, Carrera marble statues lining both sides of the crushed stone driveway. "Wow."

Max smiled. "That's all you can say about three or four hundred Venus de Milos? *Wow*?"

The statues, and there were at least that many, were alternated, with a front view followed by a back view, followed by a front view, approximately six feet apart, all the way up the curved driveway. It was a startling sight, to say the least. The army of statues all had their arms, too.

"To say that money doesn't buy taste is the understatement of the millennium," Emily told him dryly. "Wow is all I can manage." Max didn't seem surprised. "You knew these would be here," she semi-accused.

"Yeah," Max's lips twitched.

"This is the man who owns genuine Raphaels, and Michelangelos?" She shared a smile with him, then turned quickly to look out of her window when her heart responded to the softening in his eyes and the intimacy of his smile. *Don't go there. Just don't.*

"Thank God he chose not to send me any of his Elvises on velvet," she told the others, tongue in cheek, as they eventually reached the house.

Mansion. Castle. The front of the—monstrosity—was covered with natural river rock, and three wood-trimmed balconies curved from each floor of the house for spectacular views of the pine forest on the lower levels of the property and the mountains in the distance.

The house, Emily thought, *without* the added embellishments, fit into the pine trees and natural surroundings as if it had been carved from the native rock. Unfortunately, Tillman, or someone near and dear to him, had decided that natural wasn't "pretty" enough.

On every beautifully carved wood post sat a stone cherub. Nailed to every handcrafted crossbeam was a stone medallion, or a frieze of running Grecian nymphs. A five-tier Italianate fountain, strategically placed for arriving guests' viewing pleasure in the curve of the sweeping river rock stairs, dripped ice in suspended animation.

"Who's this?" Keiko indicated the impeccably dressed man waiting for them at the foot of the steps as she pulled up close to the house. "The butler?"

"Alistair Norcroft," Emily said opening her door as the man crossed to the car. "Alistair." Slinging the handles of her tote over her shoulder, she held out both hands. "How are you?"

Max summed up Norcroft quickly. He knew the man's background, but a face-to-face meeting was always preferable. Alistair Norcroft was well-maintained. His face was smooth and unlined, lightly tanned, pleasant. His light eyes steady, and direct. He was slight of build, but fit, and of medium height. His hair was short and razor cut, not too stylish, but in keeping with the current fashion. He wore a Savile Row suit, an old-school silk tie, Allen-Edmonds shoes, and a Patek Philippe watch.

Max knew this, not because he gave a flying crap about fashion. But because he made it his business to know how much money people spent on their trappings. Hiding their wealth in plain sight. Norcroft spent a lot.

"Your trip was uneventful, I hope. This snow seems to be with us a lot longer this winter. Come back here where it's warm." Tillman's assistant said smoothly.

He lead them down a corridor, then into a two-story-high great room at the mid level of the sprawling three-story residence. A fire blazed hot in the enormous stone fireplace, and ceiling-to-floor, wall-to-wall windows offered a spectacular panorama of the snow-covered mountains. The enormous room, overlooking a tree-filled ravine, was furnished with comfortable looking brown leather furniture and so many tchotchkes there wasn't a flat surface not occupied by *something*.

"I do apologize." Norcroft didn't fit in with either the back-to-nature look of the décor, nor the outrageously tacky objets d'art. "Mr. Tillman is not well enough to see visitors today, I'm afraid. I'm so sorry you came all this way for nothing. Perhaps another time? Or is there something *I* can do to aid you?"

Despite the roaring fire in this room, the rest of the house had been cold. Surprising if there were an invalid about. Max had asked Emily to set up this meeting between the "investigators looking into the deaths of several restorers" and Tillman while they'd been en route. Norcroft had called her back within minutes assuring her that Mr. Tillman would be more than delighted to answer any questions the investigators might have.

He'd offered Emily and the others the use of Tillman's guesthouse for the night. Max had told her to decline. While he wanted his questions answered, he needed Emily inside T-FLAC headquarters, where he'd be a hundred percent assured of her complete safety.

Norcroft had told Emily how much he was looking forward to seeing her again. Max had listened to the artless conversation on speaker. The guy had sounded genuine when he'd offered to assist them in any way he could.

Now, five hours later, his boss was suddenly sick? Max thought, annoyed. Still, if the super efficient assistant couldn't grant them access to his boss, Max suspected Norcroft could answer most, if not all, of the questions. The job this guy held brought him not only a hefty paycheck, but also privileged information. Max suspected there wasn't much Tillman did without it filtering through Norcroft first.

"Perhaps he's well enough to answer just a few questions?" Max suggested politely as Norcroft directed a uniformed maid to where he wanted the two-tiered, mahogany tea cart she was wheeling into the room.

"Set up on the coffee table, please, Christine," he instructed the young woman. He watched her for a moment as she spread an embroidered cloth on the giant wormwood table, then started unloading carafes and cups and plates of little sandwiches and girlie, bite-sized frosted cakes. What the fuck? Did the guy think they'd come to a frigging tea party?

"I completely understand your frustration," Norcroft addressed Max apologetically. "You've traveled a long way. I know Mr. Tillman was so looking forward to finally meeting Emily. And he certainly wants to do his civic duty and answer whatever questions you may have. Please be seated, and help yourself to the refreshments. Christine? The sandwiches for Mr. Taurus? Ah. Thank you, good girl," he said, pleased, as she uncovered a tray of man-sized sandwiches. Enough to feed a small platoon.

Niigata, standing close by, mouthed the word "restroom?" to the woman, and the maid indicated it was down the hall.

"Where were we?" Norcroft asked, missing the exchange. "Ah, yes. I'll go and check again to see if Mr. Tillman can perhaps make an effort for just a few moments. Excuse me." He inspected the table, then apparently satisfied, thanked the maid and followed her out of the room.

Putting her monstrous bag down on the arm of the sofa, Emily wandered over to inspect a small dark painting across the room. Like Max, AJ positioned herself so she could see all the entrances.

He didn't expect trouble, not here, but Max remained ultra aware as he looked around, trying to see it the way Emily had described Brill's place.

Observant, he had to be, but Emily had taught him the iconographical approach of seeing a person's home through different eyes, and to interpret what he saw in a more personal, and intriguing way. The new perspective gave him additional insight into his host.

Jesus, he'd thought his old man's villa pretentious and over the top. Compared to Richard Tillman's place, his father's home was not only tasteful, it was restrained. This was like comparing a single-wide trailer to the Taj Mahal. And while he had no doubt everything in the house carried a hefty price tag, even he, who never cared about shit like this, knew it was all mostly in exceedingly bad taste.

The iconographical interpretation was that Tillman had never shaken free of his humble roots. Born in a government housing project in Detroit just before the birth of the Great Depression, Tillman was obviously a hoarder. He had more money than God but apparently couldn't or wouldn't get rid of bottom-of-the-barrel, mass-produced statues and vases. The exceptions being several pieces of religious art scattered around the room.

Max was hardly an expert, but he'd bet the gilt porcelain figure of the Madonna, the Byzantine rendering of St. John the Baptist on wood, and several other objects were the real deal. It was just strange seeing them displayed alongside department store art. He wouldn't have expected this from a guy with shit-loads of money and a reputation as an art aficionado.

"Vermeer's *The Little Street* is an excellent copy,"

Emily indicated the painting she'd been looking at. She crossed the football-field-sized area rug to sit on the sofa facing the fire. "The one over the fireplace is a Rembrandt and the little painting by the door is a Fra Angelico. I suspect both are the originals."

He met Niigata's eyes as she came back into the room. The woman was sharp as a tack, and had picked up on his request to search as much of the house as she could in just a few moments. AJ would go next, followed by Max himself. There was a knack to doing a down and dirty search, and T-FLAC trained them well.

Dare had e-mailed them a blueprint of the house, and they had made a grid of what they estimated they could cover in the shortest amount of time without being conspicuous or getting caught. Unfortunately it wouldn't be much, but it might be all the time and opportunity they'd have.

He glanced at Emily. "I thought you needed your equipment to tell an original from a really good fake?"

She grinned. "I do. But since I'm the one who painted that one, I pretty much know I'm not Vermeer." She poured herself a cup of fragrant coffee that Max could smell halfway across the room. "Chocolate cake, ladies," she announced, helping herself to a floral plate and a small square of the chocolate confection, which she ate with relish in one bite.

"Not right now. Thanks, Em," AJ said regretfully, just as a man strolled into the room as if he owned the place. Except he was too young to be Tillman.

Wearing slightly baggy jeans and a gray wool sweater that showed off his beer belly to perfection, Tillman's son was probably in his fifties. He was five eight, with a sharply receding hairline of light, almost downy hair. And what Max suspected was a permanently dissatisfied expression.

Ignoring the women, he walked directly to Max. "Prescott Tillman. And you are?"

He didn't offer his hand, and neither did Max. He'd met dozens of Prescott Tillmans over the years. Soft. Lazy. Entitled. Riding on a wealthy daddy's coattails, and suspicious of anyone who might tip the balance of his very cushy status quo. "Max Taurus. Global Casualty and Loss. These are my associates, Mrs. Cooper and Ms. Niigata. Ms. Greene was kind enough to accompany us to speak with your father."

Emily rose from the squishy leather sofa to intercede. If the younger Mr. Tillman were a dog his hackles would be rising. She put out her hand, forcing Prescott Tillman to take it or appear terribly rude. "Mr. Tillman, I've enjoyed a long business relationship with your father. I'm sorry to hear he's taken ill. I hope it's nothing serious?"

"He's eighty-four years old and in decline, I'm sorry to say," he said, dropping Emily's hand and addressing Max again. "Whatever you need, I'm sure I can answer any questions you might have."

"For starters we'd like a list of all the paintings he's had copied in the last five years, and the names of the artists he commissioned for each," Max informed him.

"I don't have access to that information." Prescott's voice was cold. "If you leave a card, I'll have my secretary see what she can find and mail it to you. Now, if that's all, I'll have the maid see you out. I have a meeting in a few moments."

"Your teleconference has been set up in your office, Scott," Norcroft said smoothly, entering the room with a thin file folder in one hand. "You have two minutes if you need to take care of anything before Brian and Charles are on the line."

"What's that?" Prescott demanded, jabbing a fat finger at the file folder in his hand.

"The information I believe Mr. Taurus was inquiring about." He handed Max the folder. "I took the liberty of printing out a copy for you. This is a record of all the transactions Mr. Tillman—Are you going downstairs, Scott? Would you like a cup of coffee and one of Christine's excellent ham sandwiches to take to your office?"

"I'm not a fucking child, and I don't want a goddamned fucking ham sandwich." The younger Tillman stormed out of the room. If there'd been a door to slam, Emily thought, he would have slammed it. Nice guy . . .

"I apologize for Scott's language, ladies. The copying and donation of his father's extensive art collection has been a sore point for him."

"He resents his father's altruism?" Emily asked sympathetically. Not sympathetic to Prescott, but to Tillman senior's assistant who, she guessed, had to do a lot of apologizing for his employer's son.

"I really don't want to speak out of turn . . . But the truth is Scott resents his father's generosity in giving away such a large portion of his inheritance. It's understandable, of course. But unrealistic. Mr. Tillman's wealth is such that Scott couldn't spend it all in ten lifetimes. What's left after all the artwork has been given away is still a sizable fortune."

Max glanced up from the open file in his hand. "Is this everything?"

"It is, yes. Can I accommodate you with any more information?"

"Tillman senior can't see me?" Max asked.

"I'm afraid not, Mr. Taurus," Norcroft said apologetically. "He was in so much pain, his nurse gave him a sedative just before I went in to see if he might be up to visitors. Again, I am sorry."

Max flipped the folder closed. "Has Tillman senior left the country in the last four or five years?"

Norcroft shook his head. "Mr. Tillman is something of a recluse. He hasn't left this house—truth be told—his *rooms* in over ten years. I don't want you to think he's a Howard Hughes. Mr. Tillman has enjoyed rude good health for some time. But he became something of a hermit after his wife's death. And while he isn't fond of people and dealing with the trappings of going to the office every day, let me assure you that he's still as sharp as ever, and puts in a full ten-hour day from right there in his home office."

Norcroft smiled fondly. "I wish it *were* possible for you to meet him today. I know you'd be impressed with his brain and his wit. Still, we'll save that for another time. I know he'd love to finally meet you, Emily. I've spoken about you in the last few years, and he highly admires your work."

"That's lovely, thank you for telling me. I would have liked meeting him, too. But since I can't, I wonder if there's any way I could have a peek at his private gallery before we leave?" Emily asked hopefully.

Norcroft pulled a face, making him appear charmingly boyish. "It depends on how long you'll be in the area. Unfortunately, we were installing Antelami's *Deposition from the Cross* and some of the floor joists cracked from the weight. We have a contractor working on it but I'm afraid the floor is too unstable and I would be remiss if I allowed you to go into the gallery. I'm so sorry, Emily. Please come back soon, and I'd be delighted to walk you through the museum at a leisurely pace. I'm sure Mr. Tillman would like to accompany us when you come back. He's very proud of the work he's doing, donating his precious art, so the world can enjoy it.

"Let me take that." Norcroft took the floral plate from Emily, turned, then reached for her purse. In the process, the purse fell to the floor, its contents spilling everywhere.

Flustered, he quickly dropped to his knees and began placing the items back inside the Coach bag, muttering apologies as he inched along the edge of the carpet.

"It was an accident," Emily chased down a tube of lip gloss. "I can do this."

"No, no," Norcroft countered, gripping the purse under his arm as he reached beneath the sofa and retrieved a ballpoint pen. He groaned once as his arm extended fully beneath the couch, then stood, shaking the bag to settle the contents before handing it back to Emily. Then he brushed the front of his shirt, straightened his tie, and smiled.

"There. Good as new. Everything is as it should be. Is there anything else I can do for you?"

"Max *Taurus*?" Emily smiled as she settled into the corner of the backseat, tucking one leg under her. Her cheeks were pink from the cold, and her eyes were filled with amusement as she looked at him.

Max felt a thump in the region of his heart. If he'd had one. Which he *didn't*. God damn it. "As good a name as any. Niigata, what did you uncover?"

Niigata turned in her seat. "First, the thermostat was set at seventy-four but the temperature was hovering around fifty-seven."

Max nodded. "House that size? Someone turned the heat on after Emily called. Probably thought we wouldn't notice with the fire roaring. What else?"

Niigata wriggled for a few seconds, then produced a small, rumpled slip of paper. "Found this delivery receipt in the kitchen trash can."

"You went through the trash?" Emily asked.

Niigata shrugged. "A girl's gotta do what a girl's gotta do."

Max scanned the receipt. "Bread, deli ham, mustard,

coffee, sugar, cream, salt, pepper, mayonnaise . . ."

"Hell, Max," Niigata interrupted. "I'm never home but even I have most of those staples on hand."

"Maid's uniform was new." Max sounded distracted.

"How could you possibly know that? Do you have a little device that tells you how much sizing there is on a garment?"

"Probably." His lips twitched. "But in this case the 'inspected by' sticker was still attached to the tie of her apron."

"There was dust on the brass toilet tissue stand and the pipes rattled and sputtered when I turned on the water." Niigata turned to Emily. "When a faucet isn't used for a while, the water settles and air collects in the pipe. Turn on the faucet and it chokes the air out of the pipe before you get a steady stream."

"So that whole scene back there was staged," Max concluded. The other operatives agreed.

AJ asked, "Why hide Tillman senior? Unless he's dead. But why hide that fact? Especially if junior has his boxers in a knot over the donations. As sole heir— I'm assuming—junior could nix the philanthropy and keep everything for himself with Daddy dead."

Max frowned. "I didn't get the impression that Prescott Tillman was into keeping up appearances. If the old guy was dead, he wouldn't waste a lot of time letting the world know he controlled the estate. There has to be a reason for the charade. If there is a charade."

"Got any ideas?" Niigata asked.

Max pulled in an audible breath, then exhaled slowly. "Working on it."

"Okay. Now where?" Emily asked as Niigata parked close to the jet out on the runway at Denver International.

"Monta—" A sharp sound of rifle shot cut off her words like a hot knife through butter. "Down. *Shit!*" He shoved her to the ground, at the same time he switched the Glock over to full auto and answered fire. With thirty-three rounds in a single pull and hold back on the trigger, the shots were literally "hosed" onto the target.

The spent magazine dropped to the ground with a ping, and he drove another one into the grip, and started firing again almost without pause.

"Keiko's been hit!" AJ yelled over the sound of her own bursts of answering fire.

Yeah. He'd seen her drop. Still firing at the unseen sniper, he reached down and hauled Emily to her feet by her elbow. "Keep low. Get inside!" He pushed her halfway up the metal stairs with his free hand, blocking her back with his body as he shoved her up the stairs ahead of him.

"Go. Go. Go." He turned fully and fired off covering shots in the direction of the last shot as he boxed Emily in. The snipers had a helluva lot better line of sight than he and AJ had. The runways were clear, but the edges where the fresh snow was banked were blinding white. The sharpshooter could be behind any number of snow-covered barricades. It was impossible to see a muzzle flash in the iffy light.

Niigata was facedown on the tarmac thirty feet away. Max only needed a second to know she was dead. Shot through the back of the head. God *damn* it.

"Get on the floor and stay down," he yelled at Emily, shoving her inside the open door. He took the stairs in two jumps. He spared a quick glance at the gangway to make sure Emily was inside. She was. But if the pilot and copilot weren't starting the engines, or hauling their asses out of here guns blazing, it meant they were dead.

"Give me your weapon," Max instructed AJ. "I'll cover you." Max shouted to AJ. "Go make sure there's no one inside—"

Bang!

"Jesus! Cooper?!"

With a look of startled annoyance she grabbed her chest. The M16 skittered out of her limp hand as she went down and lay still.

Thirteen

MAX BURST THROUGH THE SMALL OPEN DOORWAY OF the plane carrying AJ in his arms. Emily ran to meet them, dragging a blanket with one hand and balancing towels with the other. She hadn't known which of them would need whatever they were going to need, but she was ready. Barely. She'd had to take a moment to pull herself together after looking inside the cockpit.

From her vantage point inside the plane she'd watched, horrified, as AJ had taken a bullet seconds after Keiko and a large portion of brain matter had splattered on the ground. When AJ had crumpled to the tarmac, Emily's heart had leapt with fear for all of them out there under fire.

"What can I do?" she demanded. AJ's skin was almost translucent, she was so pale. Yet the only blood Emily saw was from a deep gash on the other woman's forehead. Surely there would be more blood from a gunshot?

"Don't worry b— me. I'm o—" AJ's eyes rolled back and she went limp in Max's arms.

"She'll be fine. She's tough."

"Not tough enough to stop a speeding bullet," Emily pointed out, racing ahead of him to lower one of the chairs so AJ could lie flat. "Did you kill them?" She jerked her chin toward the closest window as she covered the redhead with the blanket, tucking it around her body.

Clearly furious, Max shook his head. "I heard the screech of tires. Whoever was shooting ran like a chickenshit as soon as they hit Cooper."

"What about Keiko?" Emily asked, moving toward the open door.

Max grabbed her arm. "Get the fuck away from the door. Jesus, Emily, the sniper could have just repositioned or there could be more than one!"

She wasn't anywhere *near* the open door; she was going for hot water to bathe the blood off AJ's face. "You said—" *that he was gone, anyway.*

Holding her tightly by the shoulders, he crushed her mouth under his for a brief, hard kiss. When he broke away he looked almost feral. "I couldn't handle it if anything happened to you. Be careful, okay?"

"Yes," she managed, shaken by the look in his eyes. She'd have to remember it, because she didn't have time to analyze what Max could possibly be thinking right now. "Keiko?"

"Dead. I've got to get her body, and then we're out of here."

Just like in the Bozzatos' house, Emily was momentarily paralyzed to find death so up close and personal. But she didn't stay frozen in her own fear for long. Right now her priority was to see what, if anything, she could do to help AJ, and to stay out of Max's way unless he needed her to do something. She crouched down beside AJ, blotting at the cut on her temple with a cloth dipped in warm water. It needed stitches. A lot of stitches.

"I hope you know how to fly. The pilot and copilot are dead, too." She was appalled at how matter-of-fact her voice sounded. As soon as she'd seen them she'd wanted to throw up. Unfortunately, there hadn't been time. Her stomach was still roiling, but she didn't have time to indulge it.

"Fuck. Did you go to the back?"

"No time," she said. "But the door's closed."

"Take this." He reached over and flipped the blanket off AJ's legs, then slipped a small gun from a holster on her ankle.

Oh, no, no, no. She so didn't want the task of shooting someone. But she rose, dried her hands, and accepted the gun from him without comment.

"The safety's off. Point and shoot."

When this was over—and she prayed to God it would be over soon—Emily promised herself she'd go and take shooting lessons. It seemed as though she was the only one on the planet who didn't know how to fire a bloody gun. Tucking the blanket back around AJ's legs one-handed, she watched Max as he checked each bank of seats along the aisle and headed toward the door in back.

Cupping the grip with both hands, she braced her feet apart. Pretending to herself that she knew what she was doing.

The fact that she *didn't* know what the hell she was doing scared her to death. She watched Max's progress unblinkingly.

Gun first and with locked elbows, in swift, economical movements, he went all the way to the back of the plane and opened the door to disappear inside. Her heart stopped as she imagined all sorts of horrible possibilities.

Mimicking Max, it took both hands to hold the gun at eye level, but at least they didn't shake. She sucked in a breath and held it, correcting where the barrel of the gun was pointing by a fraction of an inch.

A few agonizing minutes later Max came out of the rear cabin. "All clear."

Emily let out her breath, but somehow couldn't seem to lower her locked arms. For a little thing, the gun was surprisingly heavy. Or maybe it was the weight of responsibility. If there had been someone back there, would she have had to shoot them to protect Max?

Of course. There was no doubt in her mind that if anyone, or any*thing*, threatened Max, and she had the wherewithal to protect him, she would kill without hesitation. The thought stunned her. She would *kill* for this man.

He hesitated a second when he saw the raised gun. "Now's not a good time for you to shoot me, sweetheart. But hold that thought." He sent her a smile that zinged like an electrical current straight to her heart. She let her arms down slowly, unable to answer his smile.

"I'm going outside," he said evenly as he passed her in the aisle. "Use the bulkhead to block your body from sight. Cover me. If anyone gets past me, kill them." Then he bolted down the stairs.

Cover him? Mouth so dry it was hard to swallow, she did as he'd asked. Blocking her body from view, she held the gun palmed in both hands as she looked over the snowy landscape of the runway. Had anyone heard the shots? Probably not, if no one had come to offer assistance, or at least ask what the hell was going on.

She narrowed her eyes, and followed the slow arc of the barrel of the gun as she tried to discern what was shade and what was movement. The sun was setting, casting odd shadows and highlights on and around the dirty snow banked to one side.

There! Something moved in the shadows to the left, and she swung the gun in that direction. After watching the spot for several seconds she realized it was just a piece of paper blowing in the icy breeze. In her peripheral vision she saw Max pick up Keiko, then he was sprinting back up the stairs.

"Good job," he told her, not even slightly out of breath.

"Except the part where I almost blew a hole in a newspaper," she told him, not moving from her position. "I can't tell you how happy I am that I didn't have to shoot anyone."

"The day's still young."

"God. Is this what working for T-FLAC means? Nearly being killed every waking hour?"

"No. The work I do means for every tango *I* kill, fifty people who don't know of our, or *their,* existence can sleep safely in their beds at night."

"I appreciate what you do," she told him with utmost sincerity. "And thank you from all those oblivious people you keep safe. You're a true hero." No grandstanding or photo ops. Max and his team of T-FLAC operatives were the real deal.

Keiko had given her life to protect her. That made her feel sick. But with that nausea came a rebirth of her anger. She was going to help Max and do whatever it took to find these lunatics and bring them to justice. If it was the last damn thing she did.

"Bullshit. I'm no hero. I'm nothing more than an exterminator. I'm going to take her in back; will you go ahead and pull out a bed?"

Emily swiftly went to the aft cabin, and lowered one of the beds from the wall. Even though Keiko was dead, Max put her down gently, then covered her body with the blanket Emily handed him.

"You can put that down now." He motioned to the gun she was still holding by her side in a white-knuckled grip.

"You do realize you just told a woman who's held a gun exactly *twice* in her life to cover you?" He'd trusted her. He'd *trusted* her to protect his back. The concept was mind-boggling.

They went back into the main cabin, Max looking grim, and Emily feeling shell-shocked. Again.

"Life's full of new experiences." He glanced over at AJ. "How's she doing?"

"I haven't had a chance to really check." And please, please, *please,* God, make it be a superficial wound.

"Can you figure out the door?" Max reached over, clicked on the safety and pried the gun out of her clenched hand.

"Yes." And she could. Following the printed instructions above the latch, Emily secured the door. She watched him walk into the cockpit, and bit her lower lip as she remembered clearly what he was just now seeing. He cursed.

Yeah. She'd had the same reaction, after she'd about thrown up, at the sight of the two dead men in there. They'd both been shot in the back of the head at close range.

She was starting to get a marked aversion to all shades of crimson.

"Were you shot, too?" She'd come to realize that Max Aries was the kind of guy who'd have a bullet hole in him and act as though nothing had happened until he crashed and had to be dragged, kicking and screaming, to the hospital.

"I'm fine." He emerged from the cockpit carrying the pilot in a fireman's lift. The man's head was now covered in a blanket. Thank God. "Pissed, but fucking fine."

He took the copilot to the back, and placed him beside Keiko on the bed. Silently Emily handed him another blanket, and mentally apologized for not even knowing his name. He must have a family somewhere. People whom he loved. People whose lives would be irrevocably changed by his death. People, she thought with a full body shudder, who considered him a hero.

Max didn't go back for the second man, and she guessed that he'd just moved the copilot so he could have the seat. So he could fly. And he was willing to sit next to a nearly decapitated body for the duration of the flight. He must have a stomach of steel.

He picked up the submachine gun he'd brought in with AJ. "As soon as we're airborne I want you to see what you can do for her. She's wearing LockOut under her clothing, and that will have protected her from a body piercing bullet, but I suspect the hit broke a couple of her ribs. She might have internal injuries as well. Nothing you can do about those, but I'd like you to take a look at the gash on her forehead. There's ice in the galley."

She'd seen AJ dive to make a shot. That's when she'd hit the bottom rung of the stairs. The LockOut suit wouldn't have protected her if the bullet had struck her in the head instead of the chest. "I got some before you brought her back. It's right there in the ice bucket." She motioned to the table, where she'd set out a pile of towels, the ice bucket, a bowl of hot water, and several of the first aid kits. "I'll take care of what I can. Go."

"You're going to have to apply pressure to the wound to slow the bleeding. You'll be able to reach her even if you strap into the seat next to her." Cupping her cheek he searched her face. His fingers were cool against her skin, but she welcomed his touch.

"How're you holding up?" he asked, his voice steady while his hands, she was surprised to notice, shook slightly.

He leaned down and brushed a fleeting kiss over her mouth. Her lips wanted to cling. *She* wanted to cling, but she didn't. She brushed his mouth with her fingertips. "Compared to the others, I'm terrific."

"Keep it that way," he murmured, stepping away.

"Stay in that seat until we reach cruising altitude, then see what you can do for her. We'll be at a medical facility in just over an hour."

"You should stay and get checked out, too." Max told Emily as a medic wheeled a now conscious AJ into an exam room. They were down in the bowels of the earth in the T-FLAC headquarters building in Montana. Sixth floor down was the state-of-the-art medical facility as well as the labs.

She slung her tote over her shoulder, her chin and tone belligerent. "I wasn't hurt."

"Good." He waved over the young doctor who'd been hovering nearby. "Then it won't take long for them to give you a clean bill of health, will it?"

Her eyes narrowed. "I want to help you find these people."

It wasn't a stretch to picture her doing so either. But Max had had enough of seeing Emily in the fucking thick of things. He wanted her safe and out of the way. She couldn't get any safer than underground in T-FLAC's highly secure facility.

For the duration.

And wasn't she going to be pissed as hell when she realized that she wasn't leaving here anytime soon?

Not until he found the tangos responsible, and not until all the dust—every single fucking particle of it—had settled.

"It's too late to do anything tonight. Dr. Michael Yen, meet Emily Greene." Max clasped the young doctor on the shoulder. "She's all yours, Mike, I'll be by to pick her up in—what? An hour?"

"Like a package at the lost and found?" Emily asked sweetly.

"Like a date," Max responded before strolling off, hands in his pockets.

He was going to give her a night to remember before he walked away from her.

Again.

He had T-FLAC-y things to do, Emily thought as she submitted herself to Dr. Yen's examination. Max probably had to file reports in triplicate, and be debugged or debriefed or whatever it was. He would have to report to someone. He'd have to explain what had happened at the airport, and discuss what they'd seen and heard at Richard Tillman's house. Damn it. She wished she could be there to tell them—what? That Max was a super agent? That he could take out James Bond with one hand tied behind his back? Other than a scraped elbow from the attack by the faux police the other day, she had not a scratch on her.

With a clean bill of health, she was free to go.

It didn't surprise her that a guy who looked as though he should be wearing a pocket protector came to escort her. He was waiting outside the doctor's office when she came out.

His name was Rifkin, he told her without making eye contact. No first name. He couldn't have been any older than twenty, but his reddish-blond hair was already thinning on top, and Emily knew that because she was a head taller than he was, and he tended to look at his shoes a lot. They were very ordinary shoes, as were the black pants he wore. He could be anything from a gofer to a geeky genius for all she knew.

But right now he was her escort. "Mr. Aries asked that a room be prepped—*prepared* for you." Rifkin's ears got pinker and pinker as he talked. "I had your luggage delivered there while you were in with Dr. Yen. He said—"

She was sure Max had had a lot to say. And she'd be happy to listen to it. In person. "I'd like to see AJ Cooper now, please."

"Oh—"The question had thrown him a curve. "Ah—sure. Yes. Right this way. I'm sure that a quick visit will be authorized."

"Great," Emily told him cheerfully, accompanying him down a long, pale sage green hallway. Black-and-white photographs of major cities all over the world were matted in white, and framed in simple black metal. Striking, and surprising considering where she was.

The place was also a hive of activity as doctors in lab coats, nurses in crisp white uniforms, and patients milled about, or sat in various waiting rooms despite it being at least seven in the evening. "I guess spy-types need medical attention around the clock." Emily said conversationally as her boot heels *click-click-clicked* down the linoleum floor.

Where *was* Max? She hated to admit it, but whenever he was out of her sight she expected never to see him again. She'd barely survived the first time he'd walked away. She wasn't sure her heart could take it if he decided to do it again. Not now anyway. She felt too vulnerable to deal with a broken heart as well as everything else at the moment.

"There are a great number of operatives and their family members here twenty-four seven," Rifkin informed her. "That's because we have a great number of operatives around the world. They're not all here because they sustained injury on the job. No, ma'am, they are very well trained. And operatives tend not to *need* a lot of medical attention," Rifkin told her almost apologetically, indicating that they had to turn right as if he were making a turn signal in a car. "The LockOut suit is, of course, almost impervious. The material was manufactured—uh, here's Mrs. Wright's room." He was clearly relieved that he didn't have to entertain her anymore.

Cute kid. She felt ancient. As she'd learned, looks could be deceiving. He could probably kill a person ninety-seven ways, and leap tall buildings in a single bound, while firing a machine gun. "What is it you do here, Rifkin?" she asked before pushing open the door to AJ's room.

His face flamed. "I'm training to be an operative, ma'am. In the meantime I'm, er, working in the mail room. I'll be waiting right out here for you when you're done."

Emily grinned as she pushed open the door. "Ow."

The smile disappeared as she saw AJ lying in the bed. "That's gotta hurt."

"You should see the other guy," AJ muttered. "Kane is going to kill me."

"For getting hurt?" Emily asked indignantly, tossing her tote onto a nearby chair, then going to stand by the bed. The older woman had a purple-and-blue shiner over her left eye where her head had hit the stair, and she was clearly too sore to move.

"For not getting out of the way," AJ grimaced. "I tried to tell them not to call him, but of course the dickheads had to make a stupid big deal out of me being here. I only have a couple of broken ribs and a fractured collarbone, for goodness sake! It's not that big a deal." AJ grimaced. "He's on an op, but insisted on coming right away." She didn't look unhappy about it, Emily thought, noticing the way AJ smiled and her eyes lit up when she talked about her husband.

"He loves you."

"Unconditionally."

No hesitation. No doubt. Emily couldn't even imagine what that kind of confidence in another person's love was like.

There was a tap on the door, and an orderly came in bearing a tray. "Ready for dinner?" he asked, cheerily. Whatever was on the covered tray smelled fabulous, and Emily's stomach rumbled in protest.

"Starving." The patient looked at her visitor. "Em, wanna stay and share my dinner? I'm sure we can order whatever you want."

The orderly placed AJ's meal on the bedside tray, and helped her sit up. It looked like a painful process, and AJ was sweating by the time the she was propped up by several stiff, crisp pillows.

"Thanks, no," Emily grabbed her bag and slung the handle over her shoulder. "Max has arranged for me to have a room. I'm dying to take a shower before I can even think about food."

"Oh. He'll have gotten you one of the suites." AJ picked up her fork as the door closed behind the orderly. "You're in for a treat—they're reserved for visitors like presidents and royalty. And high-up operatives like Aries."

Emily's eyes widened. She'd fallen down the rabbit hole. "You're kidding."

AJ waved her off. "Have fun."

Rifkin led her through a labyrinth of unmarked passages and two different banks of elevators until Emily wasn't sure if they'd gone up or down, left or right. Interesting place. "How does anyone find their way around without signs or a map?"

Since they hadn't spoken in about ten minutes her voice clearly startled him, and his ears immediately went bright pink. "We get a map when we start working here. We have to commit it to memory."

Maybe so. But he'd also, like a dancer learning new steps, been counting off doors and turns as they went. One, two three, one, two three.

"Then what?" Emily asked, amused and touched

by his sincerity. "You have to eat the paper?"

"It's shredded." He was serious, bless his heart. "This is your suite, ma'am." He took out a keycard, slid it into the slot in the door, and pushed the door open. Standing back he handed her the card. "Your luggage has been delivered. If there's anything—*anything,* you need, just pick up the phone and press 'zero.'"

She glanced around the room. "Thank you, Rif . . . kin." He was gone.

"Wow, neat trick," she muttered, closing the door. The room smelled of the ripe peaches piled in a gorgeous slate green Murano glass bowl on the desk. Or maybe it was specially formulated spy-type air freshener, she mused. Soft music came from a high-tech looking stereo embedded in the wall under a large plasma TV.

The suite wasn't that large, perhaps twenty-five by twenty-five, but what it lacked in size it made up for in amenities. The colors were derived from the wallpaper, an understated, milky coffee color, soft, smoky blue-greens with accents of rich chocolate. The king-size bed took up the majority of the room, and was covered with a lush spread in a subtle pattern utilizing all three colors and matching the paper on the walls.

It was like standing inside a perfect, gender-neutral gift box.

A blue-green velvet chaise was spotlit by a reading lamp that matched the bronze table lamp on a small Queen Anne desk across the room. It was elegant and sophisticated. And all Emily cared about was a shower, and seeing Max.

Tossing her tote on the foot of the bed, she bent down and unzipped her boots, then kicked them off. Happy to be out of heels, she wiggled her toes. The chocolate colored carpet was lush and soft underfoot. Ah. Happy toes.

Someone had left her suitcase—the one she'd packed a lifetime ago to take to Seattle—on a folding rack. Her clothes had been pressed and hung in a free-standing armoire.

"Thank you, whoever you are." Figuring that if her clothes were hung up, the mysterious somebodies had probably taken her toiletries to the bathroom, she went to check.

"Okay. I could live in here." The glass-fronted shower stall, tiled in ocean-colored, iridescent mosaic glass tiles, took up the entire back wall, and was big enough for six or eight people. There was a sunken tub, too, but she preferred showering, and this one was going to be hers, all hers for at least half an hour, or when the hot water ran out.

Stripping, Emily tossed her clothes in the corner and turned on all twelve massaging showerheads. The steam would come next. Taking her shampoo in with her, she closed the door and lifted her face to the spray. Only one thing could make this even more blissful—

The door snicked open, letting in a draft of cool air. Perfect, perfect timing. "Hello, Max."

273

Fourteen

Wᴇ ʜᴀᴠᴇ ᴀ sᴇʀɪᴏᴜs ᴡᴀᴛᴇʀ ʀᴇsᴛʀɪᴄᴛɪᴏɴ ɪɴ ᴛʜɪs section of the building," Max told her sternly, stepping into the shower stall and shutting the door. He was gloriously naked. He plucked the plastic bottle out of her hand, and poured a dollop of rose-scented shampoo into his own palm.

Water sluiced over his tanned chest, and clung lovingly to the crisp dark hair arrowing down his body to his groin. He was *very* happy to see her.

She arched a brow. "And I suppose operatives have to double up to conserve water?"

He turned her around, so her back was toward him, then slid his fingers into her wet hair, cradling her head between his soapy palms. "Sometimes sacrifices have to be made for God and country." His hard penis pressed against the cleft of her ass as he wedged a knee between her thighs.

"I suddenly feel *very* patriotic," she murmured throatily, resting her butt against his throbbing erection as he massaged shampoo into her hair with strong fingers. Bliss.

Her concentration was in no way divided just because he was shampooing and trailing a cool tongue across her shoulder at the same time. The sensation of him laving her skin while she was off balance in his arms was highly erotic, and it said a lot about their relationship.

Not that she wanted to analyze the symbolism of this position at the moment.

For now it was just another way to express how much she lo—she caught herself—*wanted* him.

She turned around, curling her fingers around his broad shoulders for purchase as he kissed his way over and around her sensitive breasts, his fingers spread on her back, bending her away from him and bracing her as his mouth moved slowly, maddeningly down her body. He sucked a nipple into the warmth of his mouth, nibbling the tight bud with his teeth, stroking it with the slightly rough surface of his tongue until she moaned. And all the oxygen was sucked out of her lungs at the piercingly sweet sensation.

"Not that I'm complaining," she managed, as his lips moved slowly down to her belly button while he supported her over his arm. He was, apparently, fascinated by her tattoo. "But all the blood is draining to my head."

Cupping the back of her head, he pulled her upright. "Sorry about that. Better accessibility."

His wet skin gleamed as water splashed over his shoulders. "I think we'd have excellent accessibility—to each other—if we were *suppine.* Don't you?"

"Next time."

"Kiss me," she demanded, pressing her body to his.

His skin felt hot, and slick with the water pouring over his shoulders and down his body. The rough hair

275

on his chest and groin rubbed at her sensitive skin until she wanted to purr like a cat.

"Oh, you'll be thoroughly kissed—all over, before we're done tonight," he murmured, pushing soapy hair off her face before he bent his head. Her mouth opened under his, and she tasted shampoo and Max. His tongue moved in a deep rhythm that she instantly and eagerly matched.

She wound her arms around his neck, anchoring herself by fisting strands of his too long, wet hair in both hands. She had to stand on tiptoes to reach his mouth, but the elevated position aligned her mound with the thick length of his penis, and her hips undulated slightly to get as close to him as possible. Heated pleasure radiated from every point of contact, and she moaned softly into his mouth.

One big hand traveled up her wet back moving up to cup the back of her head, the other moved down to stroke her ass.

"You turn me inside out," she whispered against his mouth, loving knowing that she was responsible for making him so hard, that he'd been aroused the second he saw her. She teased him with a little shimmy of her hips, and thrilled when he made a rough sound, almost a growl.

The shower stall was as steamy as the tropics. Max crowded her against the cool mosaic tiled wall as he watched her with a fiercely heated expression in his glittering green eyes. "How many times do you think I can make you come in the next hour?" He nuzzled the arch of her throat as his hand cupped her breast. His thumb made a lazy circle around the hardness of her nipple, as his teeth scored a tingling path up her jaw. His mouth brushed hers. Once. Twice. Teasing. Taunting.

"Hmm." she skimmed a hand down his side, then slid her palm around and over the tight mound of his behind under the pulsing spray of a dozen shower-heads. "How many times do you think *I* can make *you* come in the next five minutes?" she taunted, her voice thick. His rough palm moved from her breast down her side to her hip and across her belly.

"Soft skin," he murmured, nibbling her lower lip as his fingers brushed her silky triangle of curls. "Are you wet for me, sweetheart? Will you come in my hand if I do . . . this?"

Making a small raw sound, she shuddered as his fingers parted her slick folds. Emily's knees melted as he slid first one, then two fingers deep inside her, stroking the ultra sensitive flesh that was already pulsating with the beginning of a climax.

"Like that?" Max murmured as her entire body tensed and shuddered around his hand. He pressed his palm hard against her clit and she came hard, crying out his name as her internal muscles clenched around his fingers.

Her head spun, and her nails dug into his shoulders as wave after wave rolled through her, leaving her weak. She dropped her forehead to his chest. "Score one for you." Her voice was muffled against his chest, she felt drugged with pleasure. His laughter vibrated against her lips.

Dragging her mouth across the hard plane of his chest she closed her lips over his nipple, loving the way he sucked in a sharp breath in response. He wedged his knee between her legs and she whimpered as sensation jolted through her nerve endings. Using her tongue she outlined and stroked his nipple until it was as hard and stiff as hers became when he did the same to her.

He buried his fingers in her hair. She slowly and methodically layered kisses down his sternum to his navel, gliding her hands down his hips as she moved lower and lower, making sure she had as much contact as possible as she slid her body down his. She curled her tongue around the rim of his navel and felt him shudder. Then followed the arrow of hair down to his groin.

Her fingers found him first. Hot and silken and curved high and hard against his belly, jutting from a thatch of silky black hair. She closed her hand around him as she sank to her knees. Then took him into her mouth, loving the taste and texture of him.

She kept up the suction and a steady pressure of push-pull until his fingers tunneled in her hair, and he jerked her to her feet.

"Witch," he said hoarsely, shoving her up against the wall and hooking one strong hand under her knee to pull it up around his waist.

Crushing her mouth under his, Max positioned himself at her opening, then plunged inside her wet heat. She wrapped both legs around his waist, almost pulling them off balance, but Max pressed her between his body and the wall as he pounded into her, giving no quarter. Emily came again in a huge wave of sensation that went on and on.

Max shouted out his climax, his body almost crushing hers against the tile as he continued to move, the tendons in his neck standing out in sharp relief.

It took a while, and two more climaxes, before Max hauled Emily out of the shower. Her skin was flushed and dewy, her eyes heavy-lidded and sexy as hell. "I'll never be able to walk again," she said faintly as he lay her on the bed and followed her down.

"I'll carry you."

She curled a heavy arm around his neck and pulled him half over her damp body. "Don't you think"—she said thickly, kissing his eyelid—"that carrying me around with you while you work will limit your job performance?"

Not if he carried her in his heart, Max thought, stunned that the thought had entered his brain. Fucking *forget it,* he told himself flatly. He was a T-FLAC operative. T-FLAC operatives weren't domesticated. That was fact.

Rolling over, he pulled her against his side, wrapping his arms around her slender body. He'd like to flatter himself that she'd miss him when he left. But she'd get over it. She had before. Got herself "almost" engaged to Franco.

She'd be fine, Max thought, feeling feral and out of sorts and ruining a perfectly good orgasm buzz by overanalyzing things. Stupid. She'd forget him in a few weeks. Maybe a few months. She'd move on. She'd meet some artsy-fartsy guy, get married, have a bunch of artistic kids, and live happily ever-fucking-after.

And he'd be . . . goddamned *fine*.

But just to tide him over when she was gone, in case he forgot the texture of her hair, or the way her upper lip dipped, or the way her dark eyes widened when he touched her here. And here. And there—

Max made love to her again. Slowly.

"Uncle!" she cried weakly when he was done imprinting her on his brain.

"We're going to have to build you up, woman. No stamina."

She punched him halfheartedly, her eyes fluttering closed.

"An ant could hit harder than that." He smiled against her still damp hair as he pulled her against his chest. Stroking his palm down the small of her back.

Suddenly the monitor across the room blinked, and Daklin and Navarro were in the room with them via satellite.

Horrified, Emily jerked upright, grabbing a pillow to cover herself. "Oh, my God!" she whispered. "Tell me they can't see us?!"

"They can't. What do you have?" Max asked, crossing his ankles, and pulling her against his body.

He stroked the silky skin of her bare arm, feeling the cool weight of her breasts against his chest.

"First the bad news—"

"Let me guess," Max said dryly. "Savage is no longer in Portland?"

"Why do you even *need* a team, Aries?" Daklin wanted to know. "I'm guessing you're also aware she was the one taking potshots at you at the Denver airport?"

"I figured she wanted to get Cooper out of the picture, take her place, and have easy access to Emily," Max told them.

"Yeah," Daklin agreed. "We figured that, too. Man, it's too fucking bad she's using that fine mind for evil. She managed to give the two members of her Portland team who were following her the slip at the airport. Fifteen minutes was all she needed. They picked her up again without being any the wiser."

"Considering that it was their *job* to keep eyes on her at all times, bring them both in for desk duty. This is fucking bullshit. What about her connection to the bombings?" Max asked.

"Are you asking because you want to know, or because you want to know if *we* know? Because frankly, Daklin and I haven't a fucking clue. Not yet anyway."

Max inhaled the sweet rose fragrance of Emily's hair. "Know where she is?"

"Don't be insulting."

Max chuckled. "That's what I thought. Not answering questions I bet."

"Not yet," Navarro said grimly.

"Strip her," Emily said sitting up, and scratching her upper arm, her face animated. "Strip her and look at her back."

There was a pause, before Daklin said respectfully, "We know she'll have the black rose tattooed there."

"If she's so smart, and can outwit the lot of you, I can't imagine her working for someone else, can you? She'd want to be the boss. She'd want the biggest, most flashy rose of them all, don't you think? AJ said she was vain."

"Yeah—?"

"If her tattoo of the rose is bigger, likely she's head of the group. If it's the same she's just one of the worker bees." Rubbing her right arm, she glanced up at Max, her big brown eyes glowing. "Right?"

"Yeah," he agreed. It was simple and quick. "Strip the bitch butt naked. I'll go video. *This* I want to see."

The monitor went dark. "That's very disconcerting, having people pop in and out of the room when we're naked."

"They can't see us."

"Bet they know what we were doing."

"*Are* doing."

She laughed. "That wasn't a bet or a challenge you know. We could actually *sleep.*"

"Later. Maybe we shouldn't play Russian Roulette, and use a condom this time? What do you think?"

"I think it's a little late in the day to close that barn door but, why not?" She stretched her arms lazily over her head and stretched like a well-satiated cat. "Are they ribbed?" she asked hopefully.

Max grinned as he got up and went to open the armoire to search for the packets. He shot a subtle glance at his watch. Couple more hours with her wouldn't hurt.

"How come all your clothes look clean and pressed?" she demanded as he came back to bed with a couple of foil packets.

"If I tell you I'll have to kiss you."

She lifted her mouth for his brief kiss. "Some mysterious person here does your *laundry*?"

"She's not mysterious." He stroked her breast, loving the softness of her skin, and the responsiveness of her nipple at the lightest touch. "Her name's Natasha."

"Hmm. Exotic. Is she pretty?" Emily teased, stroking his chest.

"I've always been attracted to women who don't shave their legs or moustaches."

"I'll rush out and buy Rogaine immediately."

She closed her eyes, falling into a light doze in his arms. Max reached over and picked up the sketch Daniel had done of her. He'd stuck it in his pocket at the villa, and forgotten all about it. Until he'd found it in an envelope attached to the laundry he'd picked up after the briefing.

Christ. He was struck anew at how lovely she was, even in one dimension. And his father had captured her brilliantly with the swift stroke of his pen. In the studio, Max hadn't looked any further than the symmetry of Emily's face on the page. He'd observed nothing more than the beauty of her big, long-lashed eyes and at the slight sexy bow of her mouth. His observation of the sketch had been ridiculously short-sighted.

This sketch revealed exactly who Emily was on the *inside*. With clean simple lines, the artist had captured her resolution in the curve of her jaw. He'd unveiled the empathy and compassion in those big brown eyes. He'd drawn her mouth with just the beginning of a smile, showing her wry humor and her joy for living. He'd shown her pigheadedness by the pugnacious jut of her chin. Compassion and acceptance shone from a face filled with character. It was obvious she'd looked at the artist and seen a man. Not the brilliant artist his father was purported to be, but a man who'd made mistakes. A man who was human, and fallible. And she'd loved him anyway. How the hell had he missed all this?

It was unfortunate that his father had used this amazing sketch as a piece of scrap paper, and doodled around the edges of it. Perhaps he could have it cut down and—

He sat up so quickly he woke Emily.

She blinked, still half asleep. "What happened?"

"Take a look at this."

"Oh, Max," she said, pleased as she propped herself up on her elbow. "You kept it."

"Look at the words. Tell me what you see?"

"Um . . . OILY MAGI HAIL INFANCY? What am I missing? What does that mean?" She tilted his hand so she could see the sheet of paper better in the light from the bedside table. "HANG JUTTED SMELT?! Hmm," she murmured thoughtfully, nibbling her lip. "A DAMAGE IF NO HOT RIOT. Max, I'm sorry. But none of these word groups makes *any* sense at all. Look at this one. FETCHING HONOR TRIMS."

He got off the bed and walked over to pull on his clothes.

"Why are you getting dressed?" Emily asked, puzzled.

He grabbed a notepad and pen from the desk, and came back to sit on the bed. "I think these are anagrams."

"You do? Of what?"

"I'm not sure. But I believe Daniel knew something before he died."

"Something? Something like what?"

"What connects Daniel, you, Brill, Elaine Ludwig, and Tillman?"

"The paintings. Fine, I get that. But oh, my God, Max. You don't think your *father* was somehow involved in the *bombings*? It seems really far-fetched."

He got up again and went to the armoire, removed the file folder Norcroft had given him the day they visited Tillman's home. "Let's see if any of these paintings match his anagrams."

"You start. I have to get dressed if I'm going to be

able to concentrate." She got up and pulled on jeans and a plum colored wide-necked T-shirt that fell sexily off one shoulder. Barefoot, she padded back to the bed, sitting in the middle with her legs drawn up and her chin on her bent knees.

"I'm not good at puzzles, but I'll give it a shot. I need a piece of paper and a pen, too."

Max handed her what he was working with, and went back to get another pad and pen from the desk. They both worked silently for several minutes.

"Hand me the file— Thanks." He flipped it open, and started going through the sheets of closely typed papers, scanning the lists. "What does PENITENT MARY MAGDALENE mean to you?"

"Titian painted it in 1565 . . . You know, don't you?"

"Know what?"

"Know that Richard Tillman hired Daniel to copy that painting for his collection."

"That's what it says on this manifest. Yes. But that's not the whole story, is it?"

Even though she wasn't sure if her secret had anything to do with the bombings, she *had* to tell Max, Emily knew. Promise or no promise, it was past time. "Daniel had Guillain-Barré syndrome," she told him. "I don't know if you know anything about the illness. It's an inflammatory disorder in which one's body's immune system attacks the nerves outside the brain and spinal cord. And although it's rare, in his case, parts of the brain itself were attacked. He had severe weakness and numbness in his legs and arms, but managed to hide it for years."

"With your help."

"Yes. With my help," she wasn't ashamed that she'd helped a friend. "He was devastated that he could no longer do what he loved more than anything. You have to realize, Max, that your father was a proud man—okay—to be honest, he was vain as hell. But with just cause. He was a brilliant artist, and his inability to paint crushed his spirit, as well as his ego.

"He couldn't bear anyone knowing that he could no longer even hold a brush. He refused to go out, wouldn't even see his friends. Ironically his low profile just added to his mystique."

"You did his work for him for how long?"

"For the past six years or so. He taught me everything I know, it was the least I could do. I'm not sorry. I promised Daniel that I would never tell a living soul. But I don't think when he made me promise that he meant I had to withhold the information from *you*.

"So it was me, not Daniel who did the painting seven years ago. By the time the final sale went through, and Tillman got the provenance papers, et cetera from the Hermitage in St. Petersburg, and then had it delivered to Daniel, he could barely hold his brush."

"Christ, Emily. And it never occurred to mention this to me?"

It had occurred to her. Several times. "I didn't find it relevant," she admitted honestly.

Max's lips tightened, and his eyes were flinty with

287

annoyance. "Well apparently it is. Because it says right here in Tillman's paperwork that the Penitent Mary Magdalene was donated to the church in Australia. The same church that was bombed two weeks ago."

She put a hand to her throat. "God."

"How about this for fucking coincidence? OILY MAGI HAIL INFANCY? *The Holy Family.* That was the charred remains of the painting at La Mezquita."

"Your father was commissioned by Richard Tillman to do that. But I did it."

"Yeah. I figured. So it wasn't *Daniel's* work involved in the bombings. It was your painting that were—are. Yours and Brill's—Who else?" Max rubbed the back of his neck. "I think Daniel knew something was going on, and tried to leave clues in the form of these anagrams."

Emily chewed her lower lip. "I agree. But who was he leaving them *for*?"

"Whoever would want this drawing. You?"

"Maybe. Probably. It was one of the last things he drew. And it certainly caught my attention that he didn't use his usual methods. Wrong paper, wrong medium." Her heart clenched. "Whoever is responsible for the bombings somehow knew he knew, and killed him before he could tell anyone."

"Without a doubt." Max narrowed his eyes as he scanned the sketch, turning it this way and that to read the words written around the edges. "Can you tell me what paintings these other anagrams identify?"

Emily looked at the letters, trying—and failing to rearrange the letters to put the nonsensical words into titles. Lifting her eyes from the pad she'd been scribbling on for almost five minutes, she slowly shook her head. "I'm sorry, Max. There are thousands upon thousands of paintings out there and Tillman's collection is private, so no complete list of his holdings exists."

"So there's no way to tell if the manifest Norcroft gave us is accurate or even complete?"

"After being in his home, it's clear Tillman didn't favor a particular artist. He collected everything from Renaissance masters to Allesso Baldovenetti and Andy Warhol. And those are only the ones I know about."

Max cursed, then grabbed the phone off the bedside table. "Send a runner. ASAP." He slammed the receiver down.

"Runner?" Emily asked.

"To get this to our geek-squad. They'll probably have these unscrambled in under five minutes."

"Handy."

"Definitely," he said, his jaw tight. "In a matter of minutes, three paintings have been linked to three bombings. I think we'll find dozens more in here." He tapped his finger on the file. "Tillman commissioned hundreds of paintings, and donated the originals to possibly a hundred different religious groups. We need to know which ones. Fast."

There was a brief knock at the door. Max got up

with the file folder and his father's sketch of Emily. "Stay put. We're not done."

Max handed the file to the runner and closed the door, turning around just in time to see Emily trying to get off the bed.

"Max?" Her voice was weak, and she wasn't kidding around. What the hell? She held out her hand, then her eyes rolled back. She crumpled to the floor before he could reach her.

"Emily? *Emily!*"

Max knelt at her side and pressed two fingers to the pulse under her jaw. Thready and uneven. The bluish tinge around her mouth wasn't exactly encouraging. He reached up and grabbed the house phone with one hand, then jabbed the speaker button and pressed zero.

"Emily, honey?" he asked, hardly hearing the desperation in his tone. Nothing. His heart thumped hard against his rib cage as he leaned down and tried to gauge her condition by the strength of her breath against his cheek. Respiration shallow and strained. Christ. She was fine—fucking better than fine—not three minutes ago.

"Operator."

"Aries. Get a medic and crash cart in here now!"

Her skin felt like ice against the furnace heat of his own body. He was far enough away from the bed that he couldn't reach the covers. He considered picking her up and carrying her the few feet to the bed, but was scared to move her.

Shit! He rubbed a hand down the soft, but chilled

skin of her arm. Felt the heat near her shoulder, and turned her limp body to see what the hot patch was on her upper arm. Faint redness, slightly swollen, about the size of his palm with a couple of small bloody dots in the center. She'd been scratching it earlier, he remembered. Spider bite? Mosquito? The cause of her distress or fucking nothing to do with it?

He had never, in all the years he'd been a T-FLAC operative, been more afraid than he was right now. Where the fucking hell was the crash cart and a god-damned doctor? "How—"

"ETA one minute." The woman's voice was calm and efficient, while Max's rising panic had a stranglehold on his heart. Holding Emily against his chest, he wrapped his arms around her, trying to cover as much of her with his own body as he could to keep her warm.

"I'll stay on the phone with you until they get there, okay?"

He was no longer listening to the operator. He had enough medical field training to know that, whatever the cause, Emily was in serious trouble. She was breathing, so CPR wouldn't help. She was cold, but not shivering. Unconscious. Unresponsive. Breathing labored. Pulse erratic.

"Fuck!" he said between clenched teeth, feeling both terrified and useless as he kept half his attention fixed on the door to the room, in anticipation of the medical team ever fucking showing up, and half on the woman lying limp and unresponsive in his arms.

What would make a perfectly healthy twenty-seven-year-old woman drop like a stone?

Preexisting condition? Maybe. His brain immediately went from natural causes to something far more likely to be found in his line of work. But *poison*? Less likely since she'd been with him for the past half dozen hours, and except for the chocolate cake Norcroft had served at Chez Tillman, they'd shared every meal. Could be something topical . . .

Heart attack. Jesus. An induced heart attack. "Stay with me, sweetheart. Just hang on," he whispered into her still damp hair. It smelled of roses and promises. The door burst open and three men wearing white coats rushed in. Two guided a gurney while the third pulled a red cart and an IV pole. "Step aside, Aries."

Reluctantly, Max rose to his feet as one member of the medical team started an IV drip while Emily was still on the floor.

"Get this shirt off. Did she fall?" The doctor crouched beside her. Max whipped her T-shirt over her head and tossed it aside. The medic moved the stethoscope's floating diaphragm over every inch of Emily's chest. Her bare chest now. Christ. She'd care, damn it. Max yanked the blanket off the gurney and covered her as best he could while they worked.

The doctor didn't glance up. "Seizure?" he demanded.

"She was fine one minute, like this the next."

The doctor rose, motioning the orderlies to put Emily on the gurney. They carefully lifted her, blanket and all, and secured her to the gurney. "Let's get her down to ICU right away. I don't like the look of this."

Not exactly comforting words, Max thought sickly. "Check her left arm," he said, following them out of the room, and down the hallway at a fast clip. They weren't running, but they were covering a lot of ground. The doctor on one side, Max on the other. They weren't moving fast enough for Max. He took Emily's limp hand, threading his fingers with hers, needing the physical contact.

"Look at her left shoulder there," Max told the doctor. "I don't know if that has anything to do with this, but it looks like some kind of insect bite."

Keeping up with the orderlies, the doctor peered at her bare shoulder and upper arm. "The swollen area? Hard to tell in this light, and while we're in motion. But it does looks like some kind of bite." He felt for Emily's pulse, and frowned. "If we were in the middle of a jungle somewhere I'd say venomous snake, maybe a poison spider or even an ant. But *here* . . ." He shook his head.

T-FLAC HQ was a secure underground facility. Operatives didn't just stroll in covered with the wildlife they picked up on an op. There were procedures and fail-safes to prevent such an event from happening. "Won't rule it out," the doctor murmured, out of breath from jogging. "But a bite is unlikely. I'll know better when I can actually see the mark magnified, and under better light."

Max rubbed the back of his neck as he battled the

helplessness and panic pooling in the pit of his stomach. She looked insubstantial and so pale lying there hooked up to a portable EKG, the ceiling lights illuminating her pale face with a sharp intensity that scared him. She was too white-faced. Too cold. Too unresponsive.

They were moving far too slowly for his liking. "Then what the hell is—"

Bleep, bleep, ble-bleep, then a long, blaring—terrifying—tone that made Max's blood run cold. "Christ—"

"She's going into cardiac arrest. Any history of heart problems?" the doctor demanded, working feverishly right there in the hallway to bring her vitals back to normal.

"Not that I know of." He didn't know enough about her. He knew *nothing* about her, Max thought desperately. Nothing that mattered in the grand scheme of things anyway. Jesus—what if they never had a chance to ask and answer the really important questions? And given that chance, did he even know what those important question were?

"Paddles," the doctor instructed. "Give me two hundred!"

While Max's own heart seemed to stop in his chest, thick, clear gel was squeezed from a squirt bottle onto the flat, shiny surface of the paddles wired to the crash cart. "Clear!"

He tensed as Emily's body twitched and stiffened as the shock was delivered. The EKG chirped once before returning to the flat alarm.

"Crank it up to two-fifty," the doctor instructed, holding the paddles out while the machine recalibrated. "Clear!"

Again Emily's body jerked as the voltage shot through her.

Bleep, ble-bleep, bleep, bleep, bleep.

"We've got cardiac capture," the doctor said on a relieved breath as he motioned the orderlies to continue down the corridor with her. The elevator doors were open and they wheeled Emily inside. Max slapped a hand on the button for the hospital floor and the doors slid closed. There was no sensation of movement, but the numbers rapidly decreased as they were taken down to the sixth floor.

"I want a complete blood panel. ABGs, CBC, CPK, Chem seven and full tox," the doctor ordered, as hospital staff came on the run. "Put her on one hundred percent O2 and push ten thousand units of heparin in a nine percent solution. Wait out here," he instructed Max as they wheeled her into an exam room.

"I'll keep out of the way. But I'm staying with her," he told the doctor implacably, accompanying everyone into the room. He was holding Emily's hand again. And unless they needed to get at her from this side, he wasn't budging. If this had to have happened, Max couldn't think of a better place, he told himself. T-FLAC employed the best doctors, and had better, more up-to-the-second equipment, than many top hospitals. Emily was in excellent hands. But would they be good enough to save her?

"Draw the blood and run those labs," the doctor told a nurse as he accepted a magnifier and bright light from one of the accompanying orderlies. He shone the light on her arm while the nurse said "Excuse me," and shifted Max out of the way so she could draw blood.

As soon as the nurse was done, Max retrieved Emily's hand again. "Could she have been injected with some sort of toxin?" he demanded, frowning. "When? How? By fucking *who*?"

The doctor shook his head. "Think you called it correctly earlier. Looks more like a bite."

"From what?"

"Fangs this small? You're probably looking for a spider."

"Inside a practically hermetically sealed fucking building?"

The doctor shrugged. "People bring in outside dirt, parasites. Insects on their clothing . . ."

"There *aren't* any known spiders or other insects in Montana that produce *this* kind of reaction, *this* quickly. I'm not buying it."

"I don't buy it either. Someone brought it inside with intent." He glanced up to make eye contact. "Feeling useless and frustrated, son? Accompany a team, and sweep that room. Whatever bit her is lethal and loose."

There was a thick knot of dread wedged in Max's throat. "What's the prognosis?"

The doctor looked at him with guarded eyes. "I'll try to keep her alive while you find that spider."

Fifteen

I'M MISSING SOMETHING," MAX TOLD DARIUS, THE phone anchored between his chin and shoulder as he paced outside the infectious disease section of T-FLAC's well-equipped hospital. "*What* the fuck is it?"

"The demand," Dare told him. "What in the hell do they want? That's what's missing here. The tangos' demands."

"They don't always fucking *make* one, you know that."

"I know Savage isn't going to break and give us anything."

Dare didn't need to remind him, Max thought, frustrated as hell. Catherine Seymour had cojones of steel. Worse, as a ten-year veteran at T-FLAC, she knew all the tricks and treats operatives had to offer tangos. She was one herself. She had a foot in each camp, and had played T-FLAC for fools for months, if not years. He embraced the slow burn of anger. It was better than the icy fear lying underneath his skin. "Call Daklin and get me that picture of Savage's tat."

"Will do." Dare paused. "I know this is cold comfort, but on the plus side, what happened to Emily couldn't have happened in a better place. We have the best medical team on the planet, and she's right there to reap the benefits."

"Until they know what the fuck the venom is they can't do dick. Not until the toxin's identified. Here comes my tech guy." Max closed the phone, stuffing it into his pocket. "What'cha got?" he demanded as a bald, middle-aged man with thick black-rimmed glasses approached. The young, fairly attractive blonde walking to his right easily kept pace.

Max knew the guy from the encryption department.

"Hey, Max," Saul Tannenbaum hailed from twenty feet away. Other than the three of them there was no one else in the well-lit corridor, and all the doors were closed. Including the one behind which they were monitoring Emily.

There was a comfortable waiting area at the end of the hall, with good coffee, snacks, TV, even a computer—hell, everything that would make someone's wait more comfortable. But Max wasn't leaving until Emily was out of the woods.

"Rebecca Santos, Max Aries. I put Becky here on this Tillman list you gave us, and she's put two and two together for you and came up with five." Saul didn't appear fazed that they were holding a meeting in the hospital corridor at eleven o'clock at night. "Check this out."

He handed Max the file folder Max had gotten from Norcroft and had turned into the department for analysis. "Here's a list of all the paintings and other assorted works of art Richard Tillman has purchased in the past ten years. We figured ten years was far enough back for our purposes. And of course we only know about the work he purchased legally, and that's in the file you gave us."

Max flipped the single-spaced pages one after the other. There were hundreds of sales line itemed, with the date, seller, dollar amount, and other details. "And?"

"We cross-referenced the anagrams on the drawing you gave us to the titles of the paintings on this list," Santos told Max, pointing at the list with a short, unpainted nail. "Then compared that to the donations Tillman has made over the same ten years to various religious organizations."

Max glanced at the door, wishing to hell he had X-ray vision. Or that they'd make his life a thousand times better and open the fucking thing. Two words. That was all he needed. "She's fine." That was it. Not a lot to fucking ask was it?

"Sir?"

He forced his attention to the page. "Yeah. You cross-referenced the name of the work, and the donations to the locations. Got it. What did you find, Santos?"

"There was one more element I brought in." Max glanced at Saul, wishing the sincere young woman would hurry the hell up and tell him what he needed to know so he could start pacing again. His phone vibrated in his pocket, and he grabbed at it like a lifeline. He glanced at the screen to ID the caller. Not about Emily. "Aries. Hang on, Dare." He looked at the woman. "Keep going."

Santos stood up a little straighter, tugging the hem of her jacket down before she spoke again. "Tillman donated two hundred and seventeen paintings to churches, synagogues, and temples. If you turn to page seventy-three B, you'll see that I've indexed each work to its new location."

Max flipped to the page she indicated, his eyes scanning down the page, then turned to the next and the next. Jesus. He met her eyes. "This has all been authenticated?"

"Absolutely."

"Good job. Send this in the report to Darius on Paradise ASAP."

"Yo," he said into the phone.

"The lab found an empty vial in Emily's purse," Dare told him.

"How come I'm right here, and you're thousands of miles away, and you get this intel before I do?"

"Not a popularity contest, Aries. I'm your Control. It's my job to collect and assimilate. Nothing in the vial, of course. Manufactured in China by the billion. Which tells us squat. What they did find was a latent print."

"Alistair Norcroft," Max said grimly not waiting for Dare to tell him. "Son of a bitch. He made a big fucking production of helping Emily after her purse spilled all over Tillman's floor the other day."

"I've saved you some time," Darius told him calmly. "Having the lab run matches between the symptoms of Brill, the other restorers, and Emily."

"They better fucking be doing it *fast*," Max told the other man flatly. "They're fighting like hell to keep her alive."

300

"Everyone is on this, Max. Emily will make it. In the meantime I've dispatched Daklin and Navarro to pick up Norcroft."

"Yeah, well pick up Tillman's son, too, while they're at it." Max paused, still scanning the long list of donations and locations. "See what one or both of them have done with Tillman senior while they're at it."

"You think the assistant and the son were working together?"

"I think one or both of them is a Black Rose asset," Max said grimly. "Here's the deal with Tillman's paintings. The encryption people have linked the paintings to recent bombings. Every church, syna-gogue, and temple that has been bombed in the past ninety days received a painting donated by Richard Tillman." Sibilant voices behind the door. That was fucking *it*. Max paused to listen in the hope someone was on their way out of Emily's room to remove the garrote from around his heart. *Mind.*

"Tillman senior?" Dare's loud exhale signified his disbelief.

"I doubt old Tillman wired up those bombs himself, if he even knew what was happening. But what the hell, for all we know, the old bastard could be the head of Black Rose." Max started walking at a fast clip down the long corridor to get rid of some of the excess energy building up like a pressure cooker inside him. What the hell was taking so damn long?

He never should have taken the phone call out to the

hallway; the wily doc had locked the door behind him and wouldn't let him back in.

"And maybe *Auntie's* the head of Black Rose," Dare said sarcastically in his ear. "Auntie" ran the Paradise Island hotel where Dare was currently living.

"Thanks for that visual," Max said, amused at the image of the large Polynesian woman as the head of one of the most lethal tango groups in the world. "That woman probably could run a small kingdom from right there in her master suite. But I think we can rule her out." Black Rose assets tended to stay away from the deep-fried plantains. He turned at the end of the corridor and started back.

Saul and Santos were long gone. The only things left in the long corridor aside from him were a red molded plastic chair and an empty Styrofoam cup on the floor near Emily's door.

He picked up speed, his soft soled shoes soundless on the linoleum floor. "According to this list, we have over a hundred otherwise unconnected bombings, linked directly to Tillman's donations. Most of the explosions went unnoticed because the various religious leaders didn't want to report them. Afraid of the repercussions within the community."

"So whoever is behind this escalated the bombings."

"Yeah. Black Rose throwing us a red herring? I don't get why they didn't just claim the damage they did—hell, they still aren't raising their hands. Now a pretty freaking chilly pattern is emerging."

"Don't jump to conclusions."

Christ, Max thought, feeling the familiar rush of adrenaline as all the previously unrelated pieces started falling into place like tumblers in a safe. "Here's a fact—with each bombing, real estate and collateral damage have grown exponentially." He and Dare were on the same page here.

"The most spectacular being this latest bombing. La Mezquita," Darius finished. "How many paintings are unaccounted for?"

"Nine."

"And the final body count?"

Max stared at the closed door. "Too fucking high."

Max scanned the report for a second time. Spiders. He had a new respect for the lethal arachnid. The fact that the spider's dead body had been found squashed within the rumpled sheets of the bed where he and Emily had made love didn't give him any satisfaction. Nor had the fact that the room had been swept and fumigated, and they hadn't found any more spiders. One eight-legged killer had been enough.

Leaning against the wall, Max pulled out his cell and used his thumb to speed dial Dare.

"Darius."

"They found a Sydney Funnel-web spider in our bed," he said without greeting.

"Funnel-web?" Darius repeated, surprise in his voice. "Shiny dark brown buggers with a dark purple abdomen?"

There were several color pictures of the damned

thing in the folder. "That's the one." Max ran a hand around the back of his neck where the muscles had locked an hour ago. This particular spider's bite was lethal.

"Sure it wasn't a Trapdoor or a Mouse spider? They look very simil—"

"It wasn't," Max said grimly, pushing away from the wall.

"Has the antivenin been administered?"

"The doc just gave it to her. We won't know anything for another hour or so."

"She'll be all right, Max."

"She better be."

If Emily had been bitten en route to Montana, thousands of miles away from medical attention and the antivenom, the ending to this report might be chillingly different.

Left to its own devices, his brain wanted to connect Emily to his heart. Which was bullshit. He passed by the desk and laptop with a printer that Rifkin had set up outside Emily's room. Max wasn't leaving her, but he didn't want to disturb her either. There'd be a parade of people from various divisions coming down to report their findings. The jigsaw puzzle pieces of the op were starting to come together. The picture wasn't completely clear, but the image was starting to come into focus.

He'd been on ops where he'd lain in the wet grass/mud/water/on a rooftop, *without moving,* barely breathing, for five hours straight. Now he fucking couldn't stand still for a few minutes without feeling as though he was about to jump out of his own skin. To think he'd always thought of himself as a patient man.

Except when it came to Emily. It was an unwelcome revelation.

There were nine hundred steps to the end of the corridor. He'd walked it fifty-six times, encountered forty-four people in passing in his travels, consumed seven cups of coffee, drunk two bottles of water, gone to pee twice, and sat down once. His body was out here in the corridor, but his mind was behind that closed door with Emily and the doctors.

He could have sat dead still for hours if they'd damn well let him in there with her. Even though he had absolutely no imagination whatsoever, he couldn't get the picture of Emily's pale face out of his mind. She'd looked translucent. Insubstantial.

She'd looked, God damn it, as though she were seconds from being dead. That's what his job had done to her. That's what his trying to protect her had done.

Life vs. T-FLAC.

He realized that he hadn't heard a word Dare had said.

"What are you doing?" He could hear Darius tapping at his keyboard.

"Clearly not sleeping," Dare answered absently. "I'm cross-referencing. Let's find out which of our suspects took a side trip to New South Wales recently while we wait. Call me the second you know about Emily."

The phone went dead. Two seconds later it vibrated again. Max hadn't even dropped it in his pocket yet. "Aries." He made the turn at the end of the long hallway and headed back.

"Daklin. I have a four-one-one. Savage has the Black Rose tat on her back all right—"

Emily had been right. "No surprise there; is it any bigger or smaller than any others we've seen?"

"It's not a rosebud," Asher Daklin informed him. "It's a fully open flower."

"Jesus fuck," Max breathed. They'd been able to ID Black Rose assets over the years because of the tightly furled rosebud tattooed in the small of their backs. The full-blown rose Savage sported was sure to indicate she was the *head* of the worldwide tango group. It was hard to believe she'd been operating right under T-FLAC's noses, undetected, for years.

"The head of a tango group a T-FLAC operative? Shit. No wonder they were always two steps ahead of us. Savage had access to everything *we* knew about the Black Rose."

Max was livid. She of course knew where every safe house was located. She was the one who'd hit Wies-baden.

Savage had snuffed out the lives of the very people she was supposed to be protecting, and shielding and perpetuating the activities of the same people she was supposed to have been eliminating. "You better believe we'll close that goddamned gap ASAP. From here on out everything is going to be even *more* compartmentalized around here. Hope they take the death penalty off the table. I want to know the traitorous bitch has concurrent life sentences and will remain locked up in a small cell until the day she dies."

"You'll get your wish." Daklin didn't sound any less furious than Max felt. "But don't start mailing out congratulatory cards just yet. Savage had *two* tats in the small of her back." He paused. "The rose and a *lily* bud. Black Rose wasn't the name of the entire group, Aries. It was merely the name of a *cell*. We have a sleeper tango organization, apparently called Black *Lily* that we knew fucking *nothing* about."

Fifteen minutes later, Max was *finally* allowed into Emily's room. While it had seemed like an eternity to him, he had to thank God for the speed and effectiveness of the antivenin.

He pushed open the door and strolled in. Mildly concerned, business as usual. She didn't need to know the condition of his guts or the discomfort of the hole he'd gnawed in his cheek.

She was hooked up to a monitor and drip. The room was dim, and filled with a steady *beep-beep-beep*. Though she was still a little on the pale side, she smiled the second she saw him, and held out her hand. "Hi."

Max looked at her beautiful face, a face he now knew better than his own, and his chest hurt. Despite the previous few hours, despite her wan smile, despite it all, her large expressive brown eyes shone with her love for him.

If you love someone, set them free . . . The words came to mind out of nowhere. He didn't know where he'd heard or read them, but the truth was unmistakable. He had to send Emily as far away from himself and his job as possible. If his enemies didn't succeed in killing her—*eventually*—his own death would.

If she felt half as deeply as he did, his death would annihilate her. And in his line of work that wasn't a possibility. It was a certainty.

It had never bothered him before.

He cleared his throat as he approached the bed. "Welcome back." He took her hand, forcing himself not to gather her up against his heart—*chest*—and hug the hell out of her. Maybe not let go. He hooked a chair leg with his foot and dragged it up beside the bed. Still holding her hand, he sat down, his muscles relaxing for the first time since he'd watched her drop like a stone what felt like a year ago.

He brought her hand to his mouth and kissed her soft palm. Her touch was a temporary balm to the widening ache inside him.

An hour. He'd give himself an hour. Then he'd rip himself away from her like a bandage from an open wound. Better that way. For her. For him.

Emily reached up and stroked the side of his chin with the back of her hand. The vulnerability, fear, and . . . *something* indefinable in her big brown eyes worked like a vise around his chest. "Thank God you weren't bitten as well."

He would willingly have fielded a hundred venomous spiders' bites to protect her from the one. "Hide's too tough. How are you feeling?" he asked, taking both hands in his so she'd stop making those distracting little circles with her knuckles on his jaw.

Her smile didn't reach her eyes. "Like someone who almost died. Just guessing. It's not like I've ever actually faced my own death before. How do you do it?"

"It's my job. I've done it for so long that I don't think about dying." Until now. *Until you.* Fuck. "I've got—Hang on." Max reluctantly let go of her hand, and reached into his pocket to retrieve his phone. Some ass was cutting into the most important hour of his life. "Aries," he growled.

"We've got a problem," Dare said.

No shit. Max thought as he struggled to yank his attention away from the soft outline of Emily's breasts as she breathed. He would carry a picture of her body, of her dolphins, of her lush mouth, into the next lifetime with him.

"Yo. Aries?"

"Yeah." He got up and moved away from the bed so he could focus. "What's the problem?"

"Just heard from La Mezquita. Samples from the point of detonation taken at the bomb site showed higher levels of radiation than would be expected."

"Say what?" He really needed to concentrate. He rubbed a hand across his eyes. "The painting was rigged with nukes?"

"Nope, but it sure as hell wasn't painted in fifteen hundred and whatever. According to the geek squad, the suspect painting had to be done after 1945. Something about worldwide, post-Hiroshima radiation levels being absorbed by white paint. Bottom line? Tillman, Norcroft, Tillman junior, or any combination of the three, were passing off copies as the originals."

"So where are the originals?"

"Working on it."

Max snapped his phone closed and shoved it back in his pocket.

Emily's brow was pinched together as she struggled to sit up. "Originals?" she asked over the aggressive beeping of the monitor.

"Relax, okay?" Max helped her sit up, then shifted some of the wires and the tubing from her IV so it wasn't obstructed. He stuffed several pillows behind her. "You'll pull all this shit out of your arm if you flop around like that."

She raised a brow. "Flop—? Never mind. Original *whats*?"

"The painting that exploded in La Mezquita wasn't the original, it was a copy. An excellent copy, but a copy nonetheless. It almost fooled the lab people."

"Are you telling me that it was my copy hanging at La Mezquita? Not Mr. Tillman's original? That would be wonderful! Losing the copy would be no loss at all. But there's no way they would know that. With no modesty whatsoever, I can tell you that my copies can withstand the hardest, strongest scrutiny. It would take longer than a few hours to tell the difference. I'm good, Max. So was your father. We didn't paint

310

copies. We *replicated,* down to manufacturing our own pigments and dyes, down to producing our own canvases, down to tying our own brushes. The paintings we did were identical in almost every way possible to the original."

"The fragments came here to the T-FLAC lab."

She thought about that for a nanosecond, then said with a small smile, "Okay. Let's say that they're right, and they *could* authenticate that the painting that was blown up was my copy." Her expression said she didn't believe even T-FLAC was *that* good. *That* fast. She frowned as she leaned against the bank of pillows.

She chewed her lower lip as she pleated the sheet with her fingers. "The whole point of Tillman getting people to produce copies was so that he could donate the original and *keep* the copy." She pushed her hair out of her face and sighed. "Okay. I can see by your expression that you believe the *Canigiani Holy Family was* my copy. But what if it wasn't? Let's say for a second that your lab is wrong. It wasn't my copy, but *was* the original. Priceless paintings of that historical importance don't just waltz out of a building once they're in. There's always heavy security and a chain of custody is carefully documented to protect a painting's provenance."

He cocked his head, listening, prepared to go with a different hypothesis even though he'd pit T-FLAC's expertise—in anything—against that in the regular world. "What about before it reaches the building? How would that work?"

She pressed her lips together. "It wouldn't. Unless the owner or curator was in on the fraud."

Max sat on the chair beside the bed. "Suppose he was."

"Tillman?" she asked. "You think Tillman's donations were all a scam? That for whatever reason he had us make perfect copies, then donated the *copies* instead of his originals? To what end?" She ran her fingers through her hair and tugged. "I'm not disagreeing with you. I'm just trying to make sense of it all."

"For one thing, you and Daniel made exact replicas. It would take a normal lab weeks, if not months, to uncover the fraud. And because you're that good, it would be almost impossible to tell the original from a copy. What if the plan was to donate those excellent copies all along? What if they knew the painting would be part of an explosion. An explosion that would destroy all the evidence? Why blow up an original when they could replace it with an excellent fake?"

Emily shook her head in disgust. "Think about his house. The man doesn't exactly have discriminating taste. He wanted to look good to the media for whatever reason, but also wanted to hold onto his valuable paintings." He watched as she put two and two together. "The son of a bitch had his cake and ate it, too. What a jerk."

"That, too," Max couldn't help smiling because she was adorable when she was pissed. Pink bloomed in her cheeks and her dark eyes held a glint of fire.

I miss you already, he thought tenderly. "I believe several of Tillman's donated masterpieces, or their copies, have blown up in the last several months. Far too many to chalk up to coincidence."

She bit her lower lip as she gave that some thought. "Okay. I'll go there with you. But where's the benefit to him? Why bother? You said he's never had an altruistic bent until what was it—ten or so years ago? Why suddenly find religion and a conscience, and claim to want to give away his entire art collection? He wouldn't do something like that for a tax break. The man's got more money than Midas."

"Pretend he didn't. How would he go about switching copies for originals?"

"The switch would have to take place between the authentication process and the actual delivery. That could only happen if he handpicked the authenticator and got the receiving institution to agree to accept that authentication."

Max reached up to brush a strand of hair off her cheek with his finger. The satin feel of her now-flushed skin broke his concentration. The only way he'd be able to focus was if he put some physical distance between them. Emily was just too much of a temptation.

He got up and went to lean one shoulder against the wall. "If you were Tillman, who would you use?"

"I can think of about a hundred possibilities for authenticators."

"Can you narrow it down? Maybe concentrate on the Denver metropolitan area?"

"Jim Praley is highly regarded as a Renaissance expert," she said, though she was shaking her head as soon as the name spilled from her tempting mouth. "But I'm telling you right now, *he* wouldn't be part of any scheme."

"He wouldn't necessarily know, though, right?"

"True. There's a woman at the Denver Art Museum. Her last name is Heller, Hellman, something like that. I've heard good things about her."

"That's a start," Max said, already texting the names to Darius. "If I get you a pen and paper could you make a list?"

"Sure."

"If you're not up to it, we can do this later."

She grinned up at him. "No we can't. I am starting to understand you a little more, and I get that everything you do is time sensitive."

Sixteen

I'LL HAVE SOMEONE BRING YOU PAPER. GET SOME sleep." Max pushed away from the wall. "Gotta go."

Emily didn't point out that it was the middle of the night, nor did she ask where he suddenly had to go *to*.

He had to go. Of course he did.

It took everything in her not to toss the covers aside and beg to tag along. "You could always sleep here with me." Okay. That sounded pathetic. She fluttered her eyelashes, and tried to give him a come-hither look. It made him smile. Too bad the smile didn't reach his eyes. He was already gone. Tears burned behind her lids. "No, on second thought," she threaded a teasing smile into her voice, even though her throat had closed and it was hard to speak. "You take up too much room. Go find a bed somewhere and get some rest yourself, you look like hell."

If she knew Max, he wasn't going anywhere to sleep. As far as she knew he never slept. He was going to work. And for Max that meant danger.

"Yeah. I'll do that," he muttered, not even attempting to sound sincere. He started for the door, then spun on his heel and strode back to the bed. Sliding his fingers into her hair at the temples, he tilted her face up and crushed his mouth down on hers. The kiss was hard and wet, and as brief as it was, curled her toes.

When he released her, Emily slumped back against the pillows, her mouth throbbing and her heart doing somersaults that made the monitors beep. He brushed her hot cheek with his fingertips before he stepped away from the bed. "Write that list, then get some rest."

"You, too. See you in the morning."

He turned at the door, scanning her face as if he was trying to imprint what she looked like onto his synapses. "Sweet dreams," he muttered gruffly before walking out.

With her pulse still singing from the kiss, Emily

stared at the closed door, her eyes narrowing with suspicion. She'd seen that look before and it made her chest tight. "You bugger. What are you up to?" His scent hung in the air, fueling the desire burning in the pit of her belly.

She wasn't ready for their relationship to end. In fact, Emily rolled the edge of the sheet between her fingers absently, she'd been hoping that they could at least try to make it work. Perspiration beaded her brow as she imagined what he would do if she told him how she really felt. Reaching over to the end table for her bottle of water, she acknowledged that it would be a huge risk. A man like Max would probably go running and screaming at the mere mention of the "L" word.

He'd run before, even without the messiness of love.

On the other hand, not telling him posed a different kind of risk. If she kept quiet she'd very likely spend the rest of her life wondering "what if?" Neither option was particularly appealing, but she had to do something. Knowing was better than not knowing. Even when it hurt.

She was restless despite her recent brush with death. Or maybe because of it. Each missed opportunity was a wasted chance to be happy. As the minutes ticked off on the clock mounted on the wall, a sense of foreboding began squeezing the life out of her heart. Apparently Max Aries could succeed where the spider had failed. She sipped from the bottle before returning it to the table.

"Get a grip," she admonished aloud, her voice echoing off the sparse walls. She closed her eyes and ran her fingers over the memory of his kiss freshly tattooed on her lips.

Her eyes sprang open when she heard the door creak. "You—" Her smile slipped when she saw a young woman in a white lab coat carrying a pen and pad in one hand, and a dry-cleaning plastic bag in the other.

"Mr. Aries asked me to bring this right away." The nurse handed Emily the pen and notepad. "I'll hang these up for you," she said, holding up the plastic bag. "Cleaning washed everything to get rid of the fumigation smell." The efficient woman then proceeded to unpack and hang Emily's clothes in the narrow wardrobe.

"You caused quite a stir. And you had a lot of visitors, all strays who wanted to get a peek at the rarely sighted Max Aries pacing a hole in the floor. There, good as new." She closed the narrow door. "I'll put your undies in this drawer, shall I?"

Put my *undies* in my suitcase, wherever that may be, Emily wanted to tell her. But she was more interested in the anomaly of Max worried. "He was pacing?" Calm, collected Max Aries?

"I've never seen a man more worried. Oh, don't get me wrong," the nurse hastened to assure her. "You were in excellent hands with Dr. Howard. He's absolutely *the* best. Aries insisted. Lucky for you the doctor hadn't left the building after his shift. He got to you within those critical first few minutes. Absolutely saved your life." She closed the drawer, and gave Emily a girl-to-girl smile. "But if sheer *willpower* could have saved you, Max Aries could have done it. He's somewhat of a legend around here, you know."

"He is?" Emily again tried to imagine Max marching back and forth outside her room. The image just didn't gel.

"We don't see him in the building that often, and rarely down here. He's always in the field. Most operatives take breaks, come here to relax and/or go to the gym, which is on this floor, but not Max. He's famous for three-hour turnarounds."

Now *that* hyper-Max she could imagine. "Do you know where he is now?" *Since apparently you're his biggest fan,* Emily thought, knowing she was being overly sensitive.

"Oh, he's gone." The nurse checked the monitor, and replaced the IV drip. "Need anything before I leave?"

Yes. Max. "I'm good, thanks." She held up the pad. "Should I ring when I'm done?"

"I'll have the nurse on the next shift pick it up. Think you'll be done in an hour?"

Of course he was gone. But did that mean gone as in left the hospital floor? Or gone—left the building? Or worse—gone on a flight to God only knew where. "Sure."

The nurse left.

It took longer to come up with the names because

318

she mulled over every word and gesture Max had made in the last twenty-four hours. Trying to come up with a clear and realistic evaluation of his feelings.

Hers were clear-cut. His were murkier than week-old espresso.

Half an hour later Emily was bored and cranky and peering over the precipice of self-pity. And done with Max's list. "So glad I could be of some freaking help," she told the absent, annoying man. She should have seen it coming, she thought as she waited for someone to come and get the list. She remembered someone else, and added his name while she waited, then drummed her fingernails on the paper in her lap. She should go to sleep. Her body certainly needed it. It had been a long, eventful day. Unfortunately, her brain was like a rat on a wheel.

He's gone. Been here, done this.

"That was a good-bye kiss, wasn't it, you bastard?" She sketched Max's face on the next page, then added horns, fangs, and a pitchfork. "It isn't over until *I* say it's over," she mumbled as the door opened to reveal a stern-faced male nurse in his mid forties.

"Hi there. Iris said you'd be done with whatever needs to go to Darius?" He took the notepad Emily handed him. "I'll see this gets to him right away." His voiced lowered as if he suddenly realized how gruff he sounded. "Can I take some of those pillows to make it more comfortable for you?"

Emily shrugged and nodded, deciding that sleep would make the time pass faster. He gently extracted the extra pillows so she could lie flat and her tense muscles eased.

"Do you need something to help you sleep? No? You need to get some rest, Miss Greene. Don't worry, unlike regular hospitals I won't keep popping in to check your vitals." He smiled as he turned off the light over the bed. "You'll feel a hundred percent in the morning, I promise you. There's a bottle of fresh water right here if you want it, and I see Iris left you a couple of cookies in case you get the munchies before breakfast."

"Thanks," Emily yawned.

After straightening the covers, he turned off the overhead light, plunging the room into the dim glow of the monitor. "Ring the bell when you wake up, and someone will come in for your breakfast order. Buzz me if you need anything during the night, okay?"

"I'm exhausted, I'm sure I'll sleep like a rock. Thanks."

The door closed, cocooning her in the warm darkness. But it wasn't enough to lull her active brain. She counted all the paintings she'd copied over the years, and the ones she'd done for Daniel. She counted her winter sweaters, and her favorite sandals.

Rolling onto her side, she gave in to what was really on her mind. *Max where are you?* And will you come back?

Once she'd finally nodded off, Emily slept surprisingly well, all things considered. She rang for the nurse to unhook her from the IV and the monitor, took a shower and dressed, then ordered breakfast.

Feeling more in control wearing her own jeans, boots, and a pale lemon sweater, she flipped through the pages of a current woman's magazine while she waited. She used the word *control* loosely. She was in the bowels of a building, somewhere in the heart of Montana, with no purse, no money, and worst of all, no Max.

Since she doubted T-FLAC would put her on the payroll and leave her in ICU for the rest of her natural life, Emily figured someone would be in eventually to spring her.

The more she thought about what Tillman had done, the more angry she became. He'd used her. He'd used Daniel. He'd used all of them. Worse, if Max was right, and she believed he was, Richard Tillman and/or the people working for him—people like Norcroft—were responsible for the deaths of hundreds of people. Certainly for Jacoba Brill's death, and Daniel's. And the Bozzatos'. And almost her own.

She glanced up at the knock on the door. Max didn't knock.

"Oh, you're up and dressed already," the young woman said in the too loud, too cheerful tone one used for the mentally challenged and small children. Her short, wildly curly hair was a pretty shade of blond—natural, Emily would bet. She wore dark pants and a white, man's shirt covered by a blue-and-white striped apron. She was pretty and perky, and as friendly as a puppy. She made Emily cranky, she was so sweet.

The good news was she was carrying a loaded tray.

"I put my shoes on all by myself, too," Emily said dryly, setting aside the magazine as the young orderly slid the tray onto the table beside the bed.

The younger woman had a cute, infectious smile. "Sorry, I've been moonlighting in the nursery, and I tend to forget how to talk to adults." She removed the covers from the plates.

Eggs, grilled tomatoes, a small steak, hash browns, and freshly squeezed OJ as well as a stack of whole wheat toast and a carafe of coffee. The food smelled wonderful and Emily's stomach gurgled, reminding her that it had been forever since she'd had a decent meal. If she couldn't have Max she might as well have good food. Yum. The orderly cast a quick glance at Emily as she handed her a napkin. "God, I'd trade ten years of my life to look like you. You're stunning. I mean, *really,* stunning. Are you a model?"

The girl was sweet, but Emily was starving. "Only a model patient." She cut a bite of the juicy steak and shoved it into her mouth, savoring the taste.

The girl started straightening the bed. Probably not in her job description. Emily scooped up a forkful of fluffy eggs.

"You must have guys falling over their tongues to get at you."

"There's only one I want. And I'd prefer he didn't step on his tongue, I quite like it just as it is."

"Is it true you came in with Max Aries? Oh, my God." Her face went pink. "That man is *hot.*"

"Hmm," Emily murmured noncommittally. "Thanks—" She glanced down at the photo ID clipped to the pocket of her apron. "Carol." She cut off another bite of meat. "I've never had steak for breakfast before, but this is amazing."

"It's locally raised beef," Carol said with a smile, placing the magazine Emily had been reading on the table beside the tray. "Good choice. Local is always better. Is there anything else I can get you?"

"No, thanks, I'm . . . Actually, *yes.* I need a phone." There wasn't a phone in the room, and no one had brought her tote, which held her cell phone and charger. And her wallet. Passport and driver's license. Damn.

"This is a secure facility," the young woman began apologetically. "If there's someone you'd like us to contact—"

"I have to make a really important call. Can you find me a phone somewhere. Please?"

The girl pulled her own cell phone out of her pocket. "Here, use mine."

"It's an overseas call, I'll pay you back when I get my—"

"I have a zillion minutes." She waved a hand. "Don't worry about it."

"Great. Thanks." Emily said, snatching the phone. After dialing the country code, she quickly punched in the numbers to reach Antonio Caprio.

"Pronto?"

Thank God he was home. Carol's off-the-cuff remark

about local being the best choice got Emily thinking. If Tillman wanted an Italian Renaissance painting authenticated and to not have that authentication challenged, he'd use the best of the best. And that person was Antonio, world-renowned expert. He was definitely the go-to guy when it came to Italian Renaissance.

In rapid Italian, Emily peppered him with questions. As she suspected, Antonio had traveled to Denver several dozen times in the past few years, all at the behest of Tillman's assistant, Norcroft. As an assistant, Norcroft could have been doing his boss's bidding, or he could have been acting on his own. Not that it mattered. What mattered was that she had a solid lead to pass on to Max.

She thanked Antonio, urged him to be careful, and then hung up. "How do I get in touch with Max?" she asked Carol. One more thing Max hadn't shared with her. Not one freaking *scrap* of contact information.

The girl's blue eyes widened. "I don't know. I just serve food. I'm not an operative."

"Who would know?"

"I can ask my supervisor," Carol offered. "It may take me awhile. I'm not exactly on the 'eyes only' list around here."

"Can you have someone bring my purse, and the rest of my things?" Her cell phone was in her purse. She could try the number she'd used to call him when Daniel had died.

"Oh, sure. No prob." Carol left the room and Emily picked at the food.

When no one returned in the next half hour, Emily got up and tried to open the door. She was not prepared to sit in here all day waiting and reading the same magazine all day. She twisted the handle.

She was stunned to find the door locked.

Her heart jumped up into her throat. Why would they lock her in? To prevent her from wandering around a secret facility? Probably. The logic of that didn't annoy her any less. In fact, it pissed her off. Going back to the bed, she grabbed the buzzer and rang for a nurse. She wanted to go. Now.

She wanted the rest of her clothes, her money, and her ID. And while she didn't know where the hell Max had disappeared to, he could always find *her.*

She was going home.

Her anger mounted as her repeated summonses on the bell produced not a single freaking soul. "Where the hell *is* everybody?" she demanded, slapping a hand on the closed door. "Hey people! Patient wants out! Come and get me!"

No one came. She couldn't hear anyone outside the door either. Had she heard footsteps and voices before she'd realized the door was locked? She couldn't remember. Other than the nurse at eight, and Carol and breakfast at nine, Emily hadn't seen a soul in hours. There'd been no follow-up visit from the doctor either, which she found strange.

"This is *way* too *Twilight Zone*-ish for me." After an hour she figured they'd just forgotten about her, and were busy with other patients. *Eventually* a nurse would have an ah-ha moment and come racing in.

When nobody came racing in Emily went from furious to scared, and back to furious.

She paced the small room. Reread the magazine. Lay on the bed. Jumped up. And paced some more. Pounding on the door was a waste of time, and hurt her hands. Ringing the buzzer was useless as well. She'd run out of cuss words in the first hour.

Hour two of pacing had her imagining a nuclear attack. Everyone had vacated the building, and her decomposed body, when found, would have a half-life of a million years.

Max would be sorry as hell that he'd left her here.

It was nearly three full hours later when a man and woman entered her room.

Emily rose from the chair she'd been sitting in long enough to have the shape of the chair imprinted on her butt. "About time. I appreciate the accommodations, folks, and the T-food was great, but I have a life, and I'd really, really like to get out of here." She was so angry, she didn't want an explanation. She just wanted to get the hell out.

The man was tall and bulky and dressed from head-to-toe in black. The woman was exotic with features and coloring that made country of origin or even race indiscernible. She wore bright red lipstick, and was also dressed in sleek, tight-fitting dark clothing. They didn't introduce themselves.

Which was fine and dandy with Emily. She would be hard-pressed to be polite at the moment.

"You're getting your wish, Miss Greene." The woman, who was wearing designer, black-framed glasses, handed her a small stack of clothing—black, of course—and a pair of lighter than air black sneakers. "Please change quickly. Aries instructed us to bring you to him without delay."

Irritation warred with relief as Emily accepted the clothes. "Really? Then perhaps he shouldn't have left me here cooling my jets for hours. Where is he? And if I find out he had anything to do with my incarceration I'm going to do him bodily harm. A simple, 'Emily, I need to keep you secure. I'll be locking you in for your own safety,' would have sufficed." Her jaw ached from grinding her teeth together.

"That's on a need-to-know basis. Aries asked that your departure from the facility be discreet. Please change quickly, we have a plane waiting."

"I can assure you, I need to know."

"Then I'm sure Aries will fill you in once you're on board." The man glanced at his watch. A very nice Rolex Submariner. She recognized the ebony face. She'd given Daniel the same watch for his birthday several years ago.

It was ridiculous standing here arguing. They weren't going to tell her anything. And it wasn't as if she wanted to stay down here forever. Emily went into the bathroom to change. Max probably wanted her to go back to Richard Tillman and see if she could identify any more paintings.

Which she was happy to do. Nice of him to bother

asking her himself. But en route to wherever he was taking her, she had some personal questions she wanted answered by T-freaking-FLAC operative Max Aries.

Seventeen

IS IT ALWAYS THIS QUIET IN THE AFTERNOONS?" EMILY asked her two companions. She knew the answer. No. From what she'd seen on the two occasions she'd walked around T-FLAC's headquarters, there'd been at least a few people one bumped into in passing. Several of the doors to various offices had been open when she and Max had arrived yesterday. She could easily be in any multistory office complex. But now all the doors were closed, and the brightly lit hallways were empty. A faint slither of foreboding crawled down her back.

The kind of intuition that she would normally dismiss as an artist's imagination. But it hadn't been her imagination when a stranger had broken into her palazzo and tried to kill her. It hadn't been imagination when she'd walked into the Bozzatos' home and sensed that something was horribly wrong.

She'd ignored her rusty intuition when they'd been pulled over by the fake *polizia* and she'd almost been kidnapped.

Emily straightened her shoulders, outwardly keeping a smile on her face just as inwardly she promised never to ignore her intuition again. If she made a fool of herself, so be it.

Flanked by the two operatives, she stopped walking. They each took an extra step before halting and Emily's skin chilled. God. This was insane.

No matter how stupid she felt asking two *maybe* T-FLAC operatives to ID themselves in the counterterrorists' own building, she asked anyway. "I'd like to see your identification." Looking from him, tall and deadly, to her, who appeared just as dangerous, and back again. Every flight instinct in her body was telling her to get the hell away from these two. *Fast.*

"Are you out of your mind, Miss Greene?" The woman grabbed Emily's arm tightly just above the elbow. "Look around. We don't have time for this shit. Who do you *think* we are?"

I think that just because you dress like ducks, and carry weapons like ducks, you're turkeys. "You didn't introduce yourselves," Emily pointed out, striving to sound both puzzled and reasonable. Tipping her hand wasn't in her own best interests. They hadn't been holding onto her when they'd been walking, even though the couple had flanked her from the moment they escorted her from her room. Now the woman's fingers dug into Emily's arm like a vise.

Maintaining eye contact, Emily peeled the woman's fingers off her arm one by one. "I don't like being manhandled. I'm perfectly capable of walking on my own."

The woman's red lips thinned as she let her hand drop away. "Then *walk*. I'm Catherine Seymour," the woman introduced herself briskly, urging Emily to move. "Bob Stover. We have a finite window to reach the landing strip, Miss Greene. Aries isn't a patient man."

Definitely the bad guys, Emily knew with conviction as she reluctantly fell back into step with them. Max was the personification of patience. Annoyingly so.

Emily had seen a photograph of Catherine Seymour. The woman speaking definitely wasn't the same person she'd overheard Max and his team discussing. In addition to being a traitor, the real Catherine Seymour was a well-endowed, tall redhead. The woman next to her was barely five foot two, brunette, and built like an adolescent gymnast. Emily might not know who she was, but she definitely knew who she wasn't. The knowledge wasn't comforting. The only reason for anyone to yank her away from T-FLAC headquarters stilled her blood but her brain kicked into overdrive.

Get away. Quickly.

"Will you be going with us?" Emily asked as she scanned the corridor up ahead. *Come on T-people. Where the hell are the good guys with big guns? I need rescuing here!*

"We're to deliver you to the plane. We'll receive orders there."

Dead or alive?

Wherever the rest of the T-FLAC personnel were, they weren't *here*. While it would be dandy to sit right down on the floor and wait for the guys in the white hats to save her, Emily realized that wasn't going to happen. Any rescuing that was to be done would have to be done by herself. They were approaching a bank of elevators. If she made a run for it, they'd probably shoot her. They had the guns, and the corridor was damn straight. They wouldn't miss. She figured if these two were smart enough to get inside such a high security facility they were smart enough to kill her and efficiently dispose of her body without a trace.

The elevator doors pinged open. The three of them walked inside. The doors pinged closed and the elevator began to climb.

If they'd wanted to kill her, Emily reasoned, watching the numbers above the doors climb from five, to four to three, then she'd be dead by now.

Two.

One.

Ground level. They wanted her outside. Alive.

Good. She was fine with that. Outside was open space. Outbuildings. Places to hide. The chance of someone seeing them and alerting other someones.

The man used two key cards at the front doors. Then held up something half wrapped in plastic and pressed it to a scanner.

Emily choked back bile as the man slipped the severed finger back into his pocket.

OhGodohGodohGod. Definitely the bad guys.

Snow lay thick on the ground, and the icy air bit into her lungs with each rapid breath she dragged in. Sunlight reflected back from the stark whiteness as they stepped through the doors of what, from the outside, looked like a modest ranch-style office building. Emily knew the airport was less than five minutes away by car. If they were actually going to the airport.

A black car with tinted windows sat in the driveway about fifty feet away. If she was going to make a run for it, she'd damn well better do it before they got her into that car.

If she was wrong, and they'd really been sent to bring her to Max, then she'd apologize like hell. Later. But she was trusting her instincts and making a run for it.

Now.

To the left was a row of low buildings, beyond that an enormous open field, beyond that—*way* beyond that—trees, beyond that, mountains. Boy, talk about being out of her comfort zone. Not an art gallery for miles, Emily thought as panic continued to build, almost choking her. How in God's name was she going to get away from two armed and determined people?

All she knew was she would die trying because it was either make a break for it here, or get into that car and die somewhere else.

It was a lose/lose proposition.

"Bob" went around and opened the driver's side door and got in.

"Turn the heat on. I'm freezing," "Catherine" instructed, then placed a hand on Emily's back and shoved her toward the car. "Get in front."

Catching her balance as she staggered, Emily dropped to one knee on the stamped concrete walkway. "Go ahead, I just need to retie my sh—"

She felt a prick on the side of her neck and tried to swat away the hand beside her face. "Nooo da . . . mn i . . ." The ground came up to meet her, and everything went black.

"You fucking let them *take* her?" Darius demanded.

"Someone with inside knowledge sent them in to take Greene," Marc Savin, head of T-FLAC, said calmly. He and five of his key strategists were seated in the secure boardroom on the third floor. Darius, one of his best operatives, and the one who had decided to waste his training to live in Paradise, looked incongruous in his Hawaiian shirt on the big screen at T-FLAC HQ. Dare was another loose end that needed tidying, Marc thought, draining the cold coffee in his cup.

"We were impressed that they managed to get inside and activate that particular alarm code," he told Dare. The alarm code that placed everyone inside their respective offices, and locked the doors from the outside. The thought was that if anyone—anyone at all—somehow managed to breach T-FLAC's intense security at ground level, it would be almost impossible for them to breach any of the floors below. And if somehow they managed *that* near impossible feat, then they couldn't access any of the labs or sensitive communication stations.

In theory, the plan had worked. If Marc hadn't permitted the first fingerprint/keycard entry, the couple wouldn't have gotten farther than the lobby on ground level. While the couple were his guests he'd been secretly collecting data about them. While his people ran face recognition scans and X-rayed their bodies, Marc had watched their bold progress through the building on his monitor.

They'd known *exactly* where Emily Greene was located. Not just the floor, but her room number. They were in a labyrinth of offices and labs filled with custom-designed electronics, state-of-the-art encryption software, surveillance technologies, military-grade and prototype weaponry, sensitive and classified scientific and forensic equipment. A veritable buffet of tools any terrorist organization would give their eyeteeth to acquire. All that at their fingertips and yet Greene had been the prize.

"We've only ever run that as an exercise," he told the irate Control evenly. "It worked without flaw."

"Great to know tangos can masquerade as operatives and lock down the entire facility," Dare said, angry. He was a giant, a bear of a man, and an angry Darius was a frightening sight indeed.

Marc wanted him back doing what he did best. The man was wasted as a Control, no matter how good he was at that aspect of the business. He should be back in the field. But that problem was for another time.

"They didn't," Marc pointed out, dragging the coffee carafe across the table, and pouring himself the umpteenth cup of the day. "We made them before they hit the perimeter. At no time was Emily in any danger while they had her in the building. The tangos weren't informed that the codes for lockdown changed three times a day. Doesn't mean we couldn't let it *appear* to work."

"Bullshit."

"We had them under surveillance at all times."

"She's not under surveillance *now*," Darius snapped. "And before you tell me we have their flight plan monitored, we can't see what the hell they're doing to her *inside* that aircraft. We'd better be able to explain this to Aries or he'll ream us all new ones."

"Message received," Marc told him. "But the end justifies the means, and you know it. Savage is a key player in Black Rose, and we have her in custody and being interrogated as we speak. Yet she *still* managed to grant her people access to this facility."

"No," Dare said dangerously. "You granted them access to the facility."

"Six of one. And since I'm the one the buck stops at, that's my prerogative," Savin reminded the other man. He didn't owe his people any explanations for his actions. He'd taken a risk. That was his job. "I wanted to see what lengths they'd go to. If they wanted her dead, either of them was capable of snapping her neck in the first few minutes.

"They didn't," Marc pointed out. "And even if they'd *tried,* someone was close enough to prevent them from physically harming her. They were under tight surveillance the entire time. After trying their damndest to kill her, suddenly they appear to want Miss Greene *alive*. I want to know why. And, God damn it, I want to know *who*."

"Could be Black Lily," Darius offered. "But so far we have nothing, nada on this new group. Why did they suddenly pop out of the woodwork full grown to demand a billion dollars?"

"By four tomorrow."

"Yeah. By four tomorrow."

"We don't know that these two yahoos are part of Black Lily. Jesus, we're not even sure that there *is* a Black Lily." Dare was like a pugnacious dog with a bone.

"Yeah," Marc smiled. "We are. Body scanning revealed they both have the black lily tattoo on their backs. Same as the rose faction. Who is in fucking charge? I want *that* person. And these two were entrusted to break in here, a big fricking deal. They'll lead us up the food chain. Unfortunately, Miss Greene is collateral damage."

"Jesus, Savin," Darius spluttered, in no way intimidated by who he was talking to. "Try telling *that* to Aries. As soon as he hears what you allowed to happen, he's going to go in there and have your guts for garters for authorizing this, then he's going to start reaming new assholes."

"He has bigger problems at the moment."

"Yeah," Dare said grimly. "The tangos are planning to detonate a bomb somewhere in twelve hours. Aries thinks it's the Vatican. That *would* take precedence." Darius rubbed an enormous hand across his jaw. "When this all shakes out, Max'll ask . . .You're tracking their flight plan. Where are they taking her?"

Marc hesitated. "Rome."

"You better be sure about this, Aries," Asher Daklin muttered as he, Max, and Navarro strode down the 218-meter-long nave of St. Peter's Basilica. Even though they were only a few feet apart, the only way Max could hear Daklin was through his headset. They were like lemmings going against the tide as thousands of people swarmed in the opposite direction.

" 'One of the biggest sacred sites in the world' was what they claimed. Could be any of a hundred *biggest*. I pick this one." He wasn't doing this alone. T-FLAC had called in everyone they could. Time was passing as millions of objects all over the world were simultaneously being searched for bombs.

They had people at the Seville Cathedral in Spain. In China, at the Giant Buddha of Leshan Temple. In Indonesia, at Borobudur, the largest Buddhist temple. Cathedral of Saint John the Divine in New York, as well as Temple Emanu-El, the largest synagogue in the world. In Russia, they were frantically searching the Church of Christ the Savior, and in Utah, the Salt Lake Temple. More operatives searched the largest churches, synagogues, temples, and churches in England, Thailand, Mexico, and India. T-FLAC had called in every local, national, and international law enforcement agency and all counterterrorist forces they could get their hands on to assist them on this worldwide bomb hunt.

Max's gut told him the device was here in Rome. Here in the Vatican. Here in St. Peter's.

"What if I'm wrong?" he said into his lip mic. "The Pope will run me out of town on a rail? I'm not even a practicing Catholic."

"Some of us are," Navarro pointed out.

Max spared a glance for the unhappy crowds being moved around them to the exits. Italian police and military personal had been activated to help with crowd dispersal and control. It was a daunting task moving thousands of people without causing a riot. Even the Swiss guards, in their ridiculous yellow-and-red costumes, were doing a great job moving people along. "Yeah, all these people who came in for the eleven A.M. Mass." Tourists by the ton, locals, residents. The Vatican was wall-to-wall people, every one of whom had to be cleared to a safe distance. Just in case.

They were frightened, confused, angry, and irritated.

Not that he wasn't sympathetic to their confusion, but Max was inclined to tell those weeping and wailing that they'd have a hell of a lot more to cry about if they and their precious church were blown to hell and back.

"Move it, people," he muttered, wanting them out. Thousands of pairs of eyes were searching for the detonation device, sweeping every building, every nook and cranny, every painting. It would take more time than they had. Everyone knew that.

Inside the Basilica alone were forty-five altars to search, hundreds of priceless paintings to inspect and an equal amount of statuary. It was a daunting task. And that was just in the Basilica itself. The Vatican was made up of *dozens* of buildings, each holding thousands of works of art. Any one of which could be hiding the bomb.

Max switched to the open com. "This is Aries, people," he said in fluent Italian. "We have five hours, seventeen minutes, and a handful of seconds to find our target. If you find anything—anything at *all* suspicious—contact me immediately. Good luck."

"We're all gonna need it," Daklin said in his ear.

"Amen." That was Navarro.

Eighteen

BRING HER OUT OF IT. WE'RE ABOUT TO LAND. I WANT her fully aware when we arrive." Emily heard the words but her brain had a hard time focusing. The male voice sounded vaguely familiar, but when she tried to put a face to it, her thoughts slipped and slid just out of reach.

Whatever she was lying on was hard, and vibrated in time with the dull droning sound echoing inside Emily's aching skull. Even the pinprick on her upper arm went barely noticed, although a part of her struggled to make sense of it.

She drifted off, feeling a tag of terror that seemed draped in gauze. She was scared of something. Someone. Who? She dropped into a void.

She woke up to find herself slumped in the backseat of a fast-moving car. Emily slitted her eyes, searching for landmarks.

A sign read: ROMA—FUIMICINO

Rome.

What the hell was she doing in Rome? Her memory of the who and how was perfectly clear right up until the bitch sitting beside her had given her that shot that had knocked her on her ass.

Still, being back in Italy was a plus. Not only did she have tons of friends in Rome, she knew her way around extremely well. All she had to do was figure out a way to get out of the car, and she'd be home free.

"Why isn't she waking up? Did you give her enough of the drug to bring her out of it?" *Now* the voice was familiar. Alistair Norcroft.

"She's awake," the woman said, sounding amused.

Emily opened her eyes and sat up. For someone who'd been drugged for at least ten hours, she felt surprisingly good. Thirsty, but other than that, fine. "Care to tell me what you think you're doing kidnapping me?" she demanded without preamble.

"Ah, there you are. Thank you for joining us."

"Did I have a choice? Where are we going, and why are you allowed out on the street without a keeper?" Emily tried to put a hand on the back of Alistair's seat, then realized she was handcuffed with thin plastic cuffs. "Kidnapping is against the law both here and in the States. I presume you're aware of that, but don't care?"

Norcroft laughed. "You're a delight." He turned around, his elbow on the seat between them. "Do you have any idea what a charming pawn you've been to me, my dear Emily?"

"A little unfair not giving me my own pieces to move about." The lights were synchronized, and every time Emily thought she might have a shot at escaping, the light turned green again. "Isn't it just a masturbatory effort if you play alone?"

"Oh, you played, Emily. You just weren't aware of it."

"You're the one whose been doing his damnedest to kill me?" The knowledge didn't surprise her one bit.

Cocking his head, he pursed his lips. "You've proven to be a worthy adversary."

"If you've been trying to kill me, then why am I here, still very much alive?" Unless the sick bastard was like a kid pulling the wings off a bug, killing it in increments. The thought scared the crap out of her.

"Anyone who had connections to Richard and his artwork had to die. You must see that. I couldn't have anyone putting two and two together like Daniel did."

"Yet here I am."

"You'll be my pièce de résistance, my dear."

She didn't like the sound of that. Not at all. "How did Daniel figure out what you were doing? What exactly, besides killing people left and right, *were* you doing?"

"Daniel Aries and I were great friends. You weren't aware of that, were you?" Norcroft smiled, a toothy smile.

"And I'd care why?" Was a light ever freaking going to turn *red*?

"*Daniel* was the one who came up with the scheme. A brilliant man, I admired him enormously. At first he helped me amass an enviable collection of artwork. Then over the years he made copies that we sold on the black market. It was a lucrative sideline for both of us. And from there . . .Well, that story is for another time."

Nice to know she'd *have* another time.

"Richard was a selfish, uncouth man." Norcroft rested his chin on the hand he had draped over the seat back. "His humble beginnings showed in everything he touched. I tried to teach him about art, music, and the like. But he never got it. He was—"

"This isn't that interesting," Emily said cutting him off mid oration. "Can you skip to the end?"

"You're an extremely rude young woman."

"Thank you." Their eyes locked. Emily felt as though a thousand spiders walked across her skin. She kept her gaze fixed on his anyway.

He blinked first. "I decided to immortalize Richard," he continued. "Turn him from a curmudgeonly, selfish, white-trash ignoramus into an altruistic, God-fearing philanthropist."

"And how did he feel about that?" There had to be a way to get out of this damn car. *Somehow.* And she had to be ready to take whatever opportunity was presented to her. Casually she moved her right foot, resting it on the bump in the middle of the floor. Her knee now blocked Norcroft's view of her hands as she tried the door handle.

She wasn't surprised to find it locked.

They'd have to open the door at some point, and she'd be ready.

"Richard had no idea. I'm sure if he'd been aware of his surroundings, he might have had an opinion. But he was by that time a vegetable. I had to keep him alive a little longer than I'd planned because his board of trustees wanted to see him once or twice a year. Annoying and inconvenient, but I did what had to be done."

"Then you killed him. What did his board say about that?"

Norcroft's smile was bogeyman-under-the-bed scary. "He just flatly refused to see them. I was of course suitably distressed, but very helpful. They found that dealing with me was very much more to their advantage than it had ever been with Richard. They stopped asking to see him years ago."

"Cut to the chase. Why did you have his art collection copied? Were you trying to defraud the insurance company? Keep the originals to sell? Have the last laugh? What?"

"Don't jump the gun, dear Emily. That's for the end of the story." Alistair glanced at his watch. "Oh, we have a good twenty more minutes to fill before we

arrive at our destination. Let me start at the beginning." He twisted his body around a little more and
made himself comfortable.

Pompous ass. Emily turned to look out of the
window. *Via Ostiense.* Where were they taking her?

Was Max aware that she was no longer safely
ensconced at T-FLAC headquarters? Would he show
up to take her to lunch, say, and discover she'd been
abducted from beneath his very nose? And wasn't that
nose going to be ticked off.

On the other hand, he was probably off somewhere
doing his job and saving the world. It was hard to fault
a guy who did save-the-world stuff. There was a
reason the man had remained single all these years.
Emily wanted to sigh. Trust her to fall for such an
inaccessible guy.

"I'll start at the beginning, shall I?" Norcroft rested
his chin on the back of his well-manicured hand as
they passed the *Colosseo Quadrato* on the right.

Emily slewed her eyes to look at him. "Why don't
you start at the end and work your way backward?"

"Oh, the end for you will only be the beginning for
me, my dear Emily."

She redirected her gaze to the traffic passing them.
"I'm bored already." The Lungotevere. The one-way
street running parallel to the Tiber. There were *dozens*
of bridges crossing the river. Every one with a light.
Every one of which was green.

The woman beside her bit off her chuckle when
Norcroft shot her a fulminating glance. "I was an

ambitious young man," he said, pleased with himself. "But it was hard to move out of the abject poverty I lived in with my family. Oh, by the way? I've ensured that the lights will continue to remain green until we reach our destination. So you may give me your full attention. We will not be stopping between here and there.

"Now, where was I? Oh, yes. My father was an annoying drunk who could barely hold a job. I killed him for the insurance money. That was my first kill. I was seventeen, and the check was a miserly five thousand dollars, but it got my mother and me out of Idaho. A four point oh—"

She'd been watching the lights up ahead for them to change, and it had taken a second or two for what he was saying to register. "You killed your own father?" He was right. The *semafori,* the traffic lights, had been green all the way.

Norcroft gave a half shrug. "A homeless man was convicted of the brutal crime. Where was I? MBA from Wharton. All well and good. But I still had no money to repay student loans. I answered an ad to become the assistant of a very wealthy older man."

"Richard Tillman."

"No. Hugh Stillwell. He was old, wealthy, and very, very trusting. I'd only been working for him for a matter of months when he took a fall right after he attempted to fire me for some minor infraction. I couldn't have that. I was comfortably ensconced in my new life, and quite enjoying it. The fall didn't kill him, but he was incapacitated and without the power of speech until the day he died, ten years later. Extremely unfortunate to take that kind of tumble at his age. He taught me a lot."

There was an entire unsavory story behind Norcroft's casual words. Emily really didn't want to hear it, but she had to ask. "Did you push him?" They passed the old gate to the city and the gray stone pyramid called *Piramide Cestia*. They could be going *anywhere* north!

"You're astonished at my patience aren't you? I remained in his employ for every one of those ten years. A faithful and devoted right-hand man. Ten years to collect everything. In those ten years, I distributed most of his funds and made my own informed investments. He had no family, and of course left everything to me."

"He was a vegetable?"

"His eyes were very expressive."

Emily pressed her bound hands against her stomach where nausea roiled. "He knew you pushed him?"

Norcroft smiled. "Every miserable, immobile day of his life."

The car turned left on *Ponte Vittorio Emanuele*.

They were heading toward the *Vatican*.

Oh. My. God. Surely not? "Are you planning to bomb *St. Peter's*?"

"Tsk. Tsk. Now see? You've jumped to the end of the story and spoiled my surprise."

"Are you insane?!"

"Now that isn't a smart question to ask a man, my dear Emily. What if I *were* insane? And your question incensed me so much I had to do *this*." He half flung his upper body over the seat and hit her so hard across the face Emily's head bounced against the window.

She tasted blood in her mouth and brought her hands up to touch her split lip as he subsided, his elbow casually hooked over the back of his seat again. "Does that answer your question?"

Stark raving mad.

His pale eyes flickered to the woman seated next to her. "Do you have any concerns, dear Greta?"

Dear Greta with the very red lips was squished into her own corner trying to become as small as possible. "None whatsoever."

"Then," Norcroft continued as if there'd been no interruption, "I had great wealth, but no power. Power requires wealth and contacts. I merely had wealth. And wealth I wasn't eager for people to look at too closely. And I needed a hobby. Everyone should have a hobby. Richard Tillman became mine."

"A *man* became your hobby?"

"Are you asking if he was my lover?"

The thought hadn't occurred to her. "Actually, no. People usually learn to play the piano, or decoupage, or bird-watch as a hobby."

"The answer of course—turn here, Georgiou—is yes. Richard and I became lovers several years after I went to work for him. That was almost twenty-five years ago. Almost as long-term as any marriage. What made it even cozier was that I began an affair with his dear wife Esther at the same time." Norcroft smiled fondly. "Sweet woman, rather empty-headed, but well-meaning. I much prefer women as sexual partners, but since men tend to have more power I've never been adverse to sleeping with either sex to get what I want. Dear Esther became tiresome after a few years, and I had to stage a break-in to get rid of her."

The man was a sociopath.

"I found the art of death fascinating, and while I led the police around by the nose, tried my hand at various other methods of death by natural and unnatural causes. It was really too easy. Fun. But no challenge at all. The police were convinced they had *two* serial killers on their hands." He looked dreamy, and Emily shuddered. "But no. I got bored and decided to stop. Really, all that killing was better for me than any sex, any time. But I needed to keep my mind and body clean and clear to focus on what my real calling was.

"Richard was a besotted fool, introducing me to all his wealthy and influential friends over the years. I became everything to him. Friend, lover, nurse, and right-hand man." Norcroft smiled. "I gave him servitude with my right hand, and robbed him blind, and started my little hobby, with the left."

"I've become exceedingly fond of the Sydney Funnel-web spider over the years. Really, one could hardly find a better, more discreet partner in crime, could one? One bite mimics a variety of unpleasant, and fatal, deaths by natural causes.

"His son Prescott and I have been enjoying the fruits of our labor ever since. Such a pleasant young man, didn't you think?"

In the few minutes she'd been in the same room as Richard Tillman's son Prescott, she'd summed him up as an arrogant, rude ass. "Not really."

Norcroft glanced over his shoulder to see where they were, then instructed the driver to go around the back.

They'd arrived at the side entrance to St. Peter's Basilica. Despite the warmth of the spring sunshine streaming into the vehicle, Emily felt a chill permeate her blood.

"Come along, my dear. I'll finish the story when I have you neatly tucked away inside."

Max pressed the earpiece a little more firmly into his left ear as he listened to a conversation between Marc Savin and Dare.

"He's not going to believe we did a billion-dollar wire transfer that quickly," Savin argued.

"Now *that* I can agree with," Dare said, clearly puffing on one of the cigars he favored. "We hold off on the transfer until three fifty-eight."

"Christ," Max interjected. "That's cutting it damn close to the bone." He was in charge of the over two thousand men and woman who were combing their respective grids all over the Vatican's dozens of buildings. And others were still attempting to get the civilians off Vatican property.

Just under two hours to go, and that short amount of time wasn't going to make a dent in what there was left to search. With ten times as many people and a hundred times the time margin—maybe.

"My concern is this," Max said, running his hands, with the delicacy of a lover, down the sides of a small gilt picture frame. The church was cool, but he was sweating, his entire focus on finding the fucking bomb.

"We've checked all the paintings on Tillman's list of donations to the Vatican. Nada. But just in case we missed something, we've had all the paintings moved off site. The bomb disposal unit is going over them again, this time with a fine lice comb. Frankly, I don't think they're going to find a fucking thing. And if the damned device *isn't* in one of those painting's frames, then where the hell *is* it?"

"Your gut could've steered you wrong," Savin offered. "Possible it's located at any one of the hundred *other* locations. Someone will find it."

"Maybe," Darius said flatly. "But I trust Aries's gut. Still think the bomb is located where you are?" he asked Max.

"Yeah, I do." Max wiped away a bead of sweat from his temple. He was about to stake is life, and those of his team on the fact that his gut was telling him that the explosive device was *here*. Somewhere. "But I don't want any of the other teams to slow down any. Time is running out. Here or somewhere else, something holy is going to go up with a big boom, and a

350

shitload of collateral damage if we aren't fast enough, and *smart* enough to find it in time."

"Then we're screwed," Savin pointed out the obvious. "And everything that's holy goes up with a big boom! Find me that bomb."

Nineteen

LOOKING INTO THE WINDOW, EMILY COULD SEE THERE was no one inside the *Ufficio Scavi*, the telephone booth–sized office tucked against the side of the building. Tourists would stand in line for hours waiting to get tickets so that they could visit the tomb of St. Peter beneath the Basilica.

She noticed with a twist of fear that there were no tourists lined up outside the tiny office. Just two Swiss guards standing outside the closed door. She swallowed. The same two guards who'd lifted the gate so that Norcroft's car could pass through the Holy Office Gate, through the colonnade to the left, on *Via Paolo VI*. The moment their car had passed through, the gate was lowered.

Taking a better look at the two men in their Swiss costumes Emily knew immediately that they were no more Swiss guards than she was. While they wore the colorful uniforms, their jaws weren't smoothly shaved, and their hair was too long. Norcroft's men?

Yeah. Without a doubt.

Since there was nowhere for her fear to go, she got a grip on it. Panicking and getting hysterical, while appealing at the moment, wouldn't get her anywhere. There must be some big event about to happen, she thought almost absently, glancing at the crowd. The Pope making a special showing or something? The oval *Piazza San Pietro* was filled to capacity with thousands upon thousands of milling people, and the noise of their raised and agitated voices was deafening.

As soon as the car had stopped, they'd boxed her in, giving her no chance to make a break for it. Red Lips, carrying a black duffel bag, instantly came up to take her position behind Emily. The two men flanked her. Norcroft linked his arm with hers, a small handgun pressed against her ribs.

The cacophony of the masses gathered in the Piazza beyond the gate precluded conversation. Which was fine with Emily. She really, *really* didn't want to hear any more of Norcroft's sick stories. She wanted to use every atom of her concentration to wait for, and take, the first opportunity for freedom.

Norcroft guided her inside the opening to the Necropolis.

Emily's window of opportunity slammed shut with a reverberating thud.

"I don't give a rat's ass if there *is* a f—is a traffic jam," Max snarled into the lip mic. He was lying on his back on the floor near the Chapel of the Column, west of the left transept, checking beneath the pews. "I want every man, woman, and child not actively involved off this property in the next hour. No, I don't give a shit *how.* Just *do* it."

There was going to be collateral damage. No logistical way around it. People would die today. A lot of people. Max knew that no matter how good, how organized, or how motivated, his people couldn't move thousands of confused and frightened pilgrims, worshipers, and tourists out of range fast enough. He could only hope to God that they were able to move most of the crowds a safe distance away in time. They'd estimated that there were over sixty thousand people on the Vatican City's grounds. Sixty thousand people to mobilize without panic.

Christ.

He hoped God was paying attention today.

He listened to the odd conversation on his headset, but pretty much everyone was quiet, heads down, searching. Every now and then he'd hear one of the bomb-sniffing dogs give a sharp bark, and he'd feel a shaft of anticipation spear through him that they'd found something. But so far no one, not even the dogs, had found the bomb.

They might not have discovered its hiding place, but Max heard every tick of the timer in his head. He counted off the minutes. He had the actual countdown on his visual headset, but for now it was off. He knew to the second how much time was left.

And then he'd be done.

He should, he thought, sliding back another few feet, have spent five more minutes with Emily yesterday. Five minutes and the truth. She deserved that much from him.

It was a damned joke that he'd tasted love while kissing her. But he couldn't think about that, and regret left a bitter aftertaste on his tongue. He ran his fingers slowly beneath the ancient wood as he used his feet to inch his body along, used his eyes and his fingers to search for wires, for plastique, for any sort of detonation device.

All he could do now was his job. If he survived, then he'd consider his uncertain future.

He found nothing more under the pew than a bunch of little wads of chewing gum stuck to the wood. And he inspected those as well.

"After you," Norcroft gestured for Emily to descend the narrow metal stairs ahead where a Ray-Banned man, looking like he'd stepped straight out of the movie *Men in Black,* stood cradling a mean-looking gun in his muscle-bound arms.

He shifted slightly to let them pass, then repositioned himself to guard the opening to the *scavi.*

Emily moved past him and started down the stairs, the others behind her. The Bataan Death March. Their footsteps echoed in the quiet as they descended into the crypts beneath the Basilica, single file.

To keep her mind off how thirsty she was, and oh, yes, how freaking terrified she was, Emily tried to remember what she knew about the Necropolis, other than that the complex of mausoleums under the foundation of the church had been built in the early part of AD 160. That was it. And she hadn't remembered that. She'd seen a small plaque with the information near the entrance.

The air was close and humid and smelled of damp earth. The lighting was dim, but bright enough to see where she was going. Emily didn't like *where* they were they going, but at least she could *see* it, she thought a little hysterically. Thirty or forty feet under the floor of St. Peter's.

She'd been here years ago with a school group, but she didn't remember her way around the labyrinth of old streets and dead ends. And she'd forgotten this glass door that required a handprint scan on the pad to enter. Very James Bond.

Very T-FLAC.

God. Where was Max? Was he at this very moment in Denver searching for Norcroft? She took some consolation that if psycho Norcroft was here with *her,* Max was somewhere safe. Cold comfort. She'd rather they were both safe, and together somewhere.

They couldn't go any farther, she thought with relief.

Behind her Georgiou rustled some plastic, and Emily flattened her body against the side wall and closed her eyes. Because she knew he was fishing another damned body part out of his pocket to hold up to the scanner. The thought made her stomach roll as she waited.

It was warm down there. Warm and just a little bit

claustrophobic. Sweat prickled around Emily's hairline as she leaned against the gritty wall, her eyes closed so she didn't have to see what was being used to open the damn door. She wiped her damp palms down the borrowed black cotton pants she wore.

The security system accepted whatever it was Georgiou held up, and the door swung open with a soft *whoosh*.

The air inside the Roman Necropolis, the City of the Dead, was a little more musty smelling, and smoky, with the dust from previous centuries hanging in the still air. The hillside city of the dead had been built to look like a city in miniature, where wealthy pagan families entombed their dead in houses so they could continue their new lives. Eventually, hundreds of years later, a church had been built on the site, and hundreds of years after that St. Peter's had been constructed, and the tombs had been forgotten.

It was the last place anyone would look for her. If anyone was looking at all. She'd never felt more alone in her life.

"Keep walking. Then take the stairs," Norcroft instructed from directly behind her, jabbing her in the back with his gun.

"You don't have to press that damn thing into my spine so hard," Emily informed him. "I'm not *going* anywhere." There was nowhere *to* go. She was going to die here with the pagans and Christians who'd been entombed in this cemetery for centuries.

She should have forced Max to stay for five more

minutes yesterday morning. Forced him to stand still long enough for her to tell him that she loved him. That she wanted more time to build a real relationship with him. That whatever his problem was with commitment, she'd stick by him and they could work it out. Together.

Tears stung behind her lids, and it wasn't because Norcroft kept the muzzle of his damn gun pressed against her middle vertebra.

Despite everything that had happened to her in the past few weeks, she'd never really believed on a visceral level that she would die.

Now she did.

She'd wanted a lifetime with Max.

Now it was too late.

Two abreast, they walked through the winding streets lined with tombs. Red Lips and Greek guy walked a few steps behind Emily and Norcroft, who moved the gun to jab at a rib instead of her spine. Hardly an improvement.

The rough brick walls of the tombs rose to the ceiling. Niches cut into the stone held tombs and sarcophagi with pagan inscriptions and ancient Christian graffito carved side by side into the worn marble. It was as if the Christians had taken over, and just added to the existing decoration. A tiny sarcophagus had a mournful relief carving of a man and his wife holding their infant son. Emily tried to interpret some of the ancient carvings as she passed them.

Loss. Loss. And more loss. But also love. The tombs

abounded with flowery declarations of love of every kind. Mothers for their children, husbands for their wives, a child for a well-loved pet. The carved pictures painted relatable scenes of human lives hundreds of years before.

Side streets branched off and held bigger mausoleums, where the wealthy were buried with their servants to wait on them even in death.

After walking along a fairly level surface, they came to a second narrow staircase and climbed down. There was another James Bond-like door that the Greek activated, allowing them to pass through. Emily vaguely remembered that the doors were to keep the humidity down. A prosaic reason, but it was a suitably creepy touch to this surreal expedition, and a chilling indication that, for her, this was a one-way trip.

The stone street veered off to the left, then opened into a small, *very* small, courtyard. It was crowded with the four of them.

And the chair.

A banged up, metal kitchen chair, with a cracked red plastic seat and a snake pit of ominous leather straps attached to it sat in the middle of the cramped space.

Norcroft grabbed her by the arm, and shoved her toward the only seat in the house. "Sit."

She resisted the downward pressure of his hand on her arm. "I don't think so." She had nothing to lose. She was going to die here, right beside the small hole in the wall covered with Plexiglas behind which lay St. Peter himself.

She'd rather be shot, get the execution over with, than continue to be played with. "Go to hell." She backed away from them, but Georgiou grabbed her other arm. She wasn't going anywhere, it had been stupid to even try.

Norcroft shot a glance at Red Lips. "Just a light cocktail for her please, Greta."

Twenty

INSIDE
ST. PETER'S BASILICA
14:50:04

NOTHING."
"Nada."
"Zip."

"Keep looking." The order was unnecessary. T-FLAC wouldn't *stop* looking for the bomb until A: They found and deactivated it, or B: The shit hit the fan. The escape clause, of course, was the billion-dollar booby prize Black Lily was demanding. Time was ticking away. Max, Savin, and Dare had agreed that if the incendiary device was not found, they would hold off on the money transfer until 15:59:55. Five seconds before detonation.

An hour and change to find the damn bomb.

Max's HMDG—single lens Head Mounted Display Glasses—blinked the countdown into his left eye. 14:50:04.The glasses gave him lateral head freedom and look-around ability in a sleek, wraparound design. They could create the illusion of a seventy-inch image appearing thirteen feet in front of him if that's what he needed. For now, a discreet clock was all he required.

He tapped his earpiece twice for Darius.

"Patch me through to Emily," he said quietly. He wasn't a fatalist, but he wasn't leaving the building until Black Lily's bomb was found. Wherever it was hidden. Like a ship's captain, Max was prepared to go down with his ship. He never asked his men to do anything he wasn't prepared to do himself. But he had a very important loose thread to tie up before his destiny came up and hit him in the face. "Dare?"

3:25 P.M.
THE CITY OF THE DEAD

Norcroft held up his hand as Red Lips approached with a syringe between her long, dusky fingers. "I've changed my mind. Let Miss Greene enjoy all the nuances of the next hour."

Emily almost fell to her knees in gratitude, although a drug-induced sleep might be better than what was coming. Still, if she had to face her own death she'd rather do it head-on, not as a drooling, unconscious victim.

He indicated the chair. "Please sit down."

"I'd rather stand."

"Sit. Down."

"I have no idea, or interest in, what your agenda is,"

she told Norcroft as she plonked her butt on the chair. Behind him the Greek guy was emptying out the duffel bag onto the stone floor. It was like watching clowns climb out of a clown car as he placed one item after the other around him in a semicircle out of the seemly bottomless bag. Emily returned her attention to the most dangerous member of the party.

"But I can assure you, *nobody* will care that I'm missing, in fact I doubt anyone even knows that I'm missing. So kidnapping me—bringing me back to Italy—is a total waste of your time. My death is to no one's disadvantage other than my own. Let me go, I promise I won't mention you to anyone. I just want to have my life back."

"Did you share your coup with the Bozzato family, my dear Emily?"

She used her bound hands to wipe perspiration off her temple. "What coup?"

"The Tillman commission."

"But I'd been doing that for years—Oh, Lord," she said appalled. "You killed *an entire family* based on the assumption that I'd told them I was copying paintings for Richard Tillman?"

"Oh, I've killed people for a lot less, I can assure you."

She stared at him, unable to believe he was sitting there, speaking so casually about an event that would be indelibly engraved on her brain until the day she died. And oh, yeah. Today might be that day, she thought with gallows humor. "Who did you send to k-kill them? These two?"

"Oh, I like to do my own wet work. Of course, I allowed Greta and another gentleman acquaintance to assist me. Great fun. Too bad—what was his name, dear Greta?"

"Bragonier."

"Ah, yes. *Bragonier.* Had to be left behind with the spoils of war."

She forced herself to breathe, because her lungs didn't want to cooperate. "How did you get out of the U.S.? The heliport! You flew somewhere else, then switched planes."

He made a voilà gesture, like a magician pulling a rabbit out of a hat. "Quite." He rubbed his chin on his hand. "You copied thirty-four paintings at Daniel's behest," Norcroft mused, watching her like a hungry cat watched a fat mouse. He silently indicated the Greek could do—whatever. "And were hired to do another twenty-five on your own. Fifty-nine works of art. Perfect in every way—Please raise your arms, my dear. Each one practically undetectable from the original. Daniel's little protégée churning out weapons of mass destruction, and proud of it."

"I wasn't *churning out* anything," Emily snapped, resisting as Norcroft's two goons tried to force her to raise her arms. "Will you damn well stop that?! I was commissioned," she said roughly, "I *believed,* by Richard Tillman to *copy* his collection for his own private galler—"

He cut her off with a blow to the face that left her face numb, and her senses reeling. "Do not talk back.

Every bomb that has gone off, in every church, synagogue, temple, and mosque, for the past three months was secreted in the frame of one of Richard's paintings. One of *my* paintings."

He hit her again, a stunning, openhanded blow that knocked her head back and caused her to bite her tongue. Blood bloomed in her mouth. "A brilliant, and carefully choreographed plan," he told her conversationally, not missing a beat.

The entire situation was surreal. Anyone listening to Norcroft would think he was chatting easily to a friend over a cocktail, not beating the crap out of a restrained woman. Even his demeanor, face, and body language didn't reflect the violence in the slaps. And they'd been more than slaps; the sick son of a bitch had put his whole body behind them.

Red Lips and the Greek were strapping her to the chair, but Emily couldn't take her eyes off Norcroft and hardly noticed. Her cheeks were on fire, her eyes watering from the consecutive blows. She had never been struck by anyone in her life, and the fact that he could do it so casually, so without fanfare stunned her.

"Why?" she asked, exploring the reopened cut inside her lip with her tongue. "Why do you hate Catholics? Or Jews? Or Buddhists? Because you hate religions?"

"What a simplistic young woman you are. No, my dear. The bombings are my calling card. I've worked for this recognition for the past seven years. Refining my plans, putting each component carefully into place."

The straps were too tight, she could barely breathe, and her head swam sickeningly because she was scared out of her mind. "And Daniel Aries was a component?"

"Hiding the bombs in the picture frames was *his* idea. Brilliant. Truly inspired. I took it from there."

If there was a way, *any* way, to communicate with T-FLAC and/or Max, maybe she could help them. Even if—"That was pretty damn clever of you." She tried to sound admiring. It wasn't easy. "Using the copies of the originals to hide your bombs. Which painting did you use? *Madonna dell Granduca? Adoration of the Magi?*" Two of the nine paintings still unaccounted for. Two of the paintings *she'd* done.

"Hmm. Both good choices, but no. The work of art I've chosen has more value, and is considerably more beautiful than any copy of an old master."

Emily started to chew her lower lip, then winced because it hurt. Did Max have a list by now of where the other paintings might be? What was more valuable than a Raphael or a da Vinci? She tried to think of some of the other artists on the list of missing paintings. Was it the Lorenzitti? Filippo Lippi's *Madonna and Child with Angels*? There'd been two Michelangelos on the list as well. More valuable? More beautiful? Than what?

Keep him talking. The more he talks, the more he brags, the better the chances I have of someone coming down here. GodohGodohGod. No one was going to come down here, *she* knew it, and *he* knew it.

She couldn't fathom why he'd brought her halfway across the world to tie her to a chair in an empty tomb.

No matter who he paid, or bribed, or threatened, *eventually* someone would come down here. St. Peter was buried three feet behind her, for God's sake. People *cared*. About St. Peter.

Her? Not so much. Her mother was in a world of her own, Susanna her sister was busy with her family. And since they weren't close, she wouldn't miss Emily for . . . months? Years?

Max might find out that she was missing. But by then it would be too late. Throat dry, but she felt the annoying tickle of sweat running down the middle of her back. "How did Daniel go from being your buddy to a murder victim?"

Greta and Georgiou finished strapping her into the chair and moved to stand behind their boss.

"He has a son who works for T-FLAC," Norcroft leaned a shoulder casually against the wall as if he hadn't a care in the world. "It was only a matter of time before he spilled his guts to Max. I wasn't going to risk all my hard work for a moment of familial bonding."

Her left eye was swelling shut, and her lip felt fat. "How do you know Max works for T-FLAC?" God. It was hard to breathe. One strap was tight across her diaphragm, constricting her lungs. "Daniel couldn't have told you," she said, taking small, shallow breaths. "He didn't know himself."

"Oh, it all came together with perfect precision. Discovering that Daniel's son was a member of the elite, infallible T-FLAC was an unexpected bonus. I couldn't have orchestrated the players any better if I tried. One of my top lieutenants works for the organization—"

"Catherine Seymour." Perspiration prickled along Emily's hairline. She licked her dry lips, maintaining eye contact. "She's in custody." A bead of sweat ran down her temple, followed by another. The tiny room was getting hotter by the minute with the four of them confined together like this.

Norcroft shrugged. "And has already been replaced. As planned, the Black Rose cell is dead, and Black Lily has risen in its place."

"What can you possibly hope to gain by killing hundreds, possibly *thousands* of people and destroying lives? Not to mention obliterating priceless works of art that can never be replaced?"

"Because it brings me almost orgasmic pleasure? Because it brings me the power that fear of the unknown and unspeakable acts of random violence elicits? Because it brings me wealth beyond imagining? Because, my dear, I *can*." He smiled. "And the paintings I've used were all copies. But then you knew that, didn't you?"

"Why did you have to kill the very people who made your plan work?"

"The very people who, if called upon, would not only identify their own work, but lead authorities back to the mild-mannered, always helpful Norcroft? You, my dear, just wouldn't die. That was unfortunate.

Because, as I'm sure you've realized by now, I'm a perfectionist. I tend to micromanage a little. But I've turned a lemon into lemonade, and am quite pleased with the results. As in any business undertaking, being flexible and rolling with the punches is part of being an excellent manager."

He was a damn scary megalomaniac. And she, unfortunately, was a captive audience. "Why did you drag me here? Somehow I feel redundant."

"Oh, no, no, no, my dear. Not redundant at all." Norcroft patted her head as though she were a cute puppy. "I want to see just how much Mr. Aries loves you," he said in an almost teasing voice that was as inappropriate as it was scary.

"Bullshit. First of all, he *doesn't*. Second, what would it accomplish even if he *did*?"

"Will he save you, or will he save all those pious people out there?"

"No contest. Them," Emily said with conviction. The man was mad if he thought Max, or anyone at T-FLAC for that matter, would consider that an option.

"Ah. What confidence you have in him. And think how fast he'll work to defuse the bomb when he realizes that every second he wastes will be seconds shaved off *your* life."

"I repeat. No contest."

"Perhaps they'll deposit my money in the nick of time?"

"I wouldn't count on it."

"You speak for T-FLAC, do you? Imagine the chaos

in the world's population of Catholics if their precious St. Peter's were blown to kingdom come."

"I speak as someone with a modicum of intelligence. After destroying churches and synagogues for months on end, do you really think people wouldn't figure out that your final destination was the biggest, most famous cathedral of all?"

"But St. Peter's is the *second* biggest church in the world. Hadn't you heard about that monstrosity they built in Yamoussoukro, Côte d'Ivoire?"

She hadn't. She didn't even know where that was. "Is that where your bomb is?"

He grinned. "Ah . . .That would be a . . . *No.*"

"You're nuts if you don't know how many bounties are out on your head. Every law enforcement agency in the world is searching every dark rat hole looking for you right now, it doesn't matter how little time is left on your clock. *Someone* will stop you before your bomb explodes." No matter how convincing she sounded, even *she* didn't believe her.

"Well I hope for your sake you're right. Unfortunately for you, the bomb will be activated via a remote controlled device. So even if they find me, which I can assure you they *won't,* unless the money is transferred into my account, the bomb *will* detonate. Either way, I'll take myself off now, and observe the happenings from a safe distance."

"Coward."

"With as much money as I've accumulated, I don't have to be a hero." He laughed. "I'm going to be even wealthier and a good deal more powerful than anyone can imagine. With facial reconstructive surgery, I'll be able to walk up and shake the president's hand. Or marry into royalty. Or marry a beautiful artist with soulful brown eyes, and beautiful breasts. I'd thought to offer you the chance to join me, once. With my brains, and your beauty and talent, the possibilities and opportunities would be endless."

She shuddered. "Thanks, I'd rather be blown to bits."

Norcroft pushed away from the wall. "That's what I concluded, as well. I'm afraid we have to run, my dear. But don't worry, you'll have the camera to keep you company. See there near the ceiling? When the red light comes on, it will beam your picture around the world. Be sure to tell them you're a guest of the Black Lily organization, and this will be just the beginning if they don't meet my demands. They have under an hour to make that deposit."

He turned to look at the Greek. "Ready?"

Holding up what looked like a garage door opener, the Greek nodded.

"Excellent. Please don't move," Norcroft told Emily pleasantly. "The device strapped to your chest has a liquid level on it to maintain stability. And now that the bomb has been activated, we wouldn't want it to detonate early, would we?"

"What do you *mean* Black Lily has her?" Max snarled into his lip mic as Dare informed him of Emily's abduction. "*Where* do they have her?"

"Switch to channel three, Max."

Dare never called him by his first name.

Max shifted the image layers on his HMDGs, moving the countdown numerals to the back, and bringing the image on channel three forward.

"Jesus."

Emily.

He flipped down the other lens. And saw her as a stereoscopic image, a 230,000-pixel resolution video. Full color. No sound. "Jesus," he said again.

Motionless, she stared up at the camera. Max forced himself to track his gaze down her body, forced himself to ignore the blood on her face, her puffy, bleeding lip, her big, terrified brown eyes.

Strapped to her chest was a small, sleek bomb.

The timer on the face of it synchronized with the timer on the image layered behind hers on the HMDG glasses.

15:35:01

Twenty-one

DON'T PASS OUT DON'T PASS OUT DON'T PASS OUT." Without moving her head, Emily cast down her eyes to read the blinking red LED numbers on her chest upside down. Hyperventilating, her head spun and black dots danced in her vision. Perspiration trickled down her back. Blinking, she forced her eyes to focus on the individual numbers.

Three seconds later than the last time she'd looked.

Thirty-one minutes, thirteen seconds to go.

Shifting just her eyes, she redirected her gaze back to the small red eye of the camera. If it really *was* a frigging camera. For all she knew, that son of a bitch Norcroft had lied about it. She clung to the hope that he'd told the truth. That someone out there would see where she was and show up to save her. She had tried saving herself and only gotten into more trouble. But, oh, God. Even if people *were* looking right at her, even if there *was* someone out there that could put two and two together, there was nothing, absolutely nothing that would identify *where* she was. She could be in any one of a *million* small rooms with stone walls.

"I'm in the Necropolis under the Basilica," she told anyone who was listening. "I love you, Max," she told the blinking red eye, not caring if the entire universe knew it. "I love you, and we would have made it. And as badly as I want to talk to you, feel your arms around me, if I'm going to die, there are more important things that you need to know."

Thirty-one minutes.

Emily used up six of them repeating everything Alistair Norcroft had told her.

Twenty-five minutes.

Twenty-five minutes.

"Navarro? Daklin? With me. He has her down in the Necropolis." *Hang tough, sweetheart.* He ran. Faster than he'd ever run before, touching the earpiece as he went. "Dare? Get me Levine. *Now.*" There still was no sound on the video feed, and he couldn't read Emily's lips as he ran flat out. Levine was one of their lipreading translators.

A beep in his ear. He switched channels. "Aries."

"Guerrero, Seville Cathedral." The man ID'd himself and his location in Spanish. "Want us to stop searching here?"

"Nobody stop," Max replied in English so everyone was clear on their orders. "We don't know if this is the only bomb. Keep locations clear of civilians, and *keep looking.* Someone bring me Norcroft's head on a platter. Son of a bitch is watching this from a safe distance. Darius? Calculate the acceptable blast distance, and broadcast it to our network." He closed the universal com as he ran.

Past the ninety-foot-tall *baldacchino,* the monumental canopy sheltering the papal altar. Christ. Emily was right beneath his feet here. Forty feet below him. He wanted to stop watching the video feed but he couldn't. Her terrified face kept him moving.

Running balls-out across the transept, Max hauled ass up the right aisle, past the small chapels and statues of past popes. Heading toward the massive bronze front doors, he was pissed to see there were a few stragglers, and he yelled at the them to "Move it! Get out. *Now!*" as they turned, giving him disapproving glares as he ran by. He spotted Navarro and Daklin converging near the *Pietà.* "Go, go, go!"

They went. Through the wide doors, down the steps

and out into the Piazza di San Pietro, Max closing the gap behind them. Thousands of people still milled around the base of the tall, red granite Egyptian obelisk supported by bronze lions in the center of the oval created by colossal Doric colonnades, four columns deep. They were moving, albeit slowly, but they were moving. Some of them wouldn't make it. He wanted to yell at them, but he kept moving, faster. Faster. Faster.

Every goddamned second counted.

His earpiece beeped. "Aries. Yeah? Thanks." Clicked Darius off, and the lip-reader, Levine, on. "Go."

"Max, I love you," Levine said for her. Max didn't give a flying crap that Emily's words, repeated in his ear were in a baritone instead of the soft, lilting sound of her voice, the same tone that haunted his sleep. "Stupid not to have told you when I had the chance. I—I didn't want to put you in an uncomfortable—I was scared. Okay? I was scared that you'd—I don't know what I thought."

Her left eye was swollen almost shut. Her lips puffy and bloody. "Bottom line? I love you with all my heart."

Seeing her like this Max felt a killing rage sweep over him. This kind of anger was something he'd rarely felt before. He tamped it down. Kept his focus.

"I've only got twenty-nine minutes, so if anyone's out there, here's what I know. The bomb isn't in any of the museums or the Basilica. It's here." Her lashes fluttered down as she indicated the location of the bomb with her eyes.

No wires. Where the hell were the wires? Max wondered as he took three wide steps at a time without pause.

She looked back at the camera. At *him.* "It's me."

Max's heart seized. Not a painting. Emily. *Fuck.*

"You have to get everyone away," Emily continued, her eyes blank and staring off into space. "I'm scared, Max. I'm—there's so much I haven't done. So much I should have done. I should have told you how I felt. Being strapped to a bomb kind of puts things in a new perspective. In retrospect, it was really stupid of me to keep my feelings a secret."

Max picked up speed, each step fueled by desperation and determination. "Hang on, sweetheart." Unfortunately she couldn't hear him any more than he could hear her. And she didn't have Levine lip-reading in her ear.

"Norcroft is certifiable," she said. "Even if you send the money he's demanded, I'm not sure he'll keep his word. If you ever have the chance, kill the son of a bitch for me, would you?"

"You bet."

"If you were standing in front of me right now, I'd tell you how much I love you. I'm sorry I let Daniel's skewed perceptions of you color my opinions. Dumb, right? I should have trusted my own instincts and seen through all his lies. You're a good and decent man and I was never happier than I was when I was in your arms. You always made me feel safe, and special and wanted and needed. If I had it to do over again, I'd make you see that it could have worked between us. We could have found a way. I would have found a way. You probably don't want to hear any of this," she looked right at him and smiled her sweet smile, "but I've got the whole captive audience thing going on, so . . . well, I love you. Did I say that already? I don't care. I like saying it."

Max caught up with Navarro and Daklin as they flew around the corner and vaulted over the gate.

"So, while I wait," she swallowed roughly. "I'm going to close my eyes, and pretend that you're here with me."

Three local T-FLAC operatives had dragged out a man apiece, two in Swiss guard attire, one man in black, and were hauling their asses to a waiting vehicle.

"Access?" he asked as he took the first set of metal stairs in three giant steps.

"Got it." Daklin held up a micro unit. The door at the foot of the stairs then clicked open. They thundered down the ancients' stone streets, past tombs and mausoleums. Down a second flight of metal stairs, their footsteps echoing loudly through the narrow tunnels as they ran. She'd hear them. Couldn't miss. She'd take heart that she wasn't alone.

I promise. I'll never let anything hurt you. Was he going to be able to keep that promise?

"Emily!" Max yelled. Christ—"Don't move!"

The three men crossed the first tomb suspected of holding St. Peter's bones, without pause or interest, and turned the corner into the small room that housed the bones of the Saint.

"Max." Her lips moved with barely any sound.

"Max." Levine repeated in his ear.

"Yeah. Got it." He pulled off the glasses and the lip mic, dropping them on the hard packed floor as he moved toward her. He locked his eyes on hers as Navarro and Daklin got out their tools. "Hi honey, how're you doing?"

Her eyes were enormous, her skin drained of color, sweat beaded her clammy face. Blood stained her lip and chin, and one beautiful eye was almost swollen shut. *Ah, sweetheart . . .*

"Not one of my finest hours."

"Yeah, I see that. Keep perfectly still, okay?"

"Everything itches," she mumbled, not moving her lips.

He bit back a smile. "Isn't that always the way?" He took the kit Navarro handed him, and carefully placed a helmet over her head, then pulled down the clear visor. He supported her head so it didn't flop forward with the weight. "Okay?"

"That's rhetorical, right?" Her voice was muted by the headpiece.

"I'm going to let go on the count of three. I'll have my hands right here so I can support you if it's too heavy, okay?"

"Hmm."

He released her slowly, and her neck was able to sustain the weight of the headgear.

"Let me know if you need a hand holding it."

"Hmm."

The headgear had the highest ballistic integrity of any bomb disposal helmet in the world. Tested and defeated over 2000 FPS, the visor—2315 FPS. But it wasn't going to save her if the bomb detonated.

She looked at him through the clear visor, her eyes shadowed. She knew all these precautions would be moot if the bomb detonated.

Navarro was crouched down in front of her, looking the device over before he touched it. Daklin got down there with him. They were the best bomb disposal experts T-FLAC had to offer. Max was grateful, and he wanted to fucking yell at them to hurry the hell up.

He'd never take patience for granted again. Every atom of his body was jumping. He gently wrapped Emily's upper body with a LockOut blanket with the added protection of ceramic plates embedded in the fabric. He did the same for her legs and arms, careful not to jar her as he worked.

The blankets and helmet wouldn't do her a fucking bit of good either. The device was strapped right over her heart.

"Any chance of getting it off her first, then disabling it?" he asked Navarro quietly.

"No."

Yeah. What he thought. Max would've done any-thing, promised anything, to any gods, to be able to make that look of abject fear in Emily's eyes go away.

Thirteen minutes. "We have plenty of time," he told her calmly. "You have the best bomb disposal unit in the world, right here. Try to relax." *As if.*

They didn't know how to get the thing off her, Emily could tell by the way they didn't make eye contact. An eerie calm came over her and she slowly let out the breath she'd been holding.

"Max," she said softly, then waited for him to look at her. "Whatever happens—"

"Now this is really touching," Greta sneered, strolling into the room, a strange looking weapon held at waist level and pointing right at *her*. The Greek stood just behind her.

My God, Emily thought, eyes transfixed to the weapon the woman was toting. *Where had they come from? Why hadn't they gone with Norcroft?*

"*Three* heroes to save the beautiful damsel in distress. How gallan—"

Max shot her hand, causing her weapon to go flying, spewing bullets indiscriminately in all directions.

Oh my god, oh my god, oh my god. With a scream, the woman staggered backward, holding her bloody arm against her body. *Nononononono!* Emily screamed inside as bile rose in her throat. *No shooting. Bomb here, people. No freaking shooting!*

The Greek shoved the woman out of the way, and kept coming. The room wasn't that big. But three bullets to the head pretty much put paid to his approach.

Brain matter and blood splattered walls, floor, and ceiling as his head seemed to disintegrate like a watermelon under a heavy blow.

Emily's stomach heaved as the visor covering her face became red speckled.

Bullets were flying. Bits of rock and stone joined the maelstrom of projectiles as Greta staggered to her feet and returned fire.

Could the bomb explode because her heart beneath it was going manic? Either that, or it was going to go off when a stray bullet hit it, or it was going to go off because there were only—She had no idea how long. She didn't know which was worse. Watching the last few minutes of her life tick away, or being oblivious to how long she had left.

Something large and heavy fell across her lower legs, jarring her. Navarro or Daklin? She couldn't see. Everything inside her froze as she waited to be blown to kingdom come by the jolt.

Her eyes, the only thing she dared move, slewed in search of Max. He was still firing, although there was so much noise in the small space it was impossible to tell from which direction. His pant leg was dark and shiny. He'd been shot. Her heart lurchcd, but he strode over to Greta as if it were merely a scratch. Strode over to Greta as if the woman didn't have a blazing gun in her hands.

God. Was Max *insane*?

"Don't," trembled on her lips, but she bit it back. He was doing his job. A job he did brilliantly. She wasn't going to sit here and distract him. She bit the corner of her sore lip. The pain kept the worst of the fear at bay, but her heart was slamming hard against her ribs.

Max hauled Greta up by the collar and shook her hard. "Get up, you piece of crap." Max dragged the woman toward Emily. "Deactivate the bomb. Now."

"Is the billion dollars in the account?"

"Not just no, but *hell* no. Deactivate the bomb or I'll kill you now."

Across the room Daklin was securing the Greek even though Emily was sure he was dead.

Emily stared at Greta as she was shoved in her direction. She couldn't believe the bitch had come back. Since she couldn't look down, she had no idea how much time remained on the clock. But whatever small chance there'd been a minute ago, was now gone. Greta wasn't going to let *them* defuse the bomb. And *she* sure as hell wasn't going to do it.

But was she a martyr for his cause? She bet not.

The question wasn't up for debate because without warning, Max shot her in the head.

Twenty-two

MAX HADN'T LET DOWN HIS GUARD FOR A SECOND. One moment he'd been hauling Greta toward Emily and the bomb, the next, the bitch had a weapon in her hand, and pointed at Emily's chest. No contest. He blew the fucker away. It was instant and instinctual.

"You can open your eyes now," he told Emily, shoving the other woman's body out of the way and joining Navarro, who had his chamois tool pouch open on the floor beside him.

One big brown eye peered at him through the filter of the lacy red blood splatter on the visor of the helmet she wore. "I'd really, really like to throw up sometime soon."

"Give us a minute." His eyes met Navarro's. This was going to be dicey. The device was like nothing Max had ever seen before. The highest of high-tech electronics. No wires on the outside. Nothing but a sleek, oblong box of brushed aluminum. Seven inches wide, three inches high, with an LED timer blinking the countdown in one-inch-high green numerals.

Navarro gave a small nod, gaze and hands steady. "Let's do it."

With the precision of a pair of surgeons, Max and Navarro inspected what they could see to start deconstructing Norcroft's intricate bomb. It was a tightly sealed box.

"How much time?" Emily asked sounding dazed and numb, perspiration made her face glow. The room was hot, and being covered with the insulating blankets, plus the ceramic pads, was like being in a sauna.

"Minute." He glanced at Navarro's hands wielding his tools, to see how far he'd gotten in even opening the container.

Time to detonation one minute.

Time needed?

Three minutes.

Twenty-three

THEY COULDN'T OPEN IT. EMILY COULD ONLY SEE their eyes as the two men worked feverishly to defuse the bomb. But they couldn't do it. They hadn't said anything, but she couldn't feel any movement around her chest area where Norcroft had secured the damn thing. No movement meant they weren't touching it. If they weren't touching it they couldn't defuse it. Unless they had X-ray eyes.

Daklin had limped across the room, leaving a trail of blood on the stone floor. Feeling devoid of any emotion, plain numb, Emily watched him as he started feeling around the edge of the glass barrier across the tomb of St. Peter. What on earth was he doing? Trying to get inside the tomb? She frowned, remembering not to bite her lip. What on earth . . .

The glass was bulletproof! The same bulletproof glass the Vatican had been forced to use to protect the *Pietà* after a psychotic visitor had tried to destroy Michelangelo's statue many years ago.

"Max," Emily whispered. "Get out of here. All of you. Go."

"Shut up," he said in the most unlover-like tones.

What had Norcroft said? *"Unfortunately for you, the bomb will be activated via a remote-controlled device."*

"Norcroft told me the bomb was activated by remote control."

382

"Yeah?" Max was distracted. Was he listening?

"Max?" Emily waited until he lifted his eyes to hers. She was shaken to see how terrified he looked in that instant before he masked it. "There's a remote control device. Greta had it. Look in her left—Shit. No! *Right* pocket. Hurry."

"Keep working," he told Navarro as he jumped to his feet and raced over to the woman who was sprawled with what was left of her head dripping on the stone floor. Max flipped her over, then quickly searched her pockets. He pointed the small black box straight at Emily.

"Christ. *Two* buttons. Activate. Deactivate."

He looked at Emily. "I love you. Close your eyes."

Twenty-four

THREE SECONDS.
No time to debate.
Max pressed the second button.

Twenty-five

FLORENCE
ONE MONTH LATER

TURNING AT THE TOP OF THE STAIRS, EMILY WAVED goodbye to the friends who'd brought her home. With a sassy toot of her horn, Rossella eased her car into the traffic and sped off. The four women had attended an afternoon wedding in Sienna. They'd laughed a lot and drunk a little too much excellent Cristal. They'd danced and gossiped, and she hadn't mentioned Max. Not once.

For a moment Emily stood outside her front door, hugging the cashmere shawl around her bare shoulders as she watched her friend's car weave through the evening traffic. Her smile faded.

She knew she was just delaying going inside. The weather was warming up, and it had been a glorious sunny day, turning into a beautiful balmy evening. Although she still needed the light wrap around her shoulders, spring didn't seem too far off with unseasonably warm weather like this. The dark sky was already sparkling with stars, and the air was redolent with the savory smells of family dinners and the sweet evocative fragrance of the early blooming Cape jasmine in the big clay pot beside her front door.

A night for lovers, she thought, and her heart did a little hitch as she pressed her thumb on the newly installed pad beside her door. *Where are you Max? Are you well? Do you miss me half as much as I miss you, or have you already forgotten me?*

Everytime she went in or out she was reminded of who and what Max was. The high tech security had been installed when she returned from Seattle. A man she'd never seen before had been waiting to open the front door on her arrival. She'd used her pepper spray and not only managed to knee him, she'd also shoved him down all twenty-six of her front stairs.

Then he'd showed her how to get into her own home before limping off.

Recognizing her fingerprint, the door lock deactivated with a soft click. It seemed impossible that her feelings for Max had been one-sided. And yet, here she was. Alone. She fervently hoped that the gnawing empty ache inside her would, *eventually,* dissipate. As much as she wasn't ready to face her empty palazzo after spending the day with crowds of people, she knew she couldn't stand out there all night. She pushed open the door and started to walk inside, but hair on the back of her neck unexpectedly rose. Her senses alert, she hesitated on the threshold.

The little lights on the security keypad just inside the door were green, not red. The alarm had been turned off.

And hadn't she left a light on before she'd gone out? Damn right she had. Not as naïve as she'd been a month ago, she whipped the pepper spray out of her purse. She'd practiced, and was damn proud at how fast she'd become at the draw.

As she reached behind her for the light switch, a table lamp across the room blazed on, illuminating the man sprawled lazily on her floral sofa.

"About time you got home."

Max.

Her fingers shook slightly as she dropped the spray back into her bag and closed the door behind her. She told her heart to behave. He'd seen, he'd conquered, he'd disappeared too many times for her to buy into the fairy tale that he would ever stay. Not permanently, anyway. The question was, was she prepared to let him love and leave her again? And again? How many times could she survive his leaving her?

He sat up from his relaxed position. "You look"—his hot gaze tracked her body, then came to rest on her face—"Amazing."

Casually tossing her clutch onto the hall table, Emily unwrapped the shawl from her shoulders and hung it on the coat rack. Then she was sorry she had. She needed some props to keep her hands busy. "Thanks." She shouldn't care about his compliments. Or notice that if his look had a temperature, the thin silk of her new dress would've melted right off her body. His heated look made every penny she'd spent on it worthwhile.

She gave him what she hoped looked like a casual once over. He looked exhausted. A little rough around the edges. But his hair was damp, and she could smell her shampoo, so he'd apparently availed himself of her shower while he'd waited. "You look like hell." *Liar.*

Max shrugged. "It's been a long month."

She met his penetrating gaze head on, remembering her backbone and the thirty-two days and nights of wondering when she'd remember that Max didn't play for keeps. "Hasn't it, though?"

After Rome, he'd stayed just long enough to make sure she was okay before walking away. Again. Third time with Max Aries had not been the charm.

She had, honest to God, not expected to see him ever again. She'd known that—this time—he'd be gone for good. They no longer had Daniel in common, and the terrorists were caught. Max didn't need her. It didn't matter that she believed in her soul that he cared for her, his *job* was his life. No woman, not even one who loved him as much as she did, was ever going to be able to compete with that. She'd known *that* when he'd walked away without a backward glance.

She shifted from one foot to the other, her toes pinched in the sexy but too pointy, too high heels she'd worn all day. Max cocked his head, his attention on her bare shoulders and the low dip of her décolletage. Her mouth went dry, and the hollow ache in her chest started to thrum with longing.

"I had to go."

"I know." She'd known exactly what would happen when she'd allowed Max into her heart.

"I thought you'd wait."

I thought you'd wait? She blinked. "You thought I'd . . . *wait*?" she repeated with a small laugh. "Why on earth would I do a stupid thing like that?" Instead of waiting for him to return as if she were a lovesick cast-off, she'd taken the first flight out the next day and gone to see her mother in Seattle. Wishing for a confidante, hoping to find her mom sober and available, Emily had been disappointed, but not surprised to find that nothing had changed. Her mom was in rehab again.

She knew, after many years of heartache and trying,

that she couldn't give her mother what she needed to stop the craving of addiction. Once again, she was in a position where she couldn't force someone to love her as much as she loved them. It seemed to be a theme in her life.

Resolving to pick up the pieces and live happily ever after, damn it, even if she was alone, she'd returned home to Florence. And while her heart had ached with longing and loneliness, she'd immediately started putting her life back on an even keel. She'd accepted several interesting commissions, and already had enough work to keep her busy for several years.

"I had a full and interesting life before you showed up, Max. And I've resumed said life full throttle." Her heels clicked as she crossed the terrazzo floor to walk into the vast livingroom. Closer. But not *too* close.

She casually placed a hand at the base of her throat to cover the rapid and erratic beat of her heart, and stared him down. "What are you doing in Florence? Have you come back to sell your father's villa? If so, I might be interested—"

"I'm not selling." He cut her off sounding impatient, and mildly annoyed. "Not at the moment anyway. You need better security. I just walked in."

He hadn't *just walked in.* "I thought I *had* better security. Your people came and installed it while I was gone," she said dryly.

His lips twitched. "I hear you kicked Carlo down the stairs and rendered him sterile."

"He should have waited for me outside, not in."

Looking at her slim gold watch she realized that she'd left her house seven hours ago. Judging by the mess, Max had been there all that time. Glancing pointedly at the glasses, mugs and empty plates on the coffee table in front of him, she raised a brow. "I see you've helped yourself to refreshments."

"It's been a long wait." His smile slipped, and he gave her a stony look, which ruffled her feathers.

He had no idea what a long wait was. "Well, then, don't let me keep you. It's late, and I need to be up early." She suddenly felt a stab of pity for her mom, wondering if this desire to have something at all costs was what her mother battled every day.

Emily had been attempting a twelve-step plan for her Max addiction. It hadn't worked worth a damn so far. But she was willing to keep at it until it *did* work.

He rubbed a hand around the back of his neck, then leaned forward to rest his elbows on his knees. "Don't you want to know where I've been?"

"Gone?" Somehow she made her voice cool and ironic. "Isn't that your thing, Max? To be here one day and gone the next?"

"Didn't you miss me?"

"Unbearably," she said candidly. "But you know, each time you leave it gets a little easier." A lie. Nothing made missing Max easier, and seeing him again made all the feelings inside her churn up like sand in a windstorm. Her knees felt mushy, and she sat down in the big easy chair opposite him, draped her arms on the wide arm rests. Leaning back she enjoyed the way his eyes tracked her legs as she crossed them. Hmm. She let the thin silk slide up, exposing a little more bare thigh.

A nerve jumped in his cheek. "I've never seen you dressed like that. It's—You—Jesus, Emily, help me out here."

She recognized that lust-filled expression he wore, and her traitorous body responded with a curl of heat in her belly and the rapid thud-thud-thud of her heart. "Sure," she smiled. The only time he'd seen her dressed up had been to the party last year. But that gown had flowed to the floor, and covered more than it exposed. This dress consisted of about two ounces of silk. "You've never seen me in a short red dress before."

The hunger and heat in his gaze made her wonder if he had X-ray eyes and could see beneath the flimsy material to the red silk thong and demi-cup bra she wore beneath it.

He stood up with the grace of a caged tiger, so fast two pillows fell off the sofa. She forced herself not to react. But he wasn't coming to grab her—unfortunately—he was standing up so he could pace. He shoved his fingers in the front pockets of his jeans and walked around the coffee table, apparently to find more space.

"AJ's doing great." His voice sounded uncharacteristically strained.

"I know." She could win an award for how calm she sounded when inside she was sorting through confusion and desire. "I've spoken to her several times." AJ had made a point of talking about Max. A lot.

"I was in Washington, D.C. last week. Savage's arraignment." Max wandered around the room picking things up and putting them down again in an interestingly distracted, very un-Max-like way. He walked over to the French doors, looked out, turned around, his expression . . . nervous. Stoic T-FLAC operative, Max Aries, *nervous*.

Expression composed, Emily's heart was doing flip-flops and her palms were suddenly damp. Did she dare to hope? Everything she wanted, everything she loved, was right here pacing her worn antique Persian carpet. All six plus feet of leashed energy that was Max Aries.

"They have her for several counts of treason. She's facing a mandatory death penalty."

"How do you feel about that?" How do you feel about *me*?

"She'll get what she deserves. Because of her, thousands of people died. She betrayed her country, and she betrayed the people she worked with." Absently he picked up a small decorative box without looking at it.

Emily's breath caught as he absently stroked his thumb gently across the embossed filigree on the lid of the pill box in his hand. Remembering how his touch had felt on her *skin* made her nipples become achingly erect. "What happened to Tillman's son?"

He couldn't look at her any more, Max thought a

little desperately. She was unbearably exquisite in that little red number that barely covered her delectable body. He'd had a glimpse of the small hard points of her nipples, and thought he'd lose it right then. Pacing helped. Some. Picking her up, carrying her into the bedroom, and making love to her would go a long way in calming his nerves right now. He'd thought he'd known how she felt, but now . . . ?

Who had she gone out with tonight? What man had she been thinking about when she'd poured herself into that scrap of silk? If anyone had told him as recently as a month ago that he would be jealous of another man, Max would've laughed his ass off. He didn't do jealousy. God help him, he'd never cared enough about any woman to feel it.

Emily's name came up in a whole list of firsts.

He wanted her so badly his entire body pulsed with it. But first things first. He carefully set the small box back on the table, then resumed walking around the large room. "Prescott was the one who initially came up with the idea of swapping the fakes for the originals." He could smell her. Roses. Emily. He wondered across the room to look blindly at a small painting hanging on the far wall.

"Didn't like Daddy giving away his inheritance," he told her without turning around. "With a hefty bribe, he elicited Norcroft's help in getting provenance for the fakes, then had him make the switches. Prescott didn't know that Norcroft didn't need the bribe. He was already draining Tillman senior's accounts." He had to turn around to look at her, his entire body demanded it. His breath hitched. God, she was lovely. Lovely in so many ways that Max had counted and then lost track of the number.

The lamp beside her shone in her hair, made her skin look like alabaster. "Are you waiting for someone?" He tried to sound casual instead of combative.

Her head jerked up and she gave him a startled look. "Who?"

He shrugged. "Whoever you went out with earlier?" Was the bastard coming back? Expecting to take her to bed? Expecting to peel her out of that little nothing of a dress and—

"Don't be ridiculous, Max. Go on with your story."

He didn't find the idea of her being with another man ridiculous at all. He found the idea made him homicidal.

"Given another opportunity for big cash transactions, Norcroft made sure senior's generous gifts were distributed where *he* wanted them. As far as Prescott was concerned, he was merely safeguarding his inheritance from the old man."

Leaning forward, Emily's dress rose a little higher on her bare legs. Her lips were slightly parted as she watched him pace around her damned living room like a tethered tiger. He turned away before he jumped on her like an animal. Damn, he had to finish telling her about business before he could get personal.

When had he lost the ability to pick up on a woman's cues? He had no freaking idea *what* the hell she was thinking as she politely watched him.

"He didn't know about the bombs?"

"No. Norcroft did that on his own. For years he was siphoning off whatever the hell he wanted. His terrorist activities started small. Extortion mostly, then he started buying and selling weapons on a major scale." Her nipples strained against the red silk. For him? Or was she cold. Whatever the cause, it had a decided affect on his body. He shoved his fingers deep into his front pockets.

"How did he connect with your traitor? The Black Rose?"

"Savage ran into him about ten years ago, after he'd done an arms deal with a small time tango in Argentina. Savage was the T-FLAC operative sent in to retrieve the weapons. She followed the trail back to Norcroft, and made him a lucrative offer. If he cut her in, she'd help him stay one step ahead of T-FLAC."

"You live in a dangerous world, especially when you have to keep watch over your shoulder all the time."

"It took us ten years to get Black Rose."

"Only because Savage was playing both sides, and knew where and when you'd be looking. But you eventually caught her."

"Yeah."

"And Black Lily?"

"Norcroft got the idea for the name from Savage. He got off on knowing Savage thought *she* was pulling *his* strings, when all the while he was building Black Lily behind her back. Building a silent army of tangos, most of them trained by Savage, but turned by Norcroft. Assets of the Black Lily insidiously consumed the members of Black Rose over the years, keeping a low profile, and staying under our radar. Until Norcroft became more powerful than Savage could ever have imagined and he was ready for Black Lily to take full credit."

"But Alistair Norcroft is still out there *somewhere*. He could—

"No. We got him." Max had tracked the son of a bitch for three weeks. Three weeks of turning over every rock and dung heap. The image of that fucking bomb strapped to Emily's chest had kept him strongly motivated. He was prepared to die before he'd allow Norcroft to get away scot-free. Max wouldn't have left her to die alone. He would've wrapped his arms around her and gone with her to whatever afterworld there was.

And if he was willing to die for someone, maybe it was time to have the courage to love them.

He'd eventually found Norcroft in London. There'd still been the official T-FLAC questions to be answered, but Norcroft hadn't resisted, guns blazing. It had been *mano a mano,* and the fight hadn't lasted nearly long enough for Max to relieve the pent up fury he had for Norcroft using Emily the way he'd done.

"The good news is Norcroft is dead."

Emily looked up at him expectantly at the pregnant pause.

"The bad news is he had two tats on his back. The black lily and some other damned flower we're trying to identify." A little difficult due to the location of a bullet's exit wound.

Emily's eyes went wide. "My God, Max, are you telling me this *isn't* over? That there's yet another flower terrorist group out there just waiting in the wings?"

"There's always another tango group waiting in the wings." Might as well be honest, he thought a trifle nervously. He watched her eyes, and observed her expression. "There's a reason an organization like T-FLAC thrives and never runs out of work. Terrorists are like God damned cockroaches. They breed and multiply in the dark— Look, can we talk about this some other time?"

"Will there *be* some other time?"

"I want to ask where you were tonight," he said, his voice rough as he held her gaze. He scrubbed a hand around the back of his neck, his shoulders tensing again. "But I know I don't have the right." He wanted to touch her so badly his entire body ached with the need.

Emily didn't say anything.

"Who did you dress up for? Who did you go with?" He got up and stalked to the window before pivoting back to face her, his gut knotted. He held up his hand, although she hadn't said a word. "Don't tell me, I have no fu- No right to ask. But damn it, Emily. I *want* that right. I want the privilege of knowing where you are, and *how* you are. I want the right to worry about you. I want to meet your friends." He ran his fingers through his hair, feeling like a lovesick kid on his first date. "I want to see you paint. It's like this crazy need inside of me, to watch you sleep every night, to watch you wake up every morning. I want—Jesus." He paused to clear the thickness out of his throat. "This is hard. I want you, Emily Greene. I want you and everything that comes with you."

"For how long?" Her eyes narrowed and Max regretted that he'd ever given her cause to doubt his love.

"For as long as you'll give me. Forever."

"And what will I get in return?"

"You'll get a man who'll love you enough for three lifetimes. A man who will honor you, and care about you, and devote his life to making you happy." He walked toward her, tried to gauge her reactions. "A man who swears that every time he leaves he'll give you a date and time of his return."

Her honest laughter cheered him. "As if."

He smiled back, feeling light and buoyant, and so damned happy he wanted to yell it to the world. "Okay," he admitted ruefully. "That's a bit of a stretch. But I swear to you, no matter where I go, I'll always come back to you as quickly as possible. Considering that I'll be head of the Italian branch of T-FLAC, I won't have to stray too far. I need you, Emily."

She looked at him in surprise, tiny half moons of delight bracketing the corners of her mouth. "There's an Italian branch of T-FLAC?"

He leaned over, bracing his hands on the arms of her

chair, and bent his head to brush a kiss over her smiling lips. "There is now."

She stood up within the circle of his arms, then placed both palms flat on his chest. The scent of her hair and skin made Max drunk with love.

Winding her arms around his neck, she lifted her mouth to his. He felt her warm breath against his lips.

"That sounds like a promise to me."

"It is. I love you more than I could ever have imagined was possible."

"Then welcome home, my love."